Whole Latte Life

Also by Joanne DeMaio

True Blend

Snowflakes and Coffee Cakes

Blue Jeans and Coffee Beans

whole latte life

A NOVEL

JOANNE DEMAIO

To my daughter, Mary

one

RACHEL CHECKS HER WATCH AGAIN, she can't help it, she's so hungry. Three hours of shopping does that every time and it's all she can do to not down half her lunch. Sara Beth just stepped away to fix her hair, but the food's getting cold now, so she lifts her fork and tastes her lunch, picking at sliced zucchini and carrot. The seasoning is sublime, but still, their habit is to sample it all, a piece of Sara's braised lamb, the different veggies, the sauce. It makes a goulash of lunch, their silverware spearing the other's plate, but it's how they eat. And how they talk, around the food and the savoring, dodging the other's fork.

After another minute, she takes a sip of her white wine and casually glances around. Inside the Manhattan restaurant, tiny square tables, like dominoes one after the other, line the long window. Identical pale yellow linens drape precisely over each, heavy silverware anchors thick folded napkins and crystal goblets form a distinct sparkling line along the table row. Sara Beth should be back by now enjoying every bit of this.

"Excuse me," Rachel says, standing and moving past a patron on her way to the Ladies' Room. She opens the door to the lounge, a rectangular room edged with tufted-velvet benches. Unframed mirrors hang over long marble countertops. There is a woman in her thirties blotting her lipstick on a tissue, talking to a friend or sister beside her. It is so them, that image. She watches for a second, then hurries past into the lavatory. Half of the stalls are occupied; two women stand at the sinks.

"Sara Beth?" Rachel hikes up her handbag, fully expecting to hear *Okay, okay. I'm coming* as a door swings open, Sara Beth rushing to the sink, apologizing for taking so long, maybe admitting to a headache, worrying if the food was getting cold.

Instead the room quiets, heads lift, hands still beneath the soap dispenser, eyes meet. "No Sara here," a lone voice finally calls from a stall.

Okay. So she begins knocking softly at each closed door, her head bowed and leaning close. "I'm sorry, Sara? Are you there?" Her tap at the doors is light, trying to be unobtrusive, as if that's possible. "Sara?" she asks again and again, the answers disappointing. She pushes open each empty stall, pressing her hand at an angle against the door and standing back. Is she sick, unable to move? Is that why she seemed withdrawn before lunch, maybe a little sad? *Everything okay, hon?* Rachel had asked, and Sara Beth looked up from her menu. *Of course,* she'd said.

After one more glance back at the stalls, she hurries out to the dining room. In the height of lunch hour, the room got so crowded, voices rising and falling now, making her look at different tables when she hears a woman exclaim, another gently laugh, voices of friendship so recognizable. Could Sara Beth have bumped into an acquaintance? Here? And gotten sidetracked?

"Excuse me." Their waiter approaches. "Is something the matter?"

"Yes, actually. I'm waiting for my friend. It's odd, but she seems to have disappeared." She glances past his shoulder. "You took her order? The braised lamb sandwich?"

"Yes, I remember. Can I get you anything while you wait? A coffee?" He pulls out Sara Beth's chair and motions for Rachel to sit.

"No." She sinks into the seat. "I'm fine. Thank you." As soon as the waiter turns away, she digs into her purse for her cell phone. Her fingers quickly press the number. Just as quickly, the call goes to voicemail. Sara Beth's phone is off.

Funny, the way a silly delay unnerves her. Where could she have gone? Sara's shopping bags still sit beneath the table but she took her purse. "Where the heck are you?" Rachel says, twisting around in her chair and searching the restaurant. She picks up her wine and sets it right back down without sipping any. "Come on already."

To stop from imagining anything bad, she has this way of talking herself through things, things like this annoying waiting. They've missed each other somehow and will laugh about it in a few minutes. *There was a vendor outside,* Sara Beth might rationalize. *I bought you a picture of the skyline, so you can sketch it and remember our birthday weekend.* Rachel will sigh with relief, *How sweet of you! It's perfect for my collection. But I was so worried!* And Sara Beth will tuck her hair back, smile that great big smile and brush it off as she lifts her sandwich. *I was right outside. Oh this food is divine,* she'll say around a mouthful. *Try some!*

When Rachel looks to the doorway, nothing seems like she had pictured. She grabs her phone and dials Sara Beth's cell again, getting her voicemail.

"Sara Beth?" Her whole body leans into the call, turning toward the window so she can search the sidewalk as she talks. "It's me. Rach. This feels really dumb, but where the heck did you go? This isn't funny." A long second goes by. "Well. Call me at least and tell me you're fine."

"Excuse me, please," the maitre d' says from behind her, making her stand, like this urgency is uncoiling. "Your friend. The lady with the scarf."

"Sara Beth. Yes! Is she okay?"

"Apparently she had to leave, I'm afraid."

"Leave?"

He reaches into his jacket pocket. "She left this for you."

Her eyes lock onto his. "What do you mean, *leave?*"

He hands her the folded paper. "She stopped me on her way out and asked me to wait ten minutes to deliver this. She said you would understand."

"Understand?" Rachel's fingers fumble with the note, dropping it on the floor as she opens it. "You mean, she left the restaurant ten minutes ago?" she asks as she bends over to pick it up.

"A little longer than that." He motions to the crowded lunch room. "I couldn't get to you sooner."

She glances down at Sara Beth's handwriting, scanning random phrases. But they don't register; the whole thing doesn't make sense. "Did you see which way she went? Did she say anything else?"

The maitre d' shakes his head and steps back. "I only took the message from her."

"Oh," she says, and then nothing, because what can you say when your very best friend disappears without notice? A thousand thoughts, instead, swirl in your mind. Did you say something to hurt her? Is Sara angry? Sick? Is she meeting someone and coming right back? Or was it the ballet flats she saw a block over that she loved but passed on? The maitre d' turns his hands up in apology. He doesn't know more. "Well. Thank you," Rachel says. "I appreciate it." Her eyes drop to the note again as she slowly sits.

But when he starts to walk away, she can't help looking up. This is the man who last spoke to her friend. "Oh sir?" If she keeps him talking, it'll keep Sara Beth closer. "Was she upset? Or crying?"

"No." He pauses and she can see he's summoning her friend's image. If she could only follow it, walking out the door, that image. "She seemed rushed though."

"And then she walked out? Just like that?"

He gives a slight nod.

"Well. Thank you, then. Sorry to bother you."

"Not at all," he answers.

So she sits at the table with the folded paper in hand. It's like someone hit the Pause button, the way her fingers are bent, the paper so apparent, so neatly creased. The day stops with this news. Lunch, their whole birthday celebration thing stops, and she glances over her shoulder at the other tables. Should she wait here? Leave? What's she supposed to do now?

Just this morning they had coffee-to-go and split a bagel the way they always do, on country lanes searching for antique shops and at farmers' markets hunting for *thee* best tomato plants and around the neighborhood and at the mall, today on a dawn-quiet Fifth Avenue, window-shopping at Saks. Just this morning. What happened?

She opens the note again, but stops and looks out the window from where she sits, in Sara's seat, which faces the doorway. The street is narrow and the tops of the buildings reach up beyond her view. From where she *had* been sitting, her back faced the door and she would not have seen Sara Beth leave. So was this all planned?

Really, you can't plan to disappear and not show it. The plan is too big. So then is this unplanned? Carefully reading the note again, there it is, that familiar handwriting, easy cursive that graced two decades of beautiful Christmas and birthday cards with love and sentiment and wishes for *Much Happiness!* and *The Very Best!* The note is short, written on a piece of the hotel stationery. Sara Beth collects stationery when she travels, folding pieces of paper from inns and Marriotts and now the refurbished Plaza into her purse. But this doesn't jive, her strange message about life, and turning forty, not with the sweet messages of the past. Finding her way? She feels lost? Rachel's eyes fly over the words. She has to do this, she says. She can't go back home feeling this way.

"What on earth," Rachel says. "What way?"

Please don't tell Tom about this. I really need some time alone, Rachel, to sort things out. I am so sorry to do this now, on our fortieth birthdays. I know it means a lot to you and I promise you another celebration. But we go back a long time and you're the only, only person who will understand and let me do this, let me walk away from it all for a little while. Please don't worry, I'll be back. I just need these couple days alone to try to figure this out, to figure me out.

Wait. *Wait,* Rachel's thoughts cry out, as though Sara Beth can hear them. But they often do know the other's thoughts. She stops reading and looks around the restaurant again. Time alone? Here? Outside the window, the city buildings crept a step nearer in the one minute since she last looked out. She can almost yell Red Light, the way everything presses in, in a matter of seconds. Red Light!

I know that you don't see it, but my life is a mess right now and I feel so lost. I need this one weekend alone to think, to fix things, to find room for me again, my dreams. When else could I ever—

Rachel squints to read a line Sara Beth crossed out. Something about if she doesn't do this. Well now. If she doesn't do this, what? Will she come right back and resume the weekend? If she doesn't do this, what exactly will happen? What kind of nonsense is this? Will she find herself standing on the George Washington Bridge, or buying a pair of designer boots to alleviate some midlife crisis? Instead, past the crossed out line, Sara Beth writes,

Please try to understand. Like we've always done for each other. We'll talk soon. Promise. Love, Sara Beth

"Okay, enough." Rachel grabs her cell from the table and starts to dial again. "Shoot!" she whispers half way through, then disconnects and drops it in her bag. Worry has never felt so scary, not in all her livelong life. After several moments when she hopes beyond hope that Sara Beth changes her mind and comes rushing back, breathless, apologetic, *What was I thinking?* she'd ask, Rachel finally leaves enough money to cover the lunch tab, gathers the shopping bags and walks herself straight out into the city. After checking back at the hotel for Sara Beth, she flags down a mounted police officer a few blocks further.

"That's a difficult situation," he tells her.

"I know. That's why I need your help," Rachel says, stepping back when the chestnut horse shifts its stance beneath him, nodding hard against the reins. She squints, but can't see past the black sunglasses, the helmet, the dark uniform. Right now, more than anything, what she needs is a cop, and this officer is the only one in sight.

"What you should probably do is call your friend's family, or go home to your husband. She'll show up in a day or two." He glances down Fifth Avenue before pulling on the reins and turning his horse back to work. "With that note, I wouldn't worry too much." His booted foot digs in a heel, moving the animal into traffic.

There is a boutique where the cop had been standing, a small shop with pastel clutches in the window, pink and yellow and blue, and summery wrap dresses. Cars are lined up three deep on the Avenue; clear sunlight glances off steel and windows. The people, the shops, the streets connecting them all through Manhattan, it's a carousel whirling around Rachel, the city spinning and rising, standers and jumpers, all cabbage roses and flying manes and twinkling lights and contorted whinnies and she wonders how these things happen. Twice now in the past hour she's been left behind from a situation spinning around her. Gosh darn it, right when she desperately needs help, this cop brushes her off like lint from a sweater.

"Wait a minute!" Rachel calls out, squeezing through a group of students on a class trip. "I wasn't done." She's half jogging along the curb near the horse, keeping pace with it. Oh, the officer's lengthy sidelong look doesn't escape her as she shoulders herself through Manhattan. "I am *not* leaving New York without Sara Beth," she yells over the noise of a passing bus, shielding the sun from her eyes.

Stopping alongside the curb, the police officer turns back. He already told her that since there is no indication of abduction, the NYPD can't do anything. This is still the land of the free. Free to come and go, to hide and seek.

"Can't you make an exception?" Rachel asks. "Because something's really wrong." Her hand still shades her eyes, and she can't read his behind those sunglasses. "I checked back at the hotel, the restaurant. I don't know what else to do."

"You might want to stop at the Precinct to file a Missing Person Report."

"A report." It begins to feel like all this, this insistence to authority, this nerve, like it's all been summoned for nothing. Like she'd taken a deep breath but never dove in. Sara Beth could be three states away by the time a report is filed. A stream of cars moves by and she steps closer to the curb, daring to reach up and grip the horse's leather bridle, not letting them slip away again until she is finished. The soft warmth of the horse presses against her fingers.

"Listen. She's my best friend. And only an hour ago, I was sitting in a perfectly charming restaurant when the maitre d' handed me a note. We came to the city for our fortieth birthdays. A girls' weekend out, you know? Sara Beth left the table to use the Ladies' Room and never came back." Rachel's free hand feels around deep in her shoulder bag and pulls out the folded square of paper. "It's all in her note. Something about her life not being right, and before she goes back to it, she has to find some answers. Here, of all places."

She looks over her shoulder back toward the restaurant, still clutching the bridle. It's easy to not recognize someone out of context, out of their normal place beside you thumbing through boho tunics on the rack, standing behind you at Dean & DeLuca, jogging through the park. Is Sara Beth close by?

"I'm sorry I can't do more," he tells her again.

"Well, where's the Station for this Precinct? Maybe I'll file that Report."

"The 18th Precinct? Over on West 54th."

Rachel starts to walk away, leaving the officer and his horse watching. He sits with the reins folded in his crossed hands, NYPD insignia and a shining badge pinned to his leather jacket.

If she wasn't so darn busy fighting back tears, she'd have turned to ask him if they needed a recent photograph, to see the beautiful auburn hair Sara always fusses with, tucking it behind an ear whenever she gets nervous, or self-conscious. Or if it would be better for Sara's husband to file the report. He's a lawyer after all, and has lived with her for all these years, sat with her in her kitchen, slept with her, landscaped their yard, helped with the new baby, checked her car oil, and held her close when her mother unexpectedly died. Or if the Missing Persons Bureau would ask personal questions about risk factors, like the sadness Rachel hears when Sara sometimes answers her phone, or the fatigue she sees in her eyes. Or questions about any crisis Sara Beth might've had before disappearing. Something that might have pushed her over the edge, forced this weekend escape from all that filled her life. Three children, soccer, high school, dance lessons, playgroups, library fund raisers, a colonial home, grocery shopping, cooking meals, dentist appointments. Those wonderful antiques gathering dust in the garage, novels unread, a collection of vintage leather journals she hasn't used in ages, probably long tucked away in the back of a drawer now. Dreams waiting to awaken.

Rachel quickly walks another block, leaving the officer far behind and realizing that Sara Beth didn't disappear today. She turns into a coffee shop and plants herself at a window table for a couple hours, her gaze riveted on each passerby. Have any of these people done what Sara Beth did? Are they walking out on a life-in-progress? As the shock of her friend's running away wears off, the truth grows clearer. Rachel has been losing her friend in pieces over the years.

Gone was a huge piece of her heart with her mother's death a year ago.

Gone was her desire to move to a smaller historic home with her unplanned pregnancy two years ago.

Gone was her fine arts degree, folding laundry now rather than unfolding an easel.

Gone was a certain courage returning home from a college-year abroad in France with a free-spirited boyfriend, one who'd made her daisy chains and taught her to ride horses and dared her to spend her life with him there.

Carefree became careful.

Daring became denied.

Her best friend had been disappearing for a long time now.

She pays the bill and heads out into the waning afternoon sunlight, eventually turning the corner on West 54th, intent on finding her friend.

The Precinct's American flag catches her eye first, a couple of blocks ahead. As she nears, the line of police cruisers parked outside the sandstone building has her pick up her step. Help is right here, she feels that assurance as two uniformed officers walk through the black double doors, into the station house. One detailed Missing Person Report might very well reel Sara Beth right back. The department will track her down, somehow, someway.

Rachel slows as she approaches the granite stairs leading to the double doors. The day seems to pause again right here at the police station as she seriously considers what she must do next. It comes down to a choice, and with it, she feels some of the difficult choice Sara Beth must have felt a few hours ago. With each step, she's locked in one conflicting moment.

Time is so fluid. It changes its course, rises and falls like the tides, disguising eternal moments beneath a weekend of days.

Years of friendship surge into tethered memories. A moment of death becomes an ocean current of perpetual loss. A split-second relationship decision arises with waves of doubt. Hours of a regretted pregnancy stream into days of relieved love. An hour at a time, a cry at a time, a decision at a time, a worry at a time, regret, relief, love, a sea of moments, they all swell into one emotional note of paper tucked into her handbag.

It is one of the most daunting choices Rachel has ever made. Her one decisive second, right now, at the Precinct doors, will stay with her always. She can walk away and give Sara Beth the time she wants or she can try to find her. Without a second glance back, she walks up the stairs, pulls open the door and steps inside.

two

IN THE PAST, SHE'D TURNED to art for comfort, losing herself in paintings as she studied the works of the masters. If she were to commission a portrait of her family, you'd see a Tonalist painting. From a distance, no distinction would be visible in the gradations and variations of deep paint shades. From a distance you would notice, with the diffusion of tone, the atmosphere that surrounds her family rather than the family itself. There'd be mystery in the dusky painting. A dark, muted undertone. Lean in and study the details, and the family wouldn't appear whole, Sara Beth an unfinished compilation of strokes. Her edges would blend with her family's, yet she'd be nearly transparent at her heart, a part of it washed away now, a vacuity separating her from the others. Yet close or distant, you'd notice the laying of Tom's hand on her shoulder, Kat's gaze at her mother's face, Jen secretly looping arms with her sister, the baby.

Like an artist feeling inspired, she couldn't shake an idea. It would be so easy to take herself out of the portrait for a while, to restore the painting. How often do we get this chance to spend a few days alone, reflecting on who we've become, who we've lost? Maybe this was part of the painting of her self, the first thin layer of pigment laid on the canvas, making pensive, pivotal decisions. The thought had her set down the menu and take this chance, stepping out of the restaurant alone.

So this is all new, this leaving behind her steady, dependable life. She quickly walks half a dozen Manhattan blocks, grips her leather satchel close and focuses ahead on the crowded sidewalks. At each busy intersection, buses and cars pass and she waits, head up, posture straight. This is what it must feel like to fly, spreading her wings and keeping balanced. But suddenly she stops, just stops, and leans up against the warm side of a stone building. Perspiration glazes her face and dampens her neck. This, well okay, this must be the crash landing. Doubts and worry and indecision hit her head-on.

She tips her head back and closes her eyes. City people and sounds move all around and she gulps long breaths of air. So what now? She walked through the restaurant door and found herself lost.

Sometimes a feeling comes over her. More like an urge. The urge to pick up her cell and dial without thought. *Mom?* Oh to say it would help, the word a soft cloud of relief. Cumulus and soothing. The sky on a perfect summer day is what the question is. *Mom?* But when you make these decisions, you can't call Mom, no matter how badly you miss her. As a matter of fact, now would be a good time to take her off her cell phone, to shed that security blanket. So she studies her phone, gets into the menu, sees the oh-so-familiar number that is dialed right into her mind, winces and deletes. It feels exactly like it did when her mother died, the sensation making her bend at the waist, hands on her knees, inhaling deeply, trying to find a breath.

Now there are no strings attached, no ties tugging at her conscience, no easy, familiar voice whispering in her ear. She pulls the blue silk scarf from her neck and folds it into her purse, glancing at the surroundings. It's a way of orienting herself, to see exactly where she landed. She can't just stand here. But her plan was only to step back from her life, to scrutinize and soul search in solitude for three short days. With another deep breath, she turns and crosses the street to keep walking away, turning down a short flight of stairs into a clothing boutique.

"Has it warmed up outside?"

The woman's voice startles her and she tucks her hair behind her ear. "I'm sorry?"

"You're flushed," the saleswoman answers from behind the counter. Pastel clutches line three shelves behind her. Pink and yellow and blue. "Is it getting hot out there?"

"Oh." She shakes her head. "I'm in a rush."

"You're on your lunch hour then?"

"Well. Yes, actually." A display of summer wear, sleeveless wrap dresses in muted patterns, hangs on a long rack. She picks one and holds it up against her front. If only it were that easy, change your clothes and Presto! New wardrobe, new life. Only in art, she supposes, sweeping new paint over old. "Can I try this on?"

The saleswoman points toward the dressing rooms. "I'll check with you in a bit."

She selects three dresses as though she's seriously shopping and hurries into the dressing area at the rear, locking a stall door behind her. Turning and seeing her reflection, the past thirty minutes hit her so forcefully, she sinks onto the bench and drops the dresses in a soft heap.

Now she is just Sara Beth, unfettered. It is all that matters for these few days. She dares to consider her reflection and study the woman, who, at forty, had to walk out of her life to find her way back. The eyes are less assured than she had imagined, her skin drawn. Instead of a small thrill, now there's this nagging doubt. Did she do the right thing? They say that in an oil painting, colors can be painted over each other, changing the nuance of light. So maybe this is what she'll do. Change just the nuance of Sara Beth.

A small knock at the dressing room door makes her flinch.

"How are we doing in there?" the saleswoman asks.

Sara Beth stands abruptly, swiping at her eyes and straightening her top. Her handbag slips to the floor, keys jangling out of it. She runs her fingers back through her hair trying to primp, or restore order at least. This feels completely foreign; she's usually carefully put together. Matched, color coordinated outfits hang in her walk-in closet; neutral shoes fill the shoe rack. Desperation has never been part of her appearance. "Okay," she calls out, facing her reflection. "I'm okay."

"How are the sizes?" comes the voice through the door.

Sizes? What is she doing here? She half expects her mother to tap at the door and hurry her along. Mom hates dawdling over clothes. Waste of time, she thinks. You should know what you like and buy it.

"Or can I bring any accessories for the dresses? A straw tote maybe?"

"Oh. The dresses." Sara Beth grabs at two of the hangers and shakes out the rumpled fabric before opening the door enough to slip them narrowly through, as though she is undressed and desiring privacy. "Can I have the next smaller size?" While waiting, she pulls the blue scarf from her handbag and dries her face, neck, shoulders, then her face again.

"Anything else, dear?" the saleswoman asks when she returns.

Again she inches the door open and pulls the smaller dresses through. "No. Thank you, these are fine." She hangs the dresses and searches for her compact and lipstick deep in her bag, needing to freshen up.

Freshen up. That's what she told Rachel she needed to do in the restaurant. A little lipstick, a little bronzer, and she'd be back in a flash. Her whole body sinks slowly down, wondering what she has done besides leaving her dear friend deserted back at the restaurant, solo at the cabaret, standing alone with a fashion consultant, turning in front of a mirror, the silky fabric of a long summer dress catching up with the spin. *Holy moly,* Rachel might say, oh she could just hear her. *I love these threads!*

But if she turns back, there will be no other chance to take this breather, not plum in the middle of suburban life. Rachel will want to talk this out over a pot of coffee, or with lattes at a window table, or bring her home sitting close on the train, or call Tom to New York, none of which will work. For the first time in a long time, she has to do something for herself. It's too important to put off any longer.

Until now, she's only dreamt of the possibility. Her own little antique shop, with lace curtains in the windows. Mom said she'd sew them; they found beautiful hand-stitched lace at a tag sale, deep inside an old trunk. She picked it up and it unfolded like a butterfly's wing, and they talked about how the sun would shine through, throwing tatted shadows on the furniture, the brass handles. It made her think of how Monet studied the way light changed and moved on his subjects, creating fleeting colors. Sunlight shining through lace would do the same on her antiques. It would be the light shining on her own canvas, on her children, her home, her marriage, and the responsibilities that came with it all, Jenny planning her high school schedule and Katherine in braces and a new baby, and commitment. And love. Piece by piece, the illumination of her dream brightened it all as she'd built an antique inventory from the classifieds, tag sales, estate auctions. Mom would've been there more often than not, dusting the inventory, lighting scented candles, keeping coffee going for the customers.

Yes, it was all supposed to be painted onto her canvas at forty with the perfect antique shop, a place that would belong to her and her mother.

Now her mother was gone and Rachel takes her place on the canvas, no doubt worried about her. Sara Beth's hand trembles when she freshens her lipstick, so much that she blots it all off and tosses the lipstick back in her bag. The thought of hurting

Rachel bothers her enough to go back. Leaving the dresses behind, she rushes through the store, straight to the doorway.

"Oh miss!" the salesclerk calls out. The voice comes to her as she opens the door and runs up the stairs. "Have a good day now?"

The restaurant is only a few blocks away. Turning the corner on the long window filled with a row of finely set tables, Sara Beth nearly stops. Pedestrians brush past, irritated at the way she suddenly slows up. She searches for their table and as though the whole lunch thing had never happened, it has been cleared, set with new silverware and crystal, the linen napkins folded in place.

At first it is a gift, that cleared table. She has done what she set out to do, erase herself from the picture with no harm done. There, you see? The table linens are still lovely, the glasses still sparkle. She turns from the empty table to the right, toward The Plaza, then glances left, the direction she could walk to pursue three empty days of time.

Enough time to leave her best friend devastated, imagining the worst. Rachel made the reservations ages ago, wanting to stay in the refurbished landmark on their landmark birthday. She'll tell Rachel everything. How life got in the way of her dreams and she has to find a way to reach for them soon. They're forty already! Coffee cups will sit between them, there'll be a mess of those. Lattes or cappuccinos or straight up, whatever. They'll talk it out.

Heading back to The Plaza, she passes two huge concrete planters in front of a bank, planters exploding with purple and yellow pansies. Mom's favorite flowers. Until now, she tried not to think of her mother, not wanting to imagine her frown, her questions, mostly her worry. But now there's this: happy pansies with smiling faces tipping and nodding in the breeze, exactly like the ones she planted last month. She makes them what she needs them to be, an image of Mom nodding in agreement with her decision. If she could only call her to know for sure.

Stepping off the curb, Sara Beth looks down at the menu on her phone, missing her mother's number already, and walks straight into a mounted police officer, making his horse sidestep. Okay, so now she can't help it, really. Hopefully her mother will laugh about this, a big, happy pansy smile: It's like she turned Sara Beth around as she untangles from the horse, does an about-face and walks away in the opposite direction.

* * *

"Her name?"

"Sara Beth Riley."

"Does she have a history of disappearing and returning?"

"No."

"Any chemical dependency issues?"

"No, none."

"Were you aware that she was leaving, but disagreed with her going?"

"No. No. No. This is completely out of character and unexpected. That's why I'm here."

Here. At the 18th Precinct in Manhattan, and no one in the entire world knows it. Okay, so these moments have come few and far between in her life, the times when she can't see through her tears. But she sees enough to realize how dire this situation is: Nicknames. Does *Mom* count? Physical appearance. Does it happen this fast, this not being able to picture her friend's face? Last conversation. Should she have known? *Is everything all right hon?* With her hand pressed over her mouth, she tries to focus through those tears, when a formidable blue shadow of calm in this crazy city, in her suddenly crazy life, takes a seat beside her. He speaks in a slow, composed voice. "Mrs. DeMartino. You haven't found your friend then?"

Rachel looks at the man, feeling like she knows him but not sure how. He looks tired, and yet familiar. He must see the confusion, or despair, or whatever her panicked eyes are communicating, and helps her out.

"I'm Officer Micelli. You stopped me earlier on Fifth Avenue? On the horse."

"Yes, right. And the most you could do was send me here."

"With all due respect, I didn't mean to be unsympathetic. But she kind of screwed you with that note. Since she left of her own free will, technically there was nothing I could do. I thought you understood."

"Sorry. I'm having a hard time understanding people today. And this form too. I mean, our last conversation? What we talked about? How can that help?"

"Something she said might lead us to her. It's useful to create a rough timeline of the last twenty-four hours so we can eliminate certain factors."

"Well she was with me during the past day. And she was fine. That's why I'm thrown by this. I guess something might've been on her mind, but I never imagined this."

"Okay, listen. Let's start with the basics. Her appearance, her clothes. That sort of thing."

Rachel rummages through her handbag for a photograph, pulling out her wallet, then dropping it as she opens it. When she reaches to catch it, her entire purse spills to the floor and she bends, randomly scooping the contents back inside. "I'm sorry," she says, swiping at more tears. "I can't think straight, can't see straight. I'll take this with me." She grabs at the Report and starts to fold it in half.

"Mrs. DeMartino." His voice changes. She hears it lower, sees him reach for the Report. "Let me help you fill this out. You're visibly shaken by this, and—"

"Well of course I am. My friend's disappeared. Where could she have gone?" She pulls her cell phone from her purse and checks it for messages. "And here I am, sitting in a police station waiting for the worst news. I mean, what about her husband? And her children? I can't stay here any longer. Seeing all this police stuff is scaring the hell out of me."

"Wait. Wait, wait. You also can't go out into the city shook up like this. Take a few minutes and calm down. I'll get you a coffee, just hang on."

Rachel watches him cross the room, pick up the coffee pot and swirl around a few drops of cold, muddy liquid pooled in the bottom before slamming it back onto the coffee maker.

"I have to get out of here," she says, standing, when he returns empty-handed.

"Listen, I just finished my shift. I'll walk you across the street for a coffee. Pull yourself together there. For your friend's sake, okay? Come on, we'll get this Report filled out."

* * *

Michael's seen this before. The situation has to settle, to find its place in her thoughts, to make sense. He orders at the counter, then sets his key ring and food on the square table and takes a seat, shifting it to face the doorway. He lifts the top of the hard roll on his plate. "Best roast beef sandwich in town. Little mayo, horseradish. Would you like one?"

"No, thanks. I'm fine."

"Joe can make you a half. You'll feel better with a little food in you."

"Please. No."

"Okay then. Now, Mrs. DeMartino." He scoops a forkful of coleslaw.

"Rachel. Call me Rachel," she says, glancing out the door.

"Rachel. Now about this friend of yours."

"Sara Beth."

He turns when he notices her look past him at someone approaching. Joe sets down two steaming mugs of coffee. "You have enough? The food's good?" Joe asks.

"The best." Joe gives Michael's shoulder a squeeze before turning back to the counter. "He and my Pop were paisans," he explains to Rachel, shifting in his seat and glancing around the room. "Both their parents came from the Italian mountains. Let me tell you a story about them."

"Really," Rachel insists, "I don't have time for stories."

"Hear me out, the story explains something. See, both couples, my father's parents and Joe's parents, came to Ellis Island on the same boat." Rachel sips her coffee, no nod, no nothing. He waits for a second until she glances to the door. "Coming here with only the clothes on their backs, the four of them struck up a friendship on that boat. They lived in the same tenement houses and bought homes on the same block in Queens, raised their families doors apart, took turns having the holidays." He turns back toward Joe. "Always together. Ever since the boat ride."

"Okay. Nice story. Joe over there grew up next door to your father."

"See, right off the boat," he continues, "their fathers were masons. Coming from the old country, that's all they knew. Working with their hands. So with the union work around the city, bricklaying and labor work on the commercial sites, they followed the jobs." He finishes the roll and washes it down with coffee. "They worked hard and saved hard. After about ten years, they settled in Queens, on that same street. They did okay."

He sees that Rachel is about to bolt when she checks her watch. "I'm sorry, but—" she begins.

"Joe and my Pop were like brothers. Eventually Pop bought a house down the same street from Joe. They raised their families as neighbors, just like their parents. I grew up on that street."

"Well. That's great, but I think …"

He sees it coming, the way she looks at her purse, then up at the door. It's in her resigned smile and quick breath, the moment before she decides to leave.

"Wait a sec, okay?" He nods toward Joe behind the counter. "Joe's sixty-six now, could retire with a big bank account. But that would kill him. This," he motions around the small deli, "this is his, you know. His life. His bricks and his mortar and his sweat. His wife, Lena, cooks the sausages and meatballs, and brings in her specialty eggplant parmigiana. They've got another ten years in here, easy."

Rachel's eyes sweep the deli, her purse in her lap, hands through the shoulder strap. At the far end, a small counter with red-cushioned, silver stools butts up against the meat case, full of the freshest cold cuts around. Tubs of macaroni and potato salads fill the cooler case behind the counter.

"Nice, isn't it?" Michael asks. "Between the two of them, they've fed this corner of Manhattan for twenty-five years. The Manhattan that Joe's mason father and shipmate friend, *my* grandfather, helped to build."

Rachel shifts, as though to stand. "I'd like to hear more, really, but—"

"My dad was a union mason all his life, too. Had a stroke a few years ago and never fully recovered. He died last year."

"Well, I'm very sorry. But this isn't helping me—"

"Thanks. Joe took the loss hard. He was so close to Pop that I'm like a son to him, too. And that, Rachel … It's Rachel, right? That's why I understand your worry about your friend. I grew up watching a great friendship. The same expression is on your face that I saw on Joe's, when he lost my Pop."

"You take an extremely long time to get to the point," Rachel says. "And how does that point help me?"

He turns up his hands. "You've lost a good friend, and it makes me want to help. Now, since she's not a minor and hasn't been kidnapped, you can do one of two things."

"Okay." She pulls her chair in close.

"One, we sit here and get that report finished. What they'll do with it at the Station is a Risk Assessment. Prioritize it, give you a copy before they file it away. Too much else is going on, you know?" He takes a swallow of coffee and wipes his mouth with the napkin.

"And the second thing?"

Michael leans close over the table. "Sara Beth. Let me guess. Attractive, educated forty-something, leading a tame life. Nice husband, couple of smart kids, white picket fence, PTA?"

"Pretty close."

"Comes to the Big Apple for this *Ladies' Weekend* and, basically, is seduced. Manhattan looked her dead in the eye, gave her a good stiff drink, a dinner, exciting atmosphere ... Except you can't seduce a married woman unless something's wrong at home. With her old man, with her life."

"What are you saying?"

"Something's screwed up at home, or maybe in her thinking, and it's so bad that she can't go back. It happens. Anything come to mind?"

Rachel sits up straighter. "It's presumptuous of you to tell me Sara Beth's head is messed up."

He starts to stand. "I was just looking for clues. They're always there, somewhere."

"Wait." She grabs his arm. "You said I could do two things."

"Rachel." So he sits again and tries something else. "I don't see you going back to ..."

"Connecticut."

"Connecticut. Right. I don't see you leaving here without a fight. Believe me, you've made yourself clear on that. But don't go hunting her down. You'll only put yourself," he glances past her, then back at her face. "At risk. It's better to wait her out for a few days. Where are you staying?"

"The Plaza. Till Sunday."

"So she knows where she can reach you. That note means this is her *choice*. Give her time, be there for her if she calls or comes back with her tail between her legs. But let her come back to you."

"So you're telling me to spend the next few days waiting in my room. That's the best the NYPD can do?"

He pauses, not sure how to help her. "Well, no. But with no signs of foul play, and she's not a risk to herself or anyone else, our hands are tied. So go ahead and see the sights. But don't check out of The Plaza. If she tries to contact you, the desk will take a message. And she'll know you're still in the city."

"I don't have much choice, except now I'm flying solo."

"Can you call someone to stay with you? A husband? A sister?"

She eyes him for a cautious second, but he never sees this one coming. "I'm a widow."

"Now it's my turn for sympathy."

"Well thank you. And Sara Beth asked me not to bring her husband in on this."

"That's ridiculous. And there's no one else you can call?"

"No one near enough to make the trip."

"That's a tough one then. You've got a lot on your plate. Maybe call her family then."

"But she asked me not to. I mean, what's she thinking? It's not like I can just ignore this and what, go bowling?"

Lord knows he's spent his share of hours alone in desperate situations. There is nothing worse, your worries spinning like a fantastic kaleidoscope sucking you right into it. Maybe he can help her that way, to worry less. "You can, you know."

"What?"

"Just go with me on this. Go bowling."

He kind of figured it would happen, the way she abruptly stands, hikes her bag on her shoulder and reaches in for a few dollars to pay for her coffee. "What the hell? My friend is in serious trouble and you're telling me to go bowling? I'm really losing my patience."

"Hear me out, okay? Please listen."

She pauses, then slowly sits again, that bag and two dollars clutched in her lap.

"No, I don't mean definitely bowling. It's a figure of speech. But you'll imagine the worst waiting alone in your hotel. Believe me, I've been there." His voice drops. "She could be *anywhere*. So finish that report, then go out and spend a few hours bowling, or eating, or at a show, doesn't matter what. Bring your cell and it'll help you wait." Now, he stands. "That's the only thing you can do, really. Pass some time while waiting. Maybe you'll remember something she said in the meantime."

Rachel doesn't answer. She sits looking at her hands, at the counter, out the window, anywhere but at his face.

He checks his watch. "Listen. I thought it might help, you know? That's all."

Footsteps come up behind him. "Michael."

He turns around and can't help smiling. "Lena. How are you today?"

"Good, Michael. Here." Lena is small and moves quietly, a strand of gray hair slipping from her bun. She hands him a red apple she held behind her back. "For Maggie."

"You spoil her, just like she's your kid. She got spooked today, I practically ran over a woman a few blocks back and it shook her up."

"Poor horse. You tell Maggie I'm sorry, and stop by for sugar cubes tomorrow." Lena gives his hand a squeeze and turns back to the kitchen. "And be careful."

There is a second, one that he stretches into a long pause, because sometimes someone needs one, or a situation does, when all that hinges on the day can happen in that pause, before he turns back to the table and pushes in his chair. "Mrs. DeMartino. Take care now. And I hope your friend's all right. I'm sorry I couldn't do more. You let us know if anything develops." He picks up his keys and walks to the door.

* * *

25

Rachel looks out the window onto the narrow street at dusk. Too much is happening, too fast. This is not how she planned on spending her long weekend, this sitting in a Manhattan deli, scared for her friend, talking to a police officer. "Damn it," she says, scrunching up her napkin. Why did Carl have to go and die? This would never have happened if he were here.

But he wasn't, and Sara Beth was. Rachel had turned forty a month after her friend. And it felt good. There's something *new* about it, something exciting. And she always celebrates life's good days, buying herself little presents, chocolates, or silver hoop earrings. Something! And Sara knows this about her! She knows that this weekend is about celebrating a long friendship while turning the corner on forty together. And while shopping and getting mini-makeovers. The fun stuff, like the voucher in the hotel gift bag for a discounted haircut at an exclusive salon. Now she's gone and made it something else.

Rachel turns in her seat when this cop waves back to Joe as he pushes open the door to leave. Friendship or not, she is not going to lose this weekend and just sit around. Forty gives her nerve, is what it does. Is there a limit on that? On nerve? Does the pot ever run dry? Because suddenly she feels like she's been dipping in a lot.

"Excuse me!" she calls out as the door starts closing.

Michael catches the door with his boot heel and backs up into the room, holding his keys in one hand and Maggie's apple in the other. She waits for him to say something, anything, as he looks over his shoulder at her.

"And exactly where would I find a bowling alley in this city?" she finally asks, frustrated that her weekend has come to this, to killing time and worrying, worrying in spades.

"Well," Michael begins, walking back to her table. "Down at the Piers—"

"The Piers?"

He stands at his chair, looks back at the door, then checks his watch. "Okay listen. If you want, I can take you there. A little later on. I have to stop home first."

"You'd do that? You don't even know me."

He shrugs. "I've got a general picture of the situation here."

"Okay," she finally agrees after a long silence, one in which she actually has to glance away, his stare is so darn steady. Maybe it's because there's some tenderness in his look, too, in his offer of time in the city that took her friend.

"You're sure?" he asks, checking his watch again. "I'll pick you up then? At seven. Okay?" He waits, watching closely until she nods. "Get that report done too, okay?" When she agrees, he tosses the apple in the air and catches it before walking out the door.

Seven o'clock. Sometimes you have to set a precedent. Yes. This is what it will be on *her* girl's weekend out. Forty will be *her* choices. If Sara Beth returns by this evening, fine. If not, well. Well okay.

Sara Beth has to do her thing, but so does she. Forty is forty, after all.

So, at forty she thinks she did something she hasn't done in twenty years. She checks her cell phone for any messages from Sara Beth, and stands then, collecting her purse and the police report before heading out the door back to The Plaza.

She accepted a date. Well, kind of a date, anyway.

three

SHOP LIGHTS ARE COMING ON and Rachel catches her reflection in a glass building on Fifth Avenue. The city is doubled in the fading afternoon light, its image reflected in the windows, doubling her panic at the same time. There is two of everyone now. She turns quickly and squints at a passing reflection, auburn hair catching her eye. "Sara!" she calls out, brushing past people until she can reach out and turn the woman. "Sara Beth!" The woman tugs away and keeps moving in one swift motion, a few pigeons flapping in agitation around her feet. Every auburn head will draw her now, there's no getting around it.

It's strange, looking for someone so familiar, so much a part of her life. At sight of the New York Public Library, she crosses the busy street and climbs the grand staircase, finding an available computer terminal she can use inside. She takes a seat at a long wooden table with reading lamps spaced evenly across it. If Sara Beth can't be found physically, maybe there's some sign of her virtually. Maybe she updated her Facebook page, leaving some clue to her behavior today. Or tweeted her whereabouts in one hundred forty characters. Maybe someone friended her, someone who knows something Rachel doesn't know.

First she checks her own email, scanning the inbox, looking for Sara Beth's name there. Not seeing it, a feeling of vast emptiness settles on her. She glances around, moving from her cyber world on the screen to the gothic doorway rising beside her, right next to the table. Two stone pillars reach up to the soaring ceilings, framing the doorway. What a juxtaposition of old and new, the past and present. Online mailboxes and intangible correspondence exist in harmony with the substantiation and strength of this building.

Sara Beth's Facebook page isn't any help. Rachel scrolls over her friends, recognizing different town groups who've left messages on her wall: The Friends of the Library, asking her if she can collect book donations; the Beautification Committee planning the summer plantings; other local names Rachel knows well. And what they all do is suggest a virtual portrait of her friend through their connections. She clicks on Sara Beth's photo albums, coming across several of Sara with her mother in a pumpkin patch, antiquing, at Christmas. There are others, with her sister Melissa, the kids, one with her arms wrapped around Tom.

"What are you doing?"

Rachel looks up at the sound of the harsh voice. A young mother grabs a pen from her child's hand, looking around quickly to see if anyone noticed the scribblings the boy made right on the table. "Let's get out of here," she says, standing and leaving behind a messy pile of books and paper.

Rachel turns back to her screen and blocks out the distraction, focusing intently now on Google and missing person statistics. The mother and son voices echo back even after they've left the room, continuing through the building, indifferent to the people around them.

* * *

Subject: Quick Hello
From: Sara Beth
To: Elizabeth
Date: May 15 at 4:30 PM

Hey Mom, it's me. I haven't talked to you in a few days, and wanted to check in.

Sara Beth looks at the screen for a few seconds, aware of the massive concentration in this huge room. It's amazing how a place so large and full of people can be so hushed. Her eye is drawn to the endless line of long wooden tables, each with reading lamps evenly spaced across them. The old and new. Read a book beneath golden lamplight, or log on to the Internet and read virtually. Her mother loved that sense of contrast, the new adding a whimsy to her old antiques. She misses her so much.

I don't really know what I'm doing Mom. I might've screwed up, I can't tell anymore. Without you here, it's so hard to decide things. So okay, I left. I walked away from everything I knew, for a few days. And honestly, no one will even really realize it, since I wasn't home anyway. I'm just taking a few days alone in NY. I'm not sure why, it felt like I had to get out, to leave. To find answers, something. Remember that da Vinci philosophy we talked about? You know, "One can have no smaller or greater mastery than mastery of oneself." Well I really wish someone, you especially, could tell me exactly how to do that.

Love,
Sara Beth

"What are you doing?"
The voice unnerves Sara Beth, as though it would be the exact question her mother would ask. It came from the far end of the long room, but carried well. "Let's get out of here," a

woman says, and she sees a harried young mother push back her chair and grab the hand of a toddler beside her, rushing out. She looks around the room at the rows of long wooden tables and brass desk lamps and computer stations. Near the loud woman, a grand doorway is framed by two towering stone pillars. The other patrons tune out the woman, intent on their readings and research. In all her life, she'd never been in the New York Public Library, never walked up the steps between Patience and Fortitude. Until today.

four

YOU KNOW HOW TO PLAY, right?"

Rachel looks from the illuminated bowling lane before them back to Michael beside her, his words reeling her away from thoughts of her friend. But isn't that the purpose of all this? Frames and strikes and pins and gutters? "Roll the ball, knock down the pins?"

Michael bends to tie his bowling shoes. "Did you know that Manhattan is where the colonists first played this game? Lower Broadway. Place still called The Bowling Green."

"You sure know bowling," Rachel says, scanning the music video playing above the lane. "Bet they didn't keep score on plasma TVs."

"No." That's it. Nothing else. She feels him watch her and it makes her touch her hair, the feel of his look.

"What?" she asks finally.

"Nothing. And it's not really bowling I know. It's more the city stuff."

"Colonists bowling on Broadway?"

He walks to the ball return and picks up Rachel's ball. "You didn't get one that's too heavy, did you?"

She reaches for the ball but he steps back. "Don't worry," she says. "I'm not going to throw out my back."

"It's happened, is all I'm saying. Now are you a lefty or righty?"

"Righty."

"Okay, so cradle the ball in your left hand. Never pick it up with one hand. You can hurt your wrist." He gently places the ball in her hands.

"Do you know how old I am?"

"It's just, well I don't want you to get hurt." Michael takes a seat laneside, waiting for her to start the frame.

Rachel turns and pauses, bringing the ball up, then running and releasing it to knock down seven pins. "I'm a little rusty," she says.

"Given the circumstances, I'm impressed. But watch your timing."

They bowl quietly for a few frames until Rachel sits beside him on the settee.

"You know," she tells him as they watch the other bowlers around them. "I changed my mind two times today about coming here."

After a few long moments, she begins to wonder if he didn't hear her over the noise, the music and balls rolling. "I'm glad it wasn't three," Michael finally answers. He motions for two cold beers from a waitress. "To friends, old and new," he toasts, right before he touches his glass to hers.

Okay, she has to take stock. So this New York City mounted police officer knows their bowling alley outing is only keeping her busy while she waits out her friend, that's it, hoping that after the game, after they get back to The Plaza, Sara Beth will feel better and return to the hotel too.

"A little more trivia before the next frame?" Michael asks. He settles in his seat, his head tipped low, toward hers. "In World Wars One and Two, soldiers shipped out from The Chelsea Piers, which is where we are." He takes a drink of his beer and looks out at the bowling alley lights flashing, pausing long enough to make her wonder if that's the end of the trivia. "But the Piers are actually noted for something else, besides the wars. Any ideas?"

She contemplates the bowlers around her. A lot of couples, some families.

"And no hints."

Rachel sips her drink and thinks about it, this whole trivia thing, this whole cop thing as he rubs his left shoulder beside her. "Hurt yourself?" she asks pointedly.

"No, wise guy. You playing New York trivia or not?"

"Yes, but." She pauses and searches his eyes. "Wait a minute, it sort of feels like something's riding on this?"

"Could be. Have anything in mind?"

"Well. Not offhand. You?"

He gives her another long look. "Dinner? I don't know, maybe tomorrow night? If your Sara's not back? Guess Pier 59's claim to fame and it's my treat."

"And if I lose?"

Michael offers a handshake. "Nice knowing you?"

"Yeah, right," she says, shaking his hand, feeling his grip linger a second. "I'm really not a history buff, so I can only guess." She leans forward with her elbows on her knees. Runways of blinking lights line the lanes. The Piers. In her mind big steamships come rolling in, immigrants wearing long, dark clothes, women with scarves wrapped over their heads, steam trunks beside them, leaning on the rails as the new world approaches. "Does it have something to do with bringing immigrants over? To Ellis Island?"

"Four-star, or how do they say it? Cozy and off the beaten path?"

"I'm right?"

"Close enough. It is about a ship. And there were immigrants aboard."

Surprising relief is what she feels when she sits back, relief at the promise of company the next evening. Because it works. Time passes. "Wait a minute! I know it."

"What?"

"The Titanic?"

"It was scheduled to pull up to the White Star Pier at the end of her first voyage, April 16, 1912. Only the survivors were brought here, a few days later," Michael says as he stands to pay for a tray of cheese nachos delivered laneside. "I think it's your turn now. And try not to loft the ball."

When she turns back at his admonishment, he holds up a nacho and winks at her. "Good luck," he mouths.

*　*　*

Tom thought the Backwards Dinner would keep the kids distracted from the fact their mother hadn't called from New York, even though he lied and said she called when they were at school. So sue him, he had a lot to learn about his kids being savvy, seeing through his breakfast-for-dinner, wearing their clothes inside out. This wasn't his gig, hanging out with them. His thing was working on cases in his study with Sara Beth scrambling the eggs.

After an hour of Owen spilling his sippy cup, and Kat keeping a log of the two days that passed without talking to her mother, and Jenny having an attitude so big it might as well take a seat beside her, he canned the breakfast dinner and settled the kids down with bowls of fudge swirl ice cream, clouds of whipped cream and thick curlicues of hot fudge. With sundae perfection, life was good.

For the moment. Later, the girls beg Tom to call Sara Beth at the hotel.

"Maybe tomorrow."

"Tomorrow?" Jenny asks, incredulous.

"She's probably at a show," Tom stalls her.

"Why can't we call her cell?" Kat asks.

"I *did* call her cell, all day," Jenny answers. "And it's never on."

"A week ago right now, Mom was still here," Kat says.

"In the morning then?" Jenny presses, ignoring her sister. Her irritation at Kat's time log is plain as day. *A minute from right now I'm going to kill you,* her glare says.

"I don't think it's a good idea, that early. And quit being so dramatic."

"Then why not try her cell again?"

"Because I said so. And her phone'll be off in the theater. After school tomorrow."

"But Aunt Melissa said we could sleep over her house, since it's Friday," Kat reminds him.

"So what. Chelsea won't even be there," Jenny says.

"Why not?"

"She's going to some Coffee House thing at the Rec Center."

"Can't you go too?"

"Come on, Dad. You have to be in high school to go."

"Well she won't be out all night." He sees how edgy the girls are without their mother calling. "Get to bed now. We'll talk tomorrow." He softly closes their door in a way that mimics Sara Beth and walks past the baby's room where the nightlight's glow falls on the crib and he keeps on walking, straight downstairs to the liquor cabinet. Still he gives her this chance. This time. Still he believes Sara Beth will call them, call him, from New York. Still he doesn't think things are that bad.

Holding a glass of Scotch, Tom walks back upstairs and pulls down the attic ladder. The builder had laid the electrical work there and rough framed the walls but Tom finished the rest. Working with his hands satisfied him in a way legal work didn't. And with a family of five, he thought someday the kids might use an attic corner for a playroom or clubhouse. Funny, Sara Beth beat them to it, pilfering the corner for her stray antiques. White sheets shroud the pieces.

Sitting in the dark attic now feels the same way it did the time she climbed into the attic three years ago.

"What?" he asked then, smiling at her odd expression. "Sara?"

"It's a boy."

He had been sitting in the same stenciled chair as he was now, going through a box of paint scrapers while Sara Beth went out with her sister Melissa. The garage trim was peeling then and needed a coat of paint before they listed the house. "Your sister's pregnant?"

Sara Beth shook her head. "I had an ultrasound today."

"You?"

"It's a boy, Tom." She stood in a shaft of dusty light, pulled a small thin printout from her pocket and held it out to him.

Tom studied it in the light beside her. A swirl of complicated soundwaves surrounded the fetus. "What's going on?"

"I never even noticed. Between the night classes and antiquing. And the girls' games and Kat's dance class and getting the house squared away before we sell." She took a long breath. "When I got sick the other morning, I checked the calendar."

"We're having a baby?" he asked, taking her arm. She just stared at him, no smile, nothing. He pulled her closer.

"Tom, I'm thirty-eight. The girls are practically teenagers and we have to start over with a baby? Damn it, I'll be feeding and cleaning till I'm fifty."

"Wait, Sara. Maybe this is good. That's why you didn't have your tubes tied after Kat. Remember?"

"That was before. Things change."

He reached his hand beneath her chin and tipped her head up to him. "Right," he agreed. "And this changes things too. Another *baby*, Sara."

"But we were going to sell the house. I planned to start selling antiques on the side. I don't want to give that up." She pulled out of his hold and sank to a crouch, wrapping her arms around her knees.

He moved into the light and looked at the ultrasound picture again, at his *baby*.

"Dr. Drake? When she saw I wasn't happy, she asked me about an abortion. But we weren't sure how far along I was. That's when she ordered the ultrasound and nixed the abortion. I'm in the third month," Sara Beth said, still crouched.

"Come here," Tom whispered and when she didn't move, he knelt before her. A hindrance to her was like a blessing to him. This changes everything. Including their marriage.

"It's all right. We'll keep the house. There's plenty of room here. And you can still do the antique stuff. Just not right now."

He never forgot her head resting heavy on his shoulder, her body leaning into his as though her own personal plans stood no match against their busy marriage and kids and new babies.

Their lives changed then. Sometimes that scares him, the way days move along right on track and then take a sudden turn in an opposite direction. Now he wonders if it's happening again, that about-face. He checks his watch and hears Kat's child voice, *Ten thirty and still no call.* The desire to talk to his wife suddenly consumes him. He wants to say the words he assured her in the attic, "It's all right, Sara."

Instead he makes his way down the attic ladder with a small box of old baby books and right in the hallway, opens the carton and lifts out a book. Sara Beth read this story to the girls so often, and Owen needs her to do the same with him.

He slides the rocking chair close to the crib and sits there, watching. Before you know it, Owen won't be a baby; this peaceful time in the night won't happen forever. Tom hears the sigh of his son's breathing and then he does what he's been doing more and more for the past year: He figures out how to do this reading thing, how to fill in for his wife, his voice whispering about ducks and happiness and spring and puddles.

After a few pages, he pauses, closes the book, then opens it again. "Raindrops begin falling from a cloud ... Shit, Sara Beth. What are you doing?"

He props the cardboard book on the nightstand beside the crib so that Owen will see the fluffy yellow duck when he wakes in the morning and his first impression will be a happy one.

Then he walks downstairs, sits in the home office, picks up the telephone and dials first his wife's cell, which she doesn't answer, then The Plaza. He has to talk to her and hold her and make love to her. To bring her back. She has to come home first thing tomorrow. Rachel will have to understand. He can't do this all alone. He's not sure what to do with the kids.

"I'm sorry, sir. No answer. Would you like to leave a message?"

"Could you try her room one more time?"

After a half dozen rings, he hangs up. Then he goes back in the attic to retrieve the other box of books.

* * *

Each frame Rachel's allowed herself one more cell phone check, hoping for a text message or voicemail. But now this doesn't feel right, sitting in the glitzy 300 New York bowling alley, watching an incredible number of people cranking, rolling and dumping balls. With the special effect purple and pink lights flashing, it looks like a high-tech radar, like the whole place is searching out Sara Beth.

Michael stands in front of her finishing a handful of peanuts. A faded scar runs along his jaw and his eyes look tired. She cannot even imagine what his day entails. Even though he has a way of easing her worry, casting his New York magic, it's always there, that he's a cop she found for a reason. With another futile cell phone check, the reality of Sara Beth's disappearance drops over her in a sensation, a cold sweat she's known only once before.

"Sara," she had said into the phone, cupping it urgently to her mouth.

"Rachel? Is that you? What's wrong?"

"Carl's on the floor near the bathroom. I just came home and he's on the floor."

"What do you mean? Did he fall?"

A beat of silence passed. "I don't know. He can't talk."

"Oh my God. Is he breathing? Is he?"

"Yes. Yes, I'm pretty sure." Rachel heard her own voice then, some sort of cry, low and disjointed, as though it came from someone else. It made her first look at the phone, then cup it tighter to her mouth, containing the sound. "But his face, oh Sara, his face."

"Rachel, listen. Is an ambulance coming?"

"Yes. But I need you, too."

"Don't worry, I'm coming right now. As soon as I hang up the phone. You go sit with Carl, okay sweetie?"

She nodded, tears wetting her face, the phone pressed close.

"You have to hold his hand." Her friend's words were so kind. Why did the kindest words hurt so much? "Don't let go. And speak softly to him. Tell him you love him."

And that cold reality washed over her: Her husband lay dying. He was leaving. That same feeling comes now. Something is very wrong.

All that matters is that she find her friend. Or talk about her. Or think, or plan. She touches Michael's arm. "Do you think we could leave?"

When their eyes meet, hers must have said it all. "Come on," he says. "I'll get you back to The Plaza."

"You don't mind?" she asks, gathering her handbag. As if she wouldn't leave alone if necessary. A few deep breaths of the fresh air outside make her feel more optimistic. They stop at Billy's Bakery on 9th Avenue on the way.

"Listen, if she's back, you both have some hashing out to do. Billy's cupcakes, I don't know, maybe they'll make it easier."

Walking into the bakery, with its sweet aromas and pale cream brick walls, feels like walking into someone's charming home. They stop in front of a glass case, each shelf filled with trays of cupcakes, chocolate and vanilla, frosted in browns, yellows, whites, pinks. The mere sight of all those sweet pastries does something to her, lifts her somehow. They're little puffs of happiness. Cupcakes.

"Let me have a couple Yellow Daisy, three Red Velvet, and a Chocolate. Throw some sprinkles on a few, would you?" Rachel stands behind him, watching, and he catches her eye. "Food helps," he whispers.

After walking a few blocks trying for a cab, Michael, holding the bakery box, breaks their long silence.

"Twelve thousand five hundred miles."

"To where?"

"Around the city. That's how many miles of sidewalk are in Manhattan. One of the busiest transportation systems in the world. Don't you think so?"

"What I think," Rachel says as Michael snags a cab, "is that Sara Beth better be back. She better not disappear in a twelve thousand mile maze, of all places." What she doesn't say is that Manhattan is where they drank their first cup of coffee together. On an eleventh grade art class field trip, sitting at a tiny table in a shop-front window, leaning sixteen-year-old close, they watched the city go by. Doesn't Sara Beth think of that walking past the city cafés?

At The Plaza, they stop at the front desk to see if there's any word, any message, any indication that Sara Beth had been there to get in touch with Rachel. But there's nothing.

Rachel turns to Michael. So now there's this: It's nighttime in the city and it's different. She doesn't know what to do.

"Do you want to go somewhere quiet? Talk a little?" He takes her gently by the arm and they walk to The Plaza's nightclub. "I'll buy you a glass of wine before I leave, if you want."

Contrary to the dim lighting, an undercurrent of energy moves through The Oak Room. Low voices, tinkling glasses and impeccable waiters moving about charge the room perfectly. After tasting her wine, Rachel scans the patrons. Maybe Sara Beth is as close as this. Maybe she hasn't the nerve to wander much further alone at night.

"Do you really think she'd be here?" Michael asks. He shifts his seat over so that he can see the doorway into the club and sets the cupcake box off to the side.

"I don't know. I can't picture her alone out in the city, either."

"Have you called her husband?"

"Almost, but she asked me not to in her note."

Michael raises his eyebrows. "Rachel."

"Okay, okay. I know. She's asking a lot. But she *did* ask. And I almost called Tom, that's her husband, at work today, but then I thought I'd give her more time. She must have a valid reason to do this, right?" He's studying people at another table and Rachel wonders if he's even listening. "Right?" she asks again.

"A few days head start on leaving him, covering her trail maybe."

"No, Sara's not like that, I'm telling you. I mean, they have their problems. She's said a little here and there. But nothing big."

"You've known each other for long?"

"We met in the eighth grade when she was intrigued with my messy haircut and divorced family. I was the dangerous friend." She sips her wine and it goes down as easily as she needs it to.

"Do you have a picture of her?"

Rachel pulls her wallet from her shoulder bag. "It's a couple years old, but it's all I have. I forgot to leave it with the police report." The photograph has been trimmed to fit into her wallet and shows a close-up shot of two women, one with shoulder length auburn hair and a multi-colored silk scarf tied around her neck. Their heads are tipped together, smiles grinning wildly.

"I was feeling sorry for myself one day after my husband died. She hauled me into an instant photo booth at the mall."

Michael looks up from the picture, past her shoulder at a couple talking, then back at her.

She scans the nightclub with a quick sigh. "She's always been there for me, so why didn't she trust me to be there for her?"

"Maybe she does. Can I keep this?"

"What will you do with it?"

"Give it to the right people, put it into the system." He tucks the photograph into his shirt pocket. "I checked with the department before I picked you up. Nothing fit her profile. No arrests, no Jane Does."

"I thought the police couldn't do anything at this point."

"Let's say you have a connection now. Anything else I should know about this Sara Beth Riley?"

"You're very kind."

"Kind?" he asks.

"I'm sure you have a life to get back to."

"Maybe." He raises his glass and after taking a swallow, scans a small group of friends entering the room. "And maybe we can't always be too sure about people."

She studies his face, considering. He shaved after work, but the day has been long. Shadows beneath his eyes hold either fatigue or his own stories. And she notices a bead of perspiration; he's nervous now. "It's late ..."

"Tell me whatever comes to mind. Maybe something will click. A clue, an idea."

"Sara was my Maid of Honor, my daughter's Godmother. When Carl, that's my husband, when he had his heart attack, I called Sara Beth after I called 911. And she drove over faster than the ambulance. She was six months pregnant, driving all crazy like that."

"For you."

"And for my daughter. She stayed with her that night while I sat at the hospital." Rachel pauses, thinking back. "So am I repaying her now, *being there* for her? They say these *girls'* *weekends* are about the bonding, and celebrating friendship. So is this what I'm *supposed* to do? Respect her wishes?" She holds up her wine glass in a toast to their long friendship. "In twenty-five years of stories, what's scary is that none of them explains Sara Beth's behavior today." She also can't explain how she suddenly wants to be where she can wait for the door to open or the telephone to ring. She needs to be in their room, purely waiting now.

"Do me a favor then. I know you're tired. But think about those years of stories." He pats his jacket pockets. "Do you have a pen?"

She finds a pen and pad of paper in her bag and watches while he jots down information. He folds the paper and slides it across the table. "That's my home number in Queens and my cell. If you think of anything, let me know. Anytime. If she shows up, if she's in trouble. Anything. And give me your number, too. You know. In case I have to reach you, okay?"

She does, watching him write it down, crossing out a number he writes wrong, glad for someone, at least, to know where she's at.

* * *

Sara Beth drops her purse in the bathroom sink and digs her hands in, searching blindly for the aspirin bottle. Her headache is so bad, she could barely see straight at the registration desk, dropping the room key as the clerk handed it to her. Finally she dumps the whole thing, keys and wallet and makeup and cell phone and sunglasses, clattering into the sink. She fishes out the aspirin bottle and shakes three tablets into her palm.

But something happens when she reaches for the glass of water. Her reflection stops her. With it, a memory comes of her mother not in her seventies, but at this age, looking just like Sara. And she imagines the incredible lightness of talking to her, a lightness she could always float on, it is so beautiful, the closeness she shared with her mother. The idea could make a stunning abstract painting, the way her mother, the way family, can be sweet rays of light. The mirror frames her face. A Picasso, maybe.

So standing in the tiny bathroom with its pale green tiled wall, she looks again at the three aspirin tablets in her palm, then back at her mother in the mirror, imagining what she would say if she called her, pressed the phone tight to her ear.

"Sara?" her mom would ask, to be sure she was okay. Then she'd listen to Sara Beth telling how she had stepped out of her life, and rented this tiny room, and risked losing a dear friendship, and her mom would, well, she'd worry of course. First, there would be a long silence. Oh Sara Beth knew that silence. It happened when her mother didn't really like something. *"Well then,"* she'd say. *"We're going to have to get to the bottom of this. And soon. I'm not sure I really understand what you're saying. You know I can't be there, and I think you're strong enough to find your way without me. To finish the things we started. But walking out, Sara? Are you sure that's the way to clear your thoughts?"*

Looking in the mirror, her fingers light on her face like a painter brushing in the strokes, pulling her eyes up, her cheeks back. It wasn't easy walking out on forty years of life today. One uncertain step at a time, right through the restaurant doors. She couldn't go on the way she'd been, so tired, not moving forward. If she didn't take these few days to find a way to change, she'd be no use to anyone.

But her headache. She pours a glass of water and swallows the three tablets. What if it's serious? What if it's a warning headache before an aneurysm? "A brain aneurysm is a bulge in the artery in your brain," she recites quietly. "Unruptured, it presses on the brain, causing severe headache. More common in adults than children." Who would know where she is? Would anyone help her? How would Tom know? And then she can't breathe, gasping in a deep breath. When she opens her eyes, it's her mother in the mirror.

"Oh but I love what you've done to your hair," her mother might say if she saw her now, with her hair cut short, the new layers highlighted and tousled. But she wouldn't see her. She would never see Sara Beth again.

five

WHEN SHE WAKES UP, THROUGH a wall, or ceiling, Rachel notices the muffled intonations of a man and woman talking. It's hard to tell if it comes from another room or out in the hallway. But what she hears is the masculine drone of Carl's voice and it brings her to tears. "For your birthday," he had said one morning a few years ago. "Would you like that?"

She'd looked at him over a steaming coffee cup. "Paris in the springtime? I'll bet it's beautiful."

"Paris or London. It doesn't matter. Any birthday ending in zero is a big one. Let's do forty up big." But he never made it, to her forty or his fifty. He died at forty-eight.

This is the spring when Carl planned on taking her to Paris.

So she needed that sense of travel, of being away and returning home from a trip. Because what she knows is this: Intentions don't die with the body. They are of the spirit. And fulfilling Carl's intentions enables her to let go, leaving no unfinished matters in their marriage.

She slips into her robe. Sara Beth might very well be in the next room, sitting on the tapestry sofa, a mug of coffee cupped in her hands, her face wearing an apologetic smile. They can still salvage the weekend. So Rachel puts on the right expectant face and opens her bedroom door. But there is no friend on the other side, only diffused sunlight bathing the fine furniture in a golden glow.

Standing alone, she's not sure who her damn tears are for: Sara or Carl. "Couldn't you have held on?" she asks, turning around. "I don't know what to do."

As previously arranged, Room Service arrives with breakfast. She and Sara Beth had it all planned out. First, a pot of coffee, fresh-squeezed orange juice, warm muffins, New York newspapers. Okay, okay. Then a stop at The Today Show, it's totally tourist, but they'd have loved it, leaning against the railing, hoping the camera panned them, waving for Sara's kids. Then a walk in Central Park before having their nails done for tonight. Teri Alexander, their high school classmate, had a singing engagement at The Metropolitan Room. Tonight is the big planned celebration of both their fortieth birthdays.

She checks her voicemail then pours herself a cup of coffee. Doesn't Sara Beth remember this? Isn't she thinking of her as the day begins? Sara specifically ordered the apple crumb muffins. Rachel curls up on the sofa and through the large window she sees not New York, but home in Addison, and the coffee shop at the corner of Main and Brookside.

Whole Latte Life. It's a tiny place, like a delicate china cup tucked snug on the corner and facing the town Green. A place to sit and mull over their lives. Its windowed front looks out on a manicured lawn and clusters of maple trees. There are wooden benches and barrels of flowers. Locals ride their horses around the perimeter. A whole latte perfection.

They call it their salvation, meeting for coffee twice a week after Sara gets the kids off to school. Because there is always something behind the talking, some pulse being taken. *How's your life?* it says. *Let me press a vein, take a look at your heart.* They circle tag sale ads for antiques while considering going back to college; they plan early bird stops at the farmers' market for baby tomato plants and impatiens and herbs while debating daycare for Owen. It's like they're quilters weaving pieces of their lives into a patchwork quilt, their everyday stories a different patch stitched with the telling, the listening, the tears and laughter.

She sips her coffee now and looks out at Manhattan. Did Sara Beth sleep last night? Or eat? Is she still in New York? She picks up the remote and finds The Today Show on the television. Finally the cameras pan out on the Plaza, showing throngs of women holding signs, talking, arms linked. Friends, everywhere she looks there are friends. She pictures the sign she should have made. *Sara Beth! Call me!* The camera moves along the crowd as she watches for that auburn hair falling across Sara's forehead, tucked behind an ear. There are so many signs today! Is one from Sara? Does it say she's okay, don't worry? Tom planned to tape this so the kids could look for them after school.

If it wasn't for her note, for that *Please don't call Tom, please Rachel,* that call would've already been made. But she decides to give Sara Beth what she wants, for now. That privacy. While Sara Beth does … what?

Which makes Rachel go straight for her cell phone. Sara Beth is at risk, because, really, this is proof enough, this imagining desperate signs at The Today Show pleading for contact, and her husband should know. She checks her watch, then her phone.

A knock at the door interrupts her and when she rushes to open it, hoping to see Sara Beth standing on the other side, there is only this: the same Room Service Porter. "Excuse me again. This should have been delivered with your breakfast." He hands her a small package. "Sorry for the mix-up."

"Thank you," she tells him, her heart beating fast enough to get her attention. The package is four inches square and neatly addressed in Ashley's handwriting. Rachel closes the door and unwraps it right there to find a book inside. Her finger trails the inscription.

Dear Mom,

I know we had dinner on your birthday last month. But consider this a surprise party. I didn't want you thinking I forgot about you and Sara Beth. Happy B-Day! Enjoy the book and the city!

XOXO,
Ashley

Brief verses and sweet anecdotes fill the tiny book about mothers. She skims Ashley's margin notes written on dog-eared pages. It's like her daughter reads over her shoulder, pointing, *Oh look!* Her words do that, her *Sounds like us, Mom.* Or *remember that café we went to, at the beach?* They reach over her shoulder.

And that is exactly when Rachel decides she *will* celebrate her birthday today. Ashley had arrived in spirit, and maybe thoughts of their planned evening on the town will lure Sara Beth back to The Plaza, to her life. That'll be her plan. She'll give her friend until tonight.

After a shower, she brushes her hair back, touches up her makeup, grabs her jacket and steps in front of the mirror. Her hands slide flat along the black skinny jeans hugging her hips, considering a single forty-year-old woman unexpectedly alone in Manhattan for a long weekend.

The thing is, she's not really sure how to be single again. And is she even ready to leave Carl's memory this way? After all, she went bowling with a stranger last night. Her guilt brings on that gosh darn twinge in her heart. The one telling her how much she'd *love* to tell that bowling story to her missing friend, sharing details between sips of espresso. And getting a second opinion.

She slips into her jacket, walks through the living room and locks the door behind her. There are things to do, after all, things that keep her from picturing Sara Beth right now, in memory or imagination. Memory feels too sad and imagination is just too scary.

* * *

Now Michael knows what Rachel felt like yesterday searching for her friend. He's been scanning faces all morning, hoping to see her walking down the avenue or stepping out of a cab. It gets to be maddening. Did Sara Beth return? Is Rachel still in the city?

Traffic jams up a couple blocks away and by the time he gets to the heart of the congestion, the obstacle is gone but drivers are backed up. He turns Maggie and she nods hard, like she's telling him *I know, look how they drive.* So he scans the pedestrians for Rachel, or Sara Beth, then motions for the cars on 53rd to start moving, eyeing back Sixth Avenue drivers. The one limousine trying to slip through stops with a verbal warning. One more inch and he's writing a ticket.

When the traffic flow eases, Michael moves in the direction of Joe and Lena's delicatessen. The precinct radioed him a message to stop by the deli and Lena steps outside with a coffee and doughnut, bribing him with food, so he knows something's wrong. Apparently Lena saw Summer on her way to school and his daughter was upset. The news is that his ex-wife wants to move her out of Queens.

Now, a few blocks further, freshly painted crosswalks spook Maggie and she balks, sidestepping the lines. No amount of clicking, neck rubbing or stern commands budge her over the lines. He finally has to dismount and walk the big brown horse back a block to a street vendor they passed. Maggie begrudgingly nibbles at the hot dog cart umbrella as though this is *his* fault, snorting and waiting for a piece of bread. "You could win an Oscar," he tells her. The vendor gives him a roll which he breaks in half. They both need the break.

After downing a hot dog and a bottled water, he rolls a kink out of his neck then holds out his flat hand for Maggie. In one swoop, her velvet lips lift the second chunk of bread before he mounts her. They make their way back down Sixth Avenue, this time stepping over the freshly painted crosswalk with ease.

"You did that on purpose, didn't you?" he asks the horse, and her ears tip back to his voice. He pats her neck and moves into traffic, checking his cell for messages as he does. No sooner does the driver of a van ask about city parking does Maggie nod hard and slip in a sidestep prance. He pulls sharp on the reins and decides to end his tension, which his horse is obviously feeding off of. Maneuvering her over to the curb, he checks his cell again and dials Rachel's.

"Mrs. DeMartino," he says, surprised at the noise wherever she is. "It's me, Michael. NYPD? I wondered if you had any word from your friend."

Rachel pauses, then, "No. Nothing."

Maggie fidgets, turning into the traffic until he pulls on her reins and turns her back. "Where are you? It's really noisy."

"Okay, hear me out. You'll probably think it's really dumb, you know, what a tourist. But I'm at The Today Show. It's just that we—"

"You're out searching for her then," he interrupts.

"Yes, I am."

"Why don't you call her husband? It's probably time."

"No. Not till after tonight."

"What's tonight?"

"We had plans, and I'm thinking she might show up there."

"You feel like company? I don't know, maybe you want to cash in that dinner bet?"

She's quiet first, then says, "You know, company would be great. I really don't feel like doing this thing alone. We're seeing a friend at The Metropolitan Room. She's got a gig there."

"Okay. That's decent. I'll pick you up early and pay up the wager. We'll eat at Bobo's. Little place in the West Village. It's a little better than bowling, if you know what I mean. And listen, Rockefeller Plaza *is* a real central thoroughfare. If you sit on a bench and watch the people, maybe she'll pass by." He digs in a heel against the horse's side when she starts another sidestep into traffic, pulling her back hard. "But be aware of who's around you. And leave your cell on, okay?"

six

NO PRESENT COULD EVER MATCH what her mother had given her. The package arrived by courier on her fortieth birthday, shortly after the kids were on the school bus and Tom had left for work. It was a complete surprise, getting a present delivered like that months after her death.

She set it on the kitchen table, sunlight streaming in through the window, the wrapping paper shimmering. They had talked about this birthday a lot. Forty was one of the biggest. Forty meant you could take chances; the kids were older, your home was settled, risk wasn't as risky. She and her mother had planned on opening their antique shop during her fortieth year. That had been her dream until she woke up to a new reality: pregnant at thirty-eight with Owen. New babies and bottles and schedules and diapers leave little room for new businesses. And then her mother died.

So she poured herself a cup of coffee on the morning of her fortieth, sat herself down and wondered how her mother sent something to salvage a birthday started with disappointment. That the gift would be special went without saying. That it might break open Sara Beth's heart with the weight of its love never crossed her mind.

The box was square and slim, and she guessed while untying the ribbon that it might be jewelry, a special keepsake. But she was wrong. Nestled deep in tissue was a lone brass skeleton key. It was polished to a dull shine, seeming nearly liquid. Sara Beth lifted it, turned it, then opened the card.

Dear Sara Beth,

Happy birthday, hon! It's the first day of your whole new life and I wanted to be a part of that moment, that celebration. This key is like the tiniest stacking doll nestled deep inside, and will open a wonderful door for you in more ways than one ... Please try the key, which is my gift, before the day is over. 1438 Old Willow Road. It unlocks the carriage house around back. Have fun!

Love you,
Mom

Old Willow Road was down by the river, nowhere near her mother's old house. Sara Beth showered and changed into a pair of jeans and long sleeved tee before pulling her cropped vest on over it to ward off the morning damp. She couldn't imagine what her mother had arranged, or how. After dropping Owen at playgroup, for the ten minute ride to the carriage house she wanted nothing more than to call her to break the suspense, if only she could.

The driveway snaked around the side of the farmhouse. There were lots of trees in the yard and a silver ribbon of river curved off in the distance. Sara Beth sat in her car and considered the white planked carriage house, the dark green beams crisscrossing the doors. A gold balloon bobbed from the door, curled streamers on the string blowing in the breeze.

"Oh Mom," she said to herself as she got out of the car. "What have you done?" The note hadn't said anything about going to the main house, just to go to the carriage house. And there was that balloon, so this was all somehow planned. But how? Leaves and twigs crunched beneath her feet. She slipped the key into the old lock on the right hand side door. It turned easily, so she lifted the cross beam and pulled it opened.

First there were only colors. Browns that never shimmered as beautiful as they did through tears. Beneath the mahogany, oak, cherry and pine antiques spread a sea of gold and burgundy in an oriental carpet. A vase of fresh dahlias graced an heirloom hand-stitched lace runner atop a long dark table.

There wasn't as much furniture as it seemed at first, what with the surprise of it all. Just enough antiques to start organizing a shop. But that her mother accomplished this much alone was amazing. And that she believed eternally in Sara's dream, even more so. Brass candlesticks were artfully arranged on a Queen Anne mahogany drop-leaf table. What caught her eye though was the gold swirled velvet and the oak arms of the child's Morris chair from her mother's house. The kids loved that little chair, sitting in it in front of her television set when they were little. It was a valuable antique.

"Why?" Sara Beth asked, brushing tears from her face. "How can this be?"

"Is something wrong, miss?" an older fellow asks, touching her elbow.

"No. Thank you, I'm fine," she tells him, turning around at the antique shop on East 60th. But she doesn't move, instead picking up an intricately painted navy and gold Matrioshka doll from the table, opening the nesting dolls until she gets to the tiniest inside. *It's like the place where a mother keeps her love,* her mother told her once. *It's the tiniest Matrioshka doll, nestled deep within.* Just like the brass key nestled in that tissue. And she decides to buy this doll for her mother. She'll give it to her for a special occasion, this New York souvenir. And what Sara Beth knows, holding this rare collectible, is this: Sometimes her life feels like an intricate constellation, a collection of feelings and people and dreams and events spinning through her universe.

And though the stars may be light-years apart, they are still all connected, part of only one constellation.

* * *

Tom had backed Sara Beth's car out to the driveway and turned on the overhead light so they could paint in the garage. But not before moving the piecrust tip table he found wedged in the front corner. A web of fine scratches lines the dull finish, but the table is intact. Sara Beth used to bring home old pieces of furniture the way people rescue stray animals. *It's so pretty. It just needs a little shining, then I'll find it a home.*

With the girls settled in for the overnight at their cousin's, this together stuff will be good for Owen. But he worries as he sets up: Is Owen too young for painting? Will he bore quickly? Should he have his sippy cup out here? A snack? How do you know? And then there are the Sara Beth questions: Will this weekend rejuvenate her? She's been off, lately. Will she be happier, her old self, when she comes back? Should he leave her alone and not try to call her?

"Paint, Daddy. Paint," Owen says as Tom fills a bucket with water. He sets it near his own paint can and adds an inky dose of blue food coloring. "Boo."

"That's right. Blue. Here, you stir." Owen takes the paint stick and stirs the water to swirls of blue while Tom lays a piece of plywood down on the garage floor, which he had power washed last weekend. Now he sets up blocks of scrap wood and a plain wooden toy car plucked out of a bin at Stickley's Furniture. Beside it is a new bookcase for Owen's room. "Daddy paints and Owen paints."

Tom's never done stuff like this alone with his son. He always brought casework home, working in the evenings for a few hours. So the questions keep coming. Do you talk while you paint? Is just being side-by-side enough for a child? The only sound is of wet paint brushes moving over clean wood. When he stops and contemplates the bookcase for a minute,

Owen sets down his paint brush and looks from Tom to his car and blocks.

But Owen's not contemplating what Tom is: He talked to Sara Beth's sister Melissa when he dropped off the girls there after work. No one's heard from her. And he told his sister-in-law if he doesn't hear from her tonight, he's headed to Manhattan in the morning. Sara's been distracted for months now, and this is just more of the same. The way he figures, if anything were wrong, Rachel definitely would have called. So he has that. For now.

When he looks up, Owen is sweeping blue paint onto the trunk and back bumper of his car.

Not colored water. Blue paint, just like on his toy car.

"Owen! Hey, hey stop!" He grabs the brush from his son's hand. "Perfect. Now Daddy has a blue car too, exactly like yours," he says.

"Owie boo car," Owen squeals, flapping his arms against his side.

"God damn it." He throws Owen's brush into the water bucket. "I don't need this shit, Sara," he says, grabbing a clean rag. He wipes off the wet blue paint, his biggest fan wiping along right beside him. They buff it out together with a little paste wax. Finally Tom hoists him up on his hip. "Sorry guy. Daddy's a little crabby, huh? We'll let the cars dry now, okay? Let's get you cleaned up." His hand brushes through Owen's mop of hair and he carries him through the door to the kitchen.

seven

THE FIRST THING PEOPLE NOTICE is the dress, black stretch crepe sporting a side slit and halter neckline. Under the elaborate lighting, it makes her long figure look all leg. In keeping the dress central, Teri Alexander wears her dark hair pulled back in a low twist. But it is her voice that hypnotizes. From behind the lone microphone, Teri captures The Metropolitan Room with a string of sultry songs weaving a tender story of love gone wrong.

But Michael's eyes are on Rachel. What could've been, and should've been, weighs heavy in the crowded room. Sara Beth's absence is like a soft pencil, a pastel, shading the hours lightly.

"The crowd loves you," Rachel says with a proud smile. "And this dress! What is it? Valentino or vintage?"

"The secret is to leave them wondering." Teri stands after spending her break at their table. "I am so glad you made it tonight. Tell Sara I missed her?" She turns to Michael. "And it was nice to meet you," she says, reaching for his hand.

"The pleasure was mine. Wonderful show."

"I'll email you," Rachel tells her.

Michael notices, all night, the details Rachel decided to tell, to not tell. She hadn't mentioned the disappearance to Teri, saying only that Sara Beth wasn't feeling well. He waits for

Rachel to say goodbye before guiding her through the crowd to the damp night outside. A fine sheen of moisture reflects off the city streets.

"How could Sara Beth have missed this? Teri's our old friend. This is what life's about, celebrating the milestones."

"Maybe she's having a milestone of her own."

Rachel looks up at him, slowing her step.

"To disappear here? With just enough communication to buy her freedom? A breakdown can be a milestone." He turns up the collar of his overcoat as the rain gets heavier. "Let's get a cab. I know a little place not too far from here."

It takes a few minutes in the wet weather to find an empty taxi. "Why don't you call her husband now?" Michael asks when they settle into the back seat.

The rain-streaked window distorts the city lights, playing tricks on their eyes. Rachel looks out at the few passersby. "I'm going to wait a little longer. Maybe she'll come around."

"What exactly are you waiting for? Her body showing up in a dumpster? I'm sorry if it sounds harsh, but it does happen. Maybe you should call before you regret it."

"Listen, Sara Beth is an adult. This was her decision and I'm not going to chase her down. She told me *specifically* she needed this time."

"If you're sure."

"This must be what she wants," Rachel answers as she pulls her cell phone from her purse. There are no messages. "You know, this night really meant a lot to me. But she walked away from it." She gives in to a small smile, giving Sara Beth the benefit of the doubt. "I guess she has her reasons, but I've had this evening planned for months. And you have been wonderful, taking me to Bobo's and to see Teri. I really don't want it to end yet. Thank you for asking about Sara, but I'd rather go to the club you mentioned."

He doesn't push Rachel to change her mind. Lights reflect on the wet street in glistening ribbons. Leaning forward in the dark cab, he gives the driver the address. Once inside the club, he checks their coats and the host leads them to a booth along a side wall. A three-piece jazz combo holds the floor, the lighting low.

Before they settle in the booth, Rachel scans the patrons, looking for Sara Beth's face. Behind a drink, in the shadows, lost in a crowd, she searches for even a silhouette. It makes Michael wonder why Sara Beth bothered to plan this trip with Rachel. It *should* have been perfect. As time passes, this friend has to feel Rachel's disappointment. She has to think of Rachel, doesn't she? Maybe she doesn't. Maybe the situation is that bad, because Rachel seems too nice to hurt otherwise.

"What a difference a day makes," he thinks out loud.

"What do you mean?"

His gaze moves around the club. "One day, two lifelong friends arrive for this posh birthday weekend at The Plaza? And the next day, one friend falls into some midlife crisis? It's crazy."

"And the other friend?"

He touches his champagne glass to hers, looking at her eyes, fully aware of the long charcoal gray slim skirt, fitted top and unconstructed black velvet jacket specially selected for this evening. Her blonde hair is down and the jewelry of choice is all sterling.

"She looks gorgeous, in case anyone hasn't told you recently."

"Oh, you New Yorkers," Rachel says.

"Happy birthday." He takes a sip of the champagne.

"Thank you," she answers, watching him closely. The music moves through the room like wisps of fog, winding around tables, visiting at the booths. "I've been so wrapped up in Sara Beth, I don't know a whole lot about you, Officer Micelli." She reaches forward and clasps his hand briefly. "Tell me about yourself."

What that does is make him feel very aware of himself as she looks from his eyes, to his face, weathered from a life outdoors patrolling the city streets, to the gray creeping into his dark hair at the temples, sitting in this club in Manhattan.

So how do you tell someone that there isn't much to tell? That you haven't gone out two nights in a row for months? How do you explain mundane, that your life is lacking? Empty, even. Until suddenly, one screwy Thursday when you least expect it, that same someone inches right into that big empty space.

He spins his glass slowly, looking at Rachel, then beyond her, in the dim light. "There's not much to tell. You'll wish you'd never asked."

"No sir. Come on now," Rachel says, smiling.

"Okay. Well, I've been on the force for fourteen years. Five on horseback." He'll make the rest quick and painless. "I'm divorced. I live alone in my childhood home in Queens, am a Yankees rather than a Mets fan and I have a daughter, too. She's fifteen and so far on the straight and narrow." Does he mention that he's afraid that is about to change? He shifts in his seat. "I don't go out much. A drink here and there, catch some ball games, you know, see my daughter, go to the movies. Really, Rachel. It's pretty lame."

"Sounds nice to me." She watches him still.

"Okay then. Let's see ... I'm forty-four years old and liking it these days, and I love music." The piano notes tiptoe past and he nods toward the band.

"Go on," Rachel urges.

He pauses, not having put his life under a microscope like this for a long time. Does she really want to hear about his horse and what it feels like to patrol the city streets from a saddle? Does she want to know his daughter's name and what style house he lives in? What it is about forty-four that has him liking it? Would she understand the security he finds in it all?

"Only one more thing." Really, Rachel DeMartino seems too urbane to care much about a New York City cop. He doesn't want to lose her on the trivia of his days. Funny, he's finding that he doesn't want to lose this abandoned friend at all.

"I'm waiting …"

It's Friday and the hot spots are jumping in the city. Other dance floors are filled to capacity. Here, well, here the crowd swells after midnight. He pauses, then reaches for her hand. "I like to dance."

They walk to the edge of the dance floor, his hand reaching around to the small of her back as they dance a slow song that has her glance around the room briefly before she's looking right back at him.

He senses that gaze stopping at the shadows of his face, seeing his features up close, trying to catch his eye. It feels different tonight, holding her like this, compared to yesterday's coffee at Joe's deli, hearing her story. The music plays and he moves his hand over the smooth velvet jacket on her back, up to her neck, drawing her close. She rests her head on his shoulder.

"And there's one more thing," he says, bending close to her ear. "I haven't had a weekend this interesting in a long, long time." He doesn't see her smile and close her eyes as he folds her hand to his chest and they finish the dance.

* * *

"Your turn."

"For what?"

"Who are you, Rachel?"

After two dances and a drink, it seems he wants to know more. So far he only knows her as the blonde widow deserted in Manhattan on a weekend birthday jaunt. He folds his arms on the table and leans closer.

"Well, you know all about me. I'm a pesky Connecticut widow," she says, pulling out her cell phone. "Wait, let me try her again." A few seconds later, she sets it on the table with an apologetic shrug. The damp weather brings a wave to Michael's short, dark hair. His eyes that look tired at the end of a day, at the end of the week, soften now. "And I'm just waiting for my friend?"

"This isn't about Sara Beth. Last night was, bowling. The Metropolitan Room was about her too. And later we'll bring her back into the fold. But now?" He shakes his head. "Sara Beth's doing her own thing and so are you. This here," he motions between Rachel and himself, "this is about us. This feels more like a date, I think, and I'd like to know you better."

The waitress sets down two glasses of sparkling wine. Even though Rachel considers last night's bowling a date, sort of, he is right. This feels more like the real thing, with the dinner and music. This feels nice.

"If this is a date, then you're the first guy I've dated in twenty years," she finally says.

"How am I doing?" Michael asks seriously.

The thought that comes to her is that she never expected someone like this to supplant her thoughts of Carl.

"Rachel." He leans closer. "How are you with this?"

"I'm okay."

"Okay." He leans back, turning a little so his shoulder rests on the booth back. "So I'm your first date. Now tell me your story."

"The condensed version or Chapter One, which means we might not get out of here tonight."

"Chapter One, by all means."

Yesterday afternoon she had been so impatient with his slow, roundabout way of making a point when she wanted answers about her wayward friend. Now she's seeing that he never rushes anything. In fact, he has a way of savoring every fast moving moment in this city. Of catching each one and saying *Whoa! Slow down now.* Of carefully listening to and seeing every frame on the reel.

"Chapter One," she muses, filling in the background with her parents' divorce when she was thirteen, describing how it tore her childhood neatly in half. She adds detail with Sara Beth, safe and enviable at the time, coming into her life in the eighth grade courtyard. And then there's her marriage to Carl during her last year at college. With Carl she had the chance to finally heal, with her own marriage, that gaping wound left by her parents' divorce. She'd never had the Norman Rockwell stuff and she craved an old-fashioned family life like a chocoholic craves her drug of choice.

Carl was ten years older and their relationship satiated her. She started her new family right away, having Ashley within a year. "And now she's finishing her first year of college, in upstate New York."

"You miss her."

"We're very close, even when we're apart." Rachel tells him about the book Ashley had the front desk send up on her breakfast tray. "We're really mushy that way. Always thinking of each other." She waits for his eyes to meet hers; he's studying people at a table beyond them. "But I'm boring you. I'm sorry."

"What? Boring me? Far from it." He pulls his chair closer. "Ashley."

"Yes. I miss her a lot, but I've got my gardening and night courses and my walking club. That whole part of my life: marriage, raising a child, family ..." She snaps her fingers. "It flew by."

"You were happy then."

"Why do you say that?"

"That's when time flies. When you're happy."

"True. Feeling connected and at home, well you know. Like you feel about Joe and Lena. It gives you a provenance. I've been in my home for twenty years and hadn't planned on ever leaving before Carl died."

"Where would you go?" Michael asks.

"I don't know. With Ashley away at school now, maybe a condominium."

He looks her dead on. "You? The woman who managed to snag a reservation in The Plaza? You are definitely not the condominium type."

"What type am I then?" She's curious as to how he sees her, curious about why he's folding and unfolding the napkin.

"How can I say this? You're a homebody, in the best sense of the word. You need to have a comfortable home of your own."

"But you live alone. Doesn't the quiet get to you?"

"Don't forget where I spend my days. To me, quiet's beautiful." He reaches for her hand and they dance a little closer this time, a little slower. This time, when he doesn't hold her gaze, he leans in close. "Can I see you tomorrow? Whatever you had planned with Sara Beth, we'll do together."

She pulls back, a little surprised. "We planned to do some shopping, then check out the Empire State Building." The breakfast at Tiffany's she keeps to herself. You have to keep plans like that secret, like the street vendor croissants they'd buy, the dark sunglasses. If she tells them, the holes show and become the places where you lose hope, the tiny grains of it slipping through.

"I'll wait with you, okay? Say, two o'clock?" he asks.

"You don't have to do that. I'll be fine."

"Well I'd like to. But it's up to you. You know, if it's okay."

"All right, maybe for a little while. I don't want to impose though."

He clasps her hand and folds it into him, pulling her in close to his shoulder, holding her near, in a small jazz club in Manhattan.

* * *

Once Michael dropped Rachel off at her hotel, he stopped at the Precinct to check the night's reports. Dispatch said it was a slow night. The rain'll do that. Nothing on a Sara Beth Riley. No nameless arrests that fit. Now that he's finally home though, he can't relax. He thought he'd be ready to crash, but something's off.

In the kitchen, each chair is tucked up to the table. Pulling the bottled water from the refrigerator, he waits, then takes a long drink. The house is still, which only makes his noises louder. He screws the cap back on, puts it away and walks into the living room, moving open the drawn drapes. The houses outside stand neatly aligned, but different in their own way. A porch on one, two car garage on another, some stone fronted, some brick, some clapboard siding. Here and there, a lamppost shines. He turns and goes through the living room to the staircase, taking the steps two at a time. At the top, he snaps on the hall light. The spare bedroom door is ajar and so he knows.

His daughter never sleeps with the door closed tight. For all her airs of independence, whenever she spends the night, the door is opened.

The hall light falls into her room. Summer lies curled up, facing the wall, her breathing deep and regular. Her backpack sits on the floor. It isn't surprising, really, that she came looking for him tonight. He's lived in this house forever and she must have thought that she could, too.

How can he do what is best for her? How can he possibly keep her here and happy, when her mother wants to uproot her to Long Island to her big new house, upsetting the apple cart with only a couple years to go?

He grabs the backpack to check in his own room. So long as her cell phone is in it and there's no evidence of that Facebook stuff or any dope, she'll be all right. He'll call her mother in the morning and try to get a straight story out of her. If she won't budge on moving, they'll have to make joint custody arrangements. And then it'll start, her argument that Summer should spend most of her time on Long Island. It always comes down to image. It's why she left. When he didn't move up the ranks to her liking, she walked.

He pulls his keys from his coat pocket and sets them on the dresser. It's funny how with one bedroom door ajar in the upstairs hallway, his empty life begins filling up quickly. Rachel and Summer and an ex-wife and joint custody and a missing person. And a small jazz club. And tomorrow. Lunch and the Empire State Building.

He switches off the lamp and lies in bed, listening to the rain drum against the dormered window. It comes steady now.

* * *

They had a piano when she was growing up. It sat there for the longest time, unused, until she finally started taking piano lessons. It was in the den, set beneath a window where the sun fell on it, and Sara Beth liked sitting there, tinkering with the keys. But then her parents added the addition on to the house for her father's veterinary practice, using the den space, and that was that. Somewhere along the line, the piano was sold to make room for the animals. So what happened to that part of her? To the part that journeyed through music.

"Ready to order? Care for a coffee, miss?"

"Oh. Yes. How late are you open?"

"The Skylight Diner's opened round the clock, hon."

Rain streaks the diner window, warping the city lights. "You mean I can sit here all night if I want to?"

"So long as you're a paying customer." The waitress sets down the pot of coffee. "But don't you have somewhere to go? Keeping a handsome fella waiting out there?"

She smiles politely and shakes her head. Her hand reaches up to tuck her hair behind her ear, it's such a habit, the way she tips her head with a smile and does that. Having worn it long forever, she is surprised again. There is nothing to tuck. Busy, confident New York hands snipped and layered and brushed her hair back off her face. She didn't know where else to turn when she left Rachel yesterday. It seemed so natural to change your appearance after you run away. Except the hair spray's fading now and her hair falls in unkempt, short layers. She pulls her hand back down and holds it in the other. "Could I have a slice of pie please? Apple pie? A scoop of vanilla ice cream on the side?"

She doesn't even know where this Skylight Diner is, paying more attention to restoring her self than to street signs since she left the wedding reception at the hotel. The grand piano playing a beautiful love song got her attention. It was easy to slip in and steal a back seat while the bride and groom danced in the solo spotlight. The piano made her think of who she lost all those years ago when her piano lessons stopped. Then she wondered if the bride would ever cry. Would she miss who she put away today?

Forty feels like a chameleon in this big city where she can easily change the skin of mother, wife, sister. Volunteer, carpool driver, activity coordinator. Where she might find herself different through the eyes of unfamiliar people.

And so where did she end up today, after a little shopping, distractedly picking up a white knit beret, gold skinny scarf and wide leg trousers? It didn't register at the time that it was the perfect outfit to board a jet to Paris. To Claude, after all these years. So was her subconscious trying to tell her something? Maybe she only needed the same *je ne sais quoi* as in that outfit.

Even her destination paralleled Paris … East 60th, antique alley, in an exquisite French antique shop. It was as close as she could get to Claude, to a time before all this sad loss, when there was nothing but love and freedom. Her palms ran along old chair arms polished smooth by long ago grasps of hands. She studied the patina of wooden pieces. Subtle variations in color signify a sundry of uses. Did a chest sit near a sunny window or in a dusty attic? Were the people around it happy? Was Claude happy?

Her mother used to say while restoring their farmhouse that restoring is all about finding the original story. About getting to the heart of the structure. You have to see it, the heart, she'd said as she stripped woodwork and took down walls. Today Sara's fingers traced desk tops stained with ink. Who wrote there? She bought herself an old leather-embossed journal and wondered if the letters were passionate.

But how do you hold on to passion? She'd left one behind in France a lifetime ago.

She looks down the length of the diner counter, wondering what's keeping her pie, then pulls the antique journal from her handbag. Everything happens for a reason, and here's the reason for the leather journal. It'll be all about restoring, about refurbishing her own structure and taking down personal walls. She opens it to the first page. This'll be her guide to restoration, the place she can turn to for consultations with the expert.

Dear Mom,

Maybe this will help, a journal with you as my guide. I'm not sure, but it feels worth a try. You loved restoring that old farmhouse, and really? That's what I feel like I have to do. Restore me! Somehow, maybe this will help me get inside your thoughts.

It feels good just writing it, using her mother's words about restoration. It all ties in to her antiques, and connecting to people, restoring beautiful furniture for others' homes, restoring a happiness she'd lost recently and couldn't find. Maybe a journal can help define her role in life now.

But one role is friend, and she left her best one stranded at lunch. Sara Beth nudges the creamer alongside the sugar dispenser, sets her journal to the side. She'll let Rach know she's all right, so she won't worry. She pulls out her cell to send a text. Talking won't work; too much would have to be said, back and forth. But a reassuring message would be the right thing to do. She enters Rachel's cell phone number and types in: *i'm ok rach. don't worry, promise we'll talk on sunday. i'll explain when i'm back at Plaza.*

"Here you go," the waitress says. She sets the pie down on the counter right as Sara Beth's about to Send. "More coffee too?"

"Hm?"

"Coffee, hon?"

"Oh, coffee." She looks up from her phone, distracted with the question. "Yes. Please."

She slips the phone back into her purse. That's better. *The message, wait, did she hit Send?* But then her food catches her eye. The vanilla ice cream is drizzled with warm peach sauce. Mom's favorite. According to her, it's the only way to eat vanilla ice cream. She spins around in her seat, looking. The vibes are so strong, like her mother's right there. Did she sense the journal message? Oh wouldn't she love to tell her these funny coincidences. Dial her up, hear the phone ring, the voice, "Hello? Sara!" And settle in for a chat, their two voices all that matter, the inflections, the assurances.

But there's that breathing thing again, her lungs just won't fill, so she counts in her mind, slowly, to ten. She has to do this now, get her life back under her control. Alone, with an antique black leather journal.

So I think I'm going to. Wait, scratch that. I am going to begin by restoring an old passion. Another one that I lost a long time ago. When I get back home, I'm going to start piano lessons.

eight

MAYBE HOLLY GOLIGHTLY HAS THE answer. Rachel
planned on giving Sara Beth the *Breakfast at Tiffany's* DVD for a
birthday gift. They practically had the movie memorized,
including Holly's thoughts about those dreaded mean reds
leaving her so afraid. Last night she lifted off the pale blue
wrapping paper she'd specially found, peeled off the large white
bow like on a Tiffany package and watched the movie way too
late into the night, pausing and repeating certain scenes over
and over again.

When Holly had the mean reds, she headed to Tiffany's to
calm down, finding a certain peace from the essence of the
grand store. So what about Sara Beth? Where would she go in
this city to calm down?

Maybe Sara Beth has the mean reds too, when you don't
know what you're afraid of. Because she never said anything,
never told Rachel *Oh my gosh. I'm so afraid. What if?* or *Do you
think?* It could be the mean reds, then. It is enough of a
possibility to get Rachel up at the crack of dawn, donning her
dark sunglasses like they had planned and hiking over to 727
Fifth Avenue. She even buys a croissant and coffee along the
way and stops in front of the jewelry store. Her eyes look up at
the name, Tiffany & Co., before she walks to a window and

pulls the pastry from a bag. But darn it! Sara Beth is supposed to be here. They were going to walk Holly's footsteps, looking in at the chandeliers together while drinking hot coffee. If Sara Beth has the mean reds, she knows this is the place to be. It'll calm her down.

Rachel looks down the street. It really is peaceful this early. Okay. So maybe she's here for herself. Maybe she needs to believe Holly Golightly to keep hope alive for Sara Beth. Really, there's nowhere else to find it. Hope. Nowhere but here.

* * *

"Shit!" Michael says, dropping a spoon when Summer slams her bedroom door upstairs. "I told you not to slam doors," he tells her when she walks into the kitchen. Funny how she's grown into her name, tall and willowy as August's marsh grasses, her long flyaway hair the color of the sand on Anchor Beach. But what he notices is how she doesn't look him in the eye.

"Did you hear me?" he asks.

"Yes. And good morning to you too." She slides into a chair and waits at the table.

"Did your mother drive you here last night?"

"No."

"You took the bus? Jesus, it's dangerous at night. Anything could happen. And you should've called. If I knew, I'd have some decent breakfast food. The kitchen's empty."

She scoops her hair back off her face and tightens her robe. "I'll just have coffee."

"Since when do you drink coffee?" He sets a plate in front of her. "We'll split the last muffin. How's that?"

"Fine."

He pours himself a mug of black coffee, then evenly spreads butter on the blueberry muffin before warming it in the microwave. "Have some orange juice." He sits down with his hot coffee and the muffin neatly sliced in half.

Summer takes a glass from the cupboard and shakes the orange juice carton vigorously before pouring a glass. She reaches for a second glass and fills it for him.

"So are you going to tell me why you came here in the middle of the night, or do I call your mother?"

"Well how come you weren't home?"

"This isn't about me, it's about you, darling. Start talking."

"You don't know?" Summer asks between bites of the buttery muffin.

"Know what?"

She takes a quick indignant breath, the kind meant to sway him to her side. "Know that Mom and that jerk she married are making me move to Long Island this summer? So they can live closer to his stinking flooring business? And now I'm going to have to change schools and leave my friends and you and Queens and go live there?" She picks up her muffin piece and sets it back down.

"Are you sure about all of this?"

Summer nods. "Doesn't it make you mad?"

"Oh, it did."

"Did? You knew?"

"I knew a little," he let on.

"Who told you? Auntie Lena?"

"Lena knows too?"

"Never mind," Summer says. The phone rings and she stuffs the last bite of muffin into her mouth while he talks.

"Slow down, Barbara. She's right here." Michael eyes Summer and whispers the words, *Don't move*. "She didn't tell you she'd be here?"

Standing and listening to his ex-wife, he's very much aware that Summer leaves the kitchen. She's standing at the paned picture window in the living room looking out at the street of modest homes. He can't imagine his daughter not living right across town, knowing this old house and perfect street are only a bus ride away. He watches from the kitchen as Lena walks past the house, a silky scarf tied around her head. Honey prances along beside her, her nose to the cool morning air. From behind tears that Michael guesses she can't hold back any longer, his daughter waves and waves until the motion catches Lena's eye. Lena turns up the walk toward the front door.

"I can't come in," he hears Lena say when Summer opens the door. "Honey's paws are muddy from the puddles."

"Then I'm coming out, Auntie Lena." Summer pulls her robe tighter and slips out the front door. She bends to scratch the little collie-shepherd's ears.

They stand close on the front stoop. Summer's back is to the door so she doesn't see Michael hang up the phone, push her chair in to the table and clean off her muffin plate. Breakfast with his ex-wife is not what he planned for this morning. They have to talk this move out, and already it's a problem. Barbara would not agree to the last minute breakfast until he threatened a custody battle.

He had to. This is his whole world. Summer's chatting to Lena about the dog or the weather or her life. Whatever the topic, he can't hear through the door. But it doesn't matter. What matters is the ease and familiarity and comfort with which she moves and speaks on the front step of her lifelong home. It says that this is her world, too.

* * *

Subject: It's Me Again
From: Sara Beth
To: Elizabeth
Date: May 17 at 9:30 AM

Hey Mom. Got a sec? I was thinking about growing up and trying to remember if you ever just left, and I don't think you did. You always seemed happy in that big old house, redoing it over the years. See, what it feels like is I haven't been happy lately. Like I'm not taking care of me.

And I thought if I could just get away from the sadness, it might help. It felt right when I walked away, but then I worry about what Tom will think, and Rach. I'm scared, Mom. What if they don't forgive me? What if I lose them too? You always said to follow my heart, growing up. Does that still work?

Sara Beth looks up from the computer terminal. Here, in the hotel lobby, computer stations for the customers' convenience. When she rereads the email, it hits her how her mother did go away. As she restored their farmhouse, she delved deeply into its stories by journeying into old newspapers and town records and journals. So she has that now. An answer.

* * *

Back at The Plaza, Rachel has to get used to the stillness. The room should have been filled with dishes and silverware and pots of coffee and telephone calls and reservations and plans and talk. Especially talk.

For over twenty-five years, they talked when they passed notes in school and clung to the telephone in the evening, then started letter writing in college until they were living in the same town again. Then it was face to face over coffee, in the car, at their weddings, in their new homes, throughout pregnancies, at Whole Latte Life. They talked everywhere from online to Ferris wheels to Carl's wake, where Sara Beth spent the entire time fixed leaning forward in her chair giving Rachel a hushed commentary on the flower arrangements, the visitors, the greetings, eliciting a smile every now and then with a fashion comment or an almost unheard "Oy Vey."

So it's all wrong that she drink her coffee alone now. Is this how their girls' weekend out, and all that it means, will end? She really can't accept that and when the telephone rings, lunges for it.

"Sara?" A beat of silence ticks.

"Rachel?" Tom asks.

"Tom. Oh gosh, I thought you were Sara Beth."

"Why would I be? She's with you, isn't she?"

"Hold on a second." Rachel walks quickly to the window, looks pointedly down at Manhattan. People walk, cars drive past. Sara Beth might be there, right below. She returns to the telephone believing that.

"Okay, sorry to keep you waiting." Sara is just down in the courtyard, maybe glancing up before turning in to The Plaza. That's what she'll have Tom believe. "What's up?"

"What's going on Rachel? Where's my wife?"

"Well, that's why I thought you were her." She could be in the elevator right now, nearly back in the room. "I think she's downstairs at the desk."

"The desk? Put her on. I know she's there."

"No, really." Stranger things have happened; her key might be slipping into the lock as they speak. She turns to the closed door. "Not right now, she's not."

"And do you happen to know why she hasn't called home in two days?"

"Well, didn't she?" Okay, she's digging in her purse for the key. "When we got here Wednesday night."

"She hasn't called. Would you put her on?"

Rachel turns back to the door, watching the knob carefully. "Didn't she leave a voicemail?"

"No. And if you don't put her on right now, I'm coming to New York on the next train."

"No, wait. Tom. Listen." She looks around the room. It is coming, right now, reality. Like the Acela, it's coming so fast, just a blur, knocking her off the tracks. "She's really not here."

"What?"

"Oh cripe. I don't know where she is."

"Jesus Christ, if you don't start making some sense, Rachel—"

"Tom." She sinks into the chair.

"What do you mean, she's not there? Was she ever there with you?"

"Yes. Yes, of course."

"Well where the hell is my wife now?"

"Listen." She presses the phone to her ear with both hands. "Please. Don't talk. Just listen." Then she closes her eyes and waits. When he says okay, then okay again softer, like he already knows, she tells his wife's story.

"You mean she walked out of the restaurant alone? By herself?"

"Apparently."

"What's wrong with this picture?" His voice rises. "It's been two days and you haven't called me?"

"I *know* something's wrong, but for some reason she didn't want you to know. She asked me for this personal time. In her note."

"Her *note?* She planned this?"

"I don't really know."

"And you obliged her."

"Well. Yes. And no."

"Come on, already. She's fucking disappeared!"

"Wait! Now wait a minute. I didn't sit around. I went to the police right away."

"Well thank God for that. Have they found her?"

"Not exactly. The thing is, that note bought her some freedom. There's not much they can do with no criminal act." What happens next scares her. It makes her press her fingers to her temples against a headache. Tom doesn't talk. She's not sure if he is even still on the line.

"You knew this?" he finally asks. Well. She's never heard that tone before and doesn't care if she never does again. "And you didn't tell me?"

"Hey I've been *looking* for her. Constantly. And she caught me off guard asking this favor, you know? To keep it secret."

"She went over the line with that. Way over," Tom says. "And so did you."

"Me?"

"You should have called me right away. What's wrong with you?"

"No, no stop it. It's what's wrong with your *wife!* You live with her, didn't you see this coming? Don't try to pin this on me and tell me what I should have done. Not after what I've been through. You're not here, seeing what I *have* done."

"But I don't think you should be making serious decisions for Sara Beth."

"I *didn't* make them! Sara Beth did! It's in her note." She closes her eyes. "Tom, please come, okay?" she asks. "You need to be here. I need help." She hears him take a breath, changing gears, working past his anger.

"I've got the kids."

"No kids. No. Just you."

"Just me. Right. Then what?"

"Well I don't know. This is what I've been doing. I follow our itinerary in case she shows up somewhere we planned to go. Really, I can't imagine her not coming back. I mean, she's got to come back."

"My God," Tom says. "Where are you going today?"

"A few boutiques in the Village. Then the Empire State Building. I'll call you all day, I promise. Every hour."

She imagines Tom pacing, laying out some rescue plan in his head, as if you can plan for this. Like stockpiling bottled water and canned goods and extra batteries on a cellar shelf. What could you put on the shelf for this emergency? Cell phones and a tissue box, photographs maybe, favorite ones, where you are sitting at a kitchen table, laughing, relaxed, the sunlight falling like tatted lace across the linoleum, photographs to lay down and say See? Don't leave. Nursery school Mother's Day cards maybe, made with blue construction paper and white paste and glitter, sitting on the shelf next to the tissue. Ticket stubs from great concerts, when the music lifts you for an evening. Old silent 8mm home movies from a walk on the beach when you wore that big straw sunhat, during a summer vacation when you stayed in a little white cottage, flower boxes filled with scarlet geraniums and snow white petunias, a film you'd run through a projector and watch with a teary smile.

"I can't believe this. I'll get my bag packed and call Melissa," Tom is saying. "Maybe she knows something."

"Okay. That's good."

He gives her his cell phone number. "I'll be waiting for your calls. And Rachel? If you find her? Or if she shows up?"

Two days of tears streak her face now thinking of a whole life of 8mm home movies.

"Just tell her we miss her. The kids, too. And to call. To just God damn call."

"Okay," she says softly, nodding. Before he can say more, she sets the phone in the cradle.

* * *

"Maybe I should have brought her husband in from the start and let him handle this."

"Why didn't you?" Michael asks.

"I don't know. Her note asked that I keep this secret, and we've always done little favors like that for each other."

"Rachel, this is pretty big."

"Oh, so were the others. I mean, you would think they were little, but they weren't."

They are on the eighty-sixth floor observatory of the Empire State Building, standing side by side above the city. The wind always blows this high up, but this wind has spring in it, and a little of the sunshine left to the May day while dusk falls.

"Like I took her daughters on day trips after she brought the new baby home. She had a hard time adjusting to Owen. And when my daughter was born," Rachel smiles with the memory,

"I was young and overwhelmed with being a new mother. The hardest thing was making supper, so Sara froze two weeks of dinners for me. I know, big deal, she cooked some dinners. But at the time, it saved my sanity." She looks at him. "That's why I'm waiting. Maybe I'm saving her sanity."

The sun starts setting, leaving the streets below looking like silver ribbons. Building lights come on, twinkling like stars. Michael points out a few landmarks before asking Rachel what she keeps putting off herself. "It seems that by waiting for her, you believe she'll come back. What if she doesn't?" He takes her arm and steers her around a group of tourists passing too closely.

"I can't even think about that. I feel bad that I knew something was off with her, but I let it go, thinking it was just a rough patch, maybe a little grief from losing her mom. So I owe her this much, this waiting. She's my best friend, you know? Tom's not too happy about this, but I'll see what he says when he gets here."

"That'll be good. It'll take the pressure off of you."

"She's worth it," she says, stopping and looking out at the cityscape.

Michael knows Rachel worries constantly, checking her voicemail, trying Sara's cell. He drops a quarter into a coin-operated viewer. "Take a look."

"It's pretty with the lights coming on in the skyscrapers."

"Any guess what Manhattan's very first skyscraper was, back in 1664?"

"Is this another wager?"

"Could be. Loser buys coffee?"

"You're on." Rachel considers the skyscrapers. "1664? Maybe a church?"

"Gotcha on this one. A two-story windmill. You'll have to ante up."

"A windmill." The sky turns violet in the east behind the skyline. Rachel pans the viewer, and he figures she must want to turn it downward and scan the street, glancing over the pedestrians, keeping an eye out for that auburn head.

"Take your time," he tells her, watching her press blowing strands of hair away from her face. "If the wind gets too much, we can go up to the hundred and second. I mean, if you want to. It's more cramped there, but it's enclosed."

"No, I like it here." Here, where Sara Beth is supposed to be, she doesn't say. They walk the perimeter of the deck, seeing New York from all angles. He figures Rachel is hoping for a miracle, hoping to see her friend walk through the door, or hoping to turn the curve and see Sara Beth gazing out at Manhattan, waiting for her. The Empire State Building stands on the corner of Fifth Avenue and Thirty-fourth. She is looking for that miracle on Thirty-fourth Street.

The sun sets further and Rachel slowly walks, holding her jacket closed in front of her.

"Come on," he says from behind her, placing his hands gently on her waist. "You're cold. We'll go upstairs to warm up and check back here later."

She puts her hands on his and pulls them around her waist, leaning back into him. "In a minute?" The twilight sky spreads before her. "This is so peaceful," she says. "Why couldn't this be all?"

A star breaks through the violet sky, twinkling in the darkening eastern horizon.

"See that star?" Rachel asks. "Every summer my parents rented a cottage at the beach. I'd have one week with my father, one with my mother. It was a pretty place with winding roads and little old cottages."

He turns when he hears the elevator open, and she glances over her shoulder at him.

"I always brought Sara and on the first night, we'd walk down to the beach after dinner and sit on the boardwalk. When the sun set, we'd watch the big sky over Long Island Sound, searching for the very first star. Whoever spotted it first got the wish that year. The first wish was special, the one to come true."

"Were you ever first?"

"Oh sure." She keeps her eye on the lone star over Manhattan's eastern sky. "I would squeeze my eyes shut and whisper Star light, star bright. First star I see tonight ... We still do it, wish on stars every summer. It's one of those things you hold on to."

"You found it tonight."

Rachel stares at that star and silently makes her wish.

Not that he's noticing intentionally, but it twinkles a little brighter in the sky as the sun sets. Michael thinks it is part of some constellation, part of an ancient connection in the skies, old and lasting through time, still shining on Manhattan. He closes his eyes for a second before leading Rachel upstairs.

* * *

They go higher still to the enclosed observatory on the hundred and second floor where the only evidence of wind is its whistle reaching inside.

"There are some who say that this place is very close to heaven," Michael says after a quick phone call checking up on his daughter.

"An Affair to Remember." Rachel brushes a wisp of hair off her face. "Deborah Kerr?"

"I think she was right," Michael answers.

The sky has grown dark now and it's scary to look down. Rachel can't imagine being any closer to the sky. Close to the stars, she feels connected to Sara Beth.

"Do you know what stood here before this building?"

"Wasn't it always the Empire State Building?"

"This was actually the site of the first Waldorf Astoria. They tore it down and hauled it out to sea, and a year and a half later, in 1931, this building stood in its place."

They walk a little and Rachel figures he's done with the story, surprised when his voice eventually continues.

"Once the foundations were in, the construction crews framed and built this building a floor a week, every week." Michael gazes out onto the city, speaking as though he worked there when it happened. "The exterior walls are made of limestone and granite, but it's framed with steel."

"A floor a week? That's incredibly fast."

"The architects and construction company treated it like an assembly line. When the different tradespeople completed their work on one floor, they moved up to the next and repeated the same job all over again while a different crew moved in behind them." Michael glances at her. "You following?"

"I think so."

"The work overlapped," he explains, walking carefully around other tourists. "You know, electricians and plasterers worked on the lower floors, while up above them, workers put together the steel frame and got that floor ready for the electricians and plasterers behind them, while the roof was still only a drawing in the architect's office. It was a tight operation. They even had a little railroad set up on each floor to bring the supplies where they were needed. So it's an impressive building, but fourteen men were killed assembling this tinkertoy."

"Maybe it isn't the closest thing to heaven in New York. Maybe in a way, it is heaven. For those guys. They're here."

"Heaven in sixty thousand tons of steel, sixty miles of water pipe and three thousand five hundred miles of telephone and telegraph wire, with sixty-five hundred windows to look out from."

"You know a little more than the average bear about this place." With the skyline spread before her, she feels what Michael must feel so often from atop his horse, or emerging from the subway, or upon turning a corner and catching a glimpse of this landmark. "You said your grandfather was a mason. He worked on this building, didn't he?"

"Side by side with Joe's father. The two masons. And when you think that sixteen thousand people come to work here each day, and another thirty-five thousand come to either do business or just visit the building, well, it's pretty damn amazing."

"No wonder you've researched it. You've got a personal connection."

"No research. I heard it all firsthand from my grandfather and later from Pop. You know, stories like having lunch out of a pail on the fifty-third floor beams, and the wind blowing construction debris from the upper floors. Stuff you never read about in encyclopedias." Michael slips his hand into hers and they start to walk. "But that was a long time ago." They turn to the elevators. "Careful," he says as the doors open.

Stopping back on the lower deck to see if Sara Beth might be there, the wind touches Rachel's eyes, her cheeks, blows her hair. She wants to feel it, to remember Michael's New York heaven.

"What did you wish for?" he asks.

"I can't tell. It won't come true that way," she says as he leans on the wall beside her.

"No, not tonight. When you were with Sara Beth at the beach. What was your wish when you were sixteen?"

"You know how they say this is the closest thing to heaven in New York? This building? Well, where I lived, the closest thing to heaven was that beach. So every summer my wish was that some day I could have my own little cottage at the shore." She looks up at the stars. "My own little piece of heaven."

* * *

"Ready?"

"I think so. Wait." She takes a quick breath. "Yes. Yes, I'm ready," Sara Beth answers.

"Don't move now."

"I won't." She sits on a stool in a Village boutique. It feels like she's sitting at an easel, working on that oil painting. One color paints over another in oils, and color not only creates visual impact, it creates form. This is how you form yourself, adding another layer of color. It makes her think of the Matrioshka dolls she bought for her mother, the beautiful blue and gold painted dolls layered within, waiting to be discovered.

She watches every move in the mirror. Embroidered tunics are reflected behind her, racks of turquoise and yellow and red, and Pashmina scarves and skinny jeans. She longs to be some of the person who shops in a boutique like this. She used to, years ago. Just finding a little of that woman might be enough. The splash of fabric colors don't take her attention from the boutique attendant, though. It's the only way to gauge when the trigger will be pulled. Then comes the noise, just a pop really, and it's done. And she doesn't care what anyone says, it hurts when that gun shoots the post through. Both ears are twice pierced, gold studs in place.

"There's liquid cleanser you can purchase at the register. Dip a cotton swab around the hole to keep it clean, and you should be fine. Give it a few weeks to heal."

A few weeks. That's all she thinks when she lingers in the boutique buying a scarf for each of her daughters. It's hard to imagine being back in Connecticut, living some life that will, must, be different from the life she left. Maybe that's it, though. Maybe she wants back *another* life she left long ago. Already she's visually different and glad for it. But her ears sting, and her heart still stings, and her tears do too.

A ridiculously long line of people snakes along the sidewalk in front of her. She can't imagine what the draw is, until she sees the restaurant. Serendipity's. She walks past, turns on a side street, walks around the block and eventually takes a place at the end of the line. Two hours pass on her feet in a crowd where she might be anyone: Bohemian free spirit or business woman doing the weekend. Or a friend, meeting up with another. She sees that here, families and couples and friends, friends everywhere, who laugh and talk and take pictures.

Once finally seated at a tiny round table near the white fireplace with a massive vase of twigs and branches on the mantle, she orders. "The Forbidden Broadway Sundae. With extra hot fudge? And coffee."

"Extra fudge. Celebrating something?" her waiter asks.

Well why not? She'll try celebrating her decision to move forward, to paint the layers of Sara, to find her story in an antique journal. And sitting there in the crowded restaurant, she feels it. Waiting for her sundae, cupping her coffee with the hum of people and clatter of dishes around her, someone's with her. There's a ghost at the table. Its presence is almost tangible. How many times did she communicate with her with nothing more than a look? How many times did the phone ring just as she was about to call her? That same ghost is with her now, calming her, drying her tears. Just waiting with her, a presence, as she works through these days alone. Sara Beth reaches into the velvet beaded hobo bag she bought earlier and finds the leather bound journal.

Dear Mom,

Layers, layers. Layers of color on a painting, layers of your existence, layers of me. I got a second ear piercing. It feels like a layer, maybe of someone I used to be. Someone coming back again. By going back, will I find anything of you there too? Anything?

nine

THE WIND FROM EIGHTY-SIX FLOORS up doesn't reach down to the street. They decide to walk up Fifth Avenue toward The Plaza. Rachel feels more visible to Sara Beth that way. Spring is in the air and other pedestrians have the same idea, filling the sidewalks with clipping footsteps and scraps of conversation. She glances at the passing faces, especially the women together talking. It is early still, just after nine, and that type of spring night when she can feel summer coming.

"They're showing a lot of navy," Rachel comments on the dimly lit store window displays. Has Sara Beth walked past these stores and critiqued the styles? Is she still in town? She reaches to hit the walk button at the corner.

"Don't bother," Michael says. "They don't work."

"They're broken?"

"No. Believe me, the city would be gridlock if the lights turned red every time a pedestrian wanted them to. They're all on timers. Out of your control."

"You're kidding. Then why have them?"

"A legality. And if the timed system fails, then these work." He checks both ways, then back again before taking her hand and crossing quickly. "I'd like to make you a home cooked meal. At my house." Michael pauses. "In Queens."

Rachel can't believe it. He cooks too. And would, for her. But is it too much, too soon?

"You're tired," he goes on, "and a person can take only so much restaurant food."

"I'm not too hungry right now. But thanks."

"I make a pretty mean tomato sauce, you know? Pop, he liked to garden. Got me hooked on growing tomato plants. I put the seedlings in last week, but there's sauce in the freezer. Sometimes it's nice to be in a comfortable home for a change."

"It's just that I can't leave the city now. I have to get back to the hotel."

Michael takes her elbow and checks traffic before letting her step off another curb. "I understand." They walk a block before speaking. "Coffee then? I think you lost a wager I'd like to cash in."

"That sounds better," she says, aware of someone approaching. She glances over her shoulder as the lone woman passes.

"Did you ever get your wish?"

"My what?" she asks.

"Your wish. On the beach."

"Yes, I did. Carl and I bought a summer place with his brother and wife. We split July and August with them, one month each. In the spring and fall, we'd divvy up the weekends. For a few years I did have my own piece of heaven."

"So tell me about this cottage of yours." With walls of concrete and granite and glass towering around them, he links his arm through hers, slowing their pace.

Rachel takes a deep breath, clearing Sara Beth from her mind and letting her summer memories surface, the way heat waves rise, wavering, easy. "There was a lagoon behind our yard, with tall grasses and a stream of the sea winding through it. From our back porch, we had a perfect view of the swans or a blue heron fishing on the banks. It was like living in the middle of a watercolor painting. Or, going crabbing with Ashley out on the rocks and our biggest problem was a criminal seagull who liked to steal the bait."

"Wish my criminals were that bad."

"You see? Even sitting under the beach umbrella late afternoons was enough, feeling the waves at my feet." She pauses as Michael steers her off the avenue and into a coffee shop. After contemplating the full menu, they walk out into Manhattan's night holding two large cups and one cinnamon cruller.

"Do you still go?" Michael asks, then bites into the cruller.

On the street corner, she cups her coffee with two hands as though its steam becomes the salt air, the cup the warm beach sun, the sidewalk the long sandy boardwalk. "After Carl died, I sold out my half to his brother. I didn't want to go back there alone with Ashley. It felt too sad."

"Maybe some day," Michael says. It is warm, and when she slips out of her leather bomber, he uses his cruller-free hand to drape it loosely over her shoulders. "Better?"

She nods and starts walking back toward The Plaza. "That's why I teach." What she doesn't say is that she lost so much more than just Carl when he died. The cottage, summers with Ashley, peace, the sea.

"Teach?"

She pauses for a moment, lingering with thoughts of the sea. "I'm a long-term sub for a fifth grade class. If the permanent teacher doesn't return from maternity leave, the job's mine."

Michael finishes the cruller and throws her a sidelong glance. "I never pictured you a teacher."

"This is my first year. I stayed home with Ashley before that, until Carl died. Then I went back to school for my certification. Sometimes I think I was selfish to choose teaching, but it fit."

"I doubt there's a selfish bone in your body."

"Don't get me wrong," she explains. "I like kids just fine. But I couldn't stand thinking I'd never get back to the shore. That's why I teach. I'll have the summers off."

"Still wishing then?"

"A little." She takes another sip of coffee. "Do you go to the beach?"

"Sometimes I rent a cottage for a week. There's a place out on Long Island I like."

Their pace slows when Rachel looks at a large store window where two mannequins sit at a tiny table, legs crossed beneath it, the women leaning in close to each other. It is so them in the restaurant, she thinks. Is Sara Beth close by, waiting round the bend, her Huckleberry friend?

When The Plaza stands before them, she's not really ready to leave. But staying out feels like a betrayal to Sara Beth because it won't be about Sara. Staying out means something else.

What started as a police matter has changed. It feels like turning the corner on the observation deck a hundred and two floors up. Though hoping you'll see your lost friend waiting there, the reality of her absence still startles. This feels the same way. They turned a corner somewhere between a bowling alley and the Empire State Building, and the reality of it startles her. A relationship was the farthest thing from her mind this weekend.

And like being up on that hundred and second floor, although she knows she is safe, it is still scary looking out.

* * *

At the last docking, there was a mother in her thirties, old enough to know better, disembarking holding a baby with no hat on its head. At this late hour, in the damp air out on the water. Sara Beth wanted to tell her that her baby should have been home, warm, fed and put early to bed.

Who was she to talk? She, who effectively walked away from her own children. Did they sense it, back home? Did they lose an innate connection when she disappeared, like losing a signal for a radio station when you've travelled out of its range? Her gaze falls on the city that took her into its fold, its skyscraper lights an anchor. She then looks at her hands and slips off a gold bracelet, curious to see how it would feel to lose a part of her self. She doesn't fling it into the water, but lets it drop in.

And it's like a floodgate opens, the black water sweeping over it wanting more. She knows the feeling. It's the same way life swept in, other people's lives, and death too, drowning her. The old Sara Beth, the bohemian girl who backpacked Europe in college, who lived with a guy there, who dressed in flowing skirts and grew her hair long, who painted watercolors on the Seine and later on local rivers, who never missed a music festival, who made beaded jewelry with her mother and lived on a whim, that Sara Beth would've been there for her mother that day. So she reaches in her purse, feels around for her antique journal and writes in the dark.

I feel lost Mom. Like I can't find a way, some way, back to you. There has to be a path, but I can't see it. There's so much clutter blocking my way, and it makes me so mad. It's the same clutter that got in my way the day you died, and I could've helped you otherwise.

Then she grabs a lipstick and tosses it overboard. Gone. And paper, yes, paper from The Plaza, stationery she used for Rachel's note. They flutter away into the dark. She pulls herself close to the railing, looking straight down into the water as her sunglasses go next, disappearing instantly. Her wallet comes out and she fumbles with it. Her identification cards. Yes. First she takes her library card and flings it sidearmed. Her driver's license is next. Heck, she'll need a new picture now anyway with this haircut. She throws that one straight up into the night sky, losing sight of it before it hits the water.

There's a small photograph of her three kids in the wallet. It's there every time she opens it. She takes that out and squints at it in the dark, her thumb running over the surface like it's erasing something: motherhood, responsibility, cooking, cleaning, caring. That one makes her gasp when she almost drops it, catching herself and tucking it back into the wallet.

The thing is, she knows why she feels lost, and so incredibly angry, long before dumping these things overboard, and she's crying now. It surprises her when she accepts completely the root of her loss on a ferry boat pushing through deep water. The only one who can help is her mother and she's sure not showing up on the Hudson River tonight. And it gets her even angrier, the crying and her mother and struggling, enough for her to finally place the blame of her mother's death where it belongs. Enough for her right hand to move to her wedding rings, and reach them.

It was Tom's fault.

* * *

They sit together on a bench outside The Plaza. The illuminated courtyard is softened by the shadows of Central Park. Michael explains the historical Beaux-Arts exterior of the hotel.

"When we were bowling that first night, I thought it was nerves that made you tell me about the city's nuts and bolts," Rachel says.

"Some of it was."

"No. It was pure you. You're the real thing, a real New Yorker."

"We get nervous too."

"Seriously. How can I ever thank you?" Rachel asks when he turns to watch a couple behind them. "*Hey.* I'm over here."

He turns back to her. "Thank me for what?" As if he's done anything. As if Rachel isn't a ray of sunshine that has broken through his days.

"For getting me through this. It feels like I've known you a long time."

He stands up then, rolling a tense knot from his shoulder. "I should be thanking you. And that friend of yours. Sara Beth."

He glances up at the sky and wonders about the mystery woman, then offers Rachel his arm and they walk around the courtyard. "I had a nice weekend," he says as they near the entranceway. "Even though it wasn't easy for you."

"I'm so afraid for Sara, but if she hadn't disappeared, we wouldn't have met. Serendipity, huh?"

He doesn't mean to startle her; it just happens, the way he has to stop her from leaving. He takes her face in his hands, touches her hair. "I want you to come back. I want to see you again."

She places her hand on his. "Michael," she starts. "It *doesn't* seem right that you're going back to your life and me to mine as if nothing happened between us. Because something did."

His hands are still on her face like blinders blocking out the city, the time, even Sara Beth. He tips his head down close to hers. "And we want to know what it is, right? So I'm going to call you in the morning. Would that be all right?"

"Okay," she answers, pressing a finger to his lips. And her okay says that there is something there, something to pay attention to. They need another time, without the onus of a missing friend.

"I'll call you tomorrow night, too. When you get home. To find out when you're coming back. If you're sure, I mean. I don't want to push you."

Rachel doesn't speak. This weekend has turned completely on its heels for both of them. He figures her life has been turning on its heels since her husband died and she went back to school and began her career and sent her daughter off to college. And now, after years of coping alone, for this mounted police officer to simply say come back, well, he hopes it isn't one too many turns.

"I'd like that," she finally answers.

"Okay. That's good. So I'll call you?"

"Yes."

"Will you be all right? Do you have your cell on? Do you want me to come in with you?"

Rachel shakes her head. "I'll be fine. I'm anxious to talk to the desk. And I need to get upstairs and put her things together. Then I'll call Tom again."

"Lock up behind you. And I'll stop at the station and let you know if I find anything."

"Either way?"

"Either way." He tips her chin up. "Order Room Service. Have something to eat. A sandwich at least. You need to eat."

She's on the verge of tears with what she is about to face. And maybe with a little bit of something new. Of having someone worry about *her*.

"Come here," he says, and slips his hand behind her neck and pauses before kissing her one long, tentative kiss. She tastes sweet and feels as soft as he had imagined and it makes him want to hold her all night. "I'll walk you inside," he says near her ear.

He takes her arm as she hurries up the stairs past the uniformed doorman. They stop at the Reception Desk where Rachel speaks with the clerk. He shakes his head no. No Sara Beth. No messages.

Tomorrow will be a busy day for Rachel, what with packing to leave, and if Sara doesn't show, she and Tom will have to make phone calls and arrangements. The day will be difficult, as if there has been a death.

The clerk accesses his computer when she asks to extend her checkout time by a few hours. Just in case. In case Sara Beth returns and needs to pull herself together before catching the train back, or in case she doesn't return at all. All weekend, Rachel's given an old friend exactly what she asked for: time, pure and simple. But this is the end of it. As she gathers her purse, the clerk retrieves a brown paper package and has her sign it out.

She reads the handwriting, the return address. "Oh shit," she says.

"What's wrong?" Michael stands close beside her, his denim jacket open in the warm lobby.

"I've been worried sick all weekend, and now this?" She shows him the package shipped by an auction house. "She's out shopping? What does she take me for?"

"Open it."

"What?"

"It might tell us something." He takes the package from her and tears it open enough to see inside and find antique napkin rings. "Rachel. I don't know your friend. I don't know your relationship. What I do know is that you deserve a hell of a lot better than this."

"I'm so scared for her, and shoot! Now I'm mad, too," Rachel says, taking the package. "What does she need from me?"

He knows it's the closest she's gotten to her since she disappeared, these items Sara Beth touched and bought. "Right now, it doesn't matter." Michael slips an arm around her shoulder and walks her to the door. "Come on. You deserve a night in Manhattan that is all yours."

* * *

A vast vaulted ceiling mural of gold constellations set against a deep green sky rises above them in Grand Central Terminal.

"You're big on wishes, so, Pegasus, Orion, now there are some stars to wish on," Michael says. "The zodiac constellations are there too. Over two thousand lights of them."

"This is incredible," Rachel says as he guides her to a bench where they can take it all in. "I'll bet a ton of wishes are made here. Oh, it's so beautiful."

"Wishes and maybe prayers. You're seeing the constellations from God's eye view. They're all reversed, as though you're seeing them from His side."

"Wow. It feels like a church, doesn't it? What a genius artist."

"Maybe. Some people say the artisan who installed the mural accidentally reversed the constellations, some that it's based on a medieval manuscript depicting them that way. Nobody really knows, so believe what you want."

That's what so much comes down to: believe what you want. Wish what you want. Whatever gets you through, whatever validates your choices, whatever saves you. She wonders what Sara Beth is believing this weekend.

They stop at their jazz club, she likes that, that it's *theirs* now, and he orders wine. But she reaches forward and clasps his fidgeting hand. "I'd like a Scotch."

"Make it two," Michael says. "On the rocks."

And it works, in a melancholy way. During the first half of her drink, Rachel pulls out some of the sterling silver napkin rings from the puffs of tissue in Sara Beth's package. They're animals, each one a surprise: a squirrel, a parakeet, a cat. They cull from the note scribbled on the receipt that Sara Beth purchased them from a lower Manhattan antique shop, said she was staying at The Plaza, and failed to properly complete the Connecticut ship-to address. The shop couriered the package to the hotel.

"She's in the middle of a crisis and buying antiques?" Michael asks.

Rachel turns the squirrel ring over in her hand. "Antiques are what she does. She'd planned to open a shop but got sidetracked with the new baby."

Michael pulls the napkin ring from her hand, rewraps each one and fits them in the small box. "Put them away."

She takes the box, surprised at his order, and slips it into her black shoulder bag.

He glances at the patrons in the room, so much so that she wonders if he's looking for someone. But then he reaches for her hand and stands. "Listen, if she's buying napkin rings, she'll be fine. Come on."

On her feet, the Scotch warms her, its heat welling through her veins. She feels him close, feels his hand through the fabric on her back, his face touch against her hair, feels him lead her through a slow song. The liquor lets her do that, feel.

"I'll pick you up tomorrow," he whispers. "Early."

"Early?"

"I need as much time with you as I can get," he says, then kisses her once and a little longer again. "Well, if that's okay with you."

"How early?" she asks, her cheek pressed to his.

"Say, in a couple of hours?" He pulls her close and slows his step. And so it goes, shoulder to shoulder, her face near his, he looking past her, their few words reaching each other. He holds her with him, not releasing any of her, not one bit, to Sara Beth until the night is done.

"I'll take you somewhere nice. We'll be back by noon, for Sara Beth."

"Okay." And she closes her eyes as the motion of the dance lulls her like sweet ocean waves. The sea, the sea. She's on a buoyant tube, the sun on her face, salt water swaying, dipping her toes in the water with a small splash. The beach is always there.

ten

SARA BETH THOUGHT THAT RUBBING shoulders with the world's premier auction house might bring good karma. She could hear herself already, her pride swelling over a Sotheby's piece.

"Oh, it's from Sotheby's."

"I'm sorry, it's not for sale."

"Thank you. I found it at Sotheby's."

Being among all the auction house's finery inspires her to move ahead with her dream. The Chippendale Carved Mahogany Lolling Chair. A Queen Anne Cherry wood Chest. The Federal Inlaid Cherry Tall Case Clock. A Dutch Oak Renaissance Cabinet. Italian White Marble Figures, a Swiss Gothic Tapestry Panel, the Jewel Set Pendants and Chains, Impressionist and Modern Art, Americana Furniture. Oh if only her mother were here to see this. To help her choose.

The thing is, she decided to do this Sotheby's thing so late, there's little time. In a few hours she has to be back at The Plaza. All she needs is one item to bid on, to be her unveiling piece, her signature statement. It should be something more to display than to use. Maybe brass trumpet candlesticks. Or 18th century art, floral, beautifully framed. Or a small table on which to set alternating displays. That would be pretty, with an antique lace doily or small lamp.

She checks her watch. At least she'd registered when she arrived, giving her name, ship-to address, email, phone, personal preferences. Sotheby's even created a Wish List in her name so they could email her if her preferences came in for bid. She liked that service and wanted to emulate it in her own small corner of the antique world.

The piece she really wants, the eighteenth century slant front writing desk to hold her computer and store customer information, is way over the limit, not only of her budget but of her bravery, too. $20,000 to $40,000 are not feasible numbers.

But there's another piece that catches her eye. She sets her beaded bag down beside her, feeling the weight of her leather journal in it. The old journal's become her security blanket: As long as she structures her new life in it, one entry at a time, she's okay. Feeling its presence, she gets the nerve to inspect the rare snake foot candlestand. It would fit perfectly in a small space with a vase of flowers or a framed painting set on it. What a perfect way to start an antique shop, circa 1765. She checks her watch again and decides to bid. She has to move fast to get back to The Plaza, but needs to own this piece. So there's nothing to do but place her offer at the high end of the range. Her hand actually trembles with the thought of bidding. So first she has to psych herself to become who she wants to be. Before she bids, she closes her eyes, tries to unclench her stomach, touches her new earrings for luck. That's when she knows it's time. Her hand raises from her lap to the computer mouse at the Internet Café, and her online bid is placed.

Five thousand dollars. No checking with Mom. No worrying about Tom. No urgent cell calls or text messages waiting for approval. She'll come up with the money. It's a small price to pay to start living her choice life.

But she's so happy that she actually placed her first Sotheby's bid, she has to at least send her mother an email. It's become such a habit, logging on and zipping off quick one or two line messages, staying connected. She can imagine her mother reading it and keeping her fingers crossed for Sara's bid.

* * *

"Do you want to come up? I could use some company."

"You're nervous about explaining this to her husband, aren't you?"

Rachel sits beside Michael in the taxi. "I just wish none of it had to happen." It helps being able to lean against someone, to not be so alone. He kisses the top of her head and she thinks that's comforting, being kissed there. It's such an underrated thing, the way it makes your eyes drop closed, being kissed on the head, and the way his fingers barely move on her hair, like another kiss, and the way the feel of it all lingers. It's a little refuge, that kind of kiss. They'd been beneath the George Washington Bridge at The Little Red Lighthouse for two hours. Years ago it helped ships navigate into the harbor.

"Maybe this is what Sara Beth needs," Rachel had said after they'd climbed the spiral staircase in the forty-foot lighthouse to the observation deck. The Hudson River view, with the span of the George Washington Bridge crossing it, was breathtaking. "Some beacon, guiding her back."

"Don't we all," Michael had answered. "At one point or another. Maybe she'll find it."

Now, as they near The Plaza, Rachel dreads what will happen if Sara Beth hasn't found a beacon leading her back here. She's glad to have Michael with her to talk it out. "Oh, I have something for you," she says, pulling a small wrapped box from her bag.

"What's this?"

"It's a keepsake."

Michael unwraps the box to find a Christmas ornament of the Empire State Building.

"I bought it for Ashley at the gift shop there. But I thought it would be a better gift for you. Do you have one already?"

"No I don't."

"Well you should, with your grandfather working on it. Lunch on a fifty story beam and all that? He needs to be commemorated."

"You're right," he says, slipping the ornament into his jacket pocket. "I should have a tree of these."

When Rachel gets out of the cab, the sunshine is golden, the air clear. Why couldn't the day just be easy, like this?

Back in the hotel room, she checks her voicemail, her answering machine at home, and the hotel's voicemail. She feels Michael watching, and so talks while dialing her home phone. "I extended the checkout time a few hours, in case we need it for Sara."

"I know. You've really gone the extra mile. But you shouldn't pack her bags." It makes her hands stop and set down the phone. "It might be better to leave things how she left them."

She turns to him standing at the window, wearing khakis today with a button-down shirt, the sleeves rolled casually up. He'd been looking over the room, at the tapestry sofa, the Queen Anne cherry tables, the paintings. At her jacket neatly folded over the back of a chair. At her purse and keys set on the table, next to an opened pad of paper with a fountain pen laying across it.

"In case she doesn't come back," he adds.

"It's a possibility, isn't it?"

"Everything is, at this point. And her possessions could hold a clue to what happened."

"Come here," Rachel says. "I want to show you something." They go into the bedroom and stop at Sara Beth's dresser. Her hairbrush and the velvet jewelry case her daughters gave her are there. He has to see that they are fine items chosen with care. "What do you think about all this?" she asks.

"It seems like she wanted to enjoy herself."

"That's what I thought too. Which makes me feel terrible."

"Terrible? Why?"

She pulls open the closet door. "Check out the clothes she brought. But something snapped and I never saw it coming. And I *should* have. There were things going on. Like her mother dying unexpectedly last year. Sara was devastated, maybe more than I realized." Sara's cabaret night outfit hangs beside the jeans, next to a long skirt and a couple of light sweaters and jacket. "Because she's not thinking right anymore. I mean, she didn't even take her coat. And walking out like this? What the heck is she doing?"

"Rachel. We can't guess. When's her husband getting here?"

She walks to the living room window, which faces the park. Is Sara Beth somewhere in Central Park? Is she taking a horse and buggy ride, a pretty mare trotting her along, the big carriage wheels turning beneath her?

"I'm scared of what's next. My best friend, what has she done? Something's very wrong. Maybe I should have been there more for her, with the baby, and her mother. I could've helped her settle her thoughts."

"Maybe, maybe not. Let her husband handle it now." He steps closer. "If I were married, and my wife went missing, I'd want to know. I'd bring in the detectives, the works."

"Let me call his house to be sure he left. I know he had to pack the girls' school things. They're staying with Sara's sister Melissa tonight." How many times has she dialed Sara Beth's home number without a thought? Zipped right through it, anxious to share a piece of news or make plans or just, well, *talk*, damn it. Why didn't Sara Beth talk this out with her? She leaves a brief message and hangs up the phone.

"He must be on his way."

"Why don't you try his cell?" Michael asks.

"Maybe I should pack first?"

Michael walks to her and tucks a strand of hair behind her ear. "Listen, I hate what this is doing to you. But you might be staying another day, if things get bad."

"Okay." *If she doesn't come back* goes unsaid. *If she's messed up somehow.* She picks up the phone and starts dialing Tom's cell, holding her pen as though she might need to jot something down, something urgent and new that will fix this, that she'll have to write down before it gets lost in other talk.

"Rachel," Michael interrupts her dialing. He nods toward the door right as Sara Beth closes it behind her.

* * *

She's not sure what she thought. That she could breeze in easily? Like she had stepped out on a quick errand? That Rachel would say *Hey you. Did you find what you wanted?* That coffee would be poured and they'd laugh, check in at home, then leave for the train?

"Hey, Rach," she says, setting her bags down.

"Sara. Oh my God, Sara Beth." Rachel hugs her friend and doesn't let go for a long moment. "Where have you been? Are you all right?"

"I'm fine, yes. I'm so glad you're still here." She glances over at the man standing further in the room. "We have company?"

"Company?" Rachel asks. "Well, no. And of course I'm here, I was so worried about you. Michael's with the police, Sara. He's been helping me look for you."

"Look for me? Why? I told you not to worry."

"You're kidding, right? Don't worry? You disappeared."

"Do you need anything?" Michael interrupts, stepping closer, and Sara's surprised to see he's talking to her. "Something to eat? Water? A doctor maybe?"

"What? No. Why would I need a doctor?" Her eyes move from Michael to Rachel.

"It's routine," Michael explains, watching her carefully. "Medical attention, in case anything's out of sorts. In case you'd been assaulted."

"Assaulted? Rachel? Didn't you get my note?"

"Come on," Rachel says. "This was so unlike you. Disappearing like that. We're still trying to figure out what to make of it."

"You're sure you don't need anything? Maybe file a report? Were you a victim of a crime, do you need medication, an examination?"

"Stop, please. You're scaring me now."

"Listen. I need to be very sure you weren't coerced."

"No. Nobody forced me to do anything. Rachel, is this necessary?"

"Yes it is, for the record. But if you're fine," Michael says, turning for his jacket, "I'm going to take off." He takes Rachel's arm and leads her to the door, lowering his voice. "Unless you want me to stay. But you two have a heck of a lot to hash out."

"You'll wait downstairs?"

"No, I'm going home, but I'll come back in a few hours, okay? Don't leave?"

"Sara?" Rachel asks, turning. "Are you sure you're all right?"

"Yes, of course I am. You really don't need the cops here, Rach. I'm fine."

"Rachel," he says, and she turns back to him. "She looks okay, a little beat. But her eyes are clear and she's making sense. Be careful, though. You have my number. Call me if you need me, if she changes her mind about filing a report or whatever, for anything. Okay?"

She nods and glances back at Sara.

"Give her something to eat. And lock this door, too. Be sure."

And when he leaves, telling Sara Beth seriously to *take care now*, when he walks out the door, Sara sees the pallor of Rachel's face, the strain of the past days, the notes by the telephone, the police, empty coffee cups, and what it all becomes is an artist's sketch, the random form and dimensions of the weekend, the suggestion of what happened in her absence.

eleven

SARA BETH WATCHES RACHEL PACK her bag. Nothing is what it seems. Art, people, friends. They're all layers, and this layer of their friendship is not one she'd ever fathomed. She listens to Rachel as she packs, listens to the whole story: Billy's cupcakes to help ease the talk, the pacing the city, her breakfast at Tiffany's, The Today Show, the Empire State Building. Every coffee shop she passed, Rachel did a double take inside, looking. Searching. The cell phone checks. The endless worry. The text message she never got.

Sara Beth sees that. She doesn't need to hear the words. Studying art in college, she'd been trained how to look. At a showing she'd once seen of a lesser known Impressionist's work, there was a long, narrow case in the museum's exhibit room. Inside the case, a display of his sketches was set out for viewing. They had to be behind glass; they were the originals, on one-hundred year old paper, pencil and charcoal delineations of his paintings. Human touch would sully them.

Initial sketches contain rudimentary shapes and forms. They help to translate an image onto canvas, which makes sketching an important early step in the development of a piece of art. So through studying the artist's sketches behind glass, one can observe the stages of the Impressionist's paintings hung close by.

Now she can see in the ovals of Rachel's eyes and in the lines of facial expression, the past three days. Because if art is done right, no words are necessary. But still, when Rachel turns to pick up her bag to leave, the tears lining her face catch Sara Beth by surprise. Which is the intent of great art: to move, to evoke.

Rachel's words had all been sketches, rudimentary shapes and forms, leading to this image. Their friendship had reached this damaged layer, one that felt irreparable. For the past hour, no words that Sara Beth had put on the canvas, no sketches of reason, of anger at losing her displaced dream, no shading of loss within her own life, loss of her mother, of her self, no delineation of time slipping away, no word sketches of the secret carriage house holding her antiques, could change the layer at which they'd arrived.

Sometimes, in museums, Sara Beth is moved to tears. The very reach of the artists' brush strokes goes that deep, making the work more than a painting. It is a lover, a friend, a mother, a child, whispering some truth to her. So she understands her tears now, sitting alone, trying to piece together the weekend in her mind.

Everyone wants the same drawing. No one wants to sketch her in different angles or different lighting. The reach of that brush stroke devastates.

Between that and another tension headache, which scares her the way it came on so quickly, it's all she can do to stand up and open the door when someone knocks. But she wants to try to explain herself to Rachel, if she'll give her another chance.

"Tom!" she says when she opens the door. His bulky presence filling the doorway overwhelms her and she has nothing left inside to deal with it. No words, no feelings, just a headache and exhaustion. She'd sketched herself in every way imaginable all weekend.

Tom steps in and takes her arms. "Jesus, Sara Beth. What the hell's going on?" He leads her inside and sits her on the couch. "Are you okay?" After searching her face, he goes to the bathroom for a glass of cold water.

"Here. Drink this," he tells her as he sits beside her.

The cool water passes easily over her tongue, her head pounding. *A ruptured aneurysm may quickly become life threatening,* she thinks, and quaffs half the glass before stopping.

Tom reaches forward and pushes her short hair behind her ear. His fingers touch her new piercings. "Sara Beth?"

* * *

Michael figures he'll have a ham sandwich, then do a little yard work before catching up with Rachel. Pop always said that gardening clears your head. It also loosens his back and shoulder muscles, stiff after sitting on horseback all week.

Two rhododendron bushes grow at the front corner of the cape-style house. He turns over the soil beneath them, the shovel sinking into earth, slicing through dirt and stone. The sun warms his back and the street is Sunday still.

"Hey Dad," Summer calls from the sidewalk.

He leans on the shovel and brushes his arm across his forehead. His daughter could be a model straight from a fashion catalogue, the way she casually dresses. Half her hair is pulled back in a messy bun and a tangle of beaded necklaces hangs around her neck.

"Did your mother drop you off?"

"I took the bus."

"Again? Do you have your phone with you?" he asks as he sets down the shovel. "In case you had a problem?"

"Ye-e-s," Summer says as she gets nearer.

"And it's charged?"

"Dad! Can we quit with the interrogations? And hey, *your* light's burned out on the front step. When I came over the other night, it didn't work." She sits on the stoop, leaning back on her hands, tipping her face to the sun.

"Let me get a bulb inside." He walks around her and brings one out along with a rag to wipe the pollen off the mailbox and door frame.

"So what's going on?" he asks, stepping around her hands. He gives her the cover of the light fixture. "Hold this."

"I felt like coming over. Can't I visit you?"

"For no reason?"

"Well. I told this guy that I was busy so I wouldn't have to go to the movies with him. So then I had to make myself busy."

"What guy?" he asks, twisting in the new bulb. "Where'd you meet him? Not online?"

"Ryan. He goes to my school."

"How old is he?"

"Sixteen. But we only talk on the phone, you know? It's fun. Except he keeps asking me to do something, like go to the movies. Or go on a date, I guess."

"And you don't want to?"

"No. Then it gets weird, I don't know. I just like him as a friend. For now."

He glances down at the top of her blonde head knowing damn well there are fifteen-year-olds out there having sex. But with the rug pulled out from under her, first with the divorce and now moving, Summer's energy is sapped keeping her home life straight. There's nothing left for messing around with guys right now. He hopes.

"Don't be going on that Facebook. You don't know who you're talking to."

"Dad, everybody's in the book. It's what we do."

"Yeah I know. And that's the problem. Anything else on your mind?"

"No. Except I got tired of watching Mom pack up the house."

"She's not changing her mind then."

"Huh. Like shit."

"Hey." He takes the fixture cover from her. "Watch your mouth."

"Well she doesn't care what I think. And I don't want to move. Can't I live here?"

"First, you do live here, sometimes. Second, she does care and so do I. Your new home is in a better neighborhood and has a better school system." Summer rolls her eyes. "She's trying to do what's best, even though you don't think so."

"Best for her. Between watching her pack and listening to Ryan, I had to get out of there."

"Well I'm glad you came here. But tell Ryan I said no dating. You've got your whole life to go to the movies with a guy. Wait a year or two."

"Oh thank you. Now that *you* said it, he'll stop asking."

"Maybe he'll stop calling, too." He pats her shoulder, wishing he could stop the move as easily as the dating. "Emily around?" he asks, wiping the pollen off the mailbox.

"Idk." At her friend's house across the street both cars are in the driveway. "Guess I'll walk over."

There is no magic for what is eating his daughter. If she lives with him, she'll be home alone too much. But is moving to Long Island worse? Will Barbara be around for her? It ticks him off, really, after they kept Summer's life so stable, keeping her in the same town after the divorce, the same schools, same friends. She's a good kid.

"You need a ride home later?" he asks when she stands and brushes off her hands.

Summer turns back to him. "Can't I stay for dinner?"

"Not today, kiddo."

"Why not? I took the bus all the way here."

"I've got plans," he tells her as he wipes off the storm door.

"Are the Yankees playing?"

"They are, but I'm not going." Lately she hasn't wanted to go to the games, anyway.

"Then why can't I stay?"

He sees it: She thinks he never makes plans. It's either the Yankees or some day trip with her, no life other than the one laid out in front of her. "You know how I said that you have your whole life to go to the movies with a guy? Forty-four is a good age to do stuff like that."

"Wait a minute." She puts her hands on her hips. "You have a date?"

"Not a date. I have to stop in the city and see a friend."

"A friend? Who?" Summer asks.

"Someone I met at work." He checks his watch and calculates the yard work and a quick shower. "I'll drive you back home in an hour and a half."

"That's it? I get an hour and a half?"

"You'd better hurry. If you want to see Emily for a while."

Summer turns on her heel and crosses the street.

"Is your phone on?" he calls out. When she waves it in the air, he adds, "And don't be going on the computer over there."

* * *

So this is something she never saw coming. All Sara Beth saw was her own life taking the shape she'd waited years for, the shape she worked on so often with her mother. They had her story all planned out, starting at her fortieth birthday: an antique shop, a bold new venture, her passion finally defining her.

She never saw, never wrote to her mother in her antique journal that she'd have to repair the friendship gravely injured. She never jotted down that Tom would need to be placated.

It's terrible, how much he's sweating. The black pants she wore most of the weekend lay in front of him on the bed. He folds the pants into the suitcase, dropping them as though he'd like to burn them while Sara Beth paces behind him.

"I never meant to hurt anyone, Tom. I thought that what I did would be good. For you, the kids. Everyone!"

"What could you possibly have done with yourself alone for three days?" He glances at her and winces at her short, tousled hair.

"I told you already." She grabs the clothes from the closet and drops them on the bed.

"Went to auctions? To store more old tables in the garage?"

She holds it all inside. Her carriage house that she'd never told him about, keeping it still a beautiful secret between her and her mother. Telling him might risk losing it. The secrecy of the stunning antiques is like a butterfly cupped in her hands still.

"See what I don't understand." Tom turns to her, his face pale. "Is you're not yourself. I mean, the Sara Beth I know wouldn't ride a boat back and forth between Staten Island and Manhattan."

"What? What are you talking about?"

"I saw Rachel downstairs. She filled me in a little, okay?"

"I don't know, then. All right? I just did it, Tom."

"But all night? You didn't get a room somewhere? What's wrong with you?" He shoves her velvet jewelry box in the suitcase. It makes her think of the girls. Jen. What insecurities Kat must be writing in her diary and how this will make matters worse now.

"It was only last night." Only after spending hours in a cathedral she'd come upon, The Church of St. Paul the Apostle. She holds this in, too. Something led her up its stone steps, drawing her into its dark interior where she slid into a back pew. She knelt, head bowed, for how long she didn't know, trying to find a way out, or back. The only certain thing was the voice that eventually came beside her of a young Paulist priest who'd sat nearby. He must've worried about her solitude. "Sometimes," he said in a hushed tone, "it helps to look up." He motioned to the star map painted on the ceiling. "January 25, 1885. The skies of that day." He stood then, touched her shoulder, and left the church. Her eyes never left the image, knowing that the stars we see are only some of the celestial bodies. Our vision doesn't have the capability to see beyond them, to the others with their endless stories. It was only when she realized that just because we can't see them, doesn't mean they don't exist, that she blessed herself and walked out into the evening light. Afterward her troubles, her anger, everything tying her down, dropped deep into the Hudson River beneath those stars, and grief got lost in the spray.

But now life spins its web around her. "I had some things to think about and being near water helped."

"What things?" Tom turns to face her.

"Never mind."

"What?"

"Nothing."

"No. This is not nothing."

And it scares her, the tone of voice she hears. "Tom—"

He cuts her off. "Why didn't you tell me you weren't happy? I can't read your mind. I'm busy, I'm working and supporting a family and home." He drops a blouse in the suitcase, hanger and all. "Why didn't you tell me?"

"I tried."

"When?"

Sara shakes her head. "I don't know! When I wanted to go away with you. Over breakfasts. There were times when I tried to talk and—"

"Come on, Sara," he yells, cutting her off again. "Answer me this. One thing. You thought it was okay to disappear?"

"I wasn't home anyway, so no one would notice. And I was coming back."

"But what if something happened? What if I got in a car accident and Owen was hurt?"

"I had my cell phone, Tom."

"Which was turned *off* and which I left messages on that you *ignored.*"

"Well nothing happened to Owen. There was no accident."

"But what if there was? You're a mother and a wife. How can you be so irresponsible?"

"I wasn't irresponsible. And I'm not *only* a mother and a wife."

"You were more than irresponsible! You're not seeing reality. Anything could have happened. To me or the kids. And we'd have no way of contacting you. How responsible is that? Or what if something happened to you, wandering around the city alone? Do you know how dangerous that was?"

"First of all, you're very capable of handling the family for a few days. And I'm very aware of reality. The *reality* is I had to do something to change. I couldn't keep waking up practically unable to get out of bed. I can't be sad anymore. Because I had *plans* before Mom died. Forgetting that is not fair to any of us."

"No. Here's the reality. Ready? Go find yourself. Do whatever you have to do. But not while living in my house."

"What?"

"It's my house. I paid for it. I gave you a beautiful home to live in. I'm the one who worked for it."

"You bastard. That's my house too."

"Maybe. Until you abandoned us."

"What? It was three days! How can you abandon *me*?" She takes his arm and tries to squeeze in front of him at the bed, to face him while he packs. "I'm telling you I need life to change. Aren't I worth three days away to sort my thoughts? Three days? Aren't I worth your support? Your faith?"

"No. Not when you walked out of your life. Our life." He zips her overnight bag and throws it on the floor. "We're leaving. And you are not, under any circumstances, pulling any of this shit living in my house."

"Stop saying that. It's my house, too, and you know it."

"Not anymore. Not after the stunt you pulled and what you put people through this weekend. I'll take you to court for abandonment if I have to. We're going back to Connecticut and you're finding somewhere else to live while you figure yourself out."

As he bends to pick up the suitcase, Sara Beth sees past him, sees Rachel having walked back in to hear enough to know things are bad.

So the compilation is complete. Sara Beth had originally set out to sketch herself today, her words the pencil shading in the form and shape. But instead, the afternoon became a study in composition and proved invaluable in that all these images, the varying forms and shapes and elements brought to substance today, would serve another purpose. She thought there would be only her sketch, but the ones of Tom and Rachel bring different perspectives. Together, they show her exactly how she will have problems with her friendship and how shaky her marriage is, making it difficult to assemble all the sketches in a study of the final, desired, work of art.

twelve

RIVERBANKS AND COVES AND WIDE tree-lined streets
edge the town of Addison. On the eastern side of town, Olde
Addison is filled with those vintage homes Sara's always loved.
Saltbox colonials, farmhouses and old cape cods line the
historic streets. Captains' houses dot the riverbanks.

Ten years ago, they bought their Garrison Colonial in a tract
of homes built in the apple orchard. The roads wind through
the defunct orchard with apple names like Mcintosh Lane and
Cortland Drive. They planted tiny shrubs around the front of
their house, along with a white birch sapling and Japanese
maple tree. It was a hot summer that year, Tom pressing the
spade into the dirt, feeling the soil shift. His plantings were a
gauge against life, measured against the milestones: his children,
becoming partner, anniversaries. They were proof of living, the
way they filled in the yard in sync with his life filling in. He likes
his home life the way it is and works hard to keep it that way.

He never dreamt his own wife would threaten it.

At the very least, Tom was relieved Sara Beth went for an
exam with Dr. Berg. Physically, the doctor pronounced her fit.
But the family's different. Jenny walks home from school with
friends rather than have her mother pick her up. Kat takes a

new placating role, helping with chores and keeping to herself, searching for normalcy in her old diary entries. Tom stops outside her bedroom door when he hears her voice. *Last year at this time,* or *two months ago,* she says out loud before her finger traces the lines, her lips forming the words as she finds old ordinary days.

He'd assumed that once Sara Beth had her physical, this might all blow over like some temporary midlife crisis. When it doesn't, Melissa helps, taking the kids for another weekend leaving Tom and Sara talking around the issue at first, skirting it with the mundane. The lawn needs trimming, instead of the kids need you here. They plan a stop at the nursery to replace a haggard Alberta Spruce, instead of a stop at a counselor. The car needs tires. Maybe they'll trade it in for one of those smaller SUVs.

Tom worries about the kids sleeping away from home again. To him, mundane means normal. And normal means everything. Normal is sleeping in your own home. Normal is your wife living with you, not staying with her mother's old friend on the other side of town.

He cooks dinner the weekend the kids are away, sets the plates out and talks with Sara about her escape. While sitting in strained silences at the kitchen table, the sliding glass door is opened and the evening's summer sounds drift in … kids' voices in the neighborhood, crickets, moths bumping against the screen. This is the life he wants. Not a life of separation.

Sara Beth looks out at their new deck, at the round glass table and big umbrella, matching cushioned chairs, a gas grill Tom bought this spring. Pansies wilt in the deck pot; she hasn't been here to water them. But Sara Beth hasn't really been here in his mundane, his normal, for a while.

"Let me see if I got this straight," Tom says, the dinner dishes pushed aside, the wine poured. "You walked out of your life to find a way to save it?"

"You make it sound trivial. Like it's some selfish thing I did. It's not. I was coming back, Tom. I just took time to catch my breath. To be introspective. I'm not happy with the way my life is right now, I don't know. It's hard to explain."

He sees the defiance in her eyes daring him to belittle this. "And you're doing this introspection by asking for time for yourself? Wanting *me* to go grocery shopping now?"

"I see fathers there every week, *with* their kids, having a great time! So you could take Owen on Saturday mornings. Get out of the house with him. You should be more involved with the kids anyway. You never were. And is there something wrong with saying I need Saturday mornings for myself? Plus I don't live here anymore, so there's that."

"Sara, come on. We're drifting even further apart. You're not living here, you need space on Saturdays. Maybe a divorce is what we should be talking about."

"Isn't that extreme? Just because I'm trying to work things out?"

"Well if you're so unhappy. It seems like you're finding your happiness alone."

"No, that's not it. I'm saying maybe we'd have a better home life if you were more involved with the children. Thus, grocery shopping with Owen."

"I wouldn't even know what to buy."

"So I'll make the list. But it's not that hard. Cheerios, tomatoes and carrots, some cold-cuts, and have them cut a piece of cheese for Owen, a jar of instant coffee. Maybe a roaster chicken, hamburger patties. Really, Tom. A divorce? Is that what you want?"

If this is what their marriage comes down to, shopping, what's the point? He hasn't done regular grocery shopping since before the kids were born, when Sara would walk beside him in the aisles, her fingers hooked through one of his belt loops. He looks at her, remembering those days. "Fine. All right then. We'll give it a whirl. Me and Owen."

"That would really help. It gives me free time to get some things done."

"Like what?"

"I don't know. Gardening. If you'll let me do that here. In *your* home. And I've been thinking of starting piano lessons."

"Since when? We don't even own a piano."

"Since my weekend away is when. Buying a piano would be good, and there are plenty of used ones for sale."

Tom clears the table and after dinner, they talk more, kill the bottle of wine, and fall into bed. He watches his wife. Since her New York weekend, she's turned a corner without him, leaving him a step behind trying to catch up. He traces a finger along the inside of her arm.

"Sara."

"Mmmh?" Her eyes are closed.

"Did you call the therapist?"

"Tom. Even though I'm not acting exactly like who you want me to be doesn't mean I'm not okay."

"I know. I get that. But maybe it'll help with our marriage, too."

"Maybe, Tom. My first appointment is next week."

"I'll go with you?"

"No. Don't worry," she says as she opens her eyes and reaches for the hand that trails her skin.

He feels like he's having a one night stand with a stranger.

But they are communicating, and there's something hypnotic about her change. Before she leaves for the night, he starts to feel they can work their marriage out. Until the phone call came a week later.

"I'm calling about the car you have for sale?"

"Sorry. Wrong number." Tom clicks off the cordless phone and glances at the clock. Eight-fifteen on a Friday morning, car shopping.

"Felt so relaxing to use my own shower. Was that the phone?" Sara Beth stands in the hallway outside the bedroom wearing a new kimono robe.

"Wrong number," Tom answers as he ties his shoes. The phone rings again and he reaches for it.

"Hello." It sounds like the same voice. "I'm calling about the car you advertised?"

"What number are you dialing?"

"Let's see." A newspaper page rattles and the caller reads Tom's number.

"And which car are you calling about?" Suddenly something's happening that he has to catch hold of. "Sorry. It's been sold already," he lies, then hangs up the telephone and hurries down the stairs to the kitchen, pulling his tie through his collar as he goes.

Sara Beth's back is to him as she stands at the kitchen table in her robe. The newspaper lays open to the Classifieds.

"Sara Beth?" he asks, turning the pages. "What the hell's going on?"

"I wanted to see how much we could get for it. So we could plan."

"What happened to our plan to wait until we see if we can make this work?"

She turns around then and tries to walk past him, but he grabs her arm. "I'm talking to you."

She looks at his hand on her arm and he pulls her in closer. "Answer me."

"Okay," she relents. "Okay. If we got enough for it, I thought that we could look at minivans."

"A van?" Upstairs the girls thump around, bickering with each other. That's something new, that jarring interruption to conversations, to coffee. The pound of footsteps and thud of something thrown and angle of sharp words fall on him downstairs. It's because their antenna tuned to Sara Beth has gone awry. They can't find her, can't bring her in clearly. Her sleeping here only occasionally, coming and going at whim, doesn't help.

Sara Beth glances up at the ceiling. Owen sits at the kitchen table in his booster seat and Tom jumps when he drops his cereal spoon on the floor. It pisses him off, the way he jumped, and the way Sara Beth would've felt it. He gives her a look that says *See what you're doing? You happy now?* before letting go of her arm.

"Owen. Hey, there." He wipes off the spoon on a napkin and sets it back on the table. It's interesting how the kids separate them like this, getting Tom away from their mother, trying to keep peace when the tension between them tightens. Like Owen's trying to separate them now. He uses the same napkin to blot off his forehead before running after Sara Beth walking out of the kitchen. He grabs her arms from behind and spins her around with a shake.

"Tom," she says harshly. "*Please.*"

"Please what? Help me out here."

She leans back against the wall and he fences her in with his outstretched arms. How can he already be tired, so much so that he wants to go back to bed? He feels his hair lying damp and flat and Jen yells something, some dark threat flung through the air straight at her sister upstairs, something about a shirt or dirt or shit or something.

"It's late, Tom. You have to get to work."

"How can I leave like this? I want to know what you're doing."

"I'm not doing anything."

"I thought we were working things out. After last weekend?" Shiny hoops hang from her newly pierced ears and his hand moves to touch one.

"It's nothing. I just …"

"Just *what*, Sara? If you don't like your car, say so."

"Well a van might be better. You know. I'm driving three kids around now."

"You always hated vans."

"It's not just for the kids. I could use it for my furniture, too."

"Your antiques? I thought we decided to wait a few years on that."

"I could get into it gradually having my own yard sales. Things like that."

"You're certainly not ready to take on a new endeavor right now." His eyes shift to her hands. "Where are your rings?"

"My what?"

"Your wedding band, damn it. And your diamond."

Sara Beth looks at her hand, then closes her eyes for a long moment. "I lost them."

"How do you lose your wedding rings?"

"Well I don't know. I must've misplaced them when I came back from New York."

"They've been gone that long? Sara, those rings were blessed."

"It just happened, Tom. I didn't plan it."

Tom drops his head, his arms still fencing her in. "So no rings and now you want a van? I think this midlife crisis of yours needs to be more give and take. Maybe after you take some therapy, I'll give." He stares at her then, and he's tired, so tired.

Owen starts crying in the kitchen and pushes his bowl of cereal off the table.

"Jesus, this isn't working, Sara." His face is inches from hers. "We're really messing up the kids the way you come and go and stir them up. I don't want you spending the night anymore." Then he drops his arms and goes to clean up the kitchen floor.

thirteen

RACHEL LOVES THE WAY IT happens every year, as summer nears. The nurseries overflow with flats of marigolds and snapdragons, dahlias and zinnias. Black pots of scarlet geraniums sit on front stoops. Purple and white petunias grow with abandon from hanging pots hooked onto country lampposts. And bright yellow marigolds fringe vegetable gardens. Walking through Addison is like looking through a kaleidoscope of flowers.

Her phone rings early Saturday morning.

"You sound surprised to hear me," Michael says.

"I just hung up with Ashley. I thought she might call back." Rachel checks her watch. Michael must be getting ready to go to work. "Gosh she's having a hard time away at college."

"Why doesn't she come home for the summer?"

"She got a job on campus as a Research Assistant, and enrolled in a summer course."

"Well later in the summer then, after the class."

"Maybe. I get emails and text messages from her all the time. If we weren't three hours apart, she'd be visiting too. I think it's too much being away with her dad gone now."

"She's young, Rachel. And it's like you're gone too, being so far away. Can't you go spend time with her?"

His words are the thoughts Sara Beth would say if they chewed on this over a coffee at Whole Latte Life. *How about this, Can you try that,* suggestions that see right to the heart. "Maybe I'll ask her to quit her job and come home for a couple months," Rachel says. "She's only a sophomore and doesn't have to work so hard."

Ashley had cried on the phone.

After a pause when she's sure he's swallowing a quick bite of a bagel or sandwich, he tells her, "I know how you feel. The closer Summer's moving day gets, the more I find her at my place. She's reaching out too."

"But you're close enough for her to reach."

"I am. I wish there were easy answers for you."

Easy answers. Oh if life were only filled with them. She worries about her daughter and looks for answers where she always has. At Whole Latte Life. The Saturday tag sale crowd just dispersed, folded newspapers tucked under their arms, the tag sale column marked up with circled ads, coffee in-hand. She misses being part of that crowd on Sara Beth's antique hunts. Here it is mid-June and the strain of her May disappearance has turned into these tributaries of quiet now. And if ever there was a Sara Beth moment, this is it, at this table overlooking the Green. She needs to sit across from her over two large coffees, getting her through this terrible longing with a suggestion, or a smile, or a call for *Road Trip,* the spontaneous destination being Ashley's dorm.

Well, spontaneity works both ways so she calls Sara Beth's home and gets the address she is staying at from Tom, then grabs a Colombian Blend, her eyes sweeping The Green outside the window. Addison's Adopt-a-Barrel program has a few empty barrels left for planting, so a mini-road trip is in order. It isn't that far out of the way. Old Willow Road is in the historic part of town, out past the covered bridge. Willow tree branches cascade alongside the street. If Sara's staying at a friend of her mother's, maybe she'll have free time to plant their adopted barrels, like they've done every year. Some years they go all exotic in their choices, and others they overload the barrels with sweet summer geraniums. She'll stop at the nursery along the way and pick just the right flower seedlings to plant.

* * *

What are ghosts, really? Nothing more than memories stirred up, rising to haunt you. To challenge you to wonder if you made the right choice. And it didn't take much to awaken those ghosts. Sara Beth walks through the carriage house, silent but for the memories skimming her thoughts now, ghosts invited back with a couple of words.

"Where is everyone?"

"What?"

"Your family. Your parents. Aren't they going to see you off?"

They stood in the kitchen of the old farmhouse. It was the first room her mother had renovated, the heart of the home. Sara Beth walked to the sink and glanced out the window to the yard. When she turned back and looked at Claude standing there, his hair moppy, his jeans, concert tee and jacket casual, his face was still unaware. There was a moment when she saw it, though, saw actual realization. When his eyes swept the room, looking for her luggage. Duffel bags, a backpack. Backpacks were their staples when they studied abroad. A suitcase. Anything. And then he looked to her eyes.

She shook her head. "I'm not going," she whispered after a long moment.

"What do you mean?"

"I can't," she said.

He stepped out into the hallway, walked through the living room then ran up the stairs to her bedroom. She knew, oh she knew just what he was doing. And he wouldn't find the luggage he was looking for.

He nearly stumbled coming back down the steps, before stopping up short in the kitchen. "Parlez-en a moi!"

"I can't go."

"What? Pourquoi? *Nous avions prevu.*"

"Claude. No. English, please."

"*We had plans,* Sara Beth. And one of them was *no* English. We'd live in the land and speak the language. Be a part of it. A part of the art, of the masters' world. Let it assimilate us right into it."

That's what life seemed to be all about. Assimilation. Becoming who the environment around us dictated. Letting it be the arms holding us, nurturing our souls. Claude wanted her to return to France with him and become the artists the French countryside inspired. To live the carefree days of their college year abroad. But it's hard to leave safety. To leave security. To step off that edge into a dream. And she'd been falling ever since. Falling in a downward spiral since she chose a different destination. One that put her on a date with Tom two nights after Claude boarded the plane alone. Two nights after his harsh words accusing her of cowardice, accusing her family of stopping her, angry words flung across the space in the kitchen as she stood amidst all the efforts of her mother's passion. The refinished ceiling beams, the dried herbs hanging from them. The working kitchen fireplace. The antique farm table and chairs. And she defended all she was in that one moment with two simple words. Two words that set her on a plunge that it sometimes felt like she was still in.

Ghosts? Oh yes. The memory of her choice that day haunts her now. What if, what if she'd gone with Claude? All the what ifs return when she finds herself, all these years later, standing among stoneware pitchers and a cherry washstand and a chest of drawers and a secretary, oak, rosewood, cherry, leather tops, drop leafs, all beneath the ceiling beams of the carriage house.

"Holy moly," Rachel says behind her. "I can't believe my eyes."

And isn't it the same as Claude not believing his eyes. Not believing she was choosing a life, a dream, other than the one he'd assumed.

Sara Beth steps in front of her wearing jeans and a faded denim shirt, the cuffs rolled up and frayed. There are work boots on her feet and rubber gloves on her hands. Her cropped hair is tucked under a blue bandana. Grimy furniture finish drips from the rag in her hand. "Why don't we go outside. Please? We'll talk there."

And in the hesitation, Rachel's eyes sweep the room the same way Claude's did. The same realization comes over them as his. That Sara Beth had chosen differently.

And like then, questions form each time their eyes meet. *What is this, your own shop? How did you find me? Where did you get this furniture? Can you believe what I'm doing? Why did you desert me in New York?* Because it always comes down to that, beneath all the other questions. *How could you expect me to let you walk out and not reach for you, not pull you back?* It's their own sign language, the way they read each other.

Sara Beth pulls off her bandana and snaps the dripping gloves off her fingers.

"Tom told me you were staying with a friend of your Mom's. He gave me the address, and," Rachel stops then and turns around, taking in the antiques around her. "I was thinking maybe we could plant the—"

"Wait. Tom. About Tom, if you could just, I don't know, not mention this to him?"

Rachel's eyes stop on a clean change of clothes hanging over the back of a wooden chair. So she can figure Tom never sees her in her work clothes. Those stay behind in the carriage house. And the leather journal she carries everywhere, it's here, on the chair too.

"He doesn't know about this place?" Rachel asks.

"No, but wait." Sara Beth walks to the one-drawer stand she has been working on. "There's so much to tell. Sometimes, honestly, my head spins with it all."

"That's what New York was for. I waited all that weekend for you to spill big stuff like this." Rachel looks around the room. "I don't know what to make of you anymore, Sara. I don't know what to make of your marriage, if it's working, if you're getting a divorce. You've clearly planned something big here. But listen, don't tell me if you're opening a shop or if you're dealing antiques. Don't tell me anything. I'm not keeping anymore of your secrets."

"Rachel."

"No." She holds up her hand. "I wish you'd come to me in New York and talked to me about this. Because now I don't want to know what you're doing. You've taken this really considerable life of yours and twisted it all up somehow."

And so two words, said once again, will bring new memories. This one of Rachel standing outside her car, shielding her eyes from the sun. At the thought of those two words, she'll forever summon that image, and the one of Rachel dropping her keys, bending for them, straightening with a deep breath that might begin a sentence trying to get past all this.

Maybe, to salvage what remains of their friendship, she has to shut her out of her life. Not permanently, but for a while, to save Rachel from being further hurt. When her life is back on track, she'll try to recover this friendship. So she does something that scares the hell out of her. And what she realizes is that she's done this before in her life. Getting scared, making instant decisions, doing a double take at herself.

"Listen," she says, before she can change her mind. "Please don't come back. You're not a part of this."

Sara Beth feels like some sort of an arrow slung from the great heaving bow of her life. She has to move Rachel out of the way until she straightens things out. Hopefully, over a huge pot of coffee some day she can't even fathom yet, she'll be able

JOANNE DEMAIO

to explain this all. Because incredibly, she feels more like a new person, the right person, the more she follows her heart. So Tom can't know about this carriage house just yet, the risk being he might stop her somehow. And this friendship can *not* be a bitter consequence.

Sara Beth's heart almost breaks with Rachel's quick breath then. That one breath holds a possibility of saying *I'm sorry,* somehow. *Let's fix this once and for all.*

"Sara."

"No. Rachel." This is the hardest thing she will ever in her livelong life say to her best friend, to save their friendship in the long run. She glances up, praying first for a special *some day,* the kind you hope for, the kind when all the stars are aligned in your favor and magically grant a wish, hers being to find this friendship again. Because their whole life is mapped out in the constellations, in the sky, they always thought that, especially those summers at the beach. If you looked up long enough, you recognized something in the celestial life, something of yourself. Someday she hopes she can find this part of her life again, this Rachel part.

"Get out."

Rachel moves to speak, then stops and turns, getting in her car and driving away.

And Sara Beth stands there, and what she's hearing, echoing, are those words, *Get out,* as they come storming back into her life. She never dreamt she'd say them again, and doing so spins her back twenty years.

Maybe that was the mistake that landed her here today, one simple error in judgment that turned her away from her self. That ultimately cost her mother's life. One little decision two decades ago, and her life did an about-face. She chose safety.

It was between Claude or Tom. She'd chosen wrong when she'd stood in her kitchen and told Claude to "Get out."

Would it help to find that old constellation again? The one with Claude in it?

She goes back in the carriage house, drawn in by the leather journal.

Where are you Mom? I really need you right now. Because I'm not sure if I'm doing this right. Any of it. How can I be, if it feels like the carriage house just cost me Rachel? This would've been so much easier with you here. Okay listen, I don't know if it's possible, but can you at least send me a sign, somehow? Please?

fourteen

SOME PEOPLE SAY THAT WHITE is not a color, it's simply the absence of color. Sara Beth disagrees. She loves white because it is the color of beginnings. A clean palette. And the next week, she's ready to Feng Shui it into her living room because what better room to shift the energy in her *living*.

The idea to focus on the energy of her home came at the same time she won the bid on the Sotheby's antique. After lifting the carefully packed white hued snake leg candlestand from its box, she decided to keep it in her home until she had her own antique shop. It felt right, and so she finally had a little of this: A white antique, a new beginning, circa 1765.

You always loved red, Mom. Burgundy window treatments, throws, a velvet chair. Bold and daring and passionate. So I'm going to Feng Shui it into my "Living" Room.

And a can of deep red paint came into her life to cover one living room wall.

"Mom?" Kat asks, walking into the newly painted room.

"Hey there, Kat. Do you like it?" Sara Beth steps back to admire the wall.

"I guess. But red?"

"Yes. I'm doing a little Feng Shui. You know, changing the energy in our home. I like the red. Fire! Passion! Don't you feel it?"

Kat drops into the wingback chair and studies the wall. "It needs something."

"And I have just the thing!" Sara Beth sets the white candlestand at the north corner of the wall. "An accent piece. White, for clarity and balance. We'll put a vase of flowers on it."

"Do they have to be a certain color too?"

"I guess they would now. Want to help me? We'll buy silk flowers and make a big spray."

"What colors can we buy?"

"Well, it's the north wall, so a color that works in the north. According to the Feng Shui chart, that would be Earth colors, yellows and beiges. Maybe sprigs of forsythia? That would be really pretty, and the earth colors nourish our relationships."

"How about a color for money? Like green?" Tom asks as he walks into the room holding a piece of mail. "Something to nourish the bank account."

"What do you mean?"

"To cover this five thousand plus charge to Sotheby's, dated during your Manhattan escapade. And you can explain what you're doing in my house, and this red wall while you're at it."

"It's Feng Shui," Kat says, curled in the upholstered chair, mesmerized by the new color.

"Feng what?" Tom asks.

"I'm just changing things around, Tom," Sara Beth says. "It's no big deal."

"Five thousand is a big deal. And so is your being here redecorating. You're supposed to call first and clear it with me."

"I did call. No one was home. And come on, Tom." She moves closer to him and whispers, "This separation isn't forever." When he stares at her, she continues, "Or is it?"

"Dad," Kat says, and Sara Beth turns. She hears the anxiety in her voice, the worry about her parents splitting up. Kat the peacemaker. "Want to come with us to buy flowers?"

"Flowers for what?"

"For that table. The white one."

Tom looks at the white painted snake foot candlestand, then at Sara Beth. "Sotheby's?"

* * *

Rachel didn't know how else to reach out to Sara Beth and thought planting the flower barrels on The Green would be her olive branch. *Get out* or not, she got the job done regardless with a few other friends, beneath the warm June sun. Life always has a funny way of filling up Rachel's days.

But now those two words still ring. *Get out.* Last week's flower planting without her friend feels like a farewell. Today she's alone instead of patching up a broken friendship. Absence becomes a piece of her heart, a real concrete absence in place of her friend and daughter on this Wednesday morning with the sun streaming and the flowers in bloom. But fresh from the shower, when she steps into her sunroom and tunes in Stevie Nicks on the stereo, doesn't life go and give her what she needs when the doorbell rings? *Life calling. For Rachel DeMartino.*

"Holy cow," she says with a smile as she opens the front door. It's early, just after nine o'clock.

"Hi," Michael says on the other side of the screen, a cellophane-wrapped grocery store bouquet in his hand. She hasn't seen him since their New York weekend and his presence now is huge. She crosses her arms in front of her. "Hey stranger," she says through the ear-to-ear grin that life just delivered.

"Hey. Do you want to go to the beach?" Michael asks. "Maybe? With me?"

He wears a Yankees cap backwards, aviator sunglasses, plain dark T-shirt and khaki cargo shorts. Okay, she can't help it and eyes the length of his body. He has on Docksiders, with no socks.

"Is this a date?" she asks through squinted eyes, so glad she changed out of her robe and into capris and a tank top with a light cardigan.

"Could be. If you'd invite me in."

"Did you drive all the way from New York?" She swings open the screen door and sees his pickup truck parked on the street.

"I did," he says. He pulls off his cap and hands her the flowers. "For you."

"Come on in." She is still smiling and has a funny feeling that she'll be smiling all day. Half way to the kitchen, she turns, reaches up to his face and kisses him. "I can't believe you drove all the way here. It is so good to see you."

"You too," he says, taking off his sunglasses.

"How did you find my house? And, wait a minute, how did you know I'd be free today?"

"I looked you up." Michael stands near the kitchen counter while she fills a vase with water. "And I knew you wouldn't be busy. Well, prayed was more like it."

Over the sink, slats of sunlight stream in the kitchen window through its white half-shutters. She looks over her shoulder to see if the nerves and prayers that got him to Connecticut show. Not really, except that he fidgets with his cap. She sets the flowers in the vase and motions for him to take a seat. The table is small and square, a country table with a white tile top and golden pine trim. French doors open to the sunporch behind him.

"You knew I wouldn't be busy?" She places the vase on the table and sits across from him. "Am I that predictable?"

"No. It's just that today is the day of the eleventh commandment."

"I can't wait to hear this."

"Wasn't it on your teaching certificate? All teachers shall spend the first Wednesday of summer vacation at the beach, at the water's edge."

School let out Monday. "I am on summer vacation, aren't I?" She wriggles her bare toes beneath the table. "You really want to go to the beach?"

"That's why I'm here. Do you want to come with me? I mean, I just assumed, maybe."

"Let me get changed and pack a bag." She stands and starts out of the kitchen. "But can I make you a coffee first?" she asks, turning suddenly back and catching him dabbing a napkin on his forehead. "Or would you like some juice?"

Michael shakes his head no.

"We'll stop on the way and get something?"

"Sounds good, Rachel." He sits back in the chair looking a little relieved.

"Awesome." She stares curiously at him again. "Is this for real? You drove all the way from New York to do *this?* Aren't you tired?"

"Time's wasting."

"Let *me* drive to the beach then?"

"Fair enough."

She hurries from the kitchen still smiling, thinking *Yippee!* Sometimes, not often, but sometimes, it's a perfect word.

* * *

Michael stands and stretches his legs, stiff from two hours in the truck. His shoulders are tense too and he rolls out a kink. Each darn love song on the radio made him wonder if he was making a mistake, if Rachel would be glad to see him, if his feelings were exaggerated by her absence. Until he finally switched to an all-news station. Now a month of time stands between them. He rolls his shoulders and picks a ripe peach from the fruit bowl on the counter.

Music comes from the sunporch and he bites into the peach and wanders out there. Tall windows let in sunlight warming upholstered furniture and hardwood floors. Hand-painted wooden herons stand in the far corner beside spiky cattails spilling from a large clay floor vase. Soft music rises from a shelf system on a built-in bookcase where pale pink conch shells nestle among books.

The room is so intriguing, he backs right into an antique easel, its dark oak frame holding a large blank paper in place. He catches it before it falls over, but not before a case of drawing charcoals slide from the lower tray. When he sets them back in the case, the back wall has him do a double take.

Sketches mounted in silvery-gray wooden frames fill the space. Most are pencil on paper, some charcoal, and a few are pastel. He studies them, biting into the peach as he goes.

A couple of sketches portray a man at two different times in his life, a man who must be Carl. He's a little older than Rachel and he sees respect in her pencil lines. There's a sketch of a young girl with long, fine hair, and he touches the glass of the frame lightly. From the tender gaze caught in the artist's charcoal strokes, this can only be Rachel's daughter.

The next portrait is Sara Beth. But not the woman he saw in New York. This shows Rachel's personal description of her, the gentleness, in the rendering and in the artist's touch.

There are other sketches, too, filled with incredible background detail and colors. There are stone jetties and sunset scenes drawn with such a fine touch, the medium seems to be pastel, though it is pencil. He sees hot afternoons when beach umbrellas line the shoreline like a row of swirling lollipops, and dark windy days drawn in a thousand shades of gray. Seagulls perch on weathered pilings. Rachel's pencils find the softness in marsh grasses and swans and neglected wooden rowboats, contrasting with the straight lines of her summer home's imposing two stories, its large old windows opened to the sea, and salty breezes, and seagull cries.

This is her heaven.

Rachel breezes into the room carrying a large canvas tote.

"You're very talented," Michael says, turning to study the artist. She changed into black Bermuda shorts, a white tank top, flat leather sandals. Her hair is French braided in an artist side he didn't see in New York.

"Oh, my sketches. They're a hobby of mine." She glances at her work.

"You could make money with your talent. Or teach art instead of fifth grade."

"It wouldn't be the same then," she says, straightening a frame. "*Having* to do it, you know?"

"Couldn't you get used to it? Making a living doing what you love?"

"I am," she says. "With my job, I've got two empty months in front of me to spend as much time as I'd like," she pauses as she studies her pictures, "here." She points to the row of colorful beach umbrellas. "I don't go as much as I used to, but I've got this room at home when I'm not there."

"It's a great space." The large windows open onto a green lawn where a stone birdbath is tucked into a rock garden and a birdhouse hangs from the low branches of an old maple tree. Rows of baby tomato plants fill a vegetable garden off to the side, away from the cool shade of the trees.

"After I sold my share of the cottage, I used the money to build this room. My beach room."

He turns back to the wall of sketches. Their frames are a blend of grays and browns, driftwood from the beach.

Rachel picks up her tote. "I've got sand chairs and an umbrella in the garage. It'll be hot in the sun. Ready?"

On the way out of the sunroom, she reaches for one of her sketch pads and tucks it into her canvas striped tote the way a photographer might grab a camera, or a writer a notebook.

"You have everything you need? Keys, sunblock?" he asks her in the garage.

"I do."

"And you locked up the front door?"

She looks at him for a second, pausing before nodding and picking up the umbrella.

* * *

"Show me around a little," Michael says once they're in her car.

"Do you mind walking?" she asks as she drives through Addison.

"No. Walking's fine."

She parks in a spot on Main Street in front of a hardware store. The summer day is light on traffic and getting warmer as the sun moves high in the sky. He lets it slow him, this easy day outside of the city, walking past the potted flowers at the nursery, looking into the windows of a five and dime.

At the coffee shop, as they wait at the counter for their order, she points out an important landmark. "That's our table."

He considers the empty table beside a large window facing The Green. "Yours and Sara Beth's?"

"If possession is nine tenths of the law, we should own that table."

They take their coffees outside and walk across the street. Rachel explains the eclectic barrels of flowers dotting The Green. "Anyone can adopt a barrel and plant their choice of flowers. It can get pretty artsy." She points out her barrels of zinnias among the snapdragons and black-eyed Susans and roses even, mixed with ornamental vines and spikes.

"Sara and I've adopted barrels every year except this one. Some other friends helped me out this time." They walk among the flowers. "She loves this Green. It's as pretty as it is because of her volunteering."

Colorful birdhouses hang from trees. The American flag flies from a tall white pole. Even the litter baskets are placed within wood slatted containers. There are no visual sore spots. They stop at a stone wishing fountain.

"Does this have the same potency as the stars?"

The spewing water reaches for the sky and falls in an arch of infinite silver droplets, like tiny falling stars. "I like to think so."

He slips a penny into her hand. "You first."

Rachel clasps the penny to her heart and closes her eyes, then tosses it into the stream of stars. "What about you?" she asks when he continues walking.

"I'm saving mine for later."

"Later? What do you mean? At the beach?"

"Never question wishes."

fifteen

HE MADE HER A FLOWER chain necklace, his fingers weaving daisies and wildflowers and long green grasses together outside the horse stable at Chateau du Masnegre. It was a beautiful July day in Valojoulx, France, and her memory of it bears the soft, liquid qualities of a canvas painting: The brown stable with the brick red roof sitting nestled into a hilltop, the slant of sunlight falling on the sloping lawn, varying the shades of green, the wooden fence surrounding the corral, with peels of white paint curling from the wood.

Sara Beth sat in the cool grass and watched Claude's hands weaving, very much aware of the sounds around them. Has anyone ever defined the sounds of love, she wondered. Birds sang from deep in the green trees, whose leaves rustled in the breeze. An occasional nicker came from the horses in the barn, and the sound of hoofsteps rose and fell as a lone horse cantered past. The sky, watercolored blue, was the big transparent bubble around that world.

Claude finished the necklace and put it gently around her neck and she laughed, stood and spun around in the grass. "I'm so digging this, we're having our own little Be-In. Flower power and all!" And he told her Peace, and they sat cross-legged in the sun like they were in San Francisco, circa 1969. Later she bought a pair of vintage hip-hugger bell bottoms with satin cutouts stitched into the bell from a secondhand boutique and life was hippie sweet, as it can only be in Europe at twenty years old, no matter the decade.

This is what she remembers when a piece of summer slips between her and her daughters. Kat and Jenny went with her to buy silk flowers for the candlestand. Afterward they stop at Addison Cove with ice cream cones. A stone wall dating back to colonial times holds back the surrounding woods, weathered picnic tables are tucked in the shade of ancient maple trees, and lazy colorful sailboats bob in the river inlet. Beyond, the old timber Christmas Barn stands on the far bank of the cove.

They sit in the shade, lulled by the motion of colorful vessels on water, the sails snow white. "Pretty, isn't it?" Sara Beth asks.

Kat agrees, but Jenny acts too intent on licking her mocha fudge double scoop to answer. Sara Beth notices other times, when she glances up, that Jenny looks quickly away, caught observing her silently. It's how Sara Beth feels, too, observing this other woman she wants to be, trying to figure herself out with furtive glances. She gets it, gets Jenny, but they stay silent in their sentry, easy to do near water and boats of summer, both unsure of the woman Sara Beth.

What fills their quiet are the birds singing, a boat engine idling. It would be nice to catch it, she thinks, to reach to the sky and snatch some of that summer sound and put it in a flowered box and when you need it, you open the lid and a robin's call rises. Sometimes you'll hear the boat far off idling, waiting for you to board on a crystal lake framed by tall green pines. And she thinks the sound of a horse nickering would be in that box as well.

Sitting with her daughters on the slivery table, she is acutely aware that so much of what we have in life slips away. She catches Kat's eye. "Good?" she asks, and Kat tells her it's the best. Her daughters sit with her on a summer day. They're here with her, the same way Claude was. But who's to vouch for the permanence of their presence, their love? So many of her loves have faded away, layers of her self diminishing. The piano, art, old lovers.

She can't stop thinking about Claude now. About the year they spent studying abroad, walking through elaborate museums together, backpacking, trekking through Europe. So there's this scale in her head: Tom, Claude. Tom. Claude.

The birds continue singing, a dog runs past, its license tags jangling, and when the sounds of summer peace at the cove become indistinguishable from the sounds in Valojoulx, she pulls out her leather journal.

"What's that?" Jenny asks.

"This? Oh, well. It's a journal I found at an antique shop, and it's very old. I like to write my thoughts in it sometimes."

"Like I do!" Kat pipes in. "I'm going to write about this day when we get home."

"Yes. A journal like yours." And when her girls are satisfied it's nothing more than a passing fancy, an old journal to write new thoughts in, she adds one more line to her page.

I'm going to find Claude. It might help, Mom.

* * *

"Do you know what today is?" he asks. Long Island Sound's gentle waves roll along the length of the beach. The sand feels warm on his bare feet, the sun warm on his skin. They never changed into their swimsuits, content sitting together at the water's edge.

"Besides being the eleventh commandment day?" Rachel asks without moving. Her eyes are closed behind her sunglasses.

"Yes. Seriously."

"Well ..." Their heads rest back on the sand chairs as they drink in the sun's late afternoon rays. The beach umbrella is closed, looking like a colorful pod.

"It's the first day of summer," Michael says, then watches her for a reaction.

Rachel smiles in her sand chair. Its blue and white stripes are sun bleached, its wooden armrests worn smooth by summers near the sea. She opens her eyes and looks out at the water. The afternoon sun reflects a surface of diamonds.

Finally, she looks over at him. "You're very spontaneous."

His life flashes before him as he searches for indications of spontaneity. He's lived in the same town, on the same street, in the same house for that matter, all his life. He's held the same job for the past fourteen years, the past five on horseback. You can count on finding him at random Yankee games, usually with his daughter. He hasn't landed a serious relationship since his divorce and really doesn't get out too much. He likes his home. Actually, he likes his life exactly the way it is.

Except for that relationship part. But there hasn't been a woman since the divorce who held his interest, who hasn't considered his life, his job and his home as a springboard. Just like his ex, they are never content with what is at hand. He is.

"No one's ever accused me of spontaneity," he answers.

"You don't think you're spontaneous?"

"Not at all."

Rachel pulls her knees up and wraps her arms around them. "You showed up at my door today for this." She motions to the Sound. "You took me to the top of the Empire State Building, explained your version of heaven, took me to see God's view of the constellations then took me to Manhattan's lighthouse." She stops and takes off her sunglasses and he sees that she isn't joking. "You kissed me goodnight, our first kiss, and then couldn't leave me, walking into The Plaza lobby to check on Sara with me. Do you know how I felt when you did that?"

"I know how I felt."

"Well, I felt *really* good, in case I forgot to tell you. And then," she reaches over and brushes her hand over his arm, "you rode the train back to Connecticut with me so I wouldn't have to ride alone. That's not spontaneous?"

"No." He glances at his arm where she touched him.

"Then what is it?"

"It's you. And it's me. It's what I do for someone I care about."

"But how could you have cared about me last month when you'd only just met me?"

He shrugs. "I don't know. There was something about the way you grabbed Maggie's bridle in the middle of Fifth Avenue. Remember?"

Her gaze shifts to Long Island Sound, toward New York somewhere across the water, to where it all began. She sets her head back, puts on her sunglasses and closes her eyes. "I remember. What a day."

Michael stands and picks up a smooth stone from the water and skims it across the surface. He steps deeper into the water smiling as he scoops a handful of the sea in her direction, its spray reaching her in a thousand shining droplets.

* * *

The sky turns inky under the setting sun. The tide is low and they walk along the water's edge. One last sea gull, a straggler like them, perches on the end of the jetty. It's the perfect day to straggle. If she were writing a definition of it, she would say *straggle: lingering with the first day of summer, on the beach, well into dusk*. But the thing is, when you looked it up you'd get the *feeling* along with the words: the sweet June warmth and the tang of salt air and the lapping, lapping rhythm of gentle sea water.

Michael picks up a handful of small stones and places a few flat ones in her hands.

"Do you think we can pull this off?" he asks.

She knows what he is asking: Can they sustain a relationship crossing the state line? "I'd like to think so." She skims a three-skipper, not wanting to imagine him leaving.

"Do you have any suggestions?" He hands her a few more stones. "Because I'd like to see you again."

"Couldn't we try more of this back and forth? A little bit of meeting half way?"

Michael's stone skims off into the darkness. He loses count of the skips. "Sounds good. It'll make for a nice summer." When they start walking back along the beach, he slips his arm around her.

"Look," he says, pointing over the water.

"The first star." She told him on the Empire State Building the value she placed on stars, especially the first ones. It isn't so much the stars, but the power they hold in their light. She hopes for some of that magic, a bit of stardust, to fall on her own life.

"This star's different, you know," he says. "Its phenomenon only occurs once a year."

"What do you mean?" They stop walking and linger near the water. The beach is getting dark and they watch the star, a sparkle in the violet evening sky.

The several seconds between them say two months. That's all they've got ahead of them right now. He finally bends and kisses the top of her head. "It's the first star of summer."

Earlier, at the wishing fountain back in Addison, he said he wanted to save his wish for later.

This is later.

She can't believe that this is the same tense guy she met on the streets of Manhattan, the tough New York cop on horseback who barely gave her the time of day. Now he is giving her the summer.

Before she can make her wish, Michael takes her face in his hands. And really, if there is such a thing as a wish, wouldn't this be it, this delicate slice of the end of a June day? This touch of his hand, the sensation at the nape of her neck as his fingers move through her hair, thick with salt and sea breezes? That intimate effect on the skin, it's all a part of it. A wish is something your heart craves like the moment he steps closer still and she knows that he wants more than to breathe the salt air and feel the wind at the sea. And she waits in that moment, keeping herself in it while the waves break and the sea breeze kisses her first, touching her cheek, lifting a wisp of hair. And the wish is sealed then when he kisses her as softly, moving his hands around her neck, touching her hair and she can't tell the difference, sea breeze or delicate kiss.

This could be so perfect, beneath the stars at the edge of the sea. His fingers slip through her hair to her shoulders, lighting on her skin like he's tracing his way right to her heart. But her past is there, too, and he doesn't know that he scares her when he kisses her longer, sweeter. Because she can love him so much so that she won't be able to stand it when he leaves. Like Carl did. Sometimes it feels like she's still saying goodbye to Carl, the way the sadness bubbles up. And to Ashley. And Sara Beth. But she can't stop. It's too inside them, this moment on the beach, so she kisses him back, little kisses over and over, covering the fear his kiss pried loose.

Michael pulls back and caresses her cheek with his thumb. And it stops right there on the damp streak. "Rachel? You're crying."

"No I'm not."

"Yes, you are."

"It's nothing. Really." She tries to pull away but he won't let her, moving right with her in some new dance.

"What's wrong?"

She can guess his worry, that maybe she's not ready for this. Or maybe there is someone else, here in Connecticut. That of course she had a life here before he came into it. She waits, and there are only the waves breaking on the beach. It's a pivot when a few minutes ago are still with her and so is the anticipation of what is to come, the piece of time when the high tide begins to shift, motionless on top but swirling currents beneath the calm surface of the sea, switching to go out. She steps back, he steps closer.

"I'm fine. It's really nothing."

"Tell me about nothing."

"Nothing." And so, the tide changes. "It's just, sometimes it feels like people are always leaving."

"Me?"

She shrugs.

"Ashley?"

"It'll be a long summer without her here."

"And Sara Beth."

"I want to tell her about *you*."

"So that's what this is about?" He touches her damp cheek. "You're feeling lonely."

And it's the way he says it, the inflection that finds her in her loneliness because the place is familiar to him, and it makes her feel better, not worse, or sad, or embarrassed.

He puts his arm around her shoulder and they start walking again.

"Maybe I can help you with that."

"Maybe."

"Sara Beth's really on your mind, isn't she?"

"She is. Last week, after I finished planting at The Green, I took a leftover geranium to Carl's grave. The funny thing is that I felt like I'd planted flowers at Sara Beth's grave all afternoon. Like she's really gone. How can I bring her back?"

"Maybe she's not ready to come back yet."

"I had that thought too."

"Listen. Why don't you come to New York next week? Maybe Monday?"

Little does he know that Monday, Tuesday, or any day will be fine. She has no plans with Sara Beth. No plans with Ashley. Her summer lays open. "Monday's good."

"I've got tickets to a ballgame. If you don't mind going."

"The Yankees?"

"I split a pair of season tickets with some guys at work. So we could hang out, you know. Go to the game, get something to eat maybe?"

She thinks of their evening bowling last month. The game took her away from her worries about Sara Beth. He knows what matters. Bowling, baseball, it all keeps life tamed and ordered, restrained from growing wild and out of control with crazy emotions and relationships, when you're focused on the game.

"I'd love to go." And planning their next date, the Yankees supplant her troubles. In the car all the way back to Addison, they talk about the team, the new stadium, the opposing team, dinner beforehand, drinks afterward. Her life comes back, the small stuff, giving her exactly what she needs.

And after Michael is in his truck on his way back to Queens, she studies a photograph of Manhattan on her easel. Her fingers float over the tray of pencils, dipping and touching until she senses the perfect one to begin her newest sketch.

* * *

Sara Beth sits up in bed, her laptop propped against her knees. One ear is tuned to the noises in the house, waiting to hear Tom lock the front door, climb the stairs, come to bed. Her bedside lamp throws light on the computer screen, the coverlet is folded down at the foot of the bed. She pulls up one site as a cover: Sotheby's.

With that page in place, she Googles Claude and cannot believe the first few entries. A curator? In a French museum north of Paris? He never stopped living the dream! *Art is my oxygen* he used to tell her. It kept him going, apparently. Sustained his life, breathing it every day. And she thought of Monet's words, "Colour is my daylong obsession, joy and torment." It had been hers, today. And Tom actually liked the red painted wall. So she has that now. That, and their effort to keep the marriage together under one roof again.

But can she do the rest? If she'd stayed in France all those years ago, would she be happy? Would she own a small antique shop there? Would she have mastered the language? What if, what if? Would her mother still be alive? What was she looking for?

When she hears Tom coming up the stairs, she backs out of the museum site and her desktop background fills the screen. The candid photograph is of her and her mother laughing, her mom turning to her. She sighs, reaching forward and touching her face.

"What are you doing?" Tom asks.

"Oh." Sara brings up the other site. "Just cruising Sotheby's."

"As long as you're only cruising."

And she leaves that screen, too, seeing her mother again, noticing the scarf casually wrapped around her neck, feeling the chill of that autumn day when they went pumpkin picking. Autumn was her favorite time of year. The rich scents, apple cider, woodstoves, turkey cooking in the oven. When she was little, she told her mother she wanted to do this forever, linger in the pumpkin patches in the golden light of fall. And they'd never missed a year together. She looks up at Tom at his dresser. He always welcomed her mother into their home, their lives. He had taken the picture, after all.

sixteen

HOW MANY TIMES HAS SHE told those kids not to slam the door? A few days passed under the auspice of calm, broken by the slam and Sara Beth spilling her coffee in a long stain on the front of her top. Jenny storms through the kitchen, her hands clenched in tight fists, her body rigid.

"Jenny!" Sara Beth calls after her, blotting coffee off her tank top with a paper towel.

Her daughter flies up the stairs in a staccato beat before slamming her bedroom door shut. Then comes a cushion of silence before the stereo cranks. Owen looks up at the ceiling from his booster seat. The music puts him on alert, his eyes wide, his spoon frozen midair. Sara Beth goes to the kitchen window. She's surprised Kat wasn't right behind Jenny, holding on and rising upstairs with her, the tail on her sister's kite. Outside in the sun, Kat's sitting on the picnic table wearing last year's bathing suit. Her bicycle lies on the ground all cockeyed.

"Come on, fella. Let's go see Kitty Kat outside." Owen hooks his sippy cup with his fingers as she lifts him and a few drops leak out, enough to sticky the floor. Okay, so there's that, too. Cleaning the kitchen floor. And the thought brings on another headache.

"Katherine?" Sara Beth sets Owen down on the grass near the wayward bike. Her eyes squint in the sunlight. *Brain aneurysms sometimes run in families.* Please don't let it be a migraine. "What's the matter with your sister?"

Kat doesn't turn back. "Swimming lessons started today."

"Swimming lessons." She closes her eyes for a long second and says it. "Oh shit."

Now Kat turns to face her and Sara catches every bit of recent neglect she tossed their way like an old bone. Her daughter's gaze moves from her bandana to her earrings to her old jeans. Kat pulls at her pinching bathing suit strap.

"We better get you a new suit?" Sara Beth asks.

"You didn't sign us up."

"Oh Katherine." A duffel bag stuffed with their towels and goggles lies on the grass.

"We rode our bikes all the way to the pool and waited for Nicole to call our names. Nicole is my favorite lifeguard," Kat starts. "And she's teaching my level this session." She blinks her eyes against her tears.

"Except you're not in the session." The girls love to swim. Tom teases them, searching behind their ears for gills when they come out of the water all wrinkled. Every summer, they're the first to enroll in each two-week session. Until now. Sign-ups for the summer programs were held in May at the High School gym. Sara Beth never went.

"Oh gosh, I'm sorry." She sits on the bench next to her daughter, hands limp in her lap. Sometimes, well there's really nothing she can do and it's her fault, her fault, her fault.

"Jenny was going to make it to Lifeguard level this summer, and now she can't. And Nicole won't be teaching me." Kat takes her anger, jumps up from the picnic table and rushes to her bicycle, pushing Owen away from the pedal he's been spinning. He falls backward in the grass. "Stupid Owen," she yells and picks up the bike, jumping on it and wobbling off through the grass to the front of the house. Owen starts to cry.

Something that passes for music spills into the yard from Jenny's bedroom window. Sara Beth looks up, not sure who she's angry at, Jenny in her music cave, Kat for plowing into Owen, or herself for causing the whole damn mess and this killer headache. "Owie, Owie," she assures him as she scoops him up and runs her hand close over his head. Her fingers lift his hair and find no bumps.

By the time they get to his room, Owen calms and Sara Beth's wet tank top is stretched out of shape from holding him against it. "Let's pick a book from your new blue bookcase." Owen sits dead center in front of it and starts pulling all the books off the shelf. "Mommy will be right back," she says, kissing his moppy head, straightening her top.

Down the hall, she jiggles the knob and pushes at Jenny's locked door. She knocks, listening, and when she tries the knob again, the door opens.

"Just get out," Jenny says over the music.

Her gaze moves from her daughter to the stereo shelf system. The music is too loud, Jenny sounds too mad, Sara's shirt is still coffee-wet, her patience is gone and so when she glares at the stereo, the controls blur. The last thing she needs to do is seem inept fumbling with them, because won't it prove to Jenny that she is inept at everything? She walks over to the stereo and yanks the plug from the outlet. Jenny sits straight on her bed, staring out the window.

"Jenny, listen. I'm really sorry."

"Would you stop calling me that?"

"What?"

"Jenny. Jenny. It sounds like I'm four years old." She turns and glares at Sara Beth. "It's Jen."

"Since when don't you like Jenny?"

"If you can be someone else now, so can I."

"What are you talking about?"

"Why do you dress like that all the time? You're so embarrassing."

153

Sara Beth glances down at her clothes.

"God. Those crappy old jean shorts, a dirty shirt, your short hair pulled back under an ugly bandana like you're going to a rodeo. You take Owen and disappear all day, then come back all sweaty and happy. So if you can be someone else, so can I."

"Listen. Jen. I'm going down to Parks and Rec now. Why don't you come with me? We'll sign you up for swimming lessons. I really forgot about it last month."

"That's because you were too busy in New York. Kat says you were having a midlife crisis. That that's what happens when you turn forty. She heard Aunt Melissa tell Uncle Kevin that you ran away on Rachel. You left her there. Now you're probably going to get a divorce."

"Katherine? She said all that?" Sara Beth thinks of her young daughter trying to grasp those words, to lasso them into some corral where she can look at them closely and understand them. "Well, I'm *fine,* so she must have heard wrong."

But there is truth to Katherine's words. Sara Beth knows it, facing off with her sullen daughter, facing off with the knowledge of Claude's whereabouts. The truth is right there, right between them in the room glaring at her, hands on its hips. If Tom stands in her way, she really might leave. Because there *has* to be more to her days than quibbling with her kids about swimming lessons, or school, or friends. And play groups and committee meetings. There needs to be a balance, a personal balance; something for herself to keep the scales even.

She waves off Jenny's accusations. "If this swim session is filled, we'll try the next."

"Forget it." Her daughter walks to the stereo. She slides the cord from the back and calmly plugs it back into the socket, the music blaring right where it left off. With all the cool Jen can muster, she turns the unit off. "I like it better when you don't live here. And I don't want to swim anymore."

"Of course you do. You're just upset because I forgot to sign you up."

"Even Aunt Melissa went today, with Chelsea, who's a lifeguard this summer with Nicole. Auntie had her sand chair and visor to watch. And an iced coffee waiting for you. Like every year."

"Melissa did? What did she say?"

"If you want to know, ask her yourself. Because I'm not swimming anymore." She turns her stereo back on. "And I mean it!" she screams, no longer able to maintain her indifference to this odd Sara Beth, her odd mother.

"Please come with me to Parks and Rec, Jen."

Sara Beth waits. Her daughter's back is turned to her as she skims through her iPod playlist. She isn't even seeing the titles. It's like when a storm is coming but there is more than a storm. It is the humidity, the dead calm, the sky darkening, the heavy clouds.

So Sara Beth turns around and closes the bedroom door behind her, leaning against it in the hallway before going into her own room for her purse. What an enormous effort it takes to simply do something for yourself. All she wanted was to take Owen to the carriage house and spend a couple hours cleaning up some furniture. Now one glance in the mirror does her in. A half hour ago, she looked fine. Pretty even. Her clothes were clean and unwrinkled, her bandana in place. She even put on lip gloss and a stone bracelet.

Who is this woman? How can she have turned so disheveled? Her bandana is slipping off, wide strands of hair hang out the front, her tank top is soiled, her shorts are wrinkled and where the hell did those haggard eyes come from?

Sometimes the day keeps on tainting you, leaving the detritus of family life on the fabric of your clothes. Coffee stains, crumbs, wrinkles, tears, what have you. She pulls a T-shirt and denim capris from the dresser drawer. This won't be the last change of today. She kicks off her flip-flops, sending them flying across the room, then peels off her clothes before slipping into her second outfit. And it's only ten o'clock. So there are another twelve hours of possibility, of summer outfits. Even her hair is limp. And her headache, will it ever stop? *The warning headache averages about two weeks before a ruptured aneurysm. It is known as the sentinel headache.* Maybe she needs a prescription.

When she was in college, her mother would often call in the middle of the day. Just call and listen to her campus stories. And those phone calls meant so much, connecting simply over everyday life. She turns to the phone on her nightstand. Her mother's voice would fix this. They checked in with each other all their lives, from her mother poking her head into Sara Beth's bedroom to calling the dorm to sending letters to Europe to texting daily. It's all about the minutiae. Sara Beth picks up the phone, slowly presses in her mother's number, then hangs up before the connection goes through. She wants that same bond with her own daughters and has to fix things with them first.

"Jen! I'm going to Town Hall," she yells through her daughter's door before swinging it opened. Jenny sits on a chair pulled up to the window. Her feet are propped up on the sill, her arms crossed in front of her. "Keep an eye on your sister. I'm taking Owen."

Jenny looks like a mannequin. She leaned out, morphing into someone new this year, seeming more like seventeen than fourteen. Her hair is pulled back in a simple low ponytail.

"Are you sure you don't want to come?" she asks gently.

From where she is standing, she can't see her daughter's eyes. But she imagines they are brimming with hot tears that her daughter summons every bit of effort to hold back. If Jenny says anything, even one word, it will come out in a painful sob. Maybe this is better. Right now her daughter hates her guts. The silent treatment is better than crying in front of her. Especially if they are sad tears. Sara Beth has a funny feeling they are more sad than anything else. As though she misses her old mother. And longs to have her back.

* * *

Three antique children's chairs line the side wall of the Parks & Rec office. The chairs are pint-sized, dark maple, with rush seats. Sara Beth found them at a church bazaar in New Hampshire five years ago and stuffed them into the back seat of Rachel's already stuffed car that October Girls' Weekend Out. They liked to do that sometimes: Leave the kids with the dads and take off flea marketing, sightseeing, and coffee shop hopping. It was good for the kids, good for the dads and good for the town. Whole Latte Life uses her antique oak coat rack; the Savings and Loan displays her cast iron horse bank; the library houses a large country table in the Reference Room. At Parks & Rec, someone stacked old *Highlights* magazines on a table beside the chairs and the Kiddie Korner was complete.

Owen sits in one of the chairs, studying the Timbertoes page.

"I meant to call you," Margaret Grinheim says. She logs onto the computer on the countertop. "I thought it was funny that your girls weren't enrolled. They've been swimming every year since forever."

"Is there *anything* this session, even later in the morning? Maybe at another pool?"

Margaret runs down the list of names under each pool, each timeframe, her squared off, peach-painted fingernails dragging the mouse up and down each column. "Nothing. Gee, I wish I called you."

"Me too. How about a waiting list?"

Margaret turns the monitor around so that Sara Beth can see the screen. "These are the waiting lists for each session, as noted on the designated column. At least ten kids are ahead of yours. I'll put their names down, but don't hold your breath." She adds Katherine's and Jenny's names. "Give me your telephone number, hon," she says as she tabs over. When Sara Beth hesitates, Margaret looks up at her.

"You know, never mind. Maybe I'll put them in the winter lessons at the Y." Owen sits behind her swinging his legs on the antique chair.

"Are you sure? Now, wait a minute. There is one opening in the last session, at eleven-fifteen?"

"That wouldn't work with my schedule." Because Lord knows she needs a schedule. This running around arranging lessons and micromanaging kids can't be all there is. She hoists Owen up on her hip, thinking she'll hire Chelsea and Nicole for private swimming lessons. "Thank you anyway."

"Let me know if you change your mind." She smiles at Owen. "Bye bye little fella." Owen tucks his head on Sara Beth's shoulder as she turns to leave. "Oh Sara Beth, I meant to tell you. The Green came out beautiful. It was getting so we thought you had forgotten all about the flowers."

"Flowers?" She turns back and moves to tuck her short hair behind her ear.

"In the barrels. Didn't your sister tell you I saw her? You must have been busy at another barrel."

"Melissa?"

"Rachel was there, too. Of course it was the end of the day. Pete and I'd come out of Cooper Hardware and I walked over and said hello."

"Must've slipped her mind." So Rachel planted the barrels after all, with Melissa's help. Swimming lessons, flowers, even the kids' clothes shopping. Dates and routines are like sand slipping through her fingers.

"Everyone's pleased with how you plant those flowers. It's such a pretty spot."

Sara Beth hears the sympathetic tone in Margaret's voice. She can imagine the thoughts. *Maybe she's getting a divorce.* She shifts Owen on her hip. *Sometimes late babies are a last ditch effort to save a marriage. And those earrings.* The voices are almost audible as she hurries through the hallway, down the flight of stairs and outside to her car, growing louder with each pound of her headache. She snaps Owen into his seat and takes a deep breath.

That's what she needs. Relaxation and harmony. Deep breathing. Peace. She's been out of sync with herself for so long, a little life harmony would feel good.

Before driving away, she digs her leather journal out of her hobo bag and opens to the familiar page. *Did you ever take a Yoga class? Or meditate in some way?* Just writing it helps, wishing for a mantra, feeling calmer driving through town, circling The Green before pulling over beneath the shade of a tree, feeling nauseous from the headache.

She knows. You get a sense for these things; they leave a feeling in the pit of your stomach. *This* is why Rachel stopped at the carriage house that day. To invite her to plant. Each barrel brims with zinnias of red, orange and yellow, fresh green spikes and baby vinca vines. She gets out of the car and dips her fingers into the soil. It is rich and damp, freshly watered.

Owen makes a beeline to the wishing fountain. He hurries around and around the circular stone wall of the fountain, laughing each time he passes his mother. Her hand feels down to the bottom of her purse, sweeping along for a stray coin to drop in the water.

"Penny?" Owen asks.

"No pennies today."

"No penny?"

Owen looks back at the fountain and she closes her fingers around his hand. It's early still and the morning sun is hot. She planned to stop at the carriage house after lunch. But Owen needs a nap. And she yelled to the girls as she ran out that they would hit the mall later to stock up on shorts and tops and sandals. But they'll still be mad about the whole swimming lesson thing so the shopping will suck with attitude and whatever. She'll call them on her cell now and promise them tomorrow instead. An all day thing complete with tacos and fries, when they are in better moods. When even the light isn't bothering her head.

Because suddenly, cupping a fat, blossomed zinnia, none of it matters. Seeing all this planting, the velvet petals of summer framed by cool green cascading vinca vines makes her words in the carriage house, her *Get out,* seem all the more harsh. Because she knows the meaning of zinnias, oh she knows what message Rachel is sending her. They always research the meanings of the flowers before they make their barrel choice. And Rachel's zinnias break her heart with their message—thoughts of absent friends.

Apparently she can't keep anyone happy, because at forty, she has this: No penny, no clothes for the girls, and no friend. But touching a yellow zinnia, she realizes what she does have: Flowers. And her mother. Both can cheer her up.

I really need to talk, Mom. I'm going to pick a bouquet from my garden for you. And paint my nails, too. Remember when we'd do each other's? Then after lunch, when Jen can stay home with Owen, I'll come for a visit. I'll sit outside in the sunshine with you and have a long overdue heart-to-heart.

Love,
Sara Beth

seventeen

ELIZABETH," TOM SAYS. "YOU'VE GOT to help me out here. Sara misses you so much, she can't handle it anymore. It's getting worse and I don't know what to do."

Dr. Berg had suggested that a psychological emergency can trigger a breakdown. When Tom realized yesterday exactly what psychological crisis prompted Sara Beth's changes, he called Berg right away.

"What's important to know, Tom, is that there are several stages of grief. But if a person gets stuck in one stage, the grieving isn't complete. It's crucial to go through all five stages. At the same time, people can live on forever inside our hearts. So you have to carefully distinguish the difference. Is what you're seeing Denial? Or her mother living on in a new way?"

The sun's rays are low now, casting a deep color to the thick green grass, to the trees, the violet twilight sky. Tom reaches down to straighten the simple garden bouquet Sara brought to the cemetery, noticing how precisely she'd trimmed the surrounding grass. An old navy and gold Matrioshka doll is nestled on the grave side. Its colors are faded by the summer sun, the wood of the doll dried out. He pauses before touching her mother's gravestone, bowing his head as though waiting for an answer, then leaves.

The drive along Old Willow Road feels sad with what's about to come, but he's glad for one thing. Owen wasn't the emotional emergency that triggered Sara Beth's crisis. So there's relief for his son. Tom checks the house numbers. The river ribbons beyond the road to the west, where at the end of long driveways, captains' houses look out over the water. Crumbling stone walls border the properties.

He finally pulls over on the side of the road and shuts off the car, hearing only the cicada buzzing and melodic robin song. The driveway, littered with twigs and scattered leaves, winds up beside the big old house. Now he understands why Sara arranged to stay here when he'd kicked her out, because of the strong connection to her mother. Elizabeth's close friend owned the property. It all made sense, the way she sought to get closer and closer to the mother she'd lost last year. He steps out of the car and gently closes the door.

It doesn't look like anyone is home in the farmhouse. He thinks they probably went to the summer concert at the band-shell. It's where Sara Beth is supposed to meet him in a little while. Her car is parked beside an oak tree, with the library books she said she'd drop off still piled on the front seat. But the carriage house stops him. It's made with rough-hewn white planks with deep green cross beams on the two doors. Black iron hardware hangs from the cross beams, big heavy loops to get a grip on in order to pull the wide doors opened. They had to be wide, so that the buggies could fit through in colonial times.

A split rail fence butts up to either side of the carriage house, then back along the length of the property. Someone tacked coated chicken wire along it so animals, or the family dog, wouldn't slip through.

He walks closer. The door on the right is opened and the setting sun rays fall on deep browns, reds and golds inside. It is an opulence that murmurs its colors, its cherry, mahogany, oak. Hardware whispers brass. Mirrors sigh silver. If richness made a noise, you'd hear it in this space, in the smooth black lacquered hinges. Dull pewter kettles. Creamy ceramic wash basins.

He takes another step and sees his wife bent over a small table, wiping the curved legs to a bottomless glow. All her antiques have that dimension to them, where your reflection rises up as though from a deep pool of water. His foot steps on a large stick and it snaps.

Sara Beth looks up at him. The birds sense a predator with the snap of the branch and stop chirping. He walks into the carriage house wordlessly and a lone robin resumes its evening song.

* * *

There is meticulous order here, where his home life seems to have lost it all. This is where Sara Beth stops her world from spinning out of control. The furniture is precisely arranged by room, then by style and size. Smaller pieces, the pewter pitchers, stoneware, picture frames, line long shelves running along the walls.

"Tom! What did you do? Follow me here?"

He stands across the room from his wife. Her short hair curls behind her ears, her silver hoop earrings shine. The funny thing is, she looks pretty, all soft, slender curves beneath her wrap skirt and fitted tee. Gold bangles hang from her wrist. It all hints at her college-days style. He moves to a Windsor rocking chair and pulls a piece of paper from his pocket.

Sara Beth takes the paper, her eyes locked onto his. "Where did you get this?"

"When you changed your purse yesterday, you left that old journal on the dresser. You always keep it with you, so I knew something in it meant a lot. And I read it."

"You looked in my things?"

"I love you, Sara. So I looked, okay? And I saw the way you write to your mom, telling her you'll send emails, and about little things that happened, like in New York, with the peach sauce on your ice cream. So I kept looking and found her birthday letter inside the back cover. Sara." He stands still behind the rocker, his hands resting on its top. "This is pretty incredible. Elizabeth did this for you?"

"I can explain." She sets her mother's letter on the table she had been shining and wipes her hands on a rag. "Don't be mad. It's just that Mom wants me to have this."

"Sara," he says again, watching her closely. "Wanted." His gaze sweeps the room, until he finally walks over to an old table where her laptop is set up. His hand is shaking, but still he turns the laptop in order to read the screen:

Subject: Shop Status
From: Sara Beth
To: Elizabeth
Date: June 27 at 7:10 PM

Hey Mom, I finished restoring the console tables you found and did some research. You have a great eye … They're George IV Mahogany, priced now ~ 1200 for the pair! Not a bad choice if

When he looks up from the unfinished message, Sara Beth is sitting in the Windsor rocker, staring outside, her chin raised defiantly.

"We have to talk." He clicks into the Sent Mail file in her mailbox and sees the log of emails posted to her mother the past few months. "You know, Sara—"

"Don't," she warns him.

"But you have to hear this." He steps closer.

"No I don't."

"Sara," he says, taking her hand. She closes her eyes, as if that'll block what's coming. "She's gone, sweetheart. Your mom's been dead for over a year now."

"But not completely," she answers. "She gave me this! For my birthday! It's like she came back for me, Tom. To help me."

Tom moves through the space, his hands lighting on vases and candlesticks and picture frames, picking objects up and setting them silently down. A little bit of Sara and her mother, of their connection, are in each piece. It's a world purely Sara's that finally spun into his orbit. A world she's desperately trying to hold onto. He opens the desk drawer where she does her paper and computer work, brushing aside tissue paper. There's an old chain of flowers, daisies dried out and flattened, in the tissue. Someone's junk left behind.

Tom pulls up another chair, a Louis the Tenth, or Sixteenth, something from another century, that much he knows. He leans his elbows on his knees, his head dropped. Then, looking up, says "Tell me about this gift, sweetheart. Tell me about the key and this building and what your mom did for you."

* * *

"Why?" Sara Beth had asked on the morning of her birthday, brushing tears from her face. "How?"

"I went to school with your mom," Lillian March said. She'd come up behind Sara Beth as she looked at the antiques from her mother. "We're old friends, Sara. She called me last year and asked if she could store this furniture here. Just for a while, she said. Until you opened a shop."

Sara Beth looked at this Lillian, noticed how she was the same age her mother would be, the same free spirit, her jeans tucked into a pair of leather riding boots, a cashmere tunic hanging just right, a turquoise necklace, her silver hair clipped back.

"She was so excited to start this shop with you." Lillian moved into the carriage house, her hand lighting on a rolltop desk. "When we're young, we make a lot of choices, Sara. And again when we get older. Sometimes in the middle, life bogs us down. Your mom thought forty would be the right time for you to break out. And when you got pregnant," Lillian said, laughing lightly, "Elizabeth said you never took the easy path. Always roundabout. But she knew you'd get here. Oh, she knew."

"But this letter," Sara Beth said, holding up the birthday note. "Did she know she was sick? And not tell me?"

"No, not at all. She would never do that to you. Or to Melissa. My God, if you only had the grace of a goodbye. A few weeks before the brain aneurysm, she had some terrible headaches, like she'd never had before. They affected her vision and it scared her. All the *What ifs* came to mind and she panicked a little and gave me the letter. Just in case."

"So she did know," Sara Beth insisted, believing her mother aware, in her heart, of the loss to come.

"Well, maybe she sensed something. I don't know. But she gave me an envelope, to deliver to you today. That was all her doing. Even the balloons are. She left a letter for Melissa, too, but I haven't delivered that one yet. She loved you both so much."

Sara Beth turned and looked at the accumulated antiques in the carriage house. Her mother chose every piece, Sara's partner right to the end.

* * *

"So that's how it happened, Tom. It's like she knew she was going to die and was afraid I wouldn't follow through on an antique shop without her."

"Okay, I get that, as incredible as it all is. But not the rest. The haircut and the clothes and the piano lessons and Feng Shui and whatever else."

"You know, everyone told me grief takes a year and I'd feel better after that. But I didn't, Tom. Every day started out more sad missing her. Then in March, getting this birthday gift, well it was like a little of her came back. She wants this for me, expects it, knows it's me. So I felt her with me. By the time Rach and I celebrated turning forty, it was May. Two months had passed and I still didn't know how to start all this."

"Start what?"

"This. Pursuing the dream alone. So all the other stuff, I don't know. I had to refashion my life and I took it literally. Starting with my *fashion*. And actually, I kind of like that part too. It's fun. Okay? I had some fun." But she knows that as she says it, her tears say something else. She remembers the night on the ferry in New York, dumping so much of herself into the river so that she could rebuild piece by piece. Her right hand covers her left, feeling for the missing ring, still feeling her mother's death was Tom's fault. Will that resentment ever fade? Can she keep on hiding it? "But the sadness felt even worse, doing all this without Mom. I missed her even more. It got so bad, I didn't know how to stop it except to run away from it. And still, still. Sometimes I still hear her voice. Like a breeze, a wisp of it. But it's there, I swear. It really is."

Tom walks through the room, winding through the antiques. Sara Beth watches him. He wears khaki shorts and a navy polo. Sneakers and sport socks. But she sees the weariness in his eyes. He turns and meets her gaze.

"What?" she barely asks.

"Other people are regular, Sara," he says. "They're at the park waiting for the concert to begin. They're talking about what happened at work or about a noise the car is making. They're sitting together on a blanket. They're having a little wine. Maybe cheese, and crackers out of a box. They're dancing tonight, Sara Beth. Maybe that's all I wanted."

"To dance?"

He looks long at her. "To be regular. Something's happened. I don't know what we are anymore."

"We can be that again. Nothing's wrong with me," she insists.

"Okay. Then what about Claude? He's part of your plan. It's in the journal."

"Oh Tom," she says, taking his hands. "Haven't you ever wondered?"

"Not really. No."

"Not that you'll tell me anyway. I just wondered, that's all, in the middle of all this. Wondered what my life would be if I made different choices back then. Would I be in this place now? Would the sadness be gone?"

"So you're thinking of an old flame?" He tugs his hands out of hers.

"It's not Claude I'm thinking about, it's—"

She sees the anger in his eyes, sees him trying not to let that anger win, not to let anger lift his arm and sweep every ceramic vase off the shelf.

"I'm going to find Claude. It might help, Mom," he says. "That's a direct quote, from your journal. Find. Claude. So don't you dare tell me it's not about him. It's all spelled out. So have you? Have you seen him?"

"No," she says, shaking her head. She's never felt so close to losing everything. "No. Claude was a time in my life when I was free, when any opportunity was mine. That's what I wanted back. Opportunity."

"If I have to worry about Claude now, don't come back, Sara. I don't need that in my life on top of the kids and working and the house and everything else. We're over then."

"Don't you see?" she says, and though she's not sobbing, not crying, she feels the tears streaking her cheeks. "It's the options I want." And she can't say the option to live over with Claude. The option to not be so delayed that dreaded day a year ago all because of Tom. To have a chance to get to her mother sooner. "The choices."

"You're not satisfied with me then? Is that it? So you're wondering?"

"I wasn't satisfied with my life."

"Which I'm part of. So I've got to deal with that, Sara Beth. And everything else. And the bond with your mother. You have to let her go. And move on."

"Tom, I loved her, and I still love her. I don't want to lose that."

"So you're going to do this? Open a shop?"

"That was our plan, so why couldn't I? Can't we talk? Can we go get a drink, maybe?"

He stands there in her world, seeming so unsure, his hair lying flat in the heat.

"We can stop at the bandshell?" she asks, crying freely. "Dance with me there?"

"Just like that? Have a drink and a dance?"

"No, of course not. But it'll help. To start."

Tom watches her for a moment, closes his eyes and nods, then turns and walks out into the June evening.

eighteen

MICHAEL WAKES UP GLAD IT'S Friday until Rachel calls him early and cancels their Saturday.

"It's Sara Beth," she says.

"Is she okay?"

"I think so. But she left a message on my machine when I was out walking." He can tell she's moving, bending and taking off her sneakers while she speaks, the telephone cradled to her ear. "Something about if I can meet her tomorrow to go shopping."

"Shopping."

"Well. It's not really about shopping."

"No," he answers, pacing the kitchen and downing his coffee, hating to lose Saturday.

"I'm sorry. I have to give her this chance."

"Of course you do. Don't worry about it."

"Oh, and Michael. It's Ashley, too. She's here. She drove down."

"Everything all right?"

"She surprised me with a little visit, that's all. We went to the movies last night, and we're just going to hang out today."

"I know how much that means to you. But I'm still going to miss you."

Rachel pauses. "I wonder if I could ask you a favor. I want Ashley to meet you."

"Meet me? When?"

"Today. She has to drive back to campus later and if I follow her, we could meet you in New York somewhere after you get off work. Maybe for a sandwich or something?"

"This is kind of sudden."

"I know. It's just that she's here and she worries about *me* being alone now. She knows about you, and maybe it would help to meet you and see us together a little."

"It could backfire too, Rach. She might resent me, thinking I'm taking her dad's place."

"Well I told her how you helped me in New York and she seems fine with it." After another pause, she asks, "Can you do dinner tonight?"

They settle on a time and diner off one of the highway exits not too far out of their way.

What it all is, the phone call, Sara, Ashley, it's the hold Addison has on Rachel. He wonders if he's enough to draw her away, or if their summer plan will merely reveal whatever they can't leave behind.

By the time he gets to his troop's stable, that's all he's thinking. He saddles Maggie in the tack room, paints on hoof dressing and combs her tail before waiting in the locker room for roll. Maggie is tied outside the door while he sits at the square table and takes his assignment. He bums a cigarette from the sergeant.

"You okay, Micelli?" The sergeant hands him the pack.

"I feel like a smoke, all right?"

"Suit yourself."

A few drags are enough, before he tamps out the cigarette and walks over to the bulletin board. Papers hang at random: job openings and formal department procedures tacked alongside handwritten index cards announcing the summer poker league, used refrigerators for sale, a tag sale, truck for hire.

Hands clasped behind his back, he reads the ads, searching for something, but not sure what. A landscaping service? Free kittens? A tattered index card is stuck behind the kitten card. He reads it once, then again. After calling the number and leaving a voicemail, he tucks the card in his shirt pocket, walks Maggie outside and starts his shift.

* * *

Anchor Beach is situated on Long Island Sound, in the crook of a bend in the coast. The sea air lingers heavier there, embraced by the stone jetty and pine forest, the arms of the bend. A long boardwalk reaches along half the length of the beach, giving way to a small street of seaside cottages running behind the sands. The American flag flies on the white pole in front of the boardwalk and a few gulls soar, floating like low-slung kites.

Michael can't get it out of his head. As he patrols the streets, directs traffic, dismounts Maggie and writes a handful of tickets, it's there. Even having a turkey club at Dee's Sandwich Shoppe with Rachel and Ashley, he glances out the window and pictures the beach on the horizon. Ordering ice cream cones to-go and idling together outside the restaurant, it is Anchor Beach's salt air he breathes. He hasn't rented a cottage for a couple years, but this summer he needs to be there. It would be perfect.

His phone rings late that evening, after he finally gave up on a return call.

"Dave Wagnall here. You called about renting my cottage."

"Dave, how's it going?" Dave is a fellow officer with a precinct uptown. He's heard the name before.

"Not bad. Hey, where the hell'd you find my card? On the board?"

"I pulled it off this morning."

"The problem is, Micelli, that card's old. I posted it last year."

"No shit. So the cottage isn't available?"

"Well, here's the thing. It's my mother-in-law's place. She's in a convalescent home and we've been too busy to open it up. You know, with my wife keeping an eye on her mother, it's all I can do to get there and cut the grass."

"It's tough, I know."

"But if you're interested, I'll rent it for a fair price. It needs to be aired out, sweep out the cobwebs. Other than that, it's got the basics."

"Yeah, yeah, I think I'd like to do that." His vacation time's booked for the end of July.

"What do you want? A week or two?"

He needs a week definitely for his daughter and her friend. And then time with Rachel. "How about July? Can you give me the month?"

* * *

The stores open at ten at Sycamore Square, an outdoor shopping plaza in the center of Addison. The plaza, a cluster of pretty, cream-colored buildings, sits nestled at the end of a wide, tree-lined boulevard.

Sara Beth asked Rachel to meet her there at nine-thirty, so Rachel figures they're back to that, their half hour walk before the stores open, window shopping and talking along the way. She dressed for shopping: black tank, denim skirt, wedge sandals. Easy on, easy off.

She spots Sara Beth sitting on a bench in the noted spot, legs crossed, hand clutching a big straw tote. "Sara," she calls.

Sara Beth stands. Her ankle length gauzy skirt makes her look thinner than she is. Two long strings of beads hang over her fitted top. "Hey Rach. Let's walk?"

Rachel steps beside her on the cobblestone walkway. Well okay, now here's something she notices, one of the reverberations echoing since their New York weekend. No hug. "How are you, Sara Beth?"

"I'm doing okay," she says, hiking her bag to her shoulder. "I'm glad you came."

"I wasn't too sure if I should."

"I know, after the way I talked to you at the carriage house. Oy, when I think about it. So thanks," Sara Beth says, and they walk a few quiet steps. "Hey." She taps Rachel's arm. "Speaking of that day, my secret's out."

"Secret?"

"The carriage house. Tom knows."

"You told him?"

"Not exactly. He kind of stumbled on it by himself."

"And?"

"Let's say he's trying to get used to the idea."

"Idea? What idea?"

"I'm going to go ahead with my plans. To open a shop."

"That's great," Rachel tells her, glancing into a shoe store, remembering how Sara Beth kicked her out of that carriage house and out of her life.

"But I'm only in the planning stage right now. The talking stage."

"Didn't look that way to me." They approach a boutique and stop in front of a window of mannequins fitted with pastel tees and faded denim, square straw bags slung over armless shoulders. "Seems like you've got a readymade shop there. If you hung a shingle out front, you'd be in business."

"There's more to a business than that."

"I meant it as a compliment. It looks like you're past the talking stage is all I'm saying."

"Oh. I guess." They start walking.

"Is that what today is about? A formal business announcement?"

Sara Beth glances at her as they walk. "I'm just trying to make small talk."

"Well." Ship replicas crafted of mahogany and fine silk sails line Felucca's window. Seagoing vessels and schooners laden with sails fore and aft remind her of the shoreline and her day at the beach with Michael. "Good luck with your plan then. Really. You deserve it more than anything."

"Thanks. Do you want to go in here?" Sara Beth asks.

"No. That's okay." They start walking again.

"So how've you been? How's your summer, Rach?"

Rachel slips off her sunglasses and studies her, squinting. "Gosh I hate it that this is what we've become. Polite questions. Forced smiles."

Sara Beth motions toward the little café where dark green sun umbrellas have been opened at the outdoor tables. "Let's get a coffee."

When they sit side by side with two large mugs, Rachel hears Sara Beth's low voice.

"I feel it too, Rach. That strain." She reaches over and touches Rachel's arm. "But I'm trying, I'm really trying, to make a connection with you." She pauses. "And with Tom."

So there is friction between Sara Beth and her husband, too. "Sara. We're all trying to understand what you're going through, because we love you. But maybe you've lost some connections because you're not trying to understand us back."

"Well help me to. Please."

Rachel pulls in her chair and sits straight, elbows on the table, hands clasped beneath her chin. "Okay. Did you ever think that in The Plaza, Michael advised me not to touch your belongings, in case you were dead? *That's* what I lived that weekend."

"Michael? The guy with you?"

"The police officer. See what I mean about understanding? He's a cop," she says kindly, "and he helped me."

A waitress approaches and sets a glass vase crammed with yellow marigolds on the center of their table, smiling briefly before breezing to the next.

"I'm sorry," Sara Beth says, moving the vase to the side. "I'm sure you did everything you could. And I understand your worry now."

"And it's not only me. Your husband was devastated. As surprised as he was, all he cared about was that *you* were okay."

"I'm working on being okay. It's just that I turned forty and they say this is when you surrender some of your dreams. So I wondered why it can't be a time to *pursue* them. You never know from day to day when it can be too late. Look what happened with my mom, an aneurysm out of nowhere. So I tried to change my life without disrupting everyone else's." She picks up her coffee cup, pauses mid-air and sets it back down. "Which is *exactly* what I did, didn't I?"

Rachel pushes back from her chair and checks her watch. "You used to wear your heart on your sleeve. Your kids, your home, even Addison. I miss that openness. Now you're changing yourself? A secret carriage house? A new look? I don't know what's in your heart anymore." She stands in the shade of the green umbrella and pulls her sunglasses from the top of her head.

"Rachel, we have to do this." Sara Beth watches from her seat. "You're not leaving?"

"No. I saw a dress in Celeste's I want to try on."

"That new shop? Can I meet you there in fifteen minutes?" Sara Beth motions to her coffee as though she wants to finish it.

Rachel looks at her, squinting with doubt but knowing they need a breather here.

"I won't leave. Promise." Sara Beth says with a guilty smile. "Then we'll seriously shop. And talk more. Like old times."

* * *

Sara Beth comes to the dressing area and taps on the outside entrance. "Rach?"

Rachel steps out barefoot and slightly tanned wearing a plain black sleeveless sheath, her blonde hair tucked back straight behind her ears.

"The perfect 1-b-d," Sara Beth says. "You look smashing."

Rachel steps on a carpeted pedestal and turns in front of the three-way mirror. "I don't know." What she's doing is harboring thoughts of summer in Manhattan, of needing the perfect dress for dinners in the city.

"Uh huh," Sara smiles. "All dressed up with nowhere to go?"

"Oh, Sara." She eyes her friend's reflection in the mirror, wishing she could easily tell her about Michael and New York. That the words would tumble out about this guy and his horse and his ways. That they'd laugh and wink and raise an eyebrow. That she could voice her doubts, too, about his protectiveness, how it's seeming like an insecurity. Instead she turns to her own reflection.

Sara Beth crosses her arms in front of her and leans against the doorjamb.

And the silence, Rachel notices, becomes one of them, a third reflection in the mirror. She picks at a thread on the dress seam.

"I thought the note was enough." Sara Beth speaks softly and it makes Rachel raise her eyes to her reflection. "But I screwed up."

"What do you mean?" Their reflected eyes lock, so damn anxious to fix this.

"I gave you the note in the restaurant so that you *wouldn't* worry. I *thought* it would work. I should have told you clearly *when* I'd be back, but I didn't even know what to do. I just had to go. To get out of my own skin, to figure my life out, to stop dying of sadness. I never meant to hurt you. Don't you understand?"

"I'm beginning to."

"I was afraid. Since my mom died, I just fell apart. I lost her and a lot of myself too."

"Sara. I could've helped you."

"How, really? It's up to me to put myself back together. To remake myself. It's what I'm still trying to do, little by little."

Little by little. Rachel thinks that Sara Beth has this, then: the carriage house, pursuit of a dream, including Owen in her days, communicating this to her husband and girls while trying to say goodbye to her mom, and mending the fence of a friendship. Her plate is full. "But didn't you see it coming? These things don't just happen, and you never said a word. Nothing."

Sara Beth's cell phone rings and she reaches into her handbag. "Jen, Jen. Slow down," she says, bending into the call. "Where's Dad? Okay. Put some ice on it, okay? I'll be right home." She turns back to Rachel.

"Family crisis?"

"Katherine fell off her bike and her arm's swelling. Tom's out with Owen. Guess I'm going to the Emergency Room."

"Oh boy! You better get going."

She tucks her phone away. "Can we try this another time?"

"Sure," Rachel says, stepping off the pedestal. What she would like is to go with her. Or to baby-sit Owen so Tom could go, too. Or maybe sit in the hospital with all of them, like she would have in the past.

Sara Beth doesn't ask, though. She quickly leaves and Rachel returns the black dress to the rack, thumbing through a few more. So much of their morning was the same as always. The small talk, the slow walk, the browsing. But the important stuff, the easiness evaded them until the end. Then the call came.

"Rachel?"

She turns around and Sara Beth is behind her, breathless. Her sunglasses are on, car keys in her hand. "After my coffee, well ..." She holds out the Felucca's bag. "This is for you."

"Me? A boat?"

"You liked them when we walked past the window. Maybe you can use it in your beach room?" She takes the mahogany ship from the bag, pulling it from the puffs of tissue. "This is what you and I need. Some time on a boat."

"A boat? I don't know if that'll do it."

"No, really. It would." She glances at her watch and hesitates. "On a boat, with all that water, we couldn't get away from each other. No cell phones, no dressing rooms, no cars, no emergency rooms. A boat would be the perfect thing." She puts the ship back in the bag. "Please take it." She hands Rachel the bag.

* * *

"This town's feeling way too small for me."

"The shopping didn't work?" Michael asks. He had finished mowing the lawn under the noonday sun and opens a bottled water.

"It started to, but there was a family emergency. Is it too late for me to come there?"

"I'll come to Addison. I don't want you on the road."

"No, no." She walks outside with her cordless, closing the slider behind her. "I need a change of scenery. I'll be fine driving."

"When?"

"Two hours, one if I floor it."

"Very funny. I've got a double shift tomorrow. It'll be an early night."

"I need to see you."

"Okay, then. But take your time. I'll be here," he says. "Be sure to fill your gas tank."

"I will," Rachel replies.

"Good. And make sure to leave a light on a timer. Maybe check your oil before you head out."

"Michael. Please."

He doesn't say anything, just takes a long breath.

"I have to pack an overnight bag. Do I need anything? A change of clothes for dinner or a club?"

"Casual, Rachel. Dress casual."

* * *

"What a perfect surprise this is. I thought I'd be spending the weekend in the city."

They stop at the boardwalk before driving to the cottage. "Someone I met once told me salt air is the perfect remedy to any worries," Michael says. "Try it."

So Rachel does, inhaling deeply. They sit at the end of the boardwalk, a sandy beach and Long Island Sound spread before them like a watercolor painting. The waves break along the beach, the sun sits low over the western jetty.

"Listen," Rachel says, holding still.

He tips his head to concentrate on the beach noises and Rachel kisses his cheek, then gently turns his head so that he hears the comforting noise behind them. Rising and falling lightly against their moorings, the subtle pull of the current in the boat basin brings the secured boats to life. They creak and sigh against the pilings, like the sound of a huge ocean fish.

"Boat talk," Michael says.

She glances over at him. Even though his dark hair is cut short, it can't fight the salt air and a natural wave emerges. His face is tanned from being outdoors on the job, but it looks weathered, too, faint scars showing through the tan, as though he is a fisherman back from the sea instead of a Manhattan mounted police officer.

"I've missed this," she tells him. "I was so busy getting Ashley ready for college last year, we never made it to the beach. Instead it was dorm shopping and student orientation."

"Do you miss her today?"

"Oh my gosh, do I ever. She seemed pretty chill with us, don't you think?"

Michael nods. "I'm glad I met her."

"She loves the beach too. She says that she learned an important lesson from our summers at the beach."

"What's that?"

"There are two kinds of people in this world. Beach people and lake people. Whoever she ends up marrying will have to be a beach person."

"Ashley's all right."

Michael is a beach person; anyone could see that in him. He knows about the mystical healing power of the salt air and appreciates the language of the boats behind them. He skims a mean stone on the Sound's choppy water and the very first thing he did this afternoon was splash a handful of salt water on his face and neck, then run his wet, salty fingers through his hair.

"Why don't we go to the cottage? I'm not sure what we'll find. You might not like it, I don't know."

"I still can't believe you rented one. I told you you're spontaneous."

"Believe me, it was spur of the moment. Want to check it out?"

"In a minute, okay?" The late sun warms her skin. But there's more, in this one moment. There are waves lapping at the shore, a sea breeze touches her, the salty scent of the ocean rises. One moment, and all this.

* * *

They pass cottages freshly painted beach colors of white and creamy yellow and pale blue. Pots of red geraniums sit on front steps, tall shrubs of beach grass grow like natural fountains.

"There. On the right." Michael points through the windshield, scrawled directions gripped beneath his hand on the wheel. The pale gray cottage sits on a hill not far from the beach. It is an old bungalow with a big enclosed front porch. Errant branches sprout from the shrubs and brittle curls of paint peel from the wood siding.

"Goodness gracious!" Rachel leans forward in the seat. "It is so pretty." She rushes up and unlatches the old hooks and pushes open the porch lattice windows, stiff on their hinges. Breaths of summer surprise the sunny room. *Oh!* it seems to say, and it brightens and the wooden gulls and vases of sea glass stand up straighter. Michael shoulders open the inside door because his arms are holding two bags of groceries. The summer air spilling inside the dank cottage works its magic. Drab living room furniture transforms as Rachel opens the window blinds and hefts up the sticking windows. Lumpy couches and chairs become comfortable and overstuffed, slip covered in sun faded stripes and soft plaids. Golden light paints the rickety end tables a distressed white. Tabletop clutter morphs into wooden seagulls, delicious novels and clear glass lamps filled with sea glass and shells.

Rachel moves to the bedrooms, bringing along the wand of her touch. It lights on white wicker covered with pastel linens that beguile the weary eye with images of the sea. Thin cotton curtains, the kind that puff out with gentle sea breezes, frame the white-painted windows. In one bedroom, side-by-side paned windows overlooking the distant Sound bear only a crisp white valance, white as a sunstruck sail on a boat.

Michael calls to her from the kitchen. Fruit and a box of pastry are on the counter along with the extra flashlight and smoke detector he bought, and late day sunrays stream in through the window. Dried flower bunches hang from painted ceiling beams. He stands at the French doors opening to a back porch, a room big enough for a lunch table and a corner to deposit your sandy flip-flops.

"What do you think?" he asks.

Rachel turns on the kitchen tap. The water spits and sputters until finally flowing in a clear stream. Then she reaches over the sink and cranks open the window.

"Do you like it?" Michael asks. He leans against the counter, watching her.

The cottage is high on a hill and she sees the Sound through the window, blue gray on the horizon. She turns to Michael, steps close to him leaning against the counter with his wavy hair and slow smile and his hands reaching for hers.

"It's heaven," she says, and he kisses her tenderly once, then again near her ear as his arms circle her waist, pulling her close against him. She moves her thumb to his lips, sweeping it across and thinking how lucky she is when she feels his mouth on hers again, hears her whispered name.

nineteen

IT FEELS LIKE THEY'VE BEEN dating, Tom a little awkward and Sara Beth unsure. She figures it's something you have to do every ten years or so in a marriage. Go out on dates. It even made it into her journal.

We're dating again, Tom and I. Maybe it'll help, maybe I'll see he wasn't to blame for your dying. I don't know. I'm not sure anything can convince me of that. My life's all maybes lately. Maybe it's time I tell him I feel like it was his fault. We'll see.

Love,
Sara Beth

If this is going to work, he has to know how she feels. She's moved back home, and tonight Tom's taking her out to dinner.

"Dress up. We're going somewhere special."

Black, she decides. A black silky halter, black skirt, with the gold scarf from the Greenwich Village boutique and a gold bangle bracelet.

"I can't believe you cut your hair," Sara Beth says in the car, checking out the new Tom, buzz cut and all. "It's a new you."

"I wanted to see how it felt to change my life a little."

"And?"

"I guess I'm still getting used to it."

Sara Beth brushes her hand across his head. "Well the new me sent in the small business loan application. I included a business forecast, projected expenses, expected revenue, even seasonal shopping swings."

"You used to always be that way."

"What way?"

"Remember when we met, when you got back from Europe? I couldn't believe the way you took your education all the way, going to the Louvre to finish your art studies. I liked that about you, the way you were in things one hundred percent. So it's good to see that again."

Sara Beth thinks that was before he knew about Claude being in Europe with her. So there was that. Some things she didn't take all the way, like her relationship with Claude. She didn't take it all the way to marriage. Though he proposed, she could not take her life permanently all the way to Europe back then.

Taking things all the way or not, haircut or not, Tom still resents her changes, resents her running away. She feels it, little ambiguous wisps caught in a room with them, or trapped in the car doing errands. He's having a hard time with this still. Time alone at dinner will help. They'll talk.

They drive sleepy back roads, deep evening shadow laying long among the overhanging trees. Music plays softly on the radio. She never suspects anything until Tom turns onto Old Willow Road and into the carriage house driveway.

"Tom? What are you doing?"

In the low blush of twilight, wavering candlelight glows in the paned windows and spills in a pool of gold from the opened carriage house door. Impressionism. The visual effect of light and movement on objects. Beyond the historical carriage house, a field of wildflowers gives way to deep green trees rising against a violet sky. This painting captures the golden light of dusk within the carriage house, illuminating the artifacts inside.

"Wait." Tom takes her arm as she reaches to open her door. "This isn't my doing. I don't want you to go in there with false hopes."

"What do you mean?"

"Melissa planned sort of a dinner party. When you showed her the carriage house the other day, well," he pauses, squinting out the window. "She wants you to know that we understand. Whatever you find inside, *she* wanted to do for you. It's her idea."

"And you?"

"I agreed to it because I'm trying. I still don't like the *way* you went about all this, but I don't know if it's worth losing a marriage over."

So there's that now. No matter how much they try, no matter how considerate they are, the same thought's occurred to her. What is worth losing a marriage over? A chance, maybe? Or blame? Doubt, imagining life with someone else? Claude?

Tom lets go of her arm and they step out of the car in silence.

Some things she can't help. Like the gasp that escapes when she walks into the carriage house. Life moves in slow motion when her gaze sweeps the room, a room Melissa has transformed. Much of the furniture has been pushed back, leaving center space for a long mahogany pedestal dining table, with a hydrangea, twig and feather centerpiece anchoring the place settings of antique botanical plates and white glazed French dinnerware her mother chose. And candlelight, ornate silver-on-copper English candelabras on the table, French bronze on the sideboard. The room is bathed in age and elegance, even when someone sounds out a jingle on the piano Sara Beth found in the online classifieds: *Like-new condition, plays happy songs, needs a good home.* And she knew it had been loved.

"Sara Beth," Melissa says, hugging her. "When you told me you were opening an antique shop, well, I can't believe how Mom came through for you. It's sad now, but she'd be so proud. And this is what I think she'd do for you, a dinner like this." She stops then, unsure.

"What?" Sara Beth asks.

"Maybe it'll help you, in a way. With everything you've been dealing with. You know, missing Mom so much, starting a shop. That's why I'm doing this. To bring some of Mom into your plans."

So the layers build, just like in Impressionism. Wet paint is applied directly over wet paint, before the initial layer is dried. The effect is diffused edges and intermingling of colors. Exactly the way this room depicts her life's soft edges, intermingling tonight with the colors of her mother in days gone by.

And it works, Melissa's Old World dinner party. The French country chairs upholstered in a floral fabric finish the mahogany table. Tea lights adorn the dining table and candles are scattered throughout the large space, turning the furniture into shimmering pools of browns. Sara sits and looks at her life with cautious satisfaction: Tom beside her, her sister Melissa and brother-in-law Kevin, her mother's dear friends who own the property, Lillian and Edward March, and her neighbors Julie and Connor, who've lived beside her and shared in her life for many years now. Somewhere in the shimmering light, she knows her mother is there as well, watching with sweet wistfulness.

Once they are all seated, the caterer serves the Tomato Bread Salad and Roasted Rosemary Chicken, baby carrots and red potatoes and grilled zucchini, heavy goblets of wine. Someone brought an old record player and a scratchy jazz record fills the room with music.

"Your girls will love this place, Sara. When will you show them?" Julie asks.

"In the morning. Maybe we'll have breakfast here while the table's set like this." She turns to Melissa. "Let Chelsea come, too, okay? My treat for her babysitting the kids tonight."

"Sure. I just called her. They're all settled in at your place, Owen's asleep."

"Oh, I hope they love this the same way I loved Mom's antiquing," Sara Beth says. To continue this passion of hers and her mother's to the next generation means the world to her.

"Love it? They'll be arguing over who gets to help in your new shop, whenever you finally take the plunge! Kat'll be whipping out her day-planner, Jen calling dibs."

To have her kids back and understanding her, it's all that matters. Ever since her mother died and she lost her from her life, her plans, her phone calls even, she knows. Every bit of it matters. Every layer of paint. She has to build those same layers with her children.

When they settle in afterward with coffee, Julie hands Sara Beth a thin, wrapped package. "We love you, hon. Best wishes," she says with a hug.

"Oh come on. This was enough, this beautiful meal together." Sara Beth peels back the wrapping paper on a dollar bill mounted and displayed behind an old cherry frame.

"It's your first dollar earned," Julie explains. "Consider it my deposit on that piecrust tip table."

"Thank you so much," she says, laughing as she gives Julie a hug. Tom reaches over and takes the gift from her. Can't he feel it? How right this is?

Edward March excuses himself and returns carrying a cardboard carton. In the past several weeks, Lillian often brought Sara Beth a cup of chamomile tea and they sat and talked about her mother. One of those times, Lillian returned to the main house with a framed Currier and Ives print of two kittens lapping up spilled milk. She wanted to pay for it, but no way would Sara Beth let her. "It's my gratitude. For bringing Mom back to me like this."

Now Lillian, wearing a long layered skirt reaching her ankles, a necklace of coral and mother-of-pearl hanging over her loose tank top, passes the box along to Sara Beth.

"You need a mascot to keep you company here, and to breathe some life into the stuffier pieces."

The carton tips from the uneven weight of an animal crouched in one corner. She opens it to find a tiny silver tabby with silver and black stripes running down her sides in perfect unison. "You didn't," Sara Beth says.

"Remember I said we had a few wild strays on the property?" Lillian asks. "One of them had a litter and this bugger never leaves me alone. When I hang the clothes or do my gardening, she follows me everywhere! She's a real people cat."

And so it goes for the evening, timeless comfort, wine and coffee in wavering shadows of candles and antiques, easy conversation. Sara Beth feels the effort to help her move forward, to accept the place of her mother's loss in her life. Several toasts ring out, including a personal one between Tom and herself, Tom honoring her mother. Paul Cezanne's words come to her: *We live in a rainbow of chaos.* And she knows life can be that, a beautiful chaotic rainbow. Occasionally someone plucks out a bar on the piano.

"Love the piano," Melissa says.

"We're moving it home, actually. I want to have one in the house again."

Still, one thing's bothered her all night. The final place setting left in front of an empty chair, across from her own seat. She asks her sister about it.

"I've been trying to reach Rachel, but I keep getting her voicemail. I was hoping if she got the message, she'd show up."

Sara Beth thinks of how she and Rachel shopped at Sycamore Square. If in the end she lost her very best friend, was this all worth it? The carriage house doors are thrown open onto the summer night, the sky heavy with stars. Impressionists capture moments in landscapes, moments in people's lives, caught in fleeting light. There'll be more moments, that's all she can believe.

* * *

Before he opens his eyes Sunday morning, Michael breathes in the aroma of fresh brewed coffee and salt air. The salt air gives it away. No way is he at home in Queens. He sits up on the chaise to slats of sunlight streaming in through the porch lattice windows. A high shelf is filled with big white conch shells and rows of painted sea gulls, in flight, nesting, perched, mounted on driftwood.

Yesterday they were busy and now the sills are cleaned, the spider webs wiped out of corners, the walls sponge washed, the rag rugs beaten over the clothesline, the pillows fluffed. With a soapy solution, Rachel swiped out the flower boxes outside the porch, preparing them for fresh soil and summer blossoms.

Michael stands and stretches, then rubs a stiff shoulder muscle before following the coffee aroma into the kitchen. "Rachel?" he calls as he pours himself a mug.

"Out here." On the back porch, the windows are opened to the distant sea. She is freshly showered, her damp hair combed back off her face. "Good morning, you." A cup of steaming coffee sits in front of her as she surmises his tousled hair and shadow of whiskers. "Sleep well?"

"Morning," he says, and kisses the top of her head. "Sorry about last night. You should've woken me." After picking up staples at the grocery store, they returned to the cottage with a take-out fried clam dinner. That and a glass of wine were the antidote to patrolling Manhattan, to Summer's impending move, to worrying how to keep Rachel in his life. He'd fallen fast asleep on the porch. "Where'd you sleep?"

"I found the linen closet and made up a bed."

"Were you comfortable?"

"Very. I took a walk on the beach—"

"Alone? I don't know if that's a good idea."

"Michael, it was fine. There were other people around. Then I came back and found a magazine to read."

"What've you got there?" he asks, sitting beside her with his coffee.

"It was on the front porch yesterday, leaning against the lamp." Rachel turns a plaque around. "It must hang on a wall somewhere."

Michael centers it in front of him, a navy blue plaque with a sea gull painted on the bottom, blades of sea grass painted lightly around it. The words *Little Gull* curve across the top in faded silver letters.

"This belongs outside, near the door. Come on, I'll show you." He grabs a cinnamon roll she'd heated, and they pick up their coffees. She hands him a napkin and follows out through the front porch. "It's the cottage name."

"Little Gull? That explains the painted seagulls on the porch. What a cute idea."

"Didn't your cottage have a name?"

"No. Should it?"

"Rachel. It is an unspoken law that summer cottages be named. You didn't notice the others when we came in yesterday?"

"Jeepers. They're all named?"

First he rehangs *Little Gull* on its nail, finagling it precisely straight. "Bring your coffee. You'll see." They head down the street toward the boardwalk, passing a white cottage with deep blue shutters. Painted on the corners of the shutters are simple white sailboats.

"There," he says, pointing with the pastry in his hand. The sign above the cottage door says *White Sails.* A pale yellow cottage the color of the summer sun bears the name *Early Dawn. Fiesta* is next door to *Siesta.* Another snow white bungalow with board and batten siding and multi-paned porch windows seems as elegantly detailed as a *Swan's Feather.*

"It's a fairy tale," Rachel says, reading the signs while sipping her coffee. Michael finishes the sweet roll and wipes his fingers on the napkin.

"There's another." A renovated home is reshingled, reroofed and reporched. The brass knocker on its door is a golden anchor. Large crank-out windows open to the sea. *Finally* is its name.

They reach the boardwalk and at the far end of the beach, a bank of fog burns off in the rising sun. Seagulls swoop and cry, searching for washed up crabs, diving into schools of minnows.

Rachel mentions her old wish for her own place at the beach some day, for a piece of heaven. "The cottage names remind me of it."

"Of your wish?"

"Well think about it. If heaven is paved with streets of beach sand, these would be the street names. Finally and Fair Weather and Grey Mist and White Sails and Life's Dream."

Michael drinks his coffee and after a moment, agrees. "Where else could you be?"

* * *

"It's because of Sara Beth that I rented the cottage."

After their coffee, Michael took a quick shower and called his daughter to be sure she was home, before they headed back to Queens. He wants to get to work early. Rachel likes that even though the hostlers groom Maggie daily, Michael brushes her mane and tail before his shift. He says it tunes her in to him. Maggie's ears listen to his voice saying she is the prettiest horse in the department.

"Sara Beth?" Rachel turns to him in the truck cab.

He keeps his eyes on the highway. "She got me thinking, watching her have a breakdown in the city, then finding the gumption to put herself back together as someone new."

"And *that* made you rent a cottage?"

"I'm just saying that maybe she's on to something."

"I don't know." Rachel remembers how afraid she was when Sara Beth disappeared. "She's got a funny way of showing it."

"Listen. Maybe turning forty scared the hell out of her. It was like a door opening on her life. And you've got Sara Beth looking in, saying Damn it, I'm going through, come hell or high water. She saw that life's short and she resolved to make it sweet in the face of all odds."

"You've given this some thought."

"Because I see you're still bothered by her. And I see a correlation between her situation and ours."

"You're kidding, right?"

"No," Michael tells her. "We gave ourselves the summer to see what happens between us. To me, that's like Sara Beth turning forty and seeing the time she has left. Sensing some day it will end, she decides she better do something with it now."

"So forty shook her up?"

"No. What's left of life at forty shook her up. And summer's damn short, too. Kind of like life, once you're forty." He signals a lane change, then reaches over and takes her hand. "If one summer's all the time I have with you, then, like Sara Beth, come hell or high water, I'm going to make the most of it. If you're with me on this."

"So you rented the cottage." If Sara Beth only knew she was behind all this.

"I know you've got a whole life filled with people who love you in Addison. And I don't know if this can work, what we have. But I'd hate to give up without finding out." Michael slows for his exit and as he pulls off the highway, picks up a key from beside a wrapped cinnamon roll on the console. "Here." He presses it into her palm. "It's an extra cottage key. Use it Rachel. Whenever you want to. Even if I'm at work, or with Summer, just know you've got a place at the beach for the next month." He maneuvers the busy streets and the city heat works its way into the pickup. "Anytime. But be careful, okay?"

"About what?"

"Being alone there. Locking up, drawing the blinds."

"Michael, you've got to stop that." He glances over at her. "Telling me to be careful. I know you care, but sometimes you go overboard. It's a little insulting."

"I'm sorry. Of course you can take care of yourself. It's just that I worry."

After they drive along for a while, Rachel says, feeling the key in her palm, "See, here's the thing. I know what you're saying about my life back home, and it's true. But there's more. There's you. You've been my knight in shining armor, a little overprotective, but still, ever since sitting up there on your chestnut mare that day."

"Maggie."

"And you swept right into my life. We did Manhattan and The Plaza and, well, bowling and cupcakes, all in a whirlwind. And now this."

Michael turns the truck onto his street.

"Little Gull is like an answered prayer," she continues. "The easiness of the beach, and of a little cottage. But I'm afraid there's a catch, that you'll sweep right by, or change your mind, or, I don't know, worry *too* much."

Michael parks his truck in the driveway beside her car. He glances at her, then gets out and walks around. She's afraid that she hurt him and he misunderstands. When he opens her door, she explains, "What I'm saying is that Anchor Beach is the perfect place for us to—"

"Stop. Let me finish for you." He pulls her close, moves his hands to her face and kisses her. It insists, that kiss, that he will not sweep past like Sara Beth and Carl and Ashley. He pulls back and moves a strand of hair from her face. "Anchor Beach is the perfect place to find answers, okay? There's no way I'm sweeping right by you." His arms slip down around her waist, holding her close. He bends like he's going to kiss her again but stops just shy and touches her lips with his finger. He hitches his head back toward his tended home. "See that house there? This is it. This house and Manhattan and a month at the shore. It's all I have. There's nothing else. It's where I'll *always* be."

Then before kissing her again, he presses into her hand written directions to the Cross Sound Ferry back in Orient Point, assuring her it is a much more pleasurable journey back to Connecticut than the expressway. He opens her car door for her. "Did you ever think about trading this in?"

"My car? Why?"

"Well it's black. It's not that visible at night, you know? Silver is statistically the safest vehicle, with fewer accidents."

"You're doing it again," Rachel says as she gets in the car.

"Sorry." Michael gently closes the door. "But you're on the road a lot."

She starts the car and opens her window. "I know," she agrees. "Lock my doors, don't speed."

"Hey. You said it, not me."

And during the ninety minute boat ride across Long Island Sound to the Connecticut shore, she can't help thinking of what he said after that. Not of their plans to meet at Little Gull on his next day off, the day after the Fourth of July. Not that he'll miss her all week, then kissed her again, longer and deeper than the last. Well, she thinks of that too.

But that he someday wants to have a long cup of coffee with this Sara Beth, because he has a heck of a lot for which to thank her.

twenty

THE TOWN MAINTENANCE CREW USES a fire department bucket truck to string banners high above the street. Red, white and blue swags reach across The Green. In two days, it'll be crowded with smoking grills, hot dogs, hamburgers, corn on the cob, and people wearing shorts and polo shirts, tank tops and sandals. Addison High School's Marching Band always gives a Yankee Doodle concert mid-afternoon. The poor kids will wilt beneath their tubas and big drums in this heat.

Sara Beth just came from the party rental shop with a small display tent shoved into the back of her car. *Dip or dive?* It's how she and Rachel consider decisions hanging over their heads. *Dip your toes or dive headfirst? Dip,* she wanted to tell Rachel. *This is a dip,* this little tent set up with the other crafters at the town barbecue, except hers will be filled with small antiques. Staying on deck, dipping her foot in.

In the car, she had grabbed her cell and dialed Rachel's number. But the fissure is still too deep; no mere phone call can close it. She disconnected before Rachel answered and drove to Whole Latte Life instead.

What can she do? Send flowers? Write a note of apology for how she treated her friend in New York? Any attempt she comes up with seems so inadequate.

Looking out the window at the scene of Americana across the street, she sips her latte and turns to the *Addison Weekly* she picked up in town, browsing the pages alone.

* * *

"I want my nose pierced." Summer says this over her grilled cheese and tomato sandwich, sitting at a small square table at the restaurant window.

"Your what?"

"My nose. You know, get one of those super small diamond studs?"

In Manhattan, nothing tempers the heat. The concrete soaks it up and the skyscraper windows reflect it right back at you like a boomerang. Summer has to be desperate to want to meet him for lunch in the city. At least in Queens she can sit in the shade of a tree.

"Everybody's getting it done."

"Is Emily?"

"No." She plucks a French fry from her plate. "But the girls in Long Island are. They're pretty cool. I mean, like they friended me on Facebook."

There it is. Long Island. Facebook. If she has to live there, well God damn it, she isn't going to just talk the talk. She has to walk the walk. "What'd I tell you about that Facebook? I don't want you on there. There's too many nuts online."

"Everybody's on Facebook, Dad. Are they all getting stalked and assaulted?"

"Well watch what you say on there, you hear me? And don't you need a parent's permission to get your nose pierced?" Michael asks, snagging a few of her fries while turning to see who just walked in. He'd always told her if you don't want trouble, don't dress looking for it. When the city is hot and the kids are out of school, he sees it all on his post. From atop Maggie, there are no secrets.

"If you're not eighteen."

"And these girls in Long Island. Do they live near where you're moving?"

"Yeah. I talked to them last weekend when we went out to the house with the decorator. I waited outside while Mom did her thing."

He adds mustard to his pastrami on wheat. "These girls, their mothers take them to get their bodies pierced?"

"Yes, Dad." She stirs the straw in her soda. "And it's not only mothers. Caitlin's *father* took her."

"You're kidding," he says around a mouthful of sandwich. "Listen. You're not getting your nose pierced, your tongue, your eyelids, your navel, nothing. And your mother's going to hear about this, too. If that's what your new friends are up to, then you're staying in Queens."

"Fine by me."

"Oh I get it. Nice try." He sips his coffee. His daughter's blonde hair is in a low braid, cheap mall jewelry, hemp and beads, hangs from her neck. She wears Bermuda shorts and a peasant top that covers everything. "What's new with Emily?" Emily is safe. Emily only has her ears pierced, one hole each.

"I told you already."

He lifts what's left of his sandwich, then sets it down. "Told me what?"

"Dad, are you going senile? How do you get yourself dressed in the morning?"

He pats down the NYPD uniform, touching upon the badge, the gun, the club.

"The Cape? Remember I told you yesterday?"

"That's right." He sits back and finishes the sandwich. "When are you leaving?"

"Wednesday morning. Em's parents think the holiday traffic will be lighter right on the Fourth."

"Well, aren't you lucky. A vacation at Cape Cod."

"Yes!" She gives the air a mini punch. "A week and a half of getting a tan, listening to my tunes and hanging on the beach. A little mini-golf and tennis too." She pushes her glass away. "I wonder if there'll be any cute boys there."

Michael knew it. Summer hid somewhere in there, behind all the Long Island huff and bluff. She only needs a dose of her old friend. Especially ten days on the beach with your best.

"Do me a favor," he says. "When you're at the Cape? The first day there, when you guys maybe take a walk on the beach after dinner? Watch the sky for the first star you see."

"Oka-a-a-y." She spins a fat silver ring around on her finger.

"I've got it on good authority that the first star at the beach is a perfect wishing star. Make a wish, okay?" He rolls his left shoulder, working out a kink. If anyone needs a wish right now, his daughter does.

Summer scrunches her eyebrows a little. "Okay. Whatever."

He wonders if he should tell her to be careful at the Cape. Jesus, if anything ever happened to her. He tries the deep breathing exercises from the therapy he started up again, to control his controlling. Long slow breath in, hold it, exhale fully. He's mastered it so no one even notices. Maybe he'll just remind her to have her cell phone on her.

"Well," he begins, then pauses. "Call me when you get there. So I know you made it there, okay?" Then he'll tell her to be careful, over the phone. A little at a time.

"I will." Summer drinks her soda. "What are you going to do when I'm gone?"

"Work. Maybe go bowling or something."

"You? Bowling?" He shrugs. "With who?"

She likes to do that, slip in a question like one of those sleight of hand tricks with a ball beneath one of three cups. She mixes them up and you really know you've kept your eye on the right cup. Until you confidently pick it up and are wrong.

"Maybe Rachel."

"That same lady?"

"Yes." He downs the last of his coffee. "You finishing those?"

"No. I thought she lives in Connecticut."

"She does." He scoops up her fries and studies the couple sitting behind her. "But she comes to the city sometimes."

"What, for like, a date?" She waves at him looking past her, "Hello? You listening?"

"A date? I'd say so. If we have dinner afterwards, that makes it date-ish." He watches her mind spin, calculating the late hours.

"How come I haven't met her?"

"Do you want to?" He doubts she really wants to spend time with another potential stepparent. But she doesn't have a mean bone in her either, despite her daily dose of attitude.

"I don't know. Maybe some day. So, do you really like her?"

"She's a friend." He stands and picks up the bill. "And you ask too many questions."

"Just like you. And it's soo annoying. Now you know how it feels."

"Hey, I worry about you. So are you hanging around the city and coming home with me later, or are you leaving now?"

"I'm going now. It's way too hot here today."

He leaves a tip and they walk back out into the street where heat waves rise from the pavement. "Remember the rules? Stay near other people?"

"Yes, Dad. Walk confidently. Keep my ID and money in separate pockets."

"Just be alert."

"Duh. Like don't walk in front of traffic? You too, you know. Be careful patrolling."

"And call my cell right when you get home so I know you made it safely."

"Okay," she says, and gives him a quick kiss. "Where's Maggie?"

"Around back."

"I want to see her. Please?"

He checks his watch. "Just for a minute. How about we walk you to the subway."

She grins. "Cool. My own police escort."

* * *

The *Addison Weekly* is folded into thirds on the passenger seat. At every stop sign, Sara Beth glances at the picture to which it is folded. Tom holds her close as they dance in the moonlight at the concert. And she glances at the Photo Credit beneath the picture. Rachel DeMartino.

Rachel couldn't have known that she and Tom had come from the carriage house that night. That the evening had been charged with emotion. Yet in that photograph, Rachel captured it. Sara Beth and her husband are backlit by the stage lights, silhouetted against a misty evening, pressed into each other and barely moving, really. She remembers Tom's mouth against her ear. He didn't say much, but when he did, his words felt almost inside her head. They stopped for a drink before this picture, a good strong one in a local bar and got the talking started. While driving, she pulls her leather journal from her handbag and at the next red light, opens to a familiar page, to the words *It feels like the carriage house just cost me Rachel.*

Maybe this is the day the stars align to bring her friend back into her constellation.

* * *

"Sara Beth?"

"Hi." She stands outside the screen door holding a take-out tray with two citrus smoothies. "Can I come in?"

Rachel opens the door and she follows her through the house to the kitchen. That's where all the good talks happen. Food, sunlight falling on scattered newspaper pages, it's all good. It surprises her to see cooking ingredients strewn about the counter. Well. Rachel's life goes on without her. You can always make room for two smoothies, though. She pulls them from the tray and takes a seat. Old Rod Stewart tunes spill from Rachel's beach room.

"What are you cooking?" she asks.

"Lasagna."

"Oh?" A flower arrangement sits in the center of the pine table. The type of copious bouquet you don't buy for yourself fans out from a crystal vase.

Rachel sets down a bowl of meatballs and sausages in tomato sauce. She moves the flowers to the counter and returns with a placemat and a plate along with a fork and sharp knife. "I need a half dozen meatballs crumbled real fine. A few sausages, too. To add to the sauce."

This is what they do. Walk into each other's life and not interrupt, but meld right in. It's like a dance step, one you do without thought, in sync. Sara Beth picks up the fork and plucks a meatball from the bowl. Finally.

"Having company?" She's asked questions like that for twenty-five years. Except never before did a terminal breath of silence beat before Rachel answers.

"Kind of. I'm going away for the weekend and bringing the food with me."

This is the kind of thing she does, bringing Ashley comfort food at college. "To New York?"

Rachel whisks an egg at the counter. "Yes."

"Nice. All you'll have to do is reheat this. More time for girl talk that way, which is the point, right?" She slices a meatball into thin strips. "Well say hi to Ashley for me."

Rachel sits at the table and peels the lid from her drink. "Thanks for the smoothie."

"Sure." Sara Beth works on breaking up a meatball strip with a fork.

"So what's up?" Rachel watches her slice. "Was there something you wanted?"

"Actually, yes." She pushes the crumbled meatballs aside and reaches for a sausage. "I wanted to thank you for what you did."

"For what I did?" Rachel cups her smoothie in front of her.

She pulls the folded newspaper from her bag, setting the photograph in front of Rachel. "For this."

Rachel looks at the couple dancing. "It's a nice picture of the two of you." She takes a moment longer before turning the paper back, then goes to the refrigerator and pulls out fresh parsley, a tub of ricotta cheese and shredded mozzarella. Cradling it all in her arm, she piles on the whisked egg shimmying in the bowl. Her other hand grabs a large bowl before setting it all on the table.

"It's more than a nice picture," Sara Beth insists. "You captured something between us." She points to the picture, tapping it lightly. "This was the night Tom found out about the carriage house, and boy did we have an argument about it. What you see here is what got us through that evening." She pauses. "I can see, in what you captured, that he won't walk out on me."

Rachel reaches for the plate of sausages and meatballs and knives them into the large bowl of sauce she made the day before. "Here. Stir." She slides the sauce bowl over. "Walk out on you?"

Sara Beth slowly stirs. "Well. Yes. All this stuff I'm doing, and sorry to say, that I *did,* isn't just about me. I'm trying to fix things with others too." Rachel stands and pulls a glass lasagna pan from the cabinet. After greasing it lightly, she sits again and spreads a cup of the meat sauce in the bottom. "With Tom. And now with you, too." She pauses. "Are you working for the paper?"

Rachel lays lasagna noodles in the pan. "Freelancing for the summer, something to keep me busy. You were part of an assignment." She spreads a ladle of sauce over the lasagna.

"Oh!" Sara starts refolding the newspaper. "So you took pictures of the concert?"

Rachel layers the cheese mixture on the noodles. "I shot a bunch but I never know which pictures they'll use."

"I had no idea." Still. There is something in that picture, in the manner in which Rachel composed it, framed it, back-lit it. It looks like a personal written invitation that drew her here today. *Dear Sara Beth. Please come. Time: 2PM Place: Rachel's Kitchen. Coffee will be served.* And it worked. She came right away when she saw that photo.

"When did this happen?" Sara Beth asks.

Rachel walks to the refrigerator. "The concert was my first assignment." She sets a chunk of parmesan on the table along with a silver metal cheese grater. "The editor must have liked that shot."

"I thought maybe you took it with a personal intention in mind. You know, when you saw Tom and I dancing, like you made it some sort of gesture on your part. That we're still friends?" She sits still as a mannequin, her legs crossed, her long gauzy skirt draped in folds. She doesn't dare move in case she misses a gesture, expression, a tip of her head that will end all this *dreaded* formality.

Rachel finishes with the last of the noodles and spreads the remaining sauce on top. She wipes her forehead with the back of her hand. "There were aesthetic lines in your dancing. You two had a way about you that made for a good shot."

"Huh." With her smoothie cupped in front of her on the pine and tiled table, the lasagna mess scattered around the kitchen, flowers and fun music thrown in the mix, she feels the cruelty of the room. This kitchen is behind the velvet ropes of a museum now. *Look. Don't touch.* It's a painting by one of the masters, out of her reach. The function of this room, this art, is necessary to her life. But the comfort of all its goodness is roped off somehow.

"Rach?" Rachel stands and sets the oven temperature. "Could it be? You know, a starting point?"

Before she can respond, Amy and Sharon walk in through the back door carrying tomatoes from Rachel's garden.

"Sara Beth!" Amy says. She sets the tomatoes carefully on the counter and bends to give her a hug. "It's so nice to see you!"

"Thanks, Amy. You too. I didn't realize Rachel had company." She twists around to greet Sharon behind her. "How are you, Sharon?"

"Oh great. Are you walking with us today? We're doing three miles now."

"Walking?" She reaches for the cheese grater and notices that Rachel wears her good sneakers, sport socks, shorts and a sport tank. Power walk time with the girlfriends.

"We convinced Rach to walk after the lasagna bakes, and to try out our new wrist weights."

"We're headed over to Wedding Wishes," Amy says. "I bought a couple of gorgeous gowns for my shop, and gosh, you'd love them, they're right up your antique alley. Want to come see?"

"Thanks guys, but the kids are home alone." It feels like too much, the way her friends' lives go on all around her. Rachel headed to New York, Amy selling beautiful vintage gowns to the town's brides. Weddings go on, life goes on. Lately it feels like everyone's life goes on around her, around and around, making her dizzy standing in one place, stuck in a plan. She picks up her newspaper and beaded bag. "Maybe next time?" she asks Rachel.

"Sure. I'll walk you out." She wipes her hands on a dishtowel.

Without saying goodbye, Sara Beth pushes quickly out the door to the front yard.

"Hey," Rachel says. "Slow down, and why the tears?"

"I can't believe how much I miss that." She nods toward the house. "That easiness you have with them. Cooking food together, your *great* kitchen, the talking. The sweet flowers I *don't* know anything about."

Rachel sits on the garden bench. "Those aren't tears from missing a kitchen social. It's not just me, is it?"

"Not just."

Sara Beth sits beside her.

"Do you want me to cancel the walk?"

"That's all right. I can't do it now."

"Do what?"

"Fix this. Me. Us." She stands to leave. "We need more than that smoothie inside. We need a huge pot of coffee on a long voyage on that boat, with no interruptions. Like my kids, who are home alone for *way* too long now, like my long overdue grocery shopping that Tom's supposed to do, like the business that I need to find a vacant store for and is stuck in some weird dream. And lasagnas and walking friends." She runs a hand through her short hair. "Like my marriage on my mind. You get the picture."

"But we'll start. Come on."

She wanted to come back to Addison after that Manhattan weekend and set her life on its intended course. But she owes Rachel more. She owes her all the baggage she dumped deep into the Hudson River that night on the Staten Island Ferry. She owes her an explanation for abandoning her.

The folded newspaper is in her hand. "I had thought maybe … Well, your friends are waiting." She shakes her head and squeezes Rachel's hand before hurrying out to the car.

twenty-one

RACHEL SITS AT THE ANTIQUE easel, sensing the wall of sketches behind her, a life displayed. She sketched Ashley shortly after Carl's death. They needed each other intensely then, and it shows in the drawing's affecting expression. She sketched her beach cottage the first summer there, when she couldn't get enough of that heaven.

Today her camera focused on kids twirling sparklers, babies looking out from porta-playpens, men tossing horseshoes and women talking and setting out food on The Green. Someone stuck little American flags in the flower barrels. Her camera captured what the *Addison Weekly* wanted on Independence Day. People want to see themselves happy.

Now her pencil moves back and forth and it gets to the point where she no longer needs the Manhattan photograph to copy. It's better sketching from feeling, trusting her heart to guide her hand.

But it isn't working. The varying skyline is set against the light of dusk. She reaches forward and touches the Empire State Building, needing to break through this block. If she stalls on a portrait, she visits with the subject. If it is a beach scene, she needs an afternoon by the water.

It's obvious what needs to be done. She packs the sketch and charcoals into a zippered portfolio. Tomorrow afternoon she's supposed to meet Michael at the cottage. But a shiny cottage key tempts her. *Anytime*, he said. She needs to be closer to her subject. If she leaves now, it's early enough to catch the last Cross Sound Ferry. She'll sit on the deck and raise her face into the sea breeze as Long Island nears.

Summer living is easy. It takes no time to pack a suitcase: Bermudas, T-shirts, capris and a cardigan for the evenings, espadrilles and sandals. Last she tosses in the new Yankees cap she bought for Michael, a surprise day gift.

* * *

The truck's tires crunch on the stone driveway. It takes a second for Michael's eyes to make out her black car in the shadows. He doesn't get out of the pickup right away. Everything about the night has to gather together first. The darkness conceals the old cottage roof shingles and peeling paint. But it has strong lines, a bungalow with a peaked roof, a wide front porch with old lattice windows, all of it sitting on a stone foundation. The front porch light shines softly on the shelf of conch shells and gulls. It isn't a bad little place; it only needs a sprucing up.

He unlocks the front door and sets the bag of groceries, another flashlight and a package of window alarms on the kitchen counter. Rachel's easy touch fills the room with murmurs telling secrets. *Here! Look at this.* A large glass vase, the color and texture of green sea glass, overflows with pale yellow heather and blades of tall thin marsh grass. *Oh, and here, too!* Beside it, on the kitchen table, lays the novel she began last week. The windows are opened, the white shutters folded back, the sense of the beach right outside. It's always there now, that feeling of missing her, and this, her touch in the cottage, helps.

While unpacking milk and eggs and seeing the lasagna in the freezer, he worries about her on the beach alone. What if someone follows her back? Or if she forgets to lock up? He takes two deep breaths, slowly exhaling. Exercise helps, too, his therapist told him. Serious exercise. Maybe he needs to start jogging. Or just come clean with the truth. His therapist said the more he talks about it, the better he'll feel. Heading here straight from work still in uniform, he planned only to stock the refrigerator and open a window so the cottage would be ready for tomorrow. But this place has a way of changing plans. It's like one of Rachel's sketches, shading their lives right into its lines, its shadows. He steps outside, the screen door squeaking behind him. The sea air cooled at twilight.

The walk to the beach takes minutes and he notices her as soon as he steps on the boardwalk, sitting in the far shadows. He notices, too, how she turns to watch. She knows from a distance it's him. Maybe it's the uniform discernible in the dim lighting, or the leather boots sounding foreign on the boardwalk, or his silhouette in shadow.

"Hey you," he says and sits beside her, slipping his arm around her shoulders as though they always meet on the boardwalk on midsummer nights.

"Hey," she answers, and he kisses her lightly before she comfortably leans into his body.

For a moment, they only listen to the waves off in the dark. "You're a pleasant surprise," he tells her, his fingers touching her hair. She wears capris, a camisole and a cropped black cardigan to keep off the sea damp.

She settles closer. "I couldn't stay away."

"How was the drive? Okay?"

"Fine. I caught the last ferry."

"I'm glad you came," he says. "Want to walk?" The creaking boats, the waves lapping at the sand, the salt air, it all makes you want to be a part of it. He slips off his boots and they walk along the beach, he in uniform, she beach bum. His arm pulls her close and she moves along with his body, leaving him very much aware of where they touch and of where they don't.

"You're making the summer very easy," he tells her.

"What do you mean?"

"Finding you here tonight? On the beach?" He stops near the water and turns to her in the dark. "I've got to tell you something." He moves a strand of hair from her face, running his thumb over her cheek. It's routine now, the way he checks. Sometimes it's more a check for him than for any tears, touching her to believe she came all this way to see him. His thumb strokes her face back and forth. "Do you have any idea that I'm falling in love with you?" He bends then and kisses her a summer kiss, the kind that reaches somewhere inside and takes hold. His hands reach around her neck, pulling her even closer. When he feels her smile against his lips, it's enough for him to say more. "You wanted to take the summer to enjoy the beach. And I am. Right here I need to wake up with you in my arms. When I saw your things in the cottage, I knew."

Rachel turns and sits in the sand, pulling her knees up close. He sits beside her and it's all there, the moon and the stars and the sea, but not the kiss. "Talk to me," he finally says, touching her face, tipping her chin toward him.

She brushes his face with her fingers, running them behind his ear, touching his hair. But he can't tell what the touch is. Is it *I'm sorry?* Or *Not yet?* Or *Let's slow down?* He's not sure if it's a touch that will torture him with its second thoughts.

"I think about you all the time," she says. "I think about your life and things you've told me. I guess that's why I wanted to slow down here, at this cottage at the beach. I love you too." And the whole time she talks, her hand is there, tracing his face, stroking his hair, and then it slips to his neck when she leans close and kisses him three kisses, each longer than the other.

"Whoa, whoa," he says when she starts to pull away after the third. "Where you going?" he asks with a slow grin. And he puts his arm around her shoulders and folds her into one more kiss before taking her hand and helping her to her feet to finish that walk they started along the beach.

* * *

In the cottage, Rachel pours two glasses of wine. In her mind, she's still in the beach kiss. It's the kind you don't forget because it's a kiss and the sea breeze blowing wisps of hair across it and waves breaking at your feet that you step toward so the sea reaches your ankles and there's a faraway lighthouse beam flashing like a shooting star in the night sky and it *is* the stars, twinkling but playing second stage to the low amber moon painting a swath of gold onto the sea, over the water, right to your feet where you stepped deeper into it and so you're caught in a liquid moonbeam while you kiss. A beach kiss.

They sit in the dark on the porch swing and Michael picks up her sketch. The light of the moon coming through the lattice windows illuminates the city drawing the way her mind had been trying to do. When he sets it down, he takes her face in his hands and kisses her so that there is only this moment. Really, if they never stopped, it would be enough, this life behind closed eyes, this stirring in her heart. But he pulls back and his thumb grazes her cheek in the dusky light of the porch. It's sweet, how he checks. That's part of love, too. Checking, he'd told her.

"Come here," he says, standing and leading her to the bedroom.

Dappled moonlight falls across the bed. That's what she notices: The way clouds and leafy treetops dapple the night's light. She notices it until his fingers slip beneath her camisole's lace strap and the sensation, his fingertips on her skin, brings her eyes to him. A little bit of that moonlight falls on his dark hair, almost like it followed them home from their beach walk, and she is glad for that. At how you can think of simple things and see wonder in them. He lies beside her, tracing his hand down her neck, along her collarbone, down to her hip.

Giving her time. His way has grown so familiar, his way of slowing the most perfect moments. This is what he does now. His hand travels down the curve of her hip as she slowly unbuttons and slips off his shirt. But when she reaches for his shoulder, he tenses.

"Rachel," he says, pulling back.

"What's the matter?"

He cups her hand in his, starts to say something, then stops. He sits up in the shadows and kisses her hand.

"What's wrong?" she asks. Love never comes unannounced, does it? As sweet and beautiful as it is, it's really these collisions of hearts and intentions and feelings, and something else is coming with it now too. His change comes so suddenly, the way he recoils when she reaches for his shoulder. Something is there, something is in his way.

Michael opens her hand, touches each fingertip and places her palm flat on the front of his left shoulder. "This. I want you to know about it first."

"You're hurt." In the shadows, her hand moves over his skin, feeling the scar tissue, the ragged hollow of missing flesh, healed over and since repaired. "What happened?" she asks with a concern that can't fathom this man facing the horrific cause of this wound.

"I'd been shot."

"Shot?"

"I'm okay. It happened a long time ago. But you'll feel it, you'll see it."

"Tell me what happened." Her hand touches his skin again, checking. She knows where the heart is, it's so much of your life, in so many ways.

"Not tonight, no. I'll only tell you that I was lucky."

"Lucky," she whispers. To have some monster gun unloaded into your chest. It must have done this to him, though. That injury, that affront, has him find the good. *Lucky.*

He takes her hand and touches her fingers to his mouth. "Just know it's there."

With his shoulder damaged, does he still hear the gunshot ring? Explode? She closes her eyes with the image of a bomb going off in his life. What else could it have sounded like? When his fingers touch her hair, her eyes open at the feeling.

"I know everything you're thinking about that bullet," he says, then kisses her lightly. His arms cradle her shoulders, his hands frame her face. "Because believe me, I've thought it all too. But you know what I think now?"

She touches his face, his eyes, and kisses his chin, his jaw, his mouth, before telling him no.

"What I think," he says, "is that it was a gift." And he quickly puts a finger over her mouth, not letting her deny his words. "Shhh." He shakes his head, no. "I'm not going to explain now because what I'm going to do, Rachel, is love you."

She smiles in the dark, hoping, praying, he can feel every bit of it as he kisses her lips a hundred light kisses.

Moonlight fills in the shadows and she thinks it's the same moonlight they kissed beneath on the beach. The night's all about light and dark, how it shapes them and becomes them, how life, every day, is varying shades of both, some so black, some as light as the sun. The moonlight is a pale haze silhouetting his face. What he can't see is how she lifts her hand behind him, open, and sweeps it through the misty light, closing her fist on it before bringing her hand back to his wounded shoulder, letting the moonbeam fill in his shadows.

Michael talks softly in the dark, and she touches his lips with only her moonbeam fingertips until he strokes her hair, then moves over her and trails his mouth down the soft of her throat. Every touch has new meaning now.

But his way of slowing time is never more sweet than it is this night. He takes her arms, one at a time, holding them up beside the pillow and kissing her lips lightly, almost barely. When her eyes close, it is his touch on her face that has her open them, meeting his gaze. "Hello sweetheart," he says quietly, as though she'd gone somewhere in her pleasure and he just caught up, tracing his fingers along her jaw. Summer comes through the window in the glow of the moon, in the sea air touching their skin with July warmth, and it becomes a part of it all, a part of loving him, the way he leads her to hold every moment, every sensation that began with a kiss in the moonlight.

Afterward she lies in his arms. "Are you okay?" Michael asks, his hand trailing up her arm. Now that he started, he can't seem to stop touching her. And she knows just how to answer him, little by little, stretching out a moment.

One slow, slow word at a time, she whispers "I love you," each word separated by a lengthening kiss. Her lips feel his smile form in the dark and it is genuine enough, beautiful enough to be the sweetest moment of the night.

twenty-two

AT THE CARRIAGE HOUSE, A George III library table becomes her desk, with an old brass lamp throwing light on her computer, paperwork happily askew. A morning sunbeam falls through a paned window, catching mist and dust like stardust in its light. And it makes her think of the stars and constellations, and the people and feelings and dreams spinning through her days, the constellation of her own enlightening forty-year-old universe.

She's been taking pictures this morning, of the shop of her dreams nearly true, laid carefully out—straight chairs there, end tables there, mirrors on the wall, an oak sleigh bed and chest of drawers—but all stuck in a dream, that sunshine a ray of hope lighting upon it all. Now, typing in a line beneath one picture on her computer screen, just one line, she tells her mother about life being in a dream stage.

And the sound that comes a short while later when she walks among her antiques, writing their provenance into a spiral pad, seems straight out of those dreams.

Her email box chimes with incoming mail.

She stops still, her pen aloft over the page, her heart pounding. Of course she knows it's not her mother writing back. But a thought crosses her mind about the twilight zoneness of it all. There's something to be said about standing among furniture three hundred years old, in a hundred year old carriage house, being pulled back to the twenty first century through cyber space. She cautiously clicks open her mailbox.

Subject: Antique Shop
From: Melissa
To: Sara Beth
Date: July 5 at 9:03 AM

SB, how's it going? Hey, I came across this in the Addison Weekly online classifieds. I know you're looking for a vacant storefront for your shop, but would you consider this? It looks pretty, but I'm not sure it would work. Something to think about? Maybe whoever buys the house would rent you the business addition. You could call the agent and put that out there. I attached the ad. Take a look and let me know, okay? Love, Lissa

Sara Beth opens the attachment, the first words there being *Currier & Ives location.* "Mmmh. I'll take it," she says, scanning the ad. *Colonial Home. Impeccably restored with attention to detail. Crown moldings, arched doorways, stone fireplace. Spacious kitchen, dining room, family room. Four bedrooms, two and a half baths. Walk-in pantry. One acre landscaped.*

"Melissa," she says to herself. "I don't need a house. I need a vacant little store."

But there's more. *Two-room addition currently doctor office. Lots of traffic for in-home business. Zoned residential/ business. Price Reduced.*

Sara Beth reads the ad three times, the first with her sister's idea of renting out the addition in mind. The second time she reads it, she dallies on her own new idea. And the third time, she seriously considers her idea, the one about buying the house. Another thought runs through her mind: The house reminds her of the New England farmhouse in which she grew up, her mother spending a lifetime restoring it. Then of course comes this thought: This will really be suicide for her marriage.

She enlarges the picture in the ad. It has stately lines typical of an old center chimney colonial, with a pillared entranceway, alcove windows on one side wall, and the addition with matching alcove windows on the other side. Near the street. She glances outside, then pulls her cell from her purse to call the agent, maybe get the address. There's no law against being curious, after all.

But after everything she put Tom through, will she really take her plan this far?

"Maybe," she says to herself. "Maybe I will. Can't hurt to get some ideas."

"Who you talking to?" Tom asks when he walks into the carriage house. Owen tags along helping him carry the packing blankets. Melissa's husband follows behind, letting out a low whistle at the sight of her antiques.

Sara Beth slips her phone in her hobo bag and minimizes her screen. "Just Lissa."

"Well we're ready to move the piano home. Owen's going to supervise, right guy?" he asks his son.

They make their way over to the piano, inching it closer to the doorway. As Tom and Kevin finally wheel it out the door, she saves the Currier & Ives ad in a Word file, pulls out her antique journal and keeps nudging her life along.

Tour Colonial. Wish you could come too.

* * *

The Seahorse Café is not much more than a summertime watering hole. Outside, over the big window, a neon seahorse blinks from side to side as though it's swimming in the deep blue sea. The bar is a few towns over from Anchor Beach, on a strip where the cottages are stacked too close together, the arcade filled with teens and seasonal shops selling penny candy and overpriced beach tubes hanging from ropes outside their doorways. At the end of the strip, along a shabby boardwalk, a few bars rake in the summer money.

Michael sits in his seat as though he knows it well. "It was a punk," he says. "A low life with nothing to lose. We walked in right when he was booking."

"What was he running from?"

"That's the thing. A neighbor called in to report a racket in the next apartment. We thought we had a domestic on our hands. You know, arguing, yelling. You don't usually get noise in a robbery." He looks past her, running his hand through his hair. After working a full shift in the city heat, which is different from beach heat, the day shows on him. "Unless someone walks in on you."

"Oh no."

"The tenant had come home right in the middle of being robbed. The creep beat the shit out of him and left him for dead. *That* was the noise the neighbor heard."

"So you were thinking it was a domestic."

He nods before taking a swallow of his drink. "It was in a six-family tenement house. Going up the stairs, my partner Drew turned the corner on the porch landing and walked right into his gun."

A low murmur fills the bar with patrons talking, laughter ringing. A candle flickers low in its globe on their dark table and he reaches for a few pretzels in a bowl.

"I remember the incredible noise of it. The explosion, Drew blown down the stairs, hitting the wall, his boots on the steps."

"Jesus," Rachel whispers.

He finishes his drink. "I talked to Jesus a lot in those days."

"I'll bet." She studies him. "So what did this guy do? Shoot you and run?"

"He would have." Michael taps his foot under the table. That night comes out in little ways like that, little fidgets. "If he could've found a way."

"Well he shot a cop. Wait, your partner. Did he make it?"

Michael shakes his head no. "He didn't have a chance."

"Then that guy must have been put away for a long time?"

He hesitates, squinting briefly at her. "Look at you," he says with regret.

"Me?" She wears faded Levi's with a black ribbed tank, a few gold chains hang around her neck. She notices he takes a long, deep breath.

"You're beautiful. And so far removed from that crazy night, I hate to bring it to you." He pushes the pretzel bowl away and motions for another drink. "I killed him Rachel. When he turned to face me, I'm just lucky to have got the first shot," he says. "It threw off his aim, and here I am."

Rachel winces, reaching forward and clasping Michael's hand.

"I had to do it." His voice is low. "Do you know what that gun sounded like on that landing? A freaking explosion. When Drew crashed down the stairs, I did what I had to do. For Drew, too. He never deserved what he got."

"Neither did you. I'm so sorry."

Michael stares at her and again, breathes. "My eardrum was ruptured from the close range noise and I did the whole physical therapy thing. Had a problem with bone infection at the wound afterwards. My shoulder still bothers me. But I killed a man," he finally says, pulling his hand over his face. "I tell myself to this day that it wasn't a man. It was a fucking monster. But, you know …"

"It was a man."

"I almost quit the force. Didn't come back for a long time. Thought I'd never touch a gun again. For a while I considered moving to the west coast, maybe get a hot shot computer engineering degree, something as far removed from the force as I could."

"What made you stay?"

"A few things. Mostly my daughter. And then there's the games."

"The Yankees," Rachel says under her breath.

"Someone in the department pulled some strings and arranged for a pair of season tickets for me." Michael leans forward, his arms folded on the table. "When I took that guy down, the force agreed I did it for them, too. It was their thanks. The tickets." The waitress sets down Michael's drink on a paper coaster. He reaches for the pack of cigarettes on the end of the table and lights one, inhaling deeply. "It's the only time I smoke. When I go back like this. I used to smoke all the time, but I quit when I started with the Mounteds."

"That happened after you were shot then?"

"About a year later." Holding the cigarette, he lifts a carafe and fills her glass. "I took that time off and spent it in drinking establishments, not learning establishments. This place was one of my favorites." Michael turns toward the window. The bar is dim, the back wall lined with tall booths, the round tables damp with the closeness of the sea. It's the kind of place where on summer nights, the door and windows are opened so the sea breeze comes in and mixes with the smoke, the drink, and the stories told, and you feel like a fisherman who just came back from a long voyage. Who stops here right off the boat to leech the sea from his blood before heading home.

"You wouldn't have wanted to know me then. I had it in me to get even with everyone and anyone. If someone looked at me wrong, I was ready to blow. I did, a few times, right here. Lost a tooth, broke a couple of ribs. My ex-wife, and Summer, well, let's say I wasn't easy to live with."

She can't believe that the Michael she's gotten to know, the man who listens attentively to her story, who weaves his own with threads of nostalgia and family and lore, who stays in the absolute moment, she can't believe he wouldn't have shone through, somehow.

"I'll bet you weren't that bad," she says. "But bar fights?"

He winks. "Should've seen the other guy."

"So that's where it all comes from."

"What?"

"The overprotective stuff. The guard you have up."

"Hypervigilance. That's its technical name, and believe me, I'm very much aware of it. It's a post-traumatic thing I deal with. It serves a purpose, so they tell me."

"To stay safe?"

He shakes his head. "No. It's a psychological tool. My therapist says I keep it between myself and dealing with that night. You know, it's a way to *not* come to terms with the reality of killing someone, by making a new issue instead. I don't always see myself as protecting, but I'm working on it. I know it's a problem for people." He looks around the bar, then back at Rachel with another long breath. "Therapy is helping me deal with the trauma now."

"It's not permanent then?"

"Depends if, and how, I handle it. You know, the usual mumbo jumbo: deep breathing, exercise, self-talk. So if you see me talking to myself, well, there you have it. "

Rachel reaches for his hand and holds it for a minute. "So what made you take the Mounted job?"

"Some new horses arrived and the captain thought it was time I got back to work. Or leave. He made me make a decision about whether to live or die at that point." He takes a drag of the cigarette, then tamps it out. "This seemed good, because the Mounted Unit is safer. The thinking is that people won't commit crimes when they see me. I'm in their face, on the street. Not in a car, but right there in the thick of it up on a horse. It would be the *only* way I'd come back, either on a horse or behind a desk."

"Behind a desk? You?"

"Well I went in to the stable," he continues, "to check out the horses and talk to the other Mounteds. I wasn't sure, but when I walked past the stalls, Maggie pulled my Yankees cap right off my head. Like she wanted to stop me, you know? My horse was a Yankees fan."

"So she made your decision."

"Yeah, what a trip. She started out reckless and I didn't know if I wanted to deal. The first time I took her on the street, she spooked and reared up on her back legs. I thought she'd fall right back on top of me, so I whacked her on the head with my fist."

"You hit her?"

"You have to think horse. My trainer taught me that right away. Work on her level. When I hit her, she thought she hit her head *because* she reared and never pulled that stunt again. We hung in there and she calmed me down as much as I calmed her."

"She helped you through a rough time, then."

"A little Maggie, a little liquor, a few close calls. My life turned around in one long year. I used to be always on, ready for the next arrest, the next thrill." He shakes his head. "Now, I take it slow and live every damn second. Every one of them matters."

"The good that came from the bad?"

"Plenty of bad came out of it too. That day blew my marriage to smithereens. It was headed there, anyway. Barbara wanted me moving up the ranks and out of Queens. She's been itching to do what she's doing now for a long time." His right hand reaches up and rubs his left shoulder as though the sheerness of that violence lingers: the routine call, turning the corner on the landing, followed by a blast that ruptured his life. "After I took that bullet and spent a year stewing, the last thing I could do was walk away from *anything* safe and familiar. Including my home. So she left." He looks at his left shoulder and measures a half inch with his fingers. "I came this close to dying. It still scares the hell out of me."

"It's no wonder. Do you ever think about going back to school? Making a change?"

"No. No way. I'm not cut out to walk around campus with a bookbag, reading about King Arthur. Stability, that's it for me.

My home, the force, The Yankees, everything familiar. It's a control thing after a night when, let me tell you, there was no control."

"So you know about second chances."

"It's the only reason I'm here. Some God given second chance. And some fate that had Drew in front of me going up those stairs. Life can change at any corner."

"I hear you. Like mine did, in a Manhattan restaurant two months ago."

"Sometimes," Michael says, "it feels like you're talking about a death when you tell me about Sara Beth."

"Sometimes it feels like that, too."

"You care too much about her to let this go." He waits a moment. "You've got to try to get back what you had with her, before you turn some corner in your life and it's too late."

"I will," Rachel answers, squeezing his hands and trusting him. "I promise."

* * *

Afterward, the waves break along the dark beach. The salt air brushes his face as they walk the old boardwalk, her fingers laced through his. Leaving the bar behind, he glances back at the neon seahorse blinking in the window. There had been nights in that bar when he almost finished off what the bullet missed. Or his rage had. That seems long ago now.

But that road brought him to this. Later, beneath the bedroom window in the little cottage, that same sea breeze lifts off Long Island Sound and glances across his skin, soothing with its hint of salt water and waves and innate rhythm. That's what it comes down to, life. Rhythms inherent in every day, every decision, the high tide and low, every day.

He inhales deeply, reassuring himself the cottage is secure, trying desperately not to get up and look out the window, check the locks, and Rachel must sense it. She reaches up and touches his face. It's all new, this touch. And surprising. He turns to her, his fingers tangle in her hair.

"Tell me about the gift," she murmurs.

"The gift." He whispers back, not wanting to interrupt the rhythms, the waves and tides and moment at hand. "If I hadn't been shot, I wouldn't have become a Mounted, you wouldn't have stopped me in May, you wouldn't be here in this cottage, with me. This moment, right now," he explains, then stops and kisses her, "would not exist without that one."

twenty-three

TOM RINSES HIS MUG AT the sink. Outside the kitchen window, the back yard is neatly mowed. The picnic table needs staining. Maybe he'll do that later today, after waxing the cars. After getting to the bottom of things.

"What?" Sara Beth asks when he turns, leans against the counter, and stares at her.

"Your rings." He's not comfortable with their absence. Whether they're missing or put away or sold, what matters is that he hasn't seen them since New York. "I need to know what's up with your wedding rings. If you can't wear my rings, I really can't consider looking at that house for sale. Where are they?"

She pushes her coffee cup away. "I don't have them."

"You don't have them."

Her eyes drop closed. "Listen. You must figure it happened in New York. And it did. When I rode the ferry that night and I was so sad, missing Mom and wanting to change my life back, and I didn't know how to go about it."

"Sara."

Now she looks at him. "I didn't want to tell you this because you wouldn't understand. It's just something I did. I started dropping parts of my self into the river, okay? So that I could rebuild me a little at a time. You know, makeup, my sunglasses, a photograph, things like that."

"Please don't tell me you dropped your rings into the Hudson River."

"Tom," she whispers. "Don't."

He doesn't respond, doesn't ask any questions, doesn't move.

"It was dark, I was crying, okay? One thought led to another and I didn't know what we had anymore. I couldn't keep living the same old way. It all changed. Without my mother, well, I was really hurting. And the rings felt symbolic of what I wanted to break from."

"From grief, or from me?" He looks long at her. "Never mind. Don't answer." He turns to the sink, puts his glasses on the counter, runs the cold water and scoops a handful onto his face, holding his hands over his eyes for several seconds.

"All right," he says when he turns back to Sara Beth sitting at the table. She wears a turquoise tunic he's never seen, with black capris, wooden bangles on her wrist. Vintage has returned to her style this summer and it reminds him of the Sara Beth he knew a long time ago. Sitting sideways on the chair, her long legs are casually crossed, showing her bare feet, a beaded ankle bracelet. He doesn't want to lose her.

"I'll just take a *look* at that house. After I wax the car. And stop at the mall."

* * *

"Are there any coupon sales today? Or a discount if I put this on my credit card?" Tom looks closely at the diamond ring he's chosen, and then at the saleswoman plucking rings from the display case and setting them on black velvet.

"There is a coupon today, actually. Fifty dollars off any fine jewelry purchase over two hundred fifty dollars." She slides a coupon across the counter. "That particular ring is available in white gold as well. It's very stunning. Does your fiancé have a preference? Or maybe she joined our Bridal Registry?"

"Now that's a good idea, registering a ring. I think she only registered her china preferences."

"Oh, too bad. But really, that ring is one of our finest."

"You're sure? I need to do right by the mother of my son," he says. "Make an honest woman out of her. Now is this considered fine jewelry, for the coupon discount?" Tom asks.

"Oh yes, every piece in this case is. The fine jewelry department sets stringent standards the gems must meet. And congratulations on your wedding. I'm sure you'll be very happy!"

And so Sara Beth has a new wedding ring. After which Tom buys a huge watch for himself. "A wedding gift for me," he tells the saleswoman.

"Why not?" she asks, handing him the bag. "It's a celebration! Gift Wrap is located downstairs, at Customer Service. And good luck to you both!"

* * *

"See those lights?" Michael asks. The Friday evening has grown lazy, endless. Banks of stadium lights shine down on the field. "When do you think The Yankees started playing night games?"

The Yankees' batter dallies enough to finally pull a walk. He trots to first and Rachel considers the question. "That would be at the old stadium? Which is a twin of this one?"

"Yes, same dimensions, facade, fencing," Michael says.

"Nothing's different between the two stadiums?"

"This one has cup holders on the seats."

"So they built all this for cup holders?"

"And a conference center, hotel, that kind of stuff. I miss the old place. We can wager, make it interesting. Or maybe you're afraid you'll lose?"

They've been doing this bet thing since May, so she has a collection of wagers: The dinner, the time Rachel guessed right and Michael had to wash her car, the five dollar bet. "Anything in mind?" she asks.

"Not off hand." He offers her a bite of his hot dog with mustard, relish and onions.

She chews and hands him a napkin while the runners tire the pitcher with their leads. He has too many places to eye and throws a lousy pitch. The batter pops it foul.

"How about you? Anything in particular?" Michael asks, watching the pitch and finishing the dog.

This may well be the last game she watches. The end of summer is in sight. If they can't find a way to stay together, she needs to thank him for all he's done since that first bowling night. "As a matter of fact, I do have something in mind." She gives him a long look. "Dinner in the city. My treat."

Michael returns her look completely. Somehow, she knows, he sees it in her eyes, the preparation for saying goodbye the same way they began, over a dinner wager landing them in a restaurant, a carafe of wine on the table, a candle's flame flickering in a red glass globe. He turns back to the game. The pitcher studies the plate and takes too long with the pitch. Popped foul. The count stays full.

"It would be a nice way for you to meet my daughter," he says.

She hears it. He refuses to go where her wager suggested. His new Yankees cap is on backwards, his elbows on each armrest, his hands clasped against his stomach. So you'd think he's completely at ease, but he gives it away with the moment's hesitation before he meets her gaze. He's not.

"I'm not saying goodbye to you over some fancy dinner, Rachel. Not yet. As a matter of fact, not at all, sweetheart." He takes a long breath. "It's time for you to meet my daughter. At that dinner you're going to owe me when you lose this bet." He extends his hand to shake on it.

Rachel takes his hand and doesn't let go. "So lights were not always there?"

"That's right." The pitcher tries to pick off second base.

"The Depression was in the thirties, so probably not then. It's got to be either the nineteen forties or fifties." The batter calls Time and moves from the batter's box. Fifty thousand fans watch The Yankees do their dance. "The fifties was a family era. They'd be going to the ballpark a lot."

"So you think night games started in the fifties?" Finally the batter swings. The ball does a slow loop high into the sky while he trots to first. The runners advance. Fifty thousand pairs of eyes stay on that ball, a white shooting star arching right over the wall. The crowd rises, a polite ovation rings. It is that kind of night.

"Well, it could have been after the war, too." A pitching change is called. The crowd halfheartedly taunts the outgoing pitcher. Rachel studies the field, not calculating when the lights were installed, not visualizing the past. Not that past, anyway. Feeling Michael's fingers linking through hers, she remembers instead their first night bowling, when she wanted only to find her best friend. "Nineteen fifty-three."

Michael watches the next batter come on deck. "You're good."

"Hooray!"

"But not good enough."

"I'm wrong?"

"During World War II, the lights of Ebbets Field and the Polo Grounds revealed our ships at night. The ships in New York harbor. Out of respect to America, The Yankees didn't install their lighting system until after the war. They played their first night game on May 28, 1946."

"I'm wrong? Drat, I thought I was pretty tuned in to this place."

Michael lifts her hand and kisses the back of it. "Tuned in to Yankee Stadium? My grandfather would have loved you."

"Wait a minute. He worked there, didn't he? He built that wonderful old stadium."

"His very first job in America. Doing manual labor at the Yankee Stadium site. He and my grandmother lived in a tenement house a few blocks away. Walked to work every day with his toolbox and his lunch pail."

"Do you know how amazing that is? I mean, every kid dreams of playing ball. And your grandfather came to America and helped build the most famous house of dreams. Wow." She leans a little closer.

Michael slips his arm around her shoulders. "I can taste that dinner you owe me already. Chicken parm, warm Italian bread. Little side of ravioli."

* * *

Rachel pulls into her driveway the next evening and takes a deep breath. For the past hour, she drove too fast and changed lanes too often.

So now she sits for a minute and considers her ranch home, her hands still gripped on the steering wheel. Her heart slows. The lawn needs to be cut and last week's PennySaver lays beneath a bush. The impatiens she planted have spread around the maple tree like a magenta wedding band, and the petunias growing in the pot hanging from the lamp post explode into trailing vines of pink bells.

Wedding bells.

Everywhere, all she sees are weddings. The white siding on her ranch becomes the white chapel. The stone walkway winds itself into a silver carpeted aisle. Her front door is the altar.

It is this very thought that rushed her home, making her drive like crazy. Michael hasn't said anything. It's too soon to think marriage. But he won't consider the ending, either.

The thing is, the summer has grown exquisite. Rachel can spend as much time as she likes at an old cottage at a special beach. And they've gone from Manhattan dinners to take-out seafood on a screened porch where they talk softly, like in a library, revealing their selves one page at a time, little stories. And that is how she knows.

Michael is as imbedded in New York as the gnarled roots of that old maple tree are imbedded in the rich, brown soil of her front yard. As the petunia bells are pot bound in their hanging pot. There is no uprooting him. It wouldn't be fair to ask, and he wouldn't be capable of doing so. All that he loves, all of New York, it nurtures his second chance at life.

She unlocks the front door and steps inside her house. The air is closed-up stuffy, so she opens windows and considers her home. A different light shines on it now, a light cast by another life.

In her beach room, low sunlight bathes the space in golden rays. She looks at Sara Beth's portrait. Michael wants Sara Beth back in her life. Their friendship matters.

And Rachel so needs Sara Beth to dally with this Michael question and the real possibility of marriage. And the fact that he killed someone. That's in him. Eventually she'll face a huge decision. And Sara Beth will know how to find it in the tangled mess of love, and her worry about his hypervigilance along with the repercussions of ending a life, and his divorce, and Summer becoming her stepdaughter. And the danger inherent in his work. He's got nothing to fall back on should he be injured or decide to switch careers. No other experience, no advanced education.

But that's not why she rushed home.

It happened this summer over finding conch shells on the beach and lacing up bowling shoes. While standing on the Empire State Building and walking along an old, weathered boardwalk. She walked right into his life.

Now she has to look at her home in this new light, to study it and feel its history and let it possess her. Memories will surface. Emotions will rise. Especially this week, with the anniversary of Carl's death. She'll be alone that day. It'll be like a photo album in her mind, turning the pages, remembering when, smiling, crying a little too, trying to find some way to hold on to what she has of Carl, and Ashley. Of holidays and birthdays and kitchen talks and snowy nights and Sunday dinners. Some way to put white corners on pictures of her life, close the album and take them with her. It is necessary to go through this. It is the only way to know if she can ever leave it all behind. To know if she can walk out of this life and into Michael's.

But mostly, it is to say a last goodbye to Carl.

twenty-four

WHAT IS HE *DOING?*" JEN whispers to Kat on Sunday afternoon. They watch Tom taking Sara Beth's hand on bended knee. "I thought I was going to help him wax the car. He said he'd pay me extra allowance."

"Wait! I think he's *proposing!*"

"To Mom? Eeew."

"Shhh!"

Tom catches his daughters watching through the sliding glass door and motions for them to come outside onto the deck. "Stand over there and don't talk," he tells them. "You're witnessing history."

"Tom, what is going on?" Sara Beth asks. She's sitting in the shade of the deck umbrella.

Tom reaches into his cargo shorts pocket and pulls out the velvet box. "Now this one's temporary. Until we figure things out."

"What have you done?" Sara Beth lifts her sunglasses and studies him.

He turns and winks at his daughters, then raises the box to Sara Beth. "Exactly what you're thinking. But if you *lose* this one, if you get my drift, it's seven hundred dollars, not seven thousand. I need you to wear a ring. So," and he opens the box for her, "with this ring, we thee wed."

Sara Beth looks from the ring, to Tom, to their daughters who quietly inched closer.

"We?" she asks. "We thee wed?"

And he points out the three round diamonds in the center, "Jen, Kat and Owen," then the two tiny oblong diamonds on either side. "Me," he says, touching one. "And your mom. Okay?"

"Tom," Sara Beth stops him, her heart breaking with love and guilt at once.

"So I've got everybody in your life covered."

"Well." And Sara Beth wonders about it, her mother in the ring, and how she still hasn't told Tom that if things were different that day, maybe her mother would've made it. And yet here he is, trying to keep her mother alive.

"You're getting married *again?*" Kat asks, stepping closer and looking at the ring.

"Kind of," Tom says. "We can do things different now that we're forty. Help me put this ring on Mom's finger."

So when Sara Beth extends her left hand, three hands wrap around the ring and slip it in place.

"Aren't you going to kiss the bride?" Kat asks.

Sara Beth stands and watches Tom, his frameless glasses low on his nose, his hair freshly buzzed. At this point, she doesn't know what to expect.

Tom reaches for her hand.

Suddenly she feels very much alone with him, aware of his chest rising with each breath, of his eyes not leaving hers, the heat some wavering curtain around them. When he pulls her closer, she rises on tiptoe and kisses him hesitantly. The beauty of it is, he kisses her back and doesn't stop, his hands cupping her face, taking her in like he is on one long inhale needed to live. She's never felt so necessary.

"Gross," Jen whispers behind them.

* * *

The next day, Sara Beth glances at the ring while her hand is on the steering wheel. The diamonds glimmer in the sunlight in a way her old ring never did. Her mother will always be in this ring now. The spontaneity of Tom's gesture so moved her that she decides to do the same. Before taking Katherine and Owen to see their new kitten, Slinky, at the carriage house, she takes a spontaneous side trip down Rachel's street. With such a great idea, they have to start talking again. Rachel's car is backing out of her driveway so Sara toots the horn, parks at the curb and hurries over.

"I'm glad I caught you!" she calls out. She wishes she could tell her Tom's agreed to look at the house, but that will come tomorrow night, if Rachel agrees to her invitation.

"Is everything okay?" Rachel quickly rolls down her window.

"Yes! Listen, I won't hold you. Tom's got a business dinner tomorrow. I thought we could try a girls' night out and catch up with each other. We'll take the kids to the bandshell, pack the cooler?" As the words come out, she catches sight of Rachel's suitcase in the back seat. "Oh. Maybe not, then."

"Sorry. I'm on my way to see Ashley."

Something Sara Beth noticed when they talked recently were these awkward moments, the ones aching for what they used to have, when they didn't have to ask *How is she?* In artwork, a cast shadow is the shadow that falls *from* one form onto another. Their lost New York weekend is that cast shadow.

"She misses you and her dad, doesn't she?"

Rachel puts her sunglasses on top of her head. They still find the old nuances. Like right now. Nuances that make them both want Rachel to jump out of the car, pull Sara Beth over to the garden bench and tell her about Ashley calling and emailing every day. Instead she checks her watch. "I miss her too," she says.

"I'll bet," Sara Beth answers, knowing all about missing someone. All about being miles and miles apart. If they can take a few precious minutes and talk about the kids, trying that tactic to find each other again, the miles between them would lessen. So much in her life seems to be almost in her grasp, this friendship included.

Rachel puts her car in gear. "I'm late. Ashley's car needs brakes and she asked me to come and help out. You know, drive her to class, that kind of thing, while it's in the shop."

"At least that's what she says, right? It gets her mom there?"

"Maybe she's too far from home. I don't know. But I've really got to go. She'll be waiting." She starts backing out. "Sara? How's Katherine's arm?"

"A bad sprain. The bandage comes off Friday."

"At least it's not broken." She inches back out of the driveway. "Sorry I can't make the concert," she says out her window.

"Another time," Sara Beth calls out. And then comes the worst part, getting back into her car and putting her purse on the empty passenger seat, where Rachel should be sitting for a ride with her out to the country to visit Slinky, all the while planning their girls' night out at the bandshell. It's always disappointing when you turn back to your life and it's not what you wanted it to be.

* * *

The next morning, Rachel writes out a check to her daughter to cover the cost of the brake work. "Deposit this in your account. Then you can pay the shop yourself." She sits at the desk in Ashley's dorm room.

"Thanks. What'll you do while I'm in class?"

Rachel likes observing her daughter in her own college space, seeing who she is growing into. Ashley wears a frayed denim skirt with a fitted tee and flip-flops, her hair pulled back, big gold hoops in her ears. "I guess I'll do some shopping in town."

"I'm cutting my second class, Mom."

"Not on my account you're not. I'll be fine poking around the shops."

"Oh just this once. It's only Sociology. Which I still can't understand why I have to take to be a nurse."

"It gives you a wide reaching education, Ashley. That's all."

"Well I can skip it. We'll have lunch and by then my car will be ready. That way you won't have to drive home too late on the highway."

"I don't mind," Rachel says, but sees the way Ashley is worrying about her driving at night. "Okay, we'll have lunch." Ashley breathes a sigh of relief, tucks the check into her purse and gathers her books in a pile. "Ash?"

Her daughter steps to her dresser, pulls out her elastic and quickly brushes her hair.

"Do you ever think about transferring to a local college? I've got plenty room for you."

Ashley turns, elastic in her teeth, regathering her ponytail. "Mom. Why would you ask me that?" She pulls her hair through the elastic.

"I worry sometimes. Maybe you miss the whole family thing, especially with Dad gone."

"I do, sometimes. But I worry about *you*, more. All the time."

"Me?"

"If you're okay. If you can take care of that house alone." She sits on the bed. "It's the anniversary this week, Mom. I can't believe Dad's been gone two years."

"I know." Rachel moves beside her. "Time goes by so fast. Sometimes I think of him like he's still here, you know, having a coffee in the kitchen, outside raking. A part of me always misses him."

"That's why I worry, Mom. About if you're lonely, or sad."

"Sometimes? I guess I am. Boy, what a couple of worry warts we are."

"Well. I *am* your daughter. I can't help it."

"I know the feeling. But I was just thinking that if you wanted to, you could take a semester off."

"I would if you needed me to. But I'm okay. Really." She stands and goes to her dresser. "And we'll *always* worry. It's what we do, you know? It's our thing?"

Her daughter is right. They would check up on each other even living in the same house, their *How's it going?* or *How'd you sleep?* really a gauge measuring their daily emotions. She slips her checkbook back into her purse and tells her about Sara Beth suggesting a girls' night out at the bandshell.

"She's trying to fix things, Mom. Give her a chance."

"I would love to have that old friendship back. But we never find the time. She jokes about needing to go away on some boat where no one can reach us."

"What you probably need is another weekend in New York. Just to fix the first one."

Inspiration comes at the oddest times, like right now, sitting with her daughter, thinking of boats, and Sara Beth, and a difficult promise to Michael about friendships and chances. Maybe another New York weekend would do it.

"How's Michael?" Ashley asks over her shoulder.

"Oh he's fine. He asks about you, too."

Ashley rummages through a dresser drawer. "It seems like he really likes you."

"It happens when you least expect it." She watches Ashley for a reaction and gets a doozy.

"Do you think you'll ever get married?"

"You'd be the first to know, but honestly Ashley, we haven't discussed it." She doesn't tell her about Michael's personal demon, doesn't open that door to Ashley's life with those words. "We're good company for each other right now."

"Oh." Ashley sits heavy on the bed. Rachel gets the feeling she is seeing Carl somewhere in her mind, wondering what he would think, wondering if he would want her mother happy and safe. Wondering if this anniversary is a time to let go. "Well, it would probably be okay if you ever did marry him," her daughter says.

"Thanks. I'll keep that in mind. How about you?"

"What about me?"

"Any cute guys you're interested in?"

She winks at Rachel and stands with a little jump, ready to leave for class. "A couple hot TA's who make tutoring worthwhile. That's why I can miss my second class."

twenty-five

THIS IS HERS. BECOMES HER. With a spiral notebook tucked beneath her arm, she lifts a painting from the wall and finds its corresponding notes in the pad, logging the title, artist, date of painting, and condition. Her hand lingers on the heavy wood frame when she rehangs it. Possessiveness is funny like that, making you keep your hand on objects, *mine, mine, mine,* you say, trying only to believe it.

After seeing the historic house earlier, Tom seemed unsure of making a move. So she's possessive of that, too, of the possibility of moving to an antique home. It's up to her to keep that hope alive.

Earlier she pulled out her cell phone. It felt necessary to know which hope was really on her mind. Another Google search brought up the small museum north of Paris, listing Claude as curator. She took a deep breath and placed the international call, alone, from the carriage house. Her voice, it sounded foreign, too. Like it wasn't really her, the way she scared herself going back two decades asking for Claude, identifying herself first to his office.

In the silent seconds when she was put on hold, she wondered if *this* was her new beginning. If it was too late to find out if she'd chosen wrong. And then, his voice.

"Sara?"

He sounded faraway, unsure.

"Sara Beth? Is that you?"

Her eyes closed, her heart beat fast. *How do I do this?* she wondered. *What am I looking for?* Her hand pressed the phone close and she heard him say something, in French, to someone in the room. The carefree, footloose old boyfriend with whom she'd traipsed through Europe on a wing and a prayer, speaking fluent French. And the picture came to her then. His dignified stature, his knowledge and prestige. His dream demanded it and he gave.

"Sara Beth? Etes-vous la?" Then in a moment, "Are you there?"

Slowly, she pulled the phone away from her face. Years ago, his artsy ways and open thinking took her on one long magic carpet ride through France and Italy, through ancient cities and untamed countryside.

But for her whole life, to have that kind of wanderlust? Maybe it was more a freeing journey delivering her here. More a wanderlust to remember, to brush the dust off of sometimes, to know she'd once had it. In a piece of art, the stress of light or dark is the accent. Her time with Claude was her accent, necessary, but nothing more.

She disconnected the call.

Claude would wonder now, too. If it was really her or a misunderstanding in the translation. But placing herself in France with only a phone call, she stopped wondering. So there was that now.

She slips an index card into the metal box, her hands shaking at how close she'd come to putting a new layer of paint on her canvas. Far better to change the nuance of the existing layer. Maybe over tonight's champagne and candlelight, with the written appraisal of their home and her approved loan in front of them, Tom will reconsider that colonial. So there's that possibility, too. Sometimes it all comes at once like that. The whole *When it rains* thing.

She pulls the chain on her desk lamp. Even that is antique with a brass base and original label on the shade showing a 1916 patent. With the lights off, she locks up the carriage house doors, glancing up at the stars emerging in the twilight sky. How many people have stood along the riverbanks, ship captains and farmers and children and lovers, looking at the same starry sky? Wondering about their choices. There'll always be wonder. She is comforted by that, by the familiarity, by sharing the same questions with so many others.

She glances at her new diamond ring. In the constellations, stars connect time.

* * *

Early Thursday morning, Sara Beth's world shifts. She parks across the street from the old colonial right as the morning sun reaches the front windows. But it's different from all the other times she's stopped because the pretty paned windows could be hers by day's end. Tom, with some convincing, had rethought the possibilities of this house and agreed to submit an offer on it today. It's out of her control, really, the way she drove here. It's her everything, her own North Star.

But the house isn't all that has her smiling. Rachel called before her morning walk.

"July's half gone and we haven't talked in weeks," she said. "How about we get a coffee this morning and try again?"

The longer they didn't talk things out, the worse it got. All she wanted to do was tell Rachel about the colonial, but she couldn't, not with that New York weekend still unresolved. Their relationship was like a van Gogh painting: a yellow rose of friendship and pansies of tender thoughts and red tulips of admiration and wisteria of welcome and goldenrod of encouragement and even Queen Anne's lace of protection. But the vase broke one weekend, the flowers littered between them. They could try to patch their friendship up, but over a cup of coffee?

"I don't know, Rach. We've been there, done that."

"Well so what? Who hasn't? You game, girl?"

* * *

"Buckle up," Rachel says, waiting to put the car in gear.

Even though this feels like old times going antiquing or to the farmers' market, stopping for cappuccino first, Sara Beth knows not to be fooled by the easy sensation. That's how tenuous their friendship has become. It's a butterfly flitting above those van Gogh flowers, just as easily flying away.

"I'm glad you called," Sara Beth says as she shifts in the seat.

"Me too. The kids look good."

"They've missed you." She settles comfortably, turning toward Rachel. "They were so happy you came in and visited for a bit."

"I've missed them, too. And hey, great piano."

"I'm actually going to take lessons. I can't wait."

"You are? Good for you. I think you'll love it, making music."

They pass the turn-off for Whole Latte Life. "Rachel? The coffee shop's back that way."

"Oh, I have to make another stop first." She pulls her oversized sunglasses from atop her head and slips them on. "You don't mind, do you?"

"No. Go ahead." Her hairdresser appointment isn't for another two hours. But when Rachel gets on the highway, she starts to worry. "Where exactly do you have to stop? The mall?"

"No, it's only a few exits down. Okay?"

Sara Beth doesn't want anything to ruin the chance they have this morning. But when Rachel leans forward and turns on the radio, she's surprised. "Hey. Didn't you want to talk a little?" she asks over Tom Petty. "With that music playing, I can't even hear my thoughts."

"It's just a little background music. Keeping things easy, you know?"

"I guess." Trees and signs pass by at sixty-five miles an hour. Three exits later, Sara Beth lowers the music volume. "I don't know if we'll have time for our coffee now. How much farther do you have to go?"

"Oh," Rachel says as she changes lanes, "I'd say a couple hours."

"What? Where are we going?"

She glances in her side view mirror. "New York."

"We're going to Manhattan?"

"Even better. Long Island."

"Come on, are you for real?"

Rachel guns the engine, pushing the speedometer past seventy. And she suddenly looks pretty darn pleased with herself. "Sara Beth? You've just been kidnapped."

* * *

"You're kidding, right?"

"Absolutely not."

Sara Beth struggles with her seatbelt. "Shit, Rachel, turn this car of yours around."

"No way." They're cruising in the fast lane. "This vehicle's got a one-way ticket to the beach." Rachel rolls her window all the way down, the wind whipping her hair. "Whooee! It's not turning around and you're not getting out!"

"Come on!" Sara Beth tries to hold her hair back in the wind. "I have a hairdresser appointment this morning."

Rachel reaches into her handbag, pulls out her cell phone and tosses it in Sara's lap. "Cancel." Her eyes stay on the road.

"I will not. And Katherine's having a cavity filled at three-fifteen."

"Whatever."

"*Whatever?* This is some kind of a joke, right? You can't kidnap me."

"Oh yes I can. You *ran away* on me. And that's what got us into this whole mess in the first place. You!"

Sara Beth sits back and closes her eyes. This can't be happening, not with the To-Do list she has to check off today, including a one o'clock appointment with the real estate agent.

"Come on, Rachel. If you won't go back, let me out at the next exit. Up ahead there." The car flies right by it. "You don't understand!" She whips around in the seat and watches the exit fade. "We're making an offer on a house today. For my shop. My *life*, okay? Tom finally agreed. God damn it, would you *stop this car!*"

"Tom's got everything under control. He's putting in the offer as planned."

"He *knows* about this?"

"I called him last night. Who do you think put your overnight bag in my trunk when we were with the kids?"

"Overnight bag? *Overnight?* This was *planned?* What the hell are you doing?"

Rachel grips the wheel with two hands. The wind blows through the car while Petty sings about free falling. "Listen," she says over it all. "Our friendship means *way* too much to lose over one really screwed up weekend. And you've told me more than once that what we need is time on some *boat*, with no distractions, to get to the bottom of this. Well, I don't have a boat and neither do you, so I don't know where you got that from. But there *is* a little cottage out on Long Island that will do just as good. You're *not* going back home until we're finished with this thing once and for all. Got it?"

"Long Island. I don't suppose this has anything to do with that cop I guess you've hooked up with?"

"He's a Mounted Police Officer with the NYPD and he has *far* more to do with this than you realize." So now there's that, too, this whole *guy* thing Sara Beth knows nothing about. "And he's really the best thing to happen to me since, well, he's the damn best. So leave him out of this before you say something you'll really regret."

Sara Beth shifts in her seat, crosses her arms and looks out the window. They are miles from Addison now. "This is perfect. Really great. What a brainstorm you had. Owen's got BedTime Story Time at the library tonight."

"Do you hear yourself? Hair appointment, house appointment, dentist appointment, storytime. You need this kidnapping more than you think!"

"I can't *believe* Tom agreed to this. We had a huge day planned. There's no way he'd go along with such a ridiculous idea."

"Call him."

"I think I will. And I'll have him call the police while I'm at it." She dials her home phone. The announcement on the answering machine has been changed to Tom's voice. *Sara, if it's you, don't worry. Everything's under control. I'll take care of the house and get Katherine to the dentist. Relax already, and I'll see you whenever you get back.* She stares at the phone, then disconnects silently.

Rachel keeps her eyes on the road. Then, as if to say *forget-about-it, there-is-no-ransom,* she passes a car and picks up speed.

"You won't turn around no matter what I say, will you?" When she laughs, Sara Beth punches in the salon number and cancels her appointment, then redials her home. After the beep, she leaves a message. "Tom!" She turns away from Rachel. "Jesus Tom," her voice angry. "What's gotten into you? I can't believe this. Kidnapped? I've been *kidnapped?* I thought we, well, why didn't you ... Well, Owen's got story time tonight. Be sure he wears his pajamas there. All the kids do. And let me know about, oh, never mind." She disconnects and throws the phone back in Rachel's purse.

Rachel settles back, turns the music up when a Springsteen song comes on, and drives the route to the Connecticut docking of the Cross Sound Ferry. Sara Beth alternately watches her and the road without talking because sometimes you can't talk, everything that needs to be said has been, and the moment has to wind itself down.

"I made advance reservations online," Rachel finally tells her when they pull into the line waiting to board the ferry. She inches the car forward, looking a little like a rebel.

"Why? So I wouldn't have a chance to escape if you bought the ticket here?"

"That's exactly right." She maneuvers the car onto the upper level auto deck, kills the ignition and steps out. "Come on," she says, lifting her sunglasses on top of her head and taking a deep breath of the salt air. "We have to get out of the car for the crossing."

Sara Beth opens her door, seeing the water spread out before them, seagulls flying in high loops above the dock. The boat sways slightly, like it's trying to prove that, yes, she is about to cross Long Island Sound. Because, oh boy, she still doesn't believe it.

"Hey!" Rachel says as she heads for the passenger cabins on a lower deck. "I guess we found that boat after all!" she calls over her shoulder. "What a co-in-kee-dink!"

twenty-six

ARCHITECTURE AS ART. THIS IS the thought that crosses her mind when Sara Beth sees the small gray cottage Little Gull. Architecture with its inherent design, structure and style, is one of many art forms from which she'd been trained to cull the universal forms of human expression. So much of her Art History education was a visual training. Learning to look.

It comes naturally now, silently walking the flagstone path to the bungalow. She's sure Rachel thinks it's her irritation at being kidnapped that keeps her quiet. It's not. It is the innate way she employs her trained eye: Peeling paint from the flower boxes contrasting with the red geraniums and snow white petunias; lattice porch windows open to the sea; jars of sea glass sitting amidst an array of conch shells and painted seagulls mounted on driftwood; hurricane lanterns.

So what is the human expression in this beach architecture?

What function does the three-dimensional delineation serve? In a social context, this structure serves honesty. It is edifice stripped down to simplicity, leaving room for the heart to expand within its context. She feels it already.

Inside, chairs slipcovered in stripes and plaids along with whitewashed end tables all face a stone fireplace upon which sits a massive vase of heather and wild grasses. In the kitchen, dried flower bunches hang from ceiling beams. There's a mingling of human touch with structure everywhere around her.

But nowhere more so than on the kitchen table: A vase of fresh flowers sits beside a bottle of wine and a can of coffee grounds, and, almost like an afterthought, someone leaned against the vase the mall photograph of Sara Beth and Rachel smiling together.

. "He left ice cream in the freezer, too. I think there's cookie dough."

Sara Beth turns and studies her friend's face. What she sees in its space, light and color are answers to questions she never voiced: How long did Rachel wait in the restaurant that day? A long, panicked time. And did she sleep those nights, worrying? She worried a hell of a lot more than slept. And did Rachel look for her in the city? She looked in every special place their friendship has ever taken them, hoping hoping hoping Sara would return to her in some way, even by revisiting a memory. All those answers are there, human expression in the architecture of her eyes.

After being out of college for two decades, twenty years of life between herself and classroom desks, what Sara Beth knows is this: When a relationship is mounted and framed against the simple setting of a beach cottage, she finds the same emotional dimension in the relationship's symmetry, design, balance, content, layout as in the work of the great masters.

"We've been trying all summer to get back to that picture," Rachel says.

Sara Beth takes the photograph and sets her visually trained eye on it. "Oh Rach. We never really left it in the first place."

* * *

There are oil paintings and there are watercolor paintings. Both are layered. Here, at the beach, Sara Beth thinks they are watercolor. Light. Translucent. Blending. Watercolor paints are transparent, never fully covering the layer of paint beneath. So it is important, in a watercolor, to work from the lightest color to the darkest. And that is what Sara Beth does.

She drops in her feelings and motivations, tips the paper and blots them with stories of Tom, and how she'd nearly divorced him before Owen came along. From that canvas, she pulls out the bigger picture of her life, glazing over it with the color of growing up in a well worn old home and introducing more color in the hue of her mother and how she included her children in her day-to-day life, her restoration of that home, her lesson that you're never alone in its history because of the stories in the walls, the furniture.

But in her painting, it felt lately like color was being lifted out when Owen came along, taking all her time, and then even more color drained with her mother's death. Sara Beth doesn't paint in every detail; they'd been friends long enough for Rachel to know them. So she suggests her recent feelings, her frame of mind, her desperation, with mere brushstrokes.

Now and then, they step back from the work at hand and let the canvas dry. They walk on the beach, have a glass of wine, work on a plate of cheese and crackers. But always they return to the painting, their brushstrokes seeking out the texture of their friendship.

* * *

"Owen's what ended up saving me." Sara Beth stands and looks out the old porch windows facing the sea. "I love Owen so much. But differently than the girls." She leans against the sill, touching the little seagulls on the shelves. "My pregnancy stopped me from leaving my marriage."

"What? Leaving? Why didn't you ever tell me?"

"And say what?" Sara Beth asks, turning to her. "This wasn't the life I wanted? That I fell into it because Tom was my safety? The thing is, it had nothing to do with security. Choosing Tom back then, and everything that happened this year, had more to do with Mom."

"Your mother?"

"She knew me like no one else, loved me like no one else, and growing up with her, restoring that house, furnishing it with antiques she bought with me tagging along, well, it's a connection I can't lose, to the most special person I've known. Me, and a shop, are an extension of her. With Tom, I'm finding a way to do it."

After a moment, Rachel says, "We should all be so lucky, having that love in our lives. But why the mystery? Why didn't you tell me this in New York?"

"It was grief, Rach. All the furniture and treasures in that carriage house? They were a gift from Mom on my fortieth birthday."

"No way."

Sara Beth tells the story of the package delivered on the morning of her birthday and how her mother arranged the delivery with Lillian a few weeks before her death.

"Seeing that carriage house was like Mom coming back to me. And it did something else, having her return like that. The sadness of her being gone came back too. By the time we went to New York a few months later, I'd wake up some days and cry. I remember when Mom died, I couldn't breathe. I couldn't get a breath. And that started happening again, like I'm trying to fill up this big hole inside me. I didn't know how else to get away from that, to start fresh somehow, without my partner filling my life with calls and visits and emails. So I ran away from it."

Rachel picks up the wine bottle. "That's why Tom was devastated," she says as the bottle tips into Sara Beth's glass. "He didn't realize it was about your mother."

"He thought I was leaving him."

"*Are* you?"

"No." She sets down her glass. "Let's walk outside, okay?"

The late afternoon sun has faded, the tide gone out. Rachel tells her she loves this lingering time of day here, walking along the driftline, barefoot.

"Sometimes I wonder what life would have been like if I'd done things differently. Remember Claude? My old college boyfriend?" Sara Beth picks up a seashell, then another, for her daughters.

"Are you serious? He was so, I don't know, hippy? Really, really into the art thing. Studio painting, right?"

"That's right. It was Claude's passion that drew me to him. He was so free and unbounded, the same as I saw in my mother growing up. And in the end, his passion shaped his life, too."

They look across Long Island Sound, the horizon darkening.

"I imagine it's the Atlantic sometimes. That's where he is, Claude. Across the pond. He's a curator at a French museum."

They sit for a while, the waves lapping, the sand warm. "This is what the sea is for, you know," Rachel says.

"What do you mean?"

"Now I see why you said we needed time on a boat. We needed the sea to contemplate all this beside."

One of the important rules when painting is to know when to stop, to know if any further layers will add to the painting. If not, there's no reason to dab your brush, wet the canvas, blot. And with Rachel dabbing the sea onto the painting Sara Beth decides this particular picture is complete.

* * *

After dinner, Sara Beth pokes around the cottage, coming across pieces of Rachel's new life when she walks into her bedroom. Michael's worn boat shoes are set neatly beneath a dresser; his cargo shorts folded over the back of a straight chair. A man's razor and toothbrush hang in the bathroom. She picks up his razor and wonders about the connection between Michael and her friend and herself. It is intensely here, some invisible thread, or wire, or rope, tying them together.

"It's just enough, isn't it? This cottage?"

"You bet," Rachel answers from the porch glider.

"I know you're tired tonight. We'll leave in the morning?" Sara Beth asks, leaning on the front porch doorjamb.

"But we're not done, party pooper."

"What do you mean? How much more can I explain?"

"Okay fine, so far so good. You've earned your manicure points." She goes to her bedroom and comes back with a bottle of coral nail polish. "Sit down and give me your hand." And Sara Beth sets her hand on a white wicker table between them, just like old times, a lifetime of beach porches, hurricane lamps, salt air in the breeze, waves in the distance, wishing stars.

"So tell me about this Michael dude, Rach."

"Wait a minute. You're still kidnapped and I'm still feeling kind of miffed about your walking out on me in New York." Rachel brushes a line of coral down the center of one of Sara's nails. "Like, I could have helped you, you know."

"You're a tough negotiator." Sara Beth points to a nail not covered enough. "Fix that one." So Rachel applies a second coat and tells her to dry. Sara Beth waves her fingers, blowing on them gently. "First tell me about your guy. I need a little gossip."

"How did you even know we were seeing each other? I never told you."

"I saw you together. In the grocery store one day, he must've come to Connecticut." She takes the nail polish bottle and Rachel's hand.

"What are you doing?"

"Your nails! We'll be twins. Now hold them out," she orders as she dips the brush. And while she dabs on color, she doesn't say she knew they were together by the way Rachel and Michael looked at something on the shelf, and the way Michael's hand touched the small of Rachel's back, and how the gesture seemed intimate and Sara had to turn around and leave, dropping her basket in front of the store.

"I guess what you need to know about Michael, who, yes, I am seeing, is that he's behind all this. That's the kind of guy he is." Rachel watches her draw lines of coral polish along her nails. "Michael saw the other side of your story." She lays her second hand out and Sara Beth continues polishing. "He saw my side. He saw me going crazy trying to find you everywhere: on the streets, stopping women from behind, grabbing their arm when I was sure they were you. Something seemed really, really wrong and all I wanted to do was help you." The sunlight outside fades. Nearby porch lights come on, passing voices on the sandy street are hushed. "He saw me realize all the losses you've had recently," she explains.

Sara Beth closes the nail polish bottle and stands, her arms crossed in front of her.

"But see, after all that panic, even though it still feels like you used our friendship," Rachel begins, then hesitates, "I feel like maybe it was my fault too."

"Your fault? No way."

"Maybe I should've seen some of this. Or maybe, maybe I did. And I thought it would all pass with time. It would be easier to just look the other way and be busy with my own life."

"So you asked Michael if you could use his cottage to do this?"

"Partly." Rachel looks around the porch. "Someday I'll explain how we're here doing this, in this cottage, mostly *because* of him. And because of a situation that made him *ask* me to keep you close in my life. He's behind a lot of this."

"Rach," Sara Beth interrupts. "Stop. For a little while? Let's take a break." The image of a man she doesn't know encouraging all this affects her. You can stand in one place, like here on a little seaside porch, absolutely still with your pretty coral nails, and inside everything shifts, gently, the smallest wave.

* * *

They walk down to the beach and sit in the dark on the boardwalk. "What a haven this place is," Sara Beth says. She turns and looks at the pleasure boats corralled into the boat basin behind them. Nearly every slip is full. "Have you spent a lot of time here?"

"Pretty much," Rachel answers.

"Lucky." They watch the night sky over Long Island Sound. The cottages on the east side, up on the hill, are dark now. People are sleeping. The flag was taken down at sunset. Sara Beth sits with arms folded, leaning forward on crossed legs.

"Just think," Rachel says. "If you chose Claude, you wouldn't be here now."

After a moment, Sara Beth says, "No I wouldn't."

The way she looks out into the dark, toward the water, Rachel doubts she'll ever believe some choices completely.

"We should get back," Sara Beth tells her.

"In a minute."

"Oh, I get it." Sara Beth follows her gaze to the sky. Stars glimmer behind wispy clouds. "I can't believe we've been doing this every summer."

"I guess it's our thing. Twenty-five years of wishing on stars. They must hold some celestial answer for us."

"We take death to reach a star. That's what van Gogh said."

"Well," Rachel whispers. "Then your mom's up there. And I'm going to wish that she could see you right now, putting your life back together."

"Oh Rach, stop it. You'll make me cry."

"That's okay. Maybe you haven't gotten all the tears out yet."

"Wishes are a mystery to me. It's like putting your hope out there, opening a part of your heart to the constellations. Imagine if those stars could talk, and the new constellations they could make with the wishes they've heard?"

"I wished for you from the top of the Empire State Building," Rachel admits. "There," she points to the west, "that star right there. That's the one."

"You nut. How do you know? It could be any of these *thousands* of stars!"

"Sure," Rachel says as she stands and waits for Sara to come back with her. "Doubt me. No wonder you don't get wishes."

* * *

In the kitchen, Rachel fills two heaping bowls with forbidden chocolate ice cream. They sit in the living room now, the porch closed up for the night.

"What's this for?" Sara Beth asks, taking her bowl.

"You scored some Beach Weekend points. This one's for food. Sinful food."

"How did I score points?"

"By living your life, Sara. By being real. It took a lot of courage." She samples a taste. "More courage than I had. I should have seen how hard it was for you when your mom died. I could've even helped with your shop, to keep that going."

Sara Beth scoops two spoonfuls into her mouth then sets the bowl on a table. She looks at the pretty cottage, smells the beach, hears the night sounds. "Look at all this. I really know now."

Rachel digs her spoon in and takes a huge mouthful of chocolate ice cream. "Know what?"

"I know that you are my very best friend in every amazing sense of the word." Sara Beth stands and paces the room, walking around the sofa, picking up a wooden seagull and setting it back down, brushing the dust from an old book, touching a large conch shell on the fireplace mantle. "Sailors use these. Did you know that? For crossing signals. They have a beautiful rich tone." She strokes it with her fingers, her back to Rachel. "Well. You say you could've helped, but I didn't send you any signals in New York. No crossing signals, cell phone signals, nothing. And do you want to know something, Rach?

The truth is that really, I am so sorry for what I put you through, and I have been every single day since then."

"Huh," Rachel says.

"What?"

"That feels really good."

"My apology?"

"Well I feel a lot better now that you said it. But you need one too." Rachel runs into the bedroom, opening and closing drawers before walking back into the living room. "Still friends then?"

"Always were. What's this?"

"My apology gift. Open it."

"Apology?"

"The more I hear your story, the more I wish I'd been there for you. Even in little ways. More antique hunts. Or coffees on Saturday mornings." She takes a quick breath. "More really listening. If there's anything I can do to help now, please let me know."

Sara Beth is quiet, because sometimes there just are no words. There is only the friendship, ever there, that current that never stops. She loosens the gold thread of a velvet bag and tips out a pair of dangling stone earrings, the stone a translucent shade of green.

"They're sea glass. I bought them at a boutique here." Rachel pushes back her hair and shows the same pair in her ears. "To remember all our summers at the beach, collecting sea glass from the driftline, walking and talking, wishing on stars."

Sara Beth loops the gold wire through her ears. "They're so beautiful." But then, she stands and runs out of the room.

"Hey! What's the matter?"

She comes back with the half-gallon container of chocolate chip cookie dough ice cream and two clean spoons. All that is between them now is the half-gallon on the table. "Remember that time we picked all the cookie dough chunks out of the ice cream?"

Rachel stabs at a piece with her spoon, Sara Beth trying for the same piece. "Hey. Finders, keepers."

Sara Beth pulls her spoon away and sits back, grinning at her friend. "God, I missed you," she says.

"Me too." Rachel tips the carton in her direction to let her find the next cookie dough chunk. "Me, too."

* * *

A halo of sunlight colors the eastern sky, behind the cottages on the hill. The sandy boardwalk reaches across the beach. At the far end, they sit like they did last night, side by side, Sara Beth's coffee mug cupped in her lap, Rachel sitting back, her cup on the seat beside her.

"I imagined a conversation with you all summer long that was straight out of a magazine, you know? *I'm facing a midlife crisis.*" Sara Beth makes air quotes. "*Can this woman be saved?*"

A bank of fog lifts out on the rocks. "Don't feel bad," Rachel tells her, sipping her coffee. "One time when I kept rattling around my house, I thought of the day as a Hallmark moment. The empty nest syndrome. I'll bet they have a card for that, don't you think?"

"Probably."

"Then I got to thinking of *all* my Hallmark moments, and how I always had you instead of a card."

"And now Michael." Sara Beth drinks her coffee then runs her fingertip over the rim of her cup. "You deserve this. As sorry as I am that I hurt you, I'm really glad that Michael came from it."

"Me too."

It feels like there's something else to say, like it's too bad things happened the way they did, that life is funny and all that stuff. But Sara knows that sometimes you have to let it all go, let the balloon float up out of your hand into the sky, diminishing in the breeze.

"It's going to be hot today," Rachel is saying. "Tom pack a swimsuit in that bag of yours?"

"I think so."

"How about if we hang out on the beach. Afterwards, there's this place in town that sells old cottage stuff. Maybe we can pick up something for your shop. A little treasure hunting on our Beach Weekend Out."

The sun rises in the eastern sky, casting sparkles on Long Island Sound. "I don't know how I can ever thank you for kidnapping me."

"You don't have to thank me. You sitting with me on this boardwalk is thanks enough."

twenty-seven

ON A MUGGY TUESDAY MORNING the following week, Michael walks Maggie down the ramp to the ground floor of the stable.

"Hey Coach," he says to the blacksmith. "We need a pair of shoes." The blacksmith has gone through several apprentices, trying to train someone to take his place when he retires. But temperamental kicking horses and hot burning iron and hard manual labor scare off successors.

"Michael, my man. How are ya?" Coach runs his hand along Maggie's smooth neck, her velvet skin rippling beneath his touch. "And how's my girl here? Okay?"

Michael holds onto the horse's bridle as Coach crouches and picks up Maggie's heavy hind leg, resting her foot on his thigh. He pries off the old shoe and begins trimming the thick wall of her hoof with a knife.

"Been going down to a cottage this summer. Rented a little place at Anchor Beach."

"That right?" Coach asks, filing the wall smooth.

Michael moves beside his horse dressed in the department riding gear, the furthest thing from beach clothes: dark uniform, leather boots, the crop and helmet set on the table. Coach glances up at him, then turns the file to a rough edge on the hoof. "Nice place. Anchor Beach. Don't suppose you been going there by your lonesome?"

"Not exactly."

"Didn't think so." The blacksmith bends at the waist, Maggie's rear hoof gripped between his knees as he files. His heavy boots are splattered black from the anvil work, serious safety glasses are strapped onto his head. "So what's bugging you, kid?"

"Rachel."

"Ah." He drops Maggie's leg and picks up a horseshoe with tongs, thrusting it into flames to soften it before moving over to the anvil and pounding the shoe flat and hammering the toe clip. "Trouble in paradise?"

Michael strokes Maggie's mane, then picks up one of the sweet Macs kept for the horses. "No trouble." He looks at the apple and takes a bite.

With sparks flying as he pounds the shoe, Coach yells back, "I'd like to find me a little summer paradise." He moves back to Maggie and lifts her leg to check the fit of the shoe.

"The thing is, Rachel's at the cottage more than she's not. She's got the summer off and takes the ferry from Connecticut."

"So far, so good, guy."

He takes another bite of the apple, notices Maggie eyeing him and gives her what's left. "That's half the reason I rented the place. It's an old bungalow, not much to it. And the thing is, we agreed straight off to take the summer to see if we could make a go of this, long distance and all. It's pretty easy to do when you're at that place."

"That can be close quarters, too, a little beach place like that." Coach adjusts his leather apron. "If it weren't meant to be, might seem more like cabin fever." He dips the shoe into a bucket of cold water and the hot iron sizzles like bacon on a grill.

"But we're doing pretty good. Except we've only got a few more weeks. Rachel's a teacher in Connecticut. She can't stay around here forever."

"Why not?" Coach asks, lifting his heavy cap and wiping his brow. "Don't they use teachers in New York?"

"What?"

"Listen, Officer. How old are you now? Forty-five, six?"

"Forty-four."

"Ain't no spring chicken. So what are you waiting for? You got to propose, right away."

"Whoa. It's only been a couple of months."

"Think things'll change in the next few?" He bends Maggie's leg and sets the cooled shoe in place.

"Damn straight. Weekend commutes, long distance phone calls. Email."

"Ain't nothing like having that warm body close by." Coach, bent over, pounds a four-inch nail through the shoe holes into Maggie's hoof. She doesn't even flinch. "It's good you got yourself a lady after all you been through. You're doing all right. So you got to propose, that's all there is to it."

"But her life's in Connecticut. She's tight with her daughter. Her friends. Her home's there. I don't know if she'd leave and I don't know if she'd have me."

Coach glances up at him. "Make it special, guy. Treat her right, so she wants to stick around here."

Around here? It makes him think of Rachel's rush to get home recently. She spends a few days at the cottage, enjoying the beach, gardening and sketching while Michael works. One day rolls into the next, overlapping into sweet evenings when he goes there after work. They sleep beneath a cottage window open to the sky above the sea.

Then, just as suddenly, she leaves. There is mail to be checked, or yardwork to do, or a dentist appointment. Maybe driving back and forth gets too tiring. He doesn't think it's because she finally met Summer this past Sunday. With a vase of silk flowers between them at an Italian restaurant, she reached out to his daughter, thanks to a lost baseball wager.

Maybe the summer is too much about him and not enough her. Rachel misses Sara Beth and Ashley. She lost strong connections this year.

"We've only got a few weeks," Michael tells him. "And one of those weeks, Rachel won't be here. It's mine and Summer's week. Our vacation."

The blacksmith picks up Maggie's other hind leg and pulls off the shoe with a pair of pliers. "You take care of that daughter of yours. She almost lost you and needs to know you're here for her. I'm sure your Rachel understands?"

"She's a good person. Loyal too. If you could've seen what she did for her friend a few months back. It's pretty admirable."

Coach files the bottom of the hoof. "Good woman's hard to come by. Been with my old lady thirty years now. Sweetest damn years of my life." He places a hot shoe on Maggie's hoof. The fit needs adjusting. "You of all people, being shot and all, don't you want that?"

"Course I do."

"Propose on the beach or some crazy thing. Make it special for the two of you." He pounds the shoe on the anvil. Maggie turns back, watching over her shoulder. "She'll come around."

"Yeah. Maybe." Michael pats down his pockets, as though looking for his keys. "I'll be back for Maggie in a while. You okay here?"

"Oh sure. Maggie's good company. Go call your lady." He sets the refitted shoe back on the hoof, holding up her foot and pounding in a nail. "Rachel ought to be arrested for larceny," he calls after Michael. Michael doesn't know if he means for him to hear or not, but he does, even though his voice drops for the next part. "Snuck right up and stole your tough old heart but good."

* * *

"Summer," Rachel says. "When I think of what you did, it scares me." They walk along the water's edge, Rachel's camera hanging around her neck. "Hitchhiking! You could've been hurt!"

Summer shuffles her bare feet in the sand, stealing a glance at Rachel. "I couldn't take it there anymore," she says. "The kids on my new street are so weird. Like I mean, first they started mixing rum in their soda. Now guess what they're drinking?"

Rachel crouches down for a low shot of a beached rowboat. "I'm afraid to ask."

"It's gross. They sneak their parents' vodka and fill up their water bottles with it."

The rowboat is nestled in a bed of sea grass. "Sounds like they're bored. But you're getting off the subject. Couldn't your mother have given you a ride here?"

"She's at the floor place all the time. It's like a power trip for her."

"Well your father will hit the roof when he hears what you did."

"Oh, I'm so sick of his worrying. And lately he's getting worse, acting like I don't know how to leave the house. Next time, maybe I'll go somewhere else."

"No you won't. Next time, call me. If I'm here, I'd rather pick you up then have you get yourself killed. It's so dangerous! I'll always worry about it now, that you might do it again."

"Sorry. Sometimes I really hate my new house."

"Please promise me you won't hitch again. Call me, your dad, anyone!"

"Okay, okay, I promise." She tips her face up to the sun. "But I love it here."

"I know what you mean. Are you all moved in to your new home yet?"

"Yes. It sucks." She kicks sand while she walks. "I'm going to have to go to school with these jerks."

"You'll meet more friends once you start. Your dad says they have a Marine Studies program."

"They do. Half the day you go to regular classes, then after lunch you go to the Marine program." Summer watches her change to a zoom lens.

"I'll bet they take lots of field trips to the marshes and beaches around here."

"They even do work on a research vessel. How cool is that?" Summer asks. "But I could never get accepted into it. It's really competitive. And Dad will never let me go out on a research boat. What if I drown? What if it gets windy? He ruins everything sometimes."

"From what I've heard, you ace your science classes. Your dad's very proud of you, even if he doesn't show it. And if you're accepted, you'll meet more kids like you. And," she crouches to focus a long shot of the beach, "you might decide to study it in college."

"Maybe. But I'm still going to miss Emily. She's my best friend, you know?"

"I have a friend like that. We've been beachcombing all our lives. Walking and talking on the shore." They reach the stone jetty at the end of the beach. The tide is out and Rachel moves over the exposed rocks. "You're lucky to have Emily. And with email and cell phones, you'll stay in touch."

"Could I take a picture?" Summer asks.

"Here." Rachel lifts the camera strap over her head. "Do you know how to work it?"

"I think so." She lifts it to her eye and scans the area. Her blonde hair is braided and fine wisps escape and frame her face. Her feet are bare and she wears madras shorts and a pale yellow halter top, pure summer cool.

"There's a good one," she says from behind the camera.

A seagull perches on a nearly submerged rock. Rachel shows her how to control the depth of field, zoom in close, focus and shoot. "Snap a few pictures. Maybe you can use one in the Marine program."

Summer takes another shot. "Omigosh! Maybe they'll do marine photography. Wait till I tell Em. Do you mind if I take some more?"

She scrambles out over the rocky jetty, engrossed in the world a camera opens up for her. One without stepparents and new neighborhoods and schools and bored teenagers.

Rachel watches her find beach scenes, feeling like a concerned parent. The poor girl hitchhiked to the cottage sullen and unannounced. She already spent a day or two at the beach with her father, and they all had dinner together, but Rachel doesn't know her that well. So when Summer showed up at the cottage door, she did what any parent would do. She made her a grilled cheese sandwich before convincing her to walk on the beach. That part came so easy. Summer is definitely her father's daughter.

* * *

"It's a go," Tom says that evening. "Done deal, sweetheart. They accepted it."

Sara Beth cradles the cell phone tightly to her ear. This is *thee* call she's been waiting for, the one moment that's been crystal clear in her mind. Okay, for about twenty years, but still. A page just turned in her life.

"Say it again?"

"The house is ours, Sara. They've agreed to the price and to the contingency of our house selling."

"We can start packing?"

"Looks that way. Is the inventory done?"

She glances at the opened tin box of index cards. "I just need to double check some details." It is safe to imagine now. To mentally arrange the furniture in its new home in a Currier

& Ives location. She never dared to before, afraid she would jinx herself.

Melissa pulls into the carriage house driveway, her tires crunching over twigs. Sara Beth watches her sister and is bursting to tell her the news. "In here, Lissa!"

"Hey," Melissa says.

Sara Beth pulls another ladderback chair up alongside hers. "Here. Sit."

Melissa takes a seat cautiously. "Uh oh. What's going on?"

"We did it."

"You didn't."

"Uh huh."

"No way."

"Way." Sara Beth nods briskly.

"You bought the house?"

"We made a low offer, they countered higher this morning, we countered again and they signed off on it. You are now talking to the proud owner of Addison's as yet unnamed antique shop. And at the new Sara Beth, proprietor extraordinaire." She stands and curtsies.

"Well I'll be damned." Melissa looks around the room. "Tom came around?"

"We're both *really* trying. And once he saw the house as a significant home for a partner in the local law firm, you know, right off The Green in the historical district, he agreed. It's perfect for both of us."

"I'm so happy for you. So when's this all supposed to happen?"

"In my head, it's happening right now." She spins around. "I picture my shop set up with lots of crocheted doilies and small lamps on the furniture. Like this." She reaches past her index cards and pulls the chain on the brass desk lamp, then walks to the Shaker pine chest, plugs in the cord of a Steuben glass lamp and turns that on too. They cast a glow on the room. "See? Lamps give it warmth. And I'll have china dishes, and an old mantle clock on a pine shelf. One that chimes. So my clients can picture the furniture in their homes, with their lamps and knick-knacks. Oh, and, and lace curtains! Lots and lots of lace curtains on all the windows. For Mom. So that the sun always shines through."

"It sounds beautiful."

"It is. Well, it will be anyway. I wish Mom were here."

Melissa pulls a tissue from her purse and hands it to her. "Oh, she is. I can feel it."

All around Sara Beth, the deep walnut and mahogany browns and cherry reds shimmer. Tapestry upholstery and brass hinges add richness to the space. The formal paintings contrast with the whimsy of her china pieces.

Melissa picks up a small frame on her desk. "This is pretty."

It's Claude's dried flower chain, preserved on acid-free paper and custom mounted in an old gold-leaf frame. "Thanks. That one's mine. For decorating only. And the rest, well, I need a mover who specializes in antiques."

"You've got some valuable furniture under this roof. Has it been appraised?"

"Next week. The inventory is done and the appraisal is next. I'm bringing in a specialist."

"And how. He's got his work cut out for him."

"I've got a lot of information to help. I've been logging details and furniture history for weeks now." She walks through her space, hugging herself.

"Wow. All of a sudden this is happening so fast."

"I know. Listen." Sara Beth takes Melissa's hands in hers. "Come home with me! I can't think straight right now, I'm so excited. Tom's washing the car with Owen. Then we're taking the kids out for pizza. Bring Kevin and Chelsea."

"Are you sure?"

"Yes! I want to celebrate. Finally."

"Let's close up then. You done here?"

"Almost. I fed the cat and the inventory's set." The opened metal box on her desk overflows with cards and handwritten receipts and notes scribbled onto scraps of paper. "All I have to do is lock up."

She collects her daisy chain and her purse, switches off and carefully unplugs the Steuben glass lamp, then says goodnight to Slinky. "Let's go," she says, tucking the framed daisies into her satchel and triple locking the heavy carriage doors.

So now she has this: Reality, and it's as perfect as she knew it would be.

* * *

Subject: Good News!
From: Sara Beth
To: Elizabeth
Date: July 17 at 10:30 PM

Hey Mom,

It's late, but I just got in and wanted to tell you something. I've found a home for our antique shop! And that lace we bought? It'll be so perfect in the windows. So how's this for a name: I got the idea from my first Sotheby's piece, the white candlestand I told you about? It's circa 1765. That's what I'm going to call our shop, because it's where I began, with that piece, in New York that weekend. Circa 1765. Hope you like it. Miss you.

twenty-eight

SARA," LILLIAN SAYS FROM THE other side of the screen door. It isn't yet eight in the morning. "I know it's early, but do you have a few minutes?"

"Lillian? What's the matter?" Sara Beth asks, tightening her robe.

Tom comes up behind her and sees the Marches on the front step. His tie hangs loose around his collar, his top button still undone. He reaches around Sara and opens the door.

"Lillian. Edward. Come on in."

"Are you both okay?" Sara Beth asks.

"Yes, hon. We're fine."

"Edward," Tom says, shaking his hand. "What's going on?"

"Sara. Tom." Lillian takes a quick breath. "There's been an accident."

"Let's go into the kitchen," Tom says. "Please, after you," he motions to them and knots his tie as he goes. The kids, still in their pajamas, crowd behind him.

"Daddy, up!" Owen cries, his arms outstretched. "Up!"

"Katherine. Jen. Take Owen upstairs and get him dressed. And make your beds." He eyes the girls as his voice drops. "Stay upstairs until I call for you."

"Dad!" Jen insists. "Why can't I stay?"

"Because you're the oldest and I need you to be in charge of the others. Get going."

"Tom?" Sara Beth asks. You sense bad news, sometimes, and this is her way of asking if he knows it too, the way she does, how bad this is about to be.

"I'll put on more coffee. Why don't you set out some cups?"

Lillian sits beside Edward, holding his hand beneath the table while Sara Beth sets out china cups and saucers with silver spoons. Country roses edge the antique white china. She reaches for the pewter creamer and sugar bowl on the pine hutch beside the table. Lillian watches, a sad smile escaping in spite of what is to come because anyone can see this room is pure Sara Beth; the vintage china with a fine crack here and there, hinting at its pedigree. The dull glow of old pewter and a painted country hutch.

"Wait till the kids are settled upstairs," Sara Beth says as she lays out cloth napkins like this is normal. As though her guests are simply here on a social call. "I don't want to upset them."

Tom pours the coffee and they finally both sit with the Marches. "Okay then. Tell us about this accident." As the words come out, Sara Beth knows.

Lillian pours a splash of milk into her coffee. She stirs it lightly with the sterling spoon, taps it on the edge of the cup and sets it on her saucer. "I'm so sorry. There's really no easy way to say this."

"It's the carriage house, isn't it?" Sara Beth asks.

"There was a fire," Edward says quietly.

"What?" Tom pulls his chair in closer. "How bad?"

"We're so sorry," Lillian answers. "It's completely destroyed."

A silence changes the room. Pictures form in their minds, then are discarded with disbelief.

"Destroyed?" Tom asks. "What do you mean, destroyed?"

"It's gone. There's nothing left."

"Nothing?" Sara Beth's shaking her head no. Certainly, the fire only destroyed the carriage house. Somehow, her precious antiques are safe. "But the Fire Department, they got out my antiques, right?"

"Sara, dear. Your beautiful furniture," Lillian clasps her hands to her face with a gasp. "I'm sorry."

"When? How?" Tom asks.

"We're not really sure," Lillian begins. "There was a noise early this morning, after midnight. When I heard it, I ran to the window. It was the carriage house, the whole outside wall caving in under so much fire. The flames, oh my God, they were everywhere. We called for help right away, but it burned so fast. So fast! The Fire Department will investigate and find out more."

"My antiques? Everything?" Sara Beth watches Lillian closely for the slightest gentle look, the slightest smile or touch of reassurance.

"Well we can't get near the site because of hot spots. And some of the walls are barely standing. Some pieces may have survived, we don't know for sure."

"The fire trucks couldn't get there sooner?" Sara Beth asks.

"They got there in no time, but when the fire woke us, it was already extensive. We called right away, but in a matter of minutes … Oh, Sara, there wasn't much they could do with that old barn."

"Can anything be salvaged?" Tom asks. "Even a few pieces?"

"Possibly," Edward says. "But they sprayed all that water. It doesn't look promising."

Sara Beth pushes back her chair and stands. "I have to see it." She turns to Tom.

"Dad?" Jen is standing in the kitchen doorway.

"Jen. I told you to wait upstairs," Tom says.

"But Dad." Jen looks at Lillian and Edward. "What about Slinky?"

"Come here, dear," Lillian says. Jen moves beside her and Lillian takes her hands. "I don't think she could possibly have survived." Lillian brushes a wisp of hair from Jen's face. "But it all happened so quickly, I'm sure she didn't suffer."

"Maybe she escaped?" Jen's eyes fill with tears.

Sara Beth watches her daughter's heart break and it's all too much.

"Well, I could be wrong," Lillian says gently, "but I don't want you to get your hopes up. The heat, it was terrible. Even for the firefighters."

"Slinky died?" Jen doesn't seem to believe it. "She was just an innocent kitten."

"Tom," Sara Beth says, still standing. "I have to see for myself."

"You two go," Lillian and Edward say at the same time. "We'll stay here with the kids."

"Are you sure?" Tom is already standing.

"Yes, of course. Please drive carefully." Lillian reaches into her purse. "Take my house key. If you need to get inside, if you want to sit down, you feel free."

"Can I come?" Jen asks.

"It's too dangerous," Tom tells her.

"But will you look for the cat?"

Sara Beth hugs her daughter and kisses the top of her head. "We'll look everywhere, okay?" Until she sees the destruction with her own eyes, there has to be some sort of a mistake. Some sort of hope. So she has that now.

* * *

A police cruiser and the Fire Marshal's car prevent Tom from parking near the carriage house, but they're close enough to see.

"Oh God," Tom utters. Charred timber stands precariously. Black soot and ash carpet the floor and any furniture spared the flames' fury. The roof is gone, leaving jagged sections of the walls reaching skyward.

Sara Beth's hand reaches for his and he turns to her. "Sara." But there is a force to the destruction still, enough to pull his gaze back. "Maybe it's not as bad as it seems. Let's go check it out."

She shakes her head before turning away. "I've seen enough." She stares out her side window.

"That's Bob Hough over there, the Fire Marshal," Tom says. "I did the closing on his home last month. Let me see what I can find out." He sits for a moment with Sara Beth and with this monstrosity in front of them. "I'll be right back."

Bob Hough turns when he approaches. "Good to see you, Tom. Are you representing the March family?"

"No. I wish this was a business call. My wife and I leased the carriage house."

"No kidding," Bob says. "For storage?"

"Antiques. Sara Beth was about to open a shop in town."

"Now that's a damn shame. The guys fighting it last night mentioned furniture, but I had no idea."

"Looks like she lost almost everything."

Bob moves closer to what's left of the carriage house. Then he eyes Tom's summer suit, right down to his expensive leather shoes. "You game to go in there? Maybe we can salvage something."

"What are we waiting for?" Tom slips out of his suit jacket and drapes it on the fence post, rolling up his shirtsleeves. Anything he can find will only help Sara Beth, but somehow he knows it won't be enough.

Bob retrieves a couple pairs of heavy work gloves from his car. "That inside corner is more intact than the rest. Let's start there," he suggests. "Technically I'm not supposed to do this. There could still be some live spots. So be real careful."

The police officer joins them, and Tom glances over his shoulder willing Sara Beth to stay in the car. Because walking on her pieces of charred mahogany, cherry and oak is almost enough to do him in.

* * *

By the time the fire trucks got through the winding curves of Old Willow Road, only a scorched skeleton stood, illuminated by tall dancing flames inside. They brought to eerie life the antiques they consumed, the woods' twisting and turning shadows writhing like they were alive in the melting heat.

Sara Beth sees this. She sees it happening behind her closed eyes, knowing while she reached out to her mother online, sent her words, while she slept, this evil arrived.

The emptiness inside her is huge and she has to breathe great, slow breaths to fill it. It feels the same as the day her mother died, the way her lungs won't fill. She thinks back to the little Morris chair she found in the carriage house on her birthday, from her mother. All of this, every bit of it, started with an antique chair she sat in nearly forty years ago.

Art is a lie that helps us to understand the truth. So Picasso thinks art's a lie? Everything's a lie. Art, hope, and it all lets you see the truth. There is only unhappiness. You can run away, you can sit here in the country, and it's there with you.

She loses sight of the men inside until Tom backs out, bent over. He and Bob are carrying something. They set a mahogany lowboy down near the house. Using his glove, Tom brushes a film of soot from the wood. After a close inspection, he turns and gives Sara Beth the thumbs up. He and Bob hurry back inside then, nearly colliding with the officer carrying a piecrust tip table. He sets it down beside the lowboy and Sara Beth gets out of the car. Nothing more could have survived that fire. She leans against the car and watches.

The men are three magicians pulling rabbits from a tall, black, charred top hat. The process creeps along, slowed by dangerous debris in an unstable structure, but she recognizes each blackened piece.

And what she has left now is this: The estate sales and auctions from which she found her collection. The bidding and price dickering ring in her mind. Certain auctioneers came to know her and called her when they found something she'd like. There were Saturday tag sales she hunted with Owen, finding pretty candlesticks in the warm spring sunlight, his little hand in hers. She studied the classifieds, narrowing down her furniture choices before she made the phone calls. Weeks and months passed, adding to the collection her mother began. Years of knowledge. Even the sunny weekends tag saling on country outings with Mom decades ago, brushing the dust off tables and chairs, her mother holding a china plate up to the sunlight, lowering it for Sara to see.

twenty-nine

RACHEL PUSHES ASIDE HER SCRAMBLED eggs and sips her coffee. "It's only Thursday. If you want to, have Summer come down early, without Emily."

"You think that'll stop this rebelling she's going through?"

"I don't know. Maybe it's not my place to say so, but I think you have something to do with her acting out."

"Me?" He pulls over her plate and finishes her eggs, scooping them on a piece of toast.

"You're so overprotective with her. She has no breathing space. I mean, she said you wouldn't even let her apply to the Marine Studies program."

"That's bullshit."

"Is it? You'd let her go out to sea in a vessel? Like she said, what if the water gets choppy?"

"She said that?"

Rachel nods. "I know you think you're protecting her, but you're driving her away. You have to be careful."

Michael stands and looks out the window, his arms crossed in front of him. He inhales deeply. "I'm trying. But I don't know if anyone really knows where I'm coming from."

"I think we do, particularly your daughter. Maybe she'd rather see you deal with your memory instead of using this control stuff to keep it buried."

At that, he turns and eyes her. Rachel knows that if this is going to work between them, she has to be able to say what's on her mind. "You said it's a protection for you. You keep it between you and the memory. Well your hypervigilance is standing between you and people you love now, too. You've got to face that night, Michael, or you'll lose people because of it."

"I'm trying," he says, his voice rising. She hears the anger and knows it's not really because of her. "I'm in therapy, I'm talking it out, but it takes time. And that kind of felt like a threat, that shit about losing people."

"It's not a threat. It's a wake-up call. I talked to your daughter. She needs more time with *you*, not time with your vigilance."

"Rachel. One minute changed my life. Do you understand that? Really? I killed a man. Okay? And I never thought that would be me. We don't think things will happen, but they do. And it's a goddamn nightmare, Rachel. So if I can do anything to stop another horrible minute, I have to do it."

"But," she argues, "you're losing good minutes in the process. Beautiful minutes. If I leave tonight, your daughter will have a few extra days of those good minutes with you."

"Oh no. It's not only my daughter I'm worried about losing. It's you, too."

"Me?"

"Yes. You have a very full life back in Addison. I know that." He sits beside her and picks up his coffee. "That's why I'm worried."

"Because of where I live?"

"That's right. I know I'm still dealing with issues, and I know damn well that you can walk away from all that crap, if you want to. Your life's waiting for you in another state."

"I'm not walking away, that's not what I meant about losing people."

"Listen. I've only got two days with you before you're gone again." He pauses, and the cottage suddenly changes. So does the summer. It is palpable. The sea grows deeper. The heat more intense. Thoughts more serious. Michael hasn't shaved, so whiskers shade his face.

"Remember that day last month," he finally asks, "when I showed up on your doorstep?"

"Sure. The first day of summer."

"And we talked about seeing if this relationship could work. We thought we'd take the summer and see what develops."

"I remember." She picks up her coffee.

"As of Saturday, you'll leave here for more than a week while my daughter's here. And by the time I see you again, it'll be August."

"We don't have to rush anything, we'll still have a few weeks of summer left."

"That's running out of time. And as much as I'd love to imagine you coming to New York until Labor Day, you've got to be in Connecticut and set up your classroom, your class plans." He takes a deep breath. "You've spoiled me. I don't like the thought of you not here."

"I spoiled you? Michael. I've had you and this amazing beach and this amazing cottage all summer." She reaches out and takes his hand. "And you know how I feel about a beach cottage."

"Heaven. I know."

"It is. So let's not think about leaving. I'd rather imagine this going on forever."

He leans forward and folds her hands in his. "I'm not *imagining* anything. It's too risky. I don't want to lose my daughter and I don't want to lose you. Both thoughts really scare me. You call me spontaneous, but I'm really not. I want a plan, Rachel. I want us to work." He leans closer, lowering his voice. "I've got two days before you leave again. And I intend to make them unmistakably *real*, Rachel DeMartino. To convince you to come back for good."

He moves his hands to her face and pulls her into a long kiss, half rising from his seat, his mouth moving over hers, very unmistakably real.

"Michael?" she asks, touching his unshaven cheek.

He frames her face for a long moment while conspiring something, she can see it behind his serious eyes, then stands and gets the coffee pot, distracted with his thoughts while refilling their cups. "Finish your coffee, and trust me. We've got plans that I just can't change."

"Plans?"

Michael finishes his black coffee. "Definite plans."

* * *

After breakfast, Rachel waters the petunias and geraniums in the flower boxes, then sits on the front step reading her book. A jogger runs past, the sun gets warm. Michael's rattling bags and bumping things around in the truck bed, and it's driving her nuts, he just knows it.

"Are we going somewhere?" she calls over her shoulder for the second time, keeping a finger on her page.

"No. And stop looking!" he calls back. Finally he walks down the driveway, whistling casually. He's wearing cargo shorts with lots of pockets, a black T-shirt, his Yankees hat on backwards and aviators. Old leather boat shoes are on his sockless feet. One hand holds two cheap fishing nets, the other a large green plastic sand pail. Stuffed into the pail is a bag of bait. Stuffed into his cargo pockets are the crabbing line and extra sinkers. "Come on," he says. "Tide's out. Best time for crabbing."

"Crabbing?" Rachel hesitantly grabs the straw cowboy hat from the porch. They walk down the beach road, he weighted down with crabbing gear, she dressed in her clam diggers and cowboy hat, taking the fishing nets from him.

At the rock jetty on the end of the beach, boulders grow from the edge of the sea like weeds and a couple of seagulls perch there, waiting for them to turn their backs on the bait bag. The deep green water laps in a lazy reach for the rocks.

Rachel inhales deeply, breathing the scent of seaweed and salt, periwinkle snails and barnacles. When she leans up against the side of a warm boulder and clips a hunk of fried chicken onto her crabbing line, Michael pulls himself up onto the same boulder and breaks open his bait mussels. The sun rises higher and he drops his line into the water near a cluster of submerged rocks. Rachel chooses a spot further out. The beauty of crabbing is how you can close your eyes and take the sun on your face, or how sweet memories rise as you stare into the water. She's doing this, he knows it by the way she jumps when something tugs on her line, squinting to see through a clump of seaweed. A fiddler crab dangles by one claw from the chicken bait.

"Omigosh!" she exclaims, glancing around quickly for the bucket.

Michael swoops in with the fishing net and scoops up the crab. "Here," he says, handing her the big green bucket, which she dips into a wave and fills with salt water. He flips the crab out of the net into the bucket. And so the morning goes, some crabs steal the bait, some drop off the lines before they can net them, and others end up in the pail.

What Michael loves about crabbing is that pretty much you only talk crabbing, exclaiming under your breath that you've spotted one, tallying up the catch, murmuring words of encouragement to a stubborn hidden crab. And he talks to himself, to get a grip, to stop being vigilant. That self-talk therapy he's been instructed in. He uses the net to catch a tiny eel and a few minnows to add to the pail.

"What are we going to do with them?" Rachel asks, brushing a wisp of hair from her face. The bottoms of her clam diggers are wet from wading in the tide coming in now. They look in the pail where seven or eight crabs scurry, the eel floating low, off to the side.

"Lunch?" Michael suggests.

She pulls off her straw hat and squints up at him. "You're going to cook them?"

He takes the pail and gently tips the contents back into Long Island Sound, near the rocks. "Come on," he reaches for her hand. "I'll make you a ham sandwich." He swings the nets over his shoulder, she stuffs the crabbing lines into the empty pail and they walk at the water's edge, heading back to the cottage.

* * *

After lunch, Rachel separates the edge pieces from a jigsaw puzzle box Michael set on the porch table. She leans over, intent on pressing together the pieces. Outside, the mid-day heat settles. "Why don't you change into your bathing suit?" he asks. "I'll bring the umbrella down to the beach and meet you back here in a while."

She does, slipping into a black tankini and filling a canvas tote with sunscreen and visors and her sketch pad. She pulls her hair into a messy bun, folds the local newspaper into thirds and slides it into a side pocket, then throws in a couple peaches. And doing all that, she sees it. The flashlight in each room, the new fire extinguisher, the shrubs trimmed back from the cottage so prowlers can't hide, his obsession with sitting with his back to the wall in public places, his covering the windows at night. Two cell phones. His living in a way of "just in case." And she wonders if this is what she wants, this constant monitoring for safety. This inability to ease up; this inability to get out of one night. It's not good.

When Michael returns, he waits on the front porch, perspiration lining his forehead. "It's hot on the beach. You'll need your sandals."

But *that* she loves about him. Loving concern, the way he worries about little things like the sand burning her feet. How do you distinguish between the two, obsession and care?

She hikes the nautical tote over her shoulder, Michael carries two sand chairs and they walk side-by-side in the heat of the day. There's a simplicity here she likes: footsteps gritty with sand on the beach road, bees bumbling a little slower, green lawns giving way to mid-summer brown, hushed cottages, the sun high in the sky.

"Where you headed?" Rachel asks when he takes a left through the parking lot where he should turn right. "Aren't we set up on the other end of the beach?"

He turns back to her. "Any certified beach bum knows this is the way to the ice cream truck."

Okay. Something's going on here, but she's not sure what. "Of course," she says. "What was I thinking?"

They stand in line watching kids hop from one burning foot to the other on the hot pavement. Bathing suits drip, wet hair lays flipped back, dollar bills hang limp with salt water as the kids study the menu pictured on the side of the truck.

"What do you want?" Michael asks.

"Well." She looks at the pictures on the menu. "Strawberry Crunch Bar. How about you?"

"Rocky Road Sundae."

In the center of the boardwalk stretching along the beach, a wooden canopy provides shade from the glaring sun. Usually grandmothers and hot babies in strollers, their equally hot mothers rolling the sandy wheels back and forth, line the shade. But on days like today, everybody crowds under. They find a seat and Michael stands facing the marina, one foot up on the seat, his elbow resting on the top plank, working on the fudge and nut encrusted sundae. He surveys the boats below in the boat basin.

"Would you ever want a boat?" he asks.

"I'm not really into that." Her hand is cupped beneath the dripping vanilla ice cream.

"Me neither. But if you had to pick, what boat would you choose?"

Many of the slips are empty on a hot day like this, so the selection is meager. She decides on a white cabin cruiser. "It's small and sleek, with that shiny chrome. I'll bet it runs smooth."

Michael considers her choice. "Not bad. But I'd pick that one," he says, pointing in the opposite direction.

"Which one?"

"The green one." Her gaze moves past a Boston Whaler to an old wooden fishing boat with flat wood plank seats framing the back end, a higher post for the captain in the center.

"A fishing boat?" She looks up at Mr. New York City with his dark hair curling out of his Yankees cap, his face touched by scars and a shadow of a beard, his eyes street-wise. "You?"

"I'd find a little cove," he admits. She hears something, a realization that he has to change, to contemplate his stress disorder, like he might on that old boat, "throw out the anchor, set out my fishing line, lay cushions down on those planks in the back and take a nap under the sun. Hidden in the marsh grasses. When I woke up, I'd tell everybody about the one that got away."

"Oh." She considers his boat and pictures him sleeping on the water, his Yankees cap pulled over his face. "Maybe I'd sell my boat if you'd take me for a ride on yours, Skipper."

"We'll see," he says, picking up the two sand chairs. "Gilligan."

They near the end of the boardwalk and step onto the sand. "Is that our umbrella there?" She points to the green and yellow striped umbrella at the water's edge. "The one with the tubes around it?" Two inflated beach tubes, one metallic blue, the other electric pink, encircle the umbrella pole.

"That's right."

She smiles. Which she gets the feeling is fully his intention.

They open the sand chairs in front of the umbrella and Rachel gently massages sunscreen onto Michael's shoulder. Though five years have passed, the skin there still seems tender. Maybe it always will. Or should, she thinks, keeping her touch soft. Michael takes her hand in his and they settle in their low chairs. Sitting at the water's edge, the sun's hot rays pulse. Eventually he pulls off his cap.

"Race you?" He looks from her to the water.

"Sure." She takes off her sunglasses.

"Do you need a head start?"

"A head start?" she begins saying, which gives him enough time to jump from his seat and run into the water, Rachel close on his heels, splashing him when he breaks through the water's surface.

"Hey," he laughs, running his hand through his wet hair.

And they never leave the water the entire afternoon. Sitting back in their tubes, the current carries them along the length of the beach, their relaxed arms dipping into the water, their feet submerged.

Rachel knows what he is giving her: One of those days that you recall for years to come, during really hot summers, growing old together. This crystal day that shines forever. At times, Michael reaches over and pulls her a little closer, the two tubes gently bumping close, then separating.

"This is better than my overstuffed recliner." His eyes are closed when he says it.

"Any beach bum knows that," she agrees after a few moments, giving herself a slow spin. "I think it has something to do with the surroundings."

"Probably," he finally adds, stealing a look at her from behind his aviators.

Every minute passes in such a way that Rachel finally asks him if this perfect day can actually be his secret plan.

"You ask too many questions."

For dinner, he takes her to a local seaside joint where they carry cardboard pails of clams and red and white checked trays of French fries outside to stone tables overlooking saltwater tributaries running through a lagoon. They swap bellies for strips, share a cup of tartar sauce, count herons and kingfishers.

Afterward, he gets a Frisbee from the pickup truck. Rachel sidles up behind him, slipping her arms around his waist. "What else is hidden in there?"

"Never you mind," he tells her as he turns and kisses her. "Just never mind." He hands her the Frisbee then, and walks her back to the beach.

* * *

Rachel always thought of herself as an independent thinker. She prides herself on being not easily swayed, confident in her convictions. But the next day, she wakes up thinking that if indoctrination is this life, these two days, she'll gladly follow Michael's ideology. He walks into the room showered and dressed in his swimsuit, untucked navy top, boat shoes, and two cups of coffee. Rachel sits up in her nightshirt and props the pillow behind her.

"Good morning," Michael says. "Sleep well?"

"Yes." She gladly takes the coffee from him. "How about you?"

He sits alongside her facing the far window. "Great."

She cups her lighthouse coffee mug. "You're up early."

"Couldn't sleep. Too perfect of a morning. I went for a run."

A run. This is new, and she knows it's part of his therapy, exercise instead of worry. She tastes her coffee, then inhales deeply. It smells so comforting, coffee grounds, the salt air, summer. "Let me shower," she says, throwing back the sheet and swinging her legs over the bed. "Then I'll make French toast."

"Sounds good."

She wraps her robe loosely and leaves the room, smiling because he definitely has something up his sleeve. Some summertime, beach, cottage doctrine. It drives her crazy, wondering how else he plans to win, or steal, or borrow her heart with his own personal ideology. At the same time, she wonders about his silent, unspoken efforts to change, if they'll work, or if he'll tire of them and stop.

Their day takes serious shape after a second helping of French toast. Rachel hears snipping noises while drying the dishes and sees him setting small pieces of rag on the Newport table beside the couch before taking it all out to his truck. Finally, when she's back to the jigsaw puzzle, he turns the corner with his Yankees cap pulled low, carrying a big black bat kite in one hand, its wide orange eyes peering skyward. The kite tail is made out of the rag strips, hanging limp. His other hand grips a large spool of string.

On the beach, she runs with the kite while Michael manipulates the string, unwinding it as the bat climbs into the pale morning sky. Hundreds of feet above, it pulls and dips in the air currents. Occasionally Michael passes the spool over to a curious onlooker, letting them wind it in a little, then set it free, like reeling in a fish. Late morning, they pull the kite carefully in as it swoops and dive-bombs in its descent, then spend the rest of the day lazy on the beach, playing cards, reading, the waves and surrounding voices conducive to half-dozing.

But it is the shimmering summer heat which helps cast Michael's spell. In the warm sunlight, veils of responsibility and worry and schedules all drop off. Strangers nod at them and say hello. In the heat of the afternoon, having an ice cream on the boardwalk, a group of teenaged girls watches them from their blanket, laying flat on their sleek, tanned stomachs, propped on elbows. Wishing only this for themselves some day. Only having a great guy and an ice cream and the summer beach in their lives.

Rachel and Michael make it seem like enough.

* * *

After a grilled steak dinner with salad and corn-on-the-cob, Michael pulls two paddles out of his trunk. The day winds down as he leads Rachel on a well-worn path that curves behind a row of cottages down to a lagoon. Anchored in a bend, floating alongside the banks of marsh grass, she sees the rowboat.

"You have a boat?" Rachel asks as Michael helps her in. The rowboat is old, painted white with a brick red bottom. Its benches are unpainted, the color of beached driftwood.

"No." He lifts the oars, the salt water dripping, then dips them again. "I have connections."

Long Island Sound feeds the lagoon, filling it with gently flowing tidal tributaries. They pass a great blue heron standing statuesque along the banks. Schools of minnows idle in place before darting off in another direction. Kingfishers swoop and another heron flaps its mighty wings over head. They paddle into the center of the lagoon, where the water spreads out lakelike, the green grasses a velvet carpet curling through the pool. Michael drops anchor and pulls chilled wine from a small cooler, along with two glasses.

"A toast," he says, handing Rachel her glass. "To you, sweetheart."

She touches her glass to his, then listens to his stories about Anchor Beach. Of how it hasn't changed in the past twenty years. The charm of the old cottages grows simply more beguiling, the weathered boardwalk more inviting, the sea more mysterious. Anchor Beach saved him the summer after he'd been shot. He spent a lot of time here, in between bouts of serious drinking and finding bar fights. But in the end, it became simply him and the beach, considering a new job with Maggie.

"What if you ever want to stop patrolling?" she asks. "When you're older, you know? You already have an Associate's Degree, two years from a Bachelor's."

"Why would I want to stop? I love what I do."

"I'm just saying. In ten years, what if it gets difficult riding a horse every day? Don't you at least want options?"

"Options? I make my own. And besides, I could never sit in class with a bunch of twenty-year-olds. And there's tuition, and time commitment."

"Wouldn't the department pay?"

"Rachel, we already discussed this, and my answer is still no. I have no intention of going back to school."

"And I'm not trying to push you. But listen, you always worry about when Joe and Lena sell the deli. What if you wanted to take it over? Shouldn't you have a business degree?"

Michael looks long at her. "What is this really about, Rachel? Do you need a pedigree?"

"How can you say that? I'm worried about you. I've heard all your talk about your grandfather, and Pop. Your life is rich with story and I don't want you to lose it. Sometimes it seems like this place you're at right now overshadows everything else."

"This place. Meaning that I'm still dealing with a violent day in my life."

"Yes. And maybe a change would be good."

"Listen, you're right. I love what my family stands for. They really were a part of building a great city. And I used to feel that I was honoring them somehow, keeping an eye on their efforts while I patrolled." He lifts the oars and paddles silently through a bend surrounded by tall marsh grasses. "And then I screwed up."

"What? Screwed up?"

"No one else pulled that trigger. Only me. And I'm not sure Pop would understand that decision. So I've tarnished his name and now I'm trying my best to fix that. To get back out there and restore myself on his streets. To get back into good graces."

"Michael, first of all, he's gone. And you never fell out of grace. How can you think that?"

"I'm talking about Summer's grace, about what kind of *rich story* I'm living for my own daughter, for God's sake. One of a murderer who turns his back on the experience, and on everything he stands for? That's not me, and I think you know it. So stop asking." He looks long at her and says nothing more. He's going to stay exactly where he's at.

Rachel looks away, toward the distant Sound and the evening horizon. Michael knows there's something about that place where sea and sky meet, and all that passes in front of it on shore. Time and life and sadness and clarity. There's more to the beach than Rachel's ideal of star-wishing. There's truth, and the beauty and pain that comes with it. That's where she is, right now. In that pure, difficult place.

"What does Maggie do while you're on vacation?" she finally asks, not looking at him.

He pauses, then dips the paddles slowly back in the water. "She is too. The hostlers groom her and put her out in the corral behind the stable in the afternoons. That's her vacation: standing in the sun, kicking up her feet a little bit. Maybe rolling on the ground."

She doesn't respond and he starts to row back, dipping the oars again, before nightfall. The sky shades to a royal violet in the east. The birds quiet, the insects chirp louder.

But the thought doesn't leave him. She wanted more. Education. Possibility. And he gave her his version of it. As he rows, he never stops watching Rachel. She sits with her knees drawn up and hugged close, gazing at the sky. She is barefoot, wearing khaki Bermudas and her black ribbed tank, a gold chain around her neck.

For all he is, this is who she is. She'll never stop searching for the first star. He can tell when she spots it, a light glimmer against the darkening horizon. She simply closes her eyes for a moment, then looks out at Long Island Sound beyond the lagoon.

And he knows exactly what he has to do. An idea takes hold, but will take a few weeks to sort out. He can do no less for her.

The hours pass in the cottage with Rachel curled up with a book on the porch, but not turning the pages all that often. Her thoughts are so far away and he's worried he hurt her somehow. Or lost her. So late that evening, just past eleven-thirty, he checks the daily tide chart clipped to the refrigerator then hands Rachel her sweatshirt.

"I want to show you something," he says.

"Really, Michael. It's late. I'd rather stay in."

He holds the front porch door opened for a long moment, then walks out alone. The beach road is dark now, the cottages quiet and the night air damp from the sea. It's amazing how quickly the damp rises with the setting sun.

The beach is deserted, with two lights on either end of the boardwalk casting a misty glow. Small waves lap lazy at the shore. There is no other sound at this late hour as he takes a seat facing the sea, the boat basin behind him.

The tide is out and just beginning to turn. It's a moment about the earth, the sea and the moon. The surface water in the boat basin stills while the currents below gently curve onto themselves, reversing. It makes barely enough of an invisible pull to shift the docked boats in their slips. And at the turning of the tide, in the dark, he waits to hear the boat talk, without the distracting noises of day, and people, and wind.

You can't help but be deeply aware of the sea, and the stars, as you only listen at midnight. You're somehow more alive with that awareness of something ancient below the water, that ceaseless rhythm. He turns to hear more closely the boats creaking against the pilings and posts to which they are secured.

A school of minnows ruffles the dark water. They splash up through the surface, no doubt with a large bluefish coming up behind them, on the hunt.

thirty

SATURDAY MORNING ARRIVES. THE LINGERING tension makes it feel like they are awaiting test results. The two days need to be processed.

Michael leans down into her opened car window. "Are you sure you should be driving with those flip-flops on? It's a long trip."

"Michael."

"Okay, sorry. Drive safely, then," he says. "And I'm saying that because I love you."

Her hand reaches up and touches his still-unshaven face. "Me too."

He takes her hand and kisses it, feeling as though she's just saying that to get out quickly. "I'm sorry if I hurt you somehow. I didn't mean to."

"I know." She pulls her hand back. "Have a good week with your daughter."

"Call me when you get home." He backs away from the car. "See you next Monday?"

"No, that won't work for me. I've got teacher's orientation that Thursday, so I'm not sure yet when I'll be back."

He steps further away as she backs out of the driveway, then motions for her to stop.

"Wait, I forgot something." He reaches into his cargo pocket and pulls out a small wrapped box.

"What's this?" she asks.

"Just a little something. A nice-day present. From me, to you. Wait till you get home to open it."

Rachel rides the ferry home feeling a sea breeze skim off Long Island Sound. Michael had just tried giving her forty-eight hours of her heaven. No one had ever done anything as thoughtful, and somehow her questions soured it all. She opens his present while looking out at the water, touched more than she'd have thought possible by the diamond studded journey necklace. She lifts the gold chain from the velvet box and clasps it on her neck. He wants her along on his journey. She calls and leaves him a quick voicemail. "Hey Skipper," she says softly. "I'm starting to feel more like Ginger Grant, now. Thanks."

Back on the Connecticut highways, it all starts to feel dreamlike as the beach diminishes behind her, the boats creaking, the seagulls crying, the waves breaking. During the past two days, Michael tried to show her there is nothing to be afraid of. She rounded forty and he was waiting. Glancing in the rear-view mirror, she knows he's been waiting since May when she stopped him from leaving Joe's deli at the last possible second. Since tying bowling shoes and rolling balls and knocking down pins.

But pulling into her driveway, there's more doubt about leaving here. She feels it now that she's alone: How compulsive is Michael's vigilance, a caution that stems from not believing in your own safety? There will always be triggers, but can he really lessen his worry? How do you know what's merely someone's way of loving? Carl loved her and always wanted her safe, too. And for a moment, she wishes Carl were still here and that Michael's demons hadn't found her life too.

She carries in her bags, drops the mail on the kitchen table and opens the windows. A week stretches before her to tidy up the house, weed the garden and mow the lawn.

There is a message on her answering machine. A reporter with the *Addison Weekly* picked up a fire call on his scanner and asks if she can get to Old Willow Road for the photo op. He apologizes for the early hour, but a fire of this scope is big news in sleepy Addison. He gives the address quickly, a garage of some sort going up in flames.

Suddenly there is too much to do. The kettle on the stove whistles. She pours an instant coffee and pulls the telephone book from the hall closet to compare addresses. "March, March." She passes the page twice before finding the name and seeing if the address matches.

The truth of it all makes her grab the phone to call the reporter back.

* * *

Sara Beth scrubs every speck of grease from the stovetop, bent over the burner grates and control knobs, reaching into the oven walls. Her gloves are soiled with cleanser and grit, her hair tied back beneath a bandana, her breath short as she scours away every threat.

If she'd only been attentive, she thinks, scrubbing endlessly. If she'd only installed an alarm in the carriage house, or a sprinkler system. If she'd only, if she'd only, if only.

So now Sara Beth makes herself aware. She knows that in the United States, home fires take a life on average once every three hours. Kitchens are the most prevalent origin for home fires and cause the highest percentage of home fire injuries.

No more fires, no more emergencies. First came the trip to Cooper Hardware to buy fresh batteries for the smoke alarms and three additional alarms. No more chances. She bought fire escape ladders for each upstairs bedroom, something they'd always meant to do. Now, done. Yesterday she installed the new heavy-duty fireplace screen in front of the living room fireplace. No sparks could jump through that finely knit mesh. As if she can look into a fireplace and ever see anything good, anything comforting.

And every precaution breeds new threats, new sparks she imagines jumping from a heater or furnace or wick or stovetop or outlet, sparks jumping one step ahead of her, taunting her.

Like candles, there are so many candles in the house! Dozens of votives in the dining room alone, where they love to scatter them on the table for formal dinners.

And the potholders, near the stove. She takes them off the hook and shoves them deep in a drawer as she's scouring off specks of stove grease.

While she's at it, her mind spins a fire escape plan. A drill. They'll schedule drills, even during the night, and practice until all the kids have it memorized, with different variables, where the fire is, alternate escapes, testing doors for heat, learning to crawl, Owen, checkpoints.

Part of that drill is that all the windows need to open easily in case someone has to climb out, if smoke is pouring into a bedroom from beneath the door. Towels, too, she can't forget towels to stuff around the bottoms of the doors. So once the stove is cleaned, starting downstairs she unlocks and opens each window, moving through the kitchen, living room, family room, upstairs in the bedrooms, checking for ones that stick. She sprays a little oil and slides the window opened and closed repeatedly, greasing the tracks. Then she goes through the entire house again, starting downstairs and working her way through, double checking every window, just in case.

Afterward she pulls an armful of towels from the linen closet, dropping a couple in each room. They can be stored in a drawer, or beneath the beds, where they can be grabbed and stuffed into spaces where smoke gets in. Smoke spreads faster than fire. Smoke kills. They need some type of fire box, something to hold the ladders, towels, flashlights.

And the electrical outlets. Are any overloaded? Any wires frayed? She goes through each room, touching every outlet for warmth or anything out of order. Her hand cups each cord, sliding up to the stereo or clock radio or lamp.

A lamp's light bulb can burn between two hundred twelve and nearly six hundred degrees. And cotton burns at four hundred eighty-two. She's teaching herself. And in the girls' closet, a pile of clothes towers on a shelf precariously close to a bare bulb fixture. She heaves the tower of clothes onto a bed.

A bed that can cause a fire. The majority of furniture fires involve upholstery or bedding. Jen's bed is too close to the radiator. If cotton burns at four hundred eighty-two degrees, who knows what a cotton dust ruffle might heat up to, resting against a winter radiator. So she takes the headboard first and drags the bed away, then the foot, then the headboard, then the foot again until the bed is about four feet from the wall. She'll have to rearrange the whole room now, moving Kat's bed to a different angle, shifting one of the dressers to the other side. Jen wanted to Feng Shui anyway. They'll do cool colors, blues and greens. Because there's no other way. She has to keep them all safe. And so she pulls out the drawers from Kat's dresser, sets them on her bed, and begins shoving the dresser, out of breath, a little at a time, across the room.

* * *

Tom walks into the house and sets down the grocery bags, looking up at the ceiling when the loud scraping noise comes again. And again. Rhythmically, but insistently.

"Juice, Daddy. Juice!"

He pulls a juicebox from the refrigerator and pushes the straw in, keeping an ear tuned to upstairs.

"Here you go, guy. Have a seat." Owen kneels on a chair at the kitchen table while Tom starts unpacking, putting the gallon of milk in the fridge, setting the ketchup and salad dressing on the counter. But he stops then, noticing the microwave oven pulled out from the corner, leaving a full eight inches of clearance behind it. The toaster's been repositioned too. And rubber gloves lie in the sink with wet sponges and dirty rags.

So something's going on that has him scan the room. That's when he sees bags of garbage shoved beneath the breakfast bar. One is filled with candles, votives and pillars and tapers, and on the top, two small packages of birthday candles. The other is stuffed with two electric blankets, balled up and shoved in. There's a bag of newspapers and magazines, along with pieces of mail and the kids' artwork.

And the scraping noise keeps coming. So he picks up Owen and first looks into the living room, noting the new fireplace screen. The dining room seems the same except for the lack of candles in the brass candlestick holders on the table and the empty glass votives in the hutch.

With a particularly loud bang coming from a bedroom above them, Owen looks up and holds on tight.

"Let's go see what Mommy's doing, okay guy?"

Owen keeps his eyes riveted on the ceiling and Tom decides, climbing the stairs, it's better to leave him in his crib until he scopes out the situation.

"Here you go," he says, handing him a couple books and a stuffed bear. "Daddy will be right back. You wait for me, okay?"

When his son starts to whine, Tom raises his finger to his mouth. "Shhh. I'll go get Mommy. Shhhh."

He leaves Owen standing in his crib and goes to Jen and Kat's room, slowly pushing open the door. Sara Beth's back is to him as she gets behind a dresser and heaves it a few feet, then moves to the other side and gives another shove. The room is a disaster, furniture randomly moved everywhere, piles of clothes falling off the beds, Jen's stereo haphazardly sitting unplugged on a desk chair, curtains thrown up over the curtain rods.

"Sara," he says, gently taking her arm, which she wrenches away.

"Don't!" she warns, gasping a deep breath. Her hair hangs, clinging to her perspiring face, her hands are covered with oil and dirt, her clothes soiled and messy. Suddenly she goes for the head of Jen's bed and tugs it, scraping the bed along the floor, nearly tripping on a sweater tangled at her feet.

Tom doesn't say another word. He knows, watching Sara Beth's devastation, that this isn't about the fire. It took this long, this much time, for her to react to her loss. Finally, it's for her mother. He walks up behind her and enfolds her, wrapping his arms around her tightly, locking her in his embrace, pressing against her back, tipping his head down over her shoulder, closing his eyes and resisting with all he's got when she struggles fiercely, to break free.

"It's your fault," she cries. "It's your fault she died."

"What?" Tom asks, not loosening his hold. "What are you talking about?"

"Your car," she whispers. "Your tank was empty, you were running late." She inhales as though she can't get air. "You had to go to court later."

Tom releases her from his grip and turns her to face him. "And I drove your car so you could fill my tank and swap cars with me at work."

"When I was supposed to meet my mother, Tom. We had plans that morning, and you didn't care. You said my plans could wait, that you really needed your car to go to court. That Mom would wait for me. *What difference does an hour make?* Those were your exact words."

And he knows then. He looks around the devastated room in which they stand; it is the devastation she lives. It is the hour the aneurysm struck.

* * *

It's impossible to get Sara Beth on her cell, so Rachel calls their home on Sunday and gets Tom. They meet at the window booth at Whole Latte Life. He sits across from her, his hair freshly shorn in that buzz cut he won't part with. She sees he's still not used to the short trim, running his hand back through it as though it were longer.

"She's tormented by it," he says. "If she'd gotten to her mother's earlier, she thinks she could've saved her. Called for help before it was too late."

"So in her mind, it was your fault. For having her run around with the cars."

Tom looks out the window, not answering.

"You couldn't have known though. It was just bad timing."

"What if she's right?"

"Tom. She had a brain aneurysm. Once they strike …"

"I know, Rachel. I've tried telling her that."

"Well tell me about the fire. How did it all happen?"

"We don't know what started it yet. How much do you know?"

"Only what the paper told me. I tried calling Sara Beth, but she's not picking up."

"No." Outside on The Green, the geranium blossoms hang heavy and red, the spikes tall behind them. "She won't talk to anyone right now."

"It's no wonder."

"I checked with her doctor. He's concerned, especially with this coming so soon after the episode in New York."

"Can we do anything for her?"

"He says to really listen to her. Be supportive, sympathetic, you know, all that stuff. But she's completely shut down."

"Not good, Tom."

"No. Did you hear about our house?" The warmth outside makes its way through the window and he perspires, his T-shirt damp.

The waitress brings their coffees and Tom tells her about their futile hunt for a shop location. The town storefronts are booked solid. Addison is that kind of town, brimming with cottage industry shops: boutiques filled with sachets and twig wreaths and handmade birdhouses, nurseries blossoming with flats of flowers and baby vegetables, farmstands lined with native produce and honey, and the bookstore and ice cream parlor and vintage bridal shop.

"Tourists drive miles to stroll around this Green. I see them all the time, sitting at the benches, never leaving without a keepsake. That's why we were sure her antique shop would do well. So we bought the big, old house. It seemed like the right choice with that two-room addition for her antiques, and it's historical itself. The ambiance couldn't be better." He looks outside in the direction of the house while his fingers tightly pleat a napkin.

"I had no idea you got the house. Nothing survived the fire? A few pieces she could start up with?"

"Not enough to matter. A dozen or so pieces in the back. Some remnants of tables and chairs if you poke through the ash, but the rest is gone."

"Was it insured?"

Tom shakes his head. "Antiques are tough. Their value changes, depending on different variables. An appraiser's appointment was scheduled for next week."

"Oh no."

"And it's all tied in with her mom, too, because she bought half that stuff before she died. Sara feels like she's lost her all over again." The strain shows in his tired eyes, his drawn face. "It'll take a few more days for the Fire Marshal to know exactly how the fire ignited. But for Sara Beth to start over again? The God damn cards are stacked against her."

thirty-one

SARA BETH'S FEAR IS THAT the fire took her mother, too. Ravaged her spirit so much that it's lost.

"So I can only find you here now?" she asks a week later while washing the gravestone with a sudsy scrub brush. "Can't you give me little signs, like before?" She runs the brush over the edges of the stone, then rinses it with fresh water. Once Tom left for work, she dropped the kids at Melissa's and stopped here before meeting the Fire Marshal. The sun is strong and she stands then, head dropped for a long while beneath the rays. Had it been real? If she can't recall details from their life together, did her mother even exist? She feels so completely gone, now more than ever.

"Mom?" she whispers, standing with one hand clutching her velvet beaded bag, the bucket hanging from the other, standing awhile longer before turning to leave.

At the carriage house later, she wonders the same thing: If she can't remember its details, had it existed? She stands where the building had been, struggling to picture how it looked only a short time ago.

Rays of sunlight shine through the trees, dropping like sparks on the debris. She walks through the rubble, feeling her furniture crunch in burnt bits beneath her feet. One piece, though, doesn't give. She pokes through the ash, finding a mahogany cabriole leg dusty with ash but untouched by the flames. It feels cool to the touch.

It's hard to tell what's left in her life. Sometimes her dreams of the carriage house are so vivid, it's as real as it was two weeks ago. She walks over to the split rail fence. It still stands, miraculously escaping the flames … the fence she drank tea at, the fence little Slinky sunned on.

"Sara?"

Lately her mind has a way of getting so lost in thought that it shuts out all else around her. But she knows that voice, it cuts right through her sadness.

"I'm so glad I found you," Rachel says as she comes up behind her. "I wanted to tell you how sorry I am."

With the mahogany leg still in her grip resting atop the split rail fence, they look at the debris. "The Fire Marshal just left." It's all Sara Beth can say without sobbing, now that she knows about the fire's origins.

* * *

"Let's walk," Rachel says. Walking means talking. If they'd kept records, there's no telling how many miles they've walked together in twenty-five years. Walked and talked. Probably as many miles as cups of coffee they've had. And talk helps. Tom told her it's therapeutic.

"Any respectable collector or antique dealer," Sara Beth starts as they move along the fence past the black furniture remnants, "has a basic knowledge of the field of antiques. Then, they specialize. But there is first a broad, general knowledge. One of the most obvious rules regarding antique lamps would be, well, what do you think it would be, Rachel? Tell me."

"Lamps?" She watches her friend cautiously. "Rewire?"

"You see? It's so obvious, everybody knows it. Old lamps have to be rewired, and they need new sockets and new plugs.

Never, ever, ever are you supposed to take a chance with lamps. Frayed wiring is treacherous."

"Sara Beth?"

"No. Wait." She holds up her hand, still studying the charred remains. "Let me finish. I had two antique lamps. A Steuben art glass lamp and my desk lamp, a beautiful brass lamp from 1916 that I hadn't rewired yet."

"A lamp caused this?"

"My desk lamp. They traced the fire to it. Apparently I left it on that night when I rushed out to celebrate the new house. The wires ignited and spread to the electric box and the old carriage house walls went up in a flash fire." Still she looks only into the carriage house remains. "So this is all my fault."

"But the newspaper mentioned some sort of a flare-up during the fire."

"Ed March stored gasoline for the lawn mowers on the other side of the center wall."

"Oh no."

"It was a small can, and almost empty, but it didn't cause the fire. Nothing stood a chance once that lamp went. Between the dried out timber and the old electrical circuits, the flames spread so fast."

For the very first time since the kidnapping junket, their eyes meet, Sara's hand still gripping the mahogany leg. Rachel gathers her into a hug. "I'm so sorry."

"Oh Rach," Sara Beth begins. "It's my fault. I can't do anything right." Her fingers have been wrapped tightly around the cabriole leg. She tosses it in the dirt and takes a deep breath. "My antiques, my dream, and oh my God, I thought this summer I'd lost you. My best friend. And now Mom. Everything's broken. Everything's gone."

"You can start over."

"Oh, please."

"Is there much left?"

"Bits and pieces. There's a table and chairs that were in the back. And Tom pulled out a chest of drawers and a few other pieces. They're in storage now. I don't know what I'm going to do."

"Tom told me about the new house."

"You talked to him?"

"I saw him in town last week."

Sara Beth leans against the fence. Her shoulders dip, her face is drawn. "I had these plans," she says. "Like a bridal registry service to the engagement notices in the paper. Wouldn't that be sweet? Registering to receive a beautiful antique for your home? And I planned to speak at The Historical Society about what I do, how I help bring history and family stories into a home. The same way Mom did." Her voice drops. "So now what? Everything's screwed up."

"That's not true."

"Yes it is. First my pregnancy. My marriage. Then us. And now this. And, okay, I'd talk to Mom sometimes, all right? It really felt like she heard me. I *felt* her. But now, nothing."

"It's going to be okay, you'll see. Come on," Rachel insists, pulling her friend toward their cars. She glances at the charred remains behind them, knowing the time has come. If ever a wish was put to the test, this is it. "Let's go. I'll follow you down to Whole Latte Life and we'll talk there."

"Any place would be better than here right now. Jesus, Rach. I did this."

"Shh. Stop that now." Rachel dawdles in her car as Sara Beth backs out of the driveway. Her new historic home is on the way to the coffee shop. She'll have to drive right past it. *Please,* Rachel thinks, *please notice the changes and stop there.* All Rachel has to do is give her a few minutes head start before putting her car in reverse.

* * *

Sara Beth drives down Old Willow Road, slowing near the covered bridge. Coming out the other end, the view of her new home on The Green is bittersweet. All the happiness it brought turns cruel. She pulls over and pushes her sunglasses on top of her head to get a better look and wouldn't you know it? A cardinal flies right in front of her. Which is really weird, because it *could* be another one of her mother's signs, that's for sure.

Her mother used to tell her that when a cardinal crosses your path, it's like a little Christmas ornament, any time of year. You were in for a treat. That's how much she'd loved the holidays. So maybe Mom's not completely gone then. That's when she notices the new curtains hanging in the paned windows.

Delicate white lace curtains.

She turns into the driveway and sees they are the same type of pretty curtains she planned on hanging with her mom, letting the sun shine through. But shouldn't the owners be packing up? A cast iron coin bank set on the interior windowsill, framed by those lace curtains, makes her step outside and lean against the car. It looks exactly like the horse bank she donated to the Savings and Loan. She steps closer and looking in past the curtains, sees Melissa's mahogany double pedestal table, the one that Sara Beth found for her, in the center of the room.

Okay, something's definitely up, something that makes her walk quickly to the door. It inches open onto warm colors and the lingering smell of fresh paint.

So this is new, this learning what it feels like falling into a dream.

First there are only colors. Browns that never glowed as beautiful as they do through tears. Beneath the mahogany, oak, cherry and pine antiques spreads a sea of gold and burgundy in an old oriental carpet. A huge vase of fresh dahlias and zinnias and small sunflowers, yellows and pinks and reds, graces a hand-stitched white lace runner atop Melissa's dark table. Beyond that, the three children's striped tiger chairs from Parks and Recreation stand lined in a perfectly straight row. The library's oak country table is set beneath the side window, too.

Her life flashes before her, every good deed returned in beautiful technicolor.

She walks slowly into the room. There is more. Whole Latte Life's coat rack stands inside the door, right where a coat rack should be. A painted old mirror from her neighbor hangs beside it. From the top of her white Sotheby's snake foot candlestand, she picks up the ornate picture frame she gave to her niece during the Fourth of July sale at her antique tent.

Well. She sets the frame down and leans her back against the wall before sliding down into a crouch with her arms wrapped around her knees. Someone pulled off a blessed miracle. Through her tears, her blurred gaze lingers on the heavenly white lace curtains until there is something else. There is Rachel standing in the doorway with her easel under an arm.

Oh her grin is wicked as she steps in and opens the easel, the one she does her best sketching on. It looks perfect set up near the window where sunshine will fall on the paper.

"This is for you," Rachel says.

"Me?"

"For your shop. Didn't you want to open by the fall? Lots of leaf-peepers will be passing through. They love to antique, too."

"What about your sketching?"

"Oh don't worry. I'll be your first customer."

Sara Beth still crouches, leaning against the wall, her long skirt reaching her feet. "You did this for me, didn't you?"

Rachel turns around. "Do you recognize it? Tom and I gathered it from a lot of people. They're all paying you back." She slides into a crouch beside Sara Beth. "It's the best we could do on short notice. But it looks pretty amazing, don't you think?"

A collection of brass candlesticks is artfully arranged on a cherry hutch. All the brass in the room glows, the drawer pulls, the door knockers. The woods are polished to deep liquid hues. "Why?" Sara Beth asks, brushing tears from her face.

"It's simple. Everybody loves you Sara. Don't you know that? We're all here for you." Rachel eyes her closely. "You don't see it, do you?"

Sara Beth shakes her head no, afraid to talk, to jinx anything.

"Well mostly it's that you've been a best friend, all my life. Ever since that day in eighth grade when I didn't know anyone in this town."

Sara Beth presses her fingers beneath her eyes, trying to stem the flow of tears. "But I hurt you this year."

"Yes, well. I knew, really, that New York wasn't about *us*. We all knew something else was happening. Tom, and your sister. And anyway, I thought we figured out all that stuff when I kidnapped you. This is what friends do."

If ever anyone wanted something, she wants desperately this: To believe Rachel. Has her life really been restored? The shop is filled with the touch of love that she could never have accomplished herself because it comes on olive branches and silver platters and in outstretched arms.

Her gaze sweeps the room, recognizing the framed print of kittens lapping up milk, and a wooden footstool among the pieces she gave to friends over the years. The framed daisy chain hangs beside a sunny window. But the cherry hutch and a pair of oil paintings depicting thoroughbred race horses are not familiar. There are a few other new pieces, too. "How did you do this?"

"I made some phone calls to the girls. You know, Melissa, Margaret, Brooke. Oh, and Amy and Sharon helped. Let me tell you, we had a great Girls' Weekend Out. We even brought our sleeping bags, some music. And the food! Pizza, and dessert, Brooke makes a mean cheesecake! Well. You missed a really fun one."

It's all in her smile: the past weekend of everyone painting into the late hours of night, of frantically building an interim, spare collection of furniture, of hanging curtains and washing windows and decorating during sunny afternoons. Of eating and laughing, maybe dancing too, to some old rock and roll tunes, celebrating for Sara.

"You did too much," Sara Beth insists. "You must be exhausted."

"But it was fun!" Rachel explains. "We even decided to do them more often. When one of us needs a room wallpapered or a change in decorating. Or a *life* adjustment? We're really good at it. Girls' Antique Weekend or Beach Weekend or Book Club Weekend or hey, Drown Your Sorrows in Cake and Ice Cream. Whatever! Oh. And your husband's got connections too. The homeowners let us do all this before your closing, under the circumstances."

"Tom knows about this?" The antique woods reflect pools of mysterious history. This holds his touch too.

Suddenly Rachel pulls her to her feet. "There's some stuff in the other room."

"More?"

Rachel leads her through the furniture tastefully arranged in the large room. The small quantity can never match what she lost in the fire, but still they gathered enough exquisite pieces to get her started on a part time basis. Off to the side in the second room, Amy's touch is evident in an antique cream lace wedding gown hanging on a slender mannequin, and near it, a white sheet covers a small antique. It sits beside the window under bright sunlight.

"We left this one for you to uncover."

Sara Beth's hand rests on the sheet covering the piece of furniture. Rachel nods to her and beneath the sheet she sees the gold swirled velvet first, then the oak arms. It is the Morris chair from her mother, from all those years ago. Her hand moves across the soft velvet, velvet that has grown even softer with time and memories of sitting safely there growing up in an old farmhouse, of her own daughters rocking in it, happy.

"Tom pulled it out that day with the Fire Chief, and we had it professionally cleaned. It wasn't too badly damaged. Mostly soiled."

Sara Beth is safe again, right now, in this moment. Her fingers touch the smooth dark arms. The worst time of her life, losing her mother, comes back now to give her incredible strength. She crouches to inspect it, thinking of the red cardinal that drew her eye here. "I can't sell this."

"Oh believe me, we didn't think you would."

Sara Beth stands and walks to the windows. Her fingers touch the lace curtains as she considers her life reflected in these rooms.

"We tried to pick the right colors and pull it all together like you would," Rachel says.

The walls are freshly painted a warm taupe, the crown molding and window frames a pale cream. Refinished oak floors glisten golden beneath the old oriental carpet. The wedding gown's long lace train is splayed over it.

"Sharon made the curtains from the lace you and your mom had bought, and the gown? Well, that's Amy. Melissa went to a couple auctions and watched the classifieds so we could all pick up some new pieces to build your inventory. Oh, and the stuff pulled from the fire? A woodworking shop refinished them and is delivering them here tomorrow." Rachel walks over to the window, moving aside the lace and opening the view to The Green. "So you see? I had a lot of help."

"Maybe," Sara Beth says. She sits down on a velvet settee, one of the new pieces. "But without you, I wouldn't have this shop today, would I?"

"But do you like it? You're so quiet."

The lace curtains draw her back to the window, her fingers unable to resist touching their delicacy. They bring back the memory of her mother lifting the lace out of an old trunk at a tag sale. She remembers still the blue skies of that morning. "I'm afraid to say how beautiful it all is. I'm afraid someone will wake me up or take it away or say Oh sorry, you misunderstood."

"It's yours, don't worry." Rachel gazes at the rooms. "And you know something? When I did all this, I began to understand what happened to you in New York. I felt your passion in these rooms. So did Tom. We all felt incredibly driven. And yeah, I'd say I definitely felt Elizabeth. This was so meant to be, and her spirit is here."

Sara Beth's hands touch different pieces chosen specially for her. "I want to smile and laugh and get down on my knees and cry all at the same time. But especially I want to thank you." Her voice drops then. "For granting a wish I didn't even dare consider."

"You'd have done the same for me." Rachel laughs, and makes Sara Beth laugh too. It feels good, and light and clear. "Hopefully you won't have to, but ..."

"Oh I would, if you needed me to. I swear I would."

"Well. Okay." Rachel takes a deep breath. "But instead, how about a latte?"

"My treat." Sara Beth loops her arm through Rachel's. "You might think this sounds silly. But I've been waiting all summer for this."

"For a coffee?"

"You have no idea."

thirty-two

THE REST OF HER SALVAGED furniture had been delivered, and for the next couple days, Rachel helped set up Sara Beth's antique shop. Thursday morning, they ended up back in Whole Latte Life for a much needed coffee break.

"You're still in that frame of mind," Sara Beth says, glancing toward the waitress. Rachel sits across from her wearing cuffed jeans and a yellow top. Her blonde hair is twisted back into a French braid, the journey necklace on her neck. "I can see it."

"What frame of mind is that?"

"Beach bum. It's written all over you."

"You're right. Now that things are better here, with you, I can't get that little Anchor Beach out of my mind. It's really gotten under my skin."

"Isn't there a song like that?" Sara Beth sits back and does a little shimmy in the booth while humming a familiar tune.

Rachel grins. "And your point is?"

"My point is, you've got *him* under your skin."

The past two evenings, when they sat on Sara Beth's deck under the moonlight, Rachel told her about Michael, including the night at the Seahorse Café that ultimately pushed the two friends back together, and his story of killing someone, along with her worries about his hypervigilance. She wondered if he'd get it under control or if it would push even her away.

"How can he control it?" Sara Beth had asked. "Is there some trick?"

"Therapeutic tools. Self-talk, exercise, replacing worries with self-nurturing, self-soothing things, thoughts."

"Well, sweets. He is," Sara Beth assured her. "That'd be you."

Rachel glances around the familiar coffee shop now. "He is under my skin, but still. Life is so peaceful here. Do I really want to leave that behind?"

"Only you can answer that one, Rach. You'll know when you have to."

"He wanted me to come back last Sunday, but with the teacher's orientation and setting up your antiques, I can't go until tonight."

"You talk things out with him. Maybe that'll help."

"I will. But I'm glad I stuck around here, too. To see that you're all right."

Sara looks out the window the way she has a million times before with her friend. "I *am* all right. Thanks to some amazing people in my life." She squeezes Rachel's hand and senses, in another way, that it is time to let go.

"Go easy on Tom," Rachel says. "He loved your mom too. He never meant any harm that day."

"I know, Rach. It's just, well, it's easy to blame. But I know."

The waitress finally sets a chocolate birthday cake topped with two lit candles between them. Another waitress places a big silver carafe of coffee and two mugs on the table.

"What's this?" Rachel asks.

"I never did get to wish you a happy birthday that May weekend. So I'm doing it now."

"No way."

"Way."

"Only if it's a joint celebration, then."

"How else would we do it?" The waitresses sing a quick verse of Happy Birthday, leaving them to blow out the candles.

"Make a wish," Rachel says, leaning forward on her folded arms and gazing into the two flickering flames.

"I wish for love. For you. It's worth it, Rach."

"Well, okay. And I'm going to wish on you. All the success and happiness you deserve." Rachel puffs out the candles.

"Thank you," Sara Beth tells her.

"In a strange and mysterious way, thank *you*. If it weren't for your weekend escape, I would never have met Michael and wouldn't be going back to Little Gull for a couple more days. Michael has it rented until Saturday."

Sara Beth slices the cake, putting the biggest piece on Rachel's plate. "You're the best girlfriend in the world. And I'd been meaning to buy you a gift, something special for your fortieth."

"You don't have to buy me anything," Rachel answers, tasting a wisp of frosting.

"Well, the thing is, I already did. Two vintage Adirondack chairs, being delivered to your backyard as we speak," Sara Beth says around a mouthful of cake. "Perfect for looking up at the sky and finding that first star with your best friend."

The door to the coffee shop opens and a customer walks in behind Rachel. Sara Beth squints, trying to place his face. He is tanned, wearing cargo shorts, a faded polo shirt, boat shoes and a baseball cap turned backwards. A light beard covers his face. When he pulls off his aviators, his dark eyes scan the room until they stop at hers.

Oh she knows, suddenly, exactly, precisely, who it is approaching their table; New York is written all over him. "No *way!*"

"What's the matter?" Rachel asks right as Michael taps her on the shoulder.

"Way," Sara Beth answers herself, grinning widely.

"Is this seat taken?" Michael asks, removing his cap and running his hand back through his dark hair.

Rachel hasn't said a word and hasn't taken her eyes off him. So Sara Beth looks back at him to be sure. He wears a heavy watch, one with the chronograph dial like Tom bought, and he's tanned, but oh boy, it's him. There's only one way to rescue Rachel. She swiftly kicks her under the table. And it's just right, that perfected girlfriend kick, she can tell by the way Rachel jumps and slides over, and when he sits beside her, her hand reaches to his face.

"Michael," Rachel says into his smiling kiss. "I don't believe it."

"Believe what?"

She pulls back. "That you're here!" She touches his cheek before looking across the table. "Both of you are here. Sara Beth? This is Michael Micelli. Michael? My best friend Sara Beth Riley."

"I think we've had the pleasure before." Michael extends his hand.

"Oh please." She shakes his hand, surprised that it's cold with nerves. Cold while a bead of perspiration slips down his temple. "It would mean so much to me if we could start over?"

"You bet."

"Oh, you are so nice. No wonder my friend here is smitten. Coffee?"

He nods and turns to Rachel beside him. "Smitten?" he asks with a wink, his cap in his hands, which haven't stopped turning it over and over again.

"Huh," Rachel says while Sara Beth motions to the waitress for another cup, then fills it from the carafe. "Maybe a little," she admits.

Michael sips the coffee and Rachel touches his cheek again. "You haven't shaved it off?"

"Not yet."

She looks at his forehead. "You're sweating. Is everything okay?"

"Just a little warm," he says, shifting in his seat, glancing at Sara Beth.

"Aren't you supposed to be at work?" Rachel asks.

"I haven't gone back." He picks up his cup and sets it down without drinking any.

"Is everyone all right? Summer is okay?"

"She is," he says, snagging a piece of her cake. "She got in to the Marine Studies Program, so she's pretty psyched."

"Wow! Go Summer! And Joe and Lena?"

"Everyone's fine." He spears another hunk of cake, so Sara Beth takes his cup off the saucer and slides a fresh piece of cake on that. He nods at her, then turns back to Rachel. "I had something to take care of."

"Oh," Rachel says, sounding left out of things. Absence has a way of doing that. She told Sara Beth just the night before that the time came to decide which absence she'd prefer: Addison or New York.

"Sara," Michael says. "I was sorry to hear about the fire. It must have been tough."

It takes her a moment to get her thoughts about the fire together. She's still sizing up Rachel's new guy. But something seems off; he's perspiring around his hairline, which he keeps dabbing at, and he's tapping his foot.

"I lost everything," she finally says. Sometimes something is too huge to put into words, like this, right now. "I can't say how grateful I am to have Rachel as my friend. She saved me in more ways than one."

"Here, here," Rachel says, forking a piece of chocolate cake. She sits back straight and eyes Michael sitting with them at their coffee table, pressing his fork into the cake crumbs. "And you. What *are* you doing here today? And how did you track me down?"

"Tracking you down was the easy part. I stopped at your house first, and when you weren't there, I thought *coffee*." He turns to Sara Beth. "Now for the hard part. Sara. Would you mind if I borrowed your friend?" He clears his throat and rolls his shoulder. "Just for a little while, outside?"

"Actually I've got to run," she answers. "I promised the kids some shopping."

Michael turns to Rachel. "Can we take a walk?"

Sara Beth motions for Rachel to go. "Don't worry. I'm just going to finish my coffee."

"You're sure?" Rachel asks as Michael slides from the booth, sending his fork clattering to the floor.

"Definitely." She sips her coffee. "Have fun, you two."

"I'll call you," Rachel says. "Promise."

"It was good seeing you again, Sara." Michael picks up his sunglasses from the table. "And good luck with that shop."

"Come and visit when it's opened." She stands and gives him a hug so that Rachel can't hear her whisper to him. "You take care of her."

He nods, looking closely at her. And what she figures, with her wrap sundress, cork sandals, makeup, and, okay, feather earrings, is that she must look a lot different from the sorry state she was in walking into The Plaza that May morning.

"Thanks for the cake. And the chairs, I can't wait to see them," Rachel says. She gives Sara Beth a quick kiss. "And happy birthday, sweetie. Forty's a good year. Don't worry! You'll see."

The couple goes outdoors and when Sara Beth catches sight of them on The Green, she watches Rachel walk with Michael. And what it feels like, as she sips her coffee and finds it hard to look away, is this: Watching is a way of holding on to her friend a little longer, yet somehow a little less.

* * *

Michael does have a reason for being here. Seeing her now, he knows Coach was right. Make it special. They stop at his pickup to retrieve a package, then cross over to The Green and sit on a bench near the fountain.

"You really haven't been back to work?" Rachel asks. She touches a drop of perspiration on his face. "You're still warm."

"I had to extend my vacation a few days. Something important came up."

"Important?"

"It started with your phone call last Thursday." He stands then, looks at her, and sits again. There'd been a few uncomfortable silences in that talk, that's what he remembers now.

"My phone call?"

"Yes. When you said you needed to help Sara Beth and weren't sure when you could make it to the cottage. Then you had your meeting for new teachers this week. I understood about helping Sara. Mostly it had to do with the meeting."

"The meeting's this afternoon. One o'clock."

"Well, you need to go, but maybe under a different pretense. Because," he takes a long breath, slow exhale, "when you told me about the meeting and about your job, I got to thinking about how you're starting a new career and making changes in your life. And I realized it's time I made changes too. There's something I've been putting off."

"You're not quitting your job?"

"Nothing like that. And it's not school either. What I've been putting off is taking chances. I haven't taken one in years. That bullet had enough chance to last."

"I'm sure it did."

"Now it's time." He pulls his cap off his head and resettles it twice. "Here." He hands her the small, flat box. His foot starts tapping, his baseball cap is pulled low against the bright sun, his aviators shade his eyes.

Rachel lays her open hands on top of it. "Are you okay? You look pale."

"I'll know in a minute. Open the box."

Rachel shakes the box a little before pulling off the cover and moving the white tissue.

Michael leans forward, his elbows on his legs, hands clasped between his knees, and after a long moment, looks back at her.

Her fingers lightly trace the wooden oval cottage sign, painted deep navy blue, the color of the twilight sky above Long Island Sound. A gold shooting star curves across the top of the sign, a trail of glittering gold stardust sparkling behind it.

But it is after she reads the name, *Wish I May*, painted in gold below the shooting star, when Michael looks away. If the answer's no, he doesn't want to see her face shift to sadness or regret. Doesn't want to remember that moment.

"Is this what I think it is?" she asks.

"What do you think it is?"

"A cottage sign?"

"That's right," he says, pulling off his cap and fidgeting with it between his knees.

"For me?"

"Yes. For you."

"But ... I get the feeling a really big something goes along with this."

He studies the stitching on the Yankees cap and clears his throat. "It does."

Rachel leans on her knees, too, and watches him. "This is really for me?"

"Well, there is one condition." He pulls off his sunglasses. Perspiration is running down his cheek now. He knows that. He knows his heart is beating fast. He knows he's at a loss for words, and that he's afraid, too. Afraid of her answer. He's so aware of every single damn thing right now. No deep breaths, no self-talk are going to stop this fear.

"A condition?"

"Yes. If you don't mind a modest diamond, because, well, my finances are a little tied up with that." He nods at the sign. "But I wondered if, I don't know, maybe instead of having this long-distance thing, maybe you'd consider marrying me."

Rachel looks at him, then drops her gaze to the *Wish I May* cottage sign and doesn't speak.

"I know I have issues to work out, and I am. I'm getting regular therapy, and doing my exercises."

Still she's silent, still looking at the sign.

"Help me out here, Rach," he finally says, his voice low. "I'm having a tough time."

"I'm the first chance you're taking since the night you were shot?"

He nods.

"You bought that cottage, didn't you? Little Gull."

"I haven't closed yet, but the contract's signed. Oh, and I painted it."

"That's what you've been doing this week, instead of working?"

"Yes." He thinks how the whole time he painted the little cottage, every second on the ladder, every bit of sanding the window trim, every eave he dabbed the brush into, he wondered if she would say yes, if he could change, if he should go back to school, which he decided no on that one, and then worried if that would make her say no.

"What color?" She can't take her eyes off of him now.

He nods at the sign. "Pale yellow. The color of a star." That night in the rowboat when she closed her eyes on the first star, that's when he knew he had to do this.

"You didn't," she says.

"I did."

"And you want to marry me?" Rachel asks, moving her hand to her heart.

"More than anything, Rachel. Okay? When you told me about the teachers' meeting today, I thought I'd better hurry.

Before you got yourself settled in the position. This way the Board of Ed would have enough time."

"Time?"

"Yes." He stops. "It shouldn't be so hard for me to say this, except I guess I'm really afraid of your answer, which, by the way, I'm still waiting for. But yes, time. The Board of Ed will need time to find your replacement. Because this is what I want, you and me. Every day, every night. At home, at the beach. I thought maybe I could ask you to marry me *and* come to New York instead of starting your new job here. I'm working on changing things, you know, with my nerves and all. I know it's a problem. But I'm trying. So if you need to think about it, I understand. I mean, it's a lot all at once."

Rachel runs her fingers across the painted sign that means a little summer cottage. "You want to do this right away?" she asks.

"The sooner the better."

"Yes." Her tears won't stop.

"What?"

"Yes, yes, a million yeses. I'm going to take that chance right with you."

He takes her face in his hands and caresses her cheek with his thumb.

"And yes, I'm crying," she says, laying her hand on his checking hand. *"I'm crying."*

"That's why I'm wondering if you're sure. Because you know it would mean leaving your home. I didn't know if you could do that. I just didn't know."

"A pretty house, a coffee shop, that can't keep me here. I want to be there with you, I'm so ready. But it's important that you know something else."

"What's the matter?"

"This cottage. My piece of heaven?"

"It is, isn't it?"

"Yes. Well. I *thought* it was, but really, I've found heaven all summer long. Bowling, in the city, at the beach, even here." She stops and kisses him once, then again, longer. "I love you."

"That's what matters, sweetheart." He kisses her tenderly, never believing that she'd settle for a regular guy like him, quirks and all, nerves and all. Rachel slips her arms around his neck and it takes him back to the Empire State Building, eighty-six floors up, gazing out at the Manhattan sky on a cool, May night. It seems so long ago now, waiting for a wayward friend to return.

And as he stood with her then, eighty-six floors up, as close to heaven as you can get in Manhattan, one thought moved him. It was the same thought that bothered him right after he'd been shot. Standing with Rachel on the observation deck of the Empire State Building worrying for Sara Beth, that *What if* crossed his mind.

What if? What if the gunman's hand was minutely lower? What if Sara Beth had never run away? What if she came back and Rachel took her home the next day? Whether he imagined the bullet's deadlier path or losing Rachel from his life, both questions scared him the same.

Wishes? On a star? Michael never believed in wishes and all that sentimental stuff. Fate is predetermined, some people say. In the stars, is how they put it.

Picturing the Manhattan sky, remembering that May night behind his closed eyes now, he pulls Rachel a little closer on Addison's Green, kisses her a little deeper and loves her a little more.

Acknowledgments

Many people and places were instrumental in the telling of this story. And so I'd like to extend my gratitude to …

My dedicated publishing team. Thank you for all your diligent work in producing and designing my books. I so appreciate your talents and am glad to know I can always count on you.

My readers. Thank you for all the support; there's no greater joy than knowing my stories and characters have touched you.

Sometimes a place is so special, it becomes a part of who we are. Thank you to Point O' Woods, a little beach nestled in a crook of the Connecticut coast. With its sandy boardwalk, whispering lagoon grasses and sweet salt air, it has wound its way into my heart, and onto the page as well.

To my husband Tony, and my daughters Jena and Mary. Especially for the research trip to New York City, visiting this novel's NY sites and walking my characters' paths. Life's a whole latte fun having you in it. Love you.

Also by Joanne DeMaio

True Blend
Snowflakes and Coffee Cakes
Blue Jeans and Coffee Beans

For a complete list of books by *New York Times*
bestselling author Joanne DeMaio, visit:

www.joannedemaio.com

About the Author

Joanne DeMaio is a *New York Times* and *USA Today* bestselling author of contemporary fiction. She enjoys writing about friendship, family, love and choices, while setting her stories in New England towns or by the sea. Currently at work on her next novel, Joanne resides with her family in Connecticut.

For a complete list of books and for news on upcoming releases, please visit Joanne's website. She also enjoys hearing from readers on Facebook.

Author Website:
www.joannedemaio.com

Facebook:
www.facebook.com/JoanneDeMaioAuthor

Made in the USA
Charleston, SC
ary 2017

ML   **3/2017**